T0354349

Some Damn Fool Thing

J. William Whitaker

SOME DAMN FOOL THING

iUniverse books may be ordered through booksellers or by contacting:

iUniverse
1663 Liberty Drive
Bloomington, IN 47403
www.iuniverse.com
1-800-Authors (1-800-288-4677)

ISBN: 978-1-5320-1491-8 (sc)
ISBN: 978-1-5320-3140-3 (hc)
ISBN: 978-1-5320-1492-5 (e)

Library of Congress Control Number: 2017905769

Print information available on the last page.

iUniverse rev. date: 08/22/2017

The Great European War will come from some damn foolish thing in the Balkans.

—Prince Otto von Bismarck
1888

PREFACE

Events of the present are muddled by prejudice and uncertainty. Events of the past are too often the sole concern of historians. As the years recede, it is all too easy to portray the past using dramatic events and prominent figures to distill a narrative to represent that time. Lost in such a construct are the effects such events produced on the multitude of lives forced to live through them. This book is dedicated to the spirit of those lives and all they endured.

BOOK 1
1905

1

AN OLD APPARITION

Awakened by the bright morning sunlight filtering into his bedroom, Robert d'Avillard turned over fitfully, trying to fall back to sleep. Then, roused by the unusual noise of a crowd on the sidewalk below, he noticed that it was nearly eight o'clock and quickly jumped from bed. He hurriedly washed his face and shaved; then, dressing rapidly, he left, hoping that he still might make his morning appointment with Professor de Rochelle.

As he hurried down the street, still trying to organize his clothing and the papers he was carrying, he silently cursed himself for having to rush to avoid being late. He hated being late to any appointment but especially a project review and planning session with Professor de Rochelle. What most disgusted him was his lack of self-discipline, which had led to this predicament. Last night he and a large group of friends had gathered to celebrate his cousin Thomas's birthday. Caught up in the spirit of the night and the seemingly endless bottles of red wine, he stayed until nearly midnight before coming home, all the while reassuring himself that he would be able to get up at his usual hour. Now he found himself engulfed by an unusually large crowd slowing his progress and only increasing his frustration.

Professor Henri de Rochelle was an old friend of Robert's uncle Jean, with whom he had served in the military, and through this friendship the professor had come to know both Robert and his cousin Thomas from the time they were young men. His skill in engineering and design had ultimately led to a distinguished position at the Ecole Polytechnique. When Robert arrived there as a student, he made it a point to visit Professor de Rochelle, and ultimately this led to a relationship that persisted throughout his years in school. Through these years that relationship had changed, reflecting Robert's maturation and development, but during that time Robert's respect for the professor had only increased. The thought of being late to a meeting with him, therefore, was unsettling.

Arriving at the Boulevard Saint Germaine, Robert encountered an even larger gathering clustered around a news kiosk, but, intent on getting to his appointment on time, he paid little attention to them. As he pushed through the crowds nearing the hill before the Ecole Polytechnique, however, his eye caught a glimpse of a headline written in unusually bold lettering as he heard a vendor crying out "German kaiser speaks in Morocco; threatens France while calling for Moroccan independence." As the import of these words sank in, Robert came to a stop and joined in line with the gathering crowd. Soon with a copy of the early edition in hand, for the next several blocks he tried to read while attempting to avoid the crush of the crowd, until at last he reached the professor's office.

As he entered the office, he was relieved to see that the professor was not in his usual location behind his large oak desk. Looking around, he did not see Madame Broullard, the professor's secretary, or many other associates or students. He walked quickly toward his own desk and spied a rumpled copy of the same journal he was carrying as he passed the professor's office, indicating that he had almost certainly been there at his usual early hour.

At the small nook that comprised the limits of his office, Robert took up the calculations and plans that he had been working on the day before, trying to project an air of concentration and industry. His thoughts, however, constantly drifted to this morning's news until, finally realizing the futility of continuing with his calculations, he set aside his work to reread the morning paper.

Robert knew that Morocco, long an area of French influence, had been granted French protection in a recent historic agreement with Britain, thereby allowing the French to more formally colonize this supposedly independent nation, as they had done earlier with Algeria. Now in a remarkable act of defiance for this agreement and French colonial rights, the German kaiser had sailed into Tangiers with a small military fleet and had given a rousing speech for Moroccan independence to the sultan and parliament. The full text of the speech and many other details remained unclear at this time, but what was clear was the German challenge to French authority and prestige in the area.

Robert was not a student of history and took little interest in politics, but despite that, he quickly realized the implications of the kaiser's actions. For more than thirty years France had been obsessed by the memory of the humiliating defeat that had been suffered at the hands of the Prussian forces directed by Bismarck. That defeat had come with a protracted siege of Paris, a bloody uprising by the lower classes, and the loss of Alsace and parts of Lorraine. In the aftermath of the Prussian victory, countless memories of German cruelty and atrocities contributed to a sense of outrage and fear by the French for this now-powerful neighbor.

In the years after his victory over the French, Bismarck had been content to let France recover while he set about consolidating Prussian power as the first among equals in the new German Reich, a consolidation forged in the aftermath of the Prussian triumph of the disparate principalities and states that had previously comprised much of the German-speaking world of Central Europe. Now, after many years, this feared neighbor to the east had reappeared in the person of the young kaiser, once again threatening France and its colonial possessions. Such a gesture, Robert realized, in light of the enmity toward Germany that simmered throughout France, could have serious consequences and certainly could not be ignored.

As Robert studied the morning dispatches, the office personnel began to reassemble. The desk where he sat was near the center of this office, which included a collective of gifted engineers, but the entire organization was also symbolically as well as functionally at the center of the wave of industrial innovation and application that was transforming Paris on nearly a daily basis. During the early years of the industrial transformation of the continent, France initially had lagged behind the British and Germans in pioneering the advances that had radically changed the quality of life throughout Europe. As the nineteenth century progressed, however, French engineers and scientists came forward with designs of their own and in so doing profoundly altered life not only in Paris but also in the most remote of provincial villages.

No better symbols of this progress could be found than the new railroad stations that served as hubs for rapid travel throughout the country and, of course, Gustave Eiffel's remarkable tower sculpted in steel. In recent years, Professor de Rochelle and his present and past students had been involved in the design of some of the most significant and innovative projects of this new age. Much of the present transportation structure of France was conceived in the offices around Robert, with many important projects designed and managed from there. For anyone interested in civil engineering, this office in Paris was a remarkable place to be.

Robert d'Avillard had arrived at his present status not by nepotism, as was common in the old order, but like everyone in this office—by merit. As a young boy growing up on his family's lands in Provence, he had an early interest in the workings of the agricultural machinery and its upkeep. In school, though an able student in all the disciplines, he found that mathematics not only was of great interest but also seemed to come to him almost as second nature. It was not long, with some guidance from his father, before he became intrigued with the application of mathematic and scientific principles in the building and maintenance of the family estate and its equipment. Such a natural aptitude, with only the mildest encouragement from his father, led him to Paris to study engineering at the Ecole Polytechnique.

He arrived accompanied by a letter of introduction from his uncle Jean, allowing Robert to become reacquainted with Professor de Rochelle. At first the professor acted much like a surrogate uncle, making sure Robert had the right lectures and information to adapt to his new circumstances. He was gratified to learn with the passing of the first school year that his young charge not only would survive the rigors of his studies but was indeed excelling. It was soon evident that Robert had an aptitude not only for the practical applied mathematics and science of the engineering curriculum but also for some of the most sublime and theoretical aspects of these disciplines. Impressed by Robert's abilities, the professor increasingly came to view Robert not as a student but as a young protégé.

It was only natural, therefore, that the professor would offer Robert an opportunity to work in his office. At first, like many an apprentice before him, his tasks were often menial, yet almost always they served to condition him for more challenging future assignments. As Robert proved his competency, he quickly advanced to the point that he was handling projects commonly assigned to men much his senior. The work he had labored over this morning involved plans for a series of large railroad bridges.

Shortly after ten, the professor at last returned to the office. He was a somewhat short man, with a round face accentuated by a well-groomed beard. As he had gotten older, his increasing girth, concealed by his usual stylish coat, added to his appearance as a most respected member of French society. Normally reserved, he appeared more animated than usual this morning. His gestures and speech when talking with his secretary and other personnel indicated an increased urgency, which contrasted with his usual more measured pace.

"I'm sorry to be off schedule this morning, Robert," he said as he entered Robert's office, "but the kaiser has certainly stirred up my military friends. No sooner had I arrived than I received several messages, and I have just come from a meeting with one of my old colleagues. This particular gentleman is at the center of the army's strategic planning and is now having to rethink some of his plans to address the possibilities implied by the kaiser's speech. It now seems that our rail lines will be more critical than ever, and if events deteriorate further, we will no doubt have to expedite our planning to help accelerate new construction. No longer does the army move on its stomach and feet, like in the old days of the emperor, but now instead on rails of steel fueled by steam power."

"I must confess that I was late myself, Professor, as I got caught up in the crowds along the boulevard. Half of Paris seems to be on the street this morning. Have you heard anything more about what the Germans might be doing or if the kaiser has said something new?"

"I probably know little more than you do or what was reported in the press," the professor replied. "It is clear, however, that the army is taking this very seriously. I have had a number of requests about the status of several projects, which will take the better part of the day to reply to. I suspect that if this continues, we will have to rearrange a number of priorities in the days ahead. For the present, I want you to continue on the work you are doing, and when I have the time in the next days, I will review your progress and answer any questions that might come up.

"I no doubt will be in and out of the office over the next few days, so if we miss connections, you may leave any messages with Madame Broullard, and I'll leave any communications that I might have for you with her as well. Any questions that you have in my absence I will try to answer through her as quickly as I can. Whether we like it or not, if matters deteriorate, the army may become our major or only client, and that project you are working on will be of great interest to them. I must go to another appointment now, but I will try to get back with you in some manner this afternoon."

Robert was glad to be alone after the professor left. The office had returned to more normal activity, with the quiet movement of associates in the hall and the rustle of work being done in offices throughout the area. His desk seemed unusually bright and warm for this hour, with sunlight streaming through the south window. He welcomed these reminders of the normalcy of his routine, but as the morning progressed, his mind continued to drift away to the Moroccan affair.

For as long as Robert could remember, much of North Africa seemed to be a rather exotic but natural extension of France. He had never been there in person, but being from Provence, he had sensed the presence of these lands from a young age. There in Provence, the sunshine and warmth that was so important to the family lands his mother would say came as a gift from the winds born over the lands of North Africa. He could remember his first visit—and almost every one since—to Marseilles, where he was astonished to see Arabs and Africans in their exotic dress, speaking in a language as strange as their appearance. He had always been intrigued by their quarters, squeezed among small streets behind the old port that appeared more like some Algerian marketplace than a city in republican France.

Mediterranean ports such as Marseilles had served as the portal by which the north of Africa and Europe had traded and communicated with each other for more than two millennia. It was only natural that as France emerged as a European power, its influence in the Mediterranean would increase. Eventually, French commercial interests and maritime power reached such prominence that the age-old problem of Barber piracy was used as a pretext to invade and colonize parts of the northern reaches of the continent. To ensuing generations of Frenchmen, this seemed a logical and beneficial spread of French influence and culture, as much a moral obligation as it was an economic opportunity.

Now in the kaiser's dramatic gesture was the implication that French rule had no place in Morocco and, by inference, was inferior to that of Germany. This was an insult that challenged not only French prestige but their legitimacy in the region, where they had already made great commitments in Algeria. It was suddenly apparent that this heretofore exotic and distant land might serve as a catalyst to bring about a crisis that would threaten the security and comfort of life so many miles away in Paris.

This stark reminder of German power made Robert acutely aware of old concerns, voiced by previous generations of Frenchmen who had suffered at the hands of this militant neighbor, prompting him to seriously think—perhaps for the first time—about the responsibilities of his birthright. He had long felt a pride and loyalty that came with the place of his birth and its values that had provided a foundation for his maturity. Now the sudden and unexpected appearance of injudicious threat, like an ancient evil reemergent in the guise of a bellicose kaiser, posed a real threat to his homeland.

The threat also compelled Robert to refocus on his work, which, given the circumstances in Morocco, now had more urgency and importance. He also chided himself for jumping to unfounded conclusions without more of substance to analyze. Robert had prided himself on his ability to reason through complex problems in a controlled and logical manner. Turning to his old methods, he could only conclude from the information available that the kaiser had chosen, with his bombastic speech, to break from the relative isolation and restrained foreign policy of his grandfather and Bismarck. Robert also knew that the German emperor had enough power vested in him that this signal that modern Germany intended to assume a more prominent role in the affairs of the continent could not be easily ignored. At this point it could be only speculation what that role might be or what means might be employed to achieve it. Robert—and indeed all of Europe—had reason for concern, however, as this modern unified Germany was born through Prussian statesmanship augmented by its military might.

If future German diplomacy might center on military threat, the question that confronted Robert was how he could best contend with such a somber reality. Instinctively, he knew that if some foreign ruler tried to disrupt his life, as it now existed, through coercion, then such threats would have to be opposed. What he might do, however, was by no means clear at this time. What he sensed was a new determination to vigorously defend his French birthright, should it be challenged.

This commitment, however open-ended it might seem at present, made it easier for Robert to concentrate on the work at hand. He soon was involved with a series of calculations necessary to ensure the safety of a bridge, the design of which he was finalizing. By the end of the afternoon he was pleased to have accomplished far more than he had ever anticipated. On leaving, he checked with Madame Broullard for any messages the professor might have left. Finding none, he left, looking forward to meeting his friends that evening for dinner to talk about the events of the day. As he passed through the large courtyard of the Ecole Polytechnique, he noted the effect of the evening sun, which had turned the stones of the building the color of burnished gold and helped to add drama to the blue, white, and red of the large tricolor that flew over the entryway, the sight of which added even more poignancy to his thoughts of the day.

2

A SERPENT IN THE GARDEN

For Thomas d'Avillard, the day had been every bit as unsettling as it had been for his cousin Robert. The previous evening's birthday festivities had taken a toll on him as well, slowing his usual morning routine. Finally motivated by hunger he had set out to find something to eat, only to encounter the same noisy crowds along the street as Robert had and quickly discovered the reason for their agitation in the reports of the kaiser's speech in Tangiers. The news helped to dispel the remaining effects from the night before, and intrigued, he dispensed with his usual leisurely breakfast, quickly eating a croissant while he drank his morning coffee and studied the journal report.

Thomas had lived much of his life close to his cousin Robert, and the two had been influenced through the years by their kinship as well as proximity to each other. Separated by one year in age, they had grown up within sight of each other in the foothills of the Luberon in the south of France. They were both of above-average height, thin-waisted with well-muscled torsos, and both had the dark eyes and curly brown hair that seemed so common among young men from Provence. Both shared a keen intelligence and had been brought up to value the use of that intellect to reason through the problems and uncertainties they encountered in their studies and in everyday life. Whereas Robert was attracted to mathematics and its application to science and design, Thomas was drawn to philosophy and theology. It was therefore not surprising that his thoughts pertaining to the events reported from Morocco were different from his cousin's.

It was not that Thomas was any less a Frenchman than Robert. The two had been frequent companions for as long as either could remember. From his earliest days, Thomas was surrounded by a world of remarkable opportunity. His home was on the grounds of an old family estate, which provided him not only opportunity to roam widely, unfettered by the constraints of the city, but also to observe the remarkable repetition of nature that occurred throughout the year in that sun-drenched land so envied by his northern relatives. This rhythm of the sun and its effect on the land would serve as a visible calendar, providing Thomas an understanding of the world around him.

Following the winter solstice, as the days lengthened, the increasing warmth of early spring would gradually make its presence felt. The chill wind that howled from the north over the Alps, turning even bright, sunny February days into excruciatingly cold walks from school, would be replaced by winds from the south, born from the deserts of North Africa. And so the dormant browns of winter, with the occasional green of the cypress, would be transformed by the spring and the burgeoning of countless flora into a palette of infinite greens. As the days lengthened, these greens would ripen into the violet of lavender and gold of sunflowers and would then turn into the bronze of the fall vineyards. As the daylight hours shortened, the land and trees would brown following the harvest to await the return of the warmth from the south. During those shortened days, the holidays were celebrated with great ceremony, with feasts supplemented by the bounteous game harvested by hunting the surrounding hillsides. In the first days of the New Year, the mistral winds would return, signaling the waning days of winter and the promise of the new spring and a return to life that would soon follow.

In time, Thomas came to appreciate not only the glorious cycle of color and the delectable bounty of its fields but also the role of the various inhabitants of Provence to its great natural stage. There were large numbers of workers in the fields, vineyards, and increasingly, the villages, whose lives seemed to be intimately involved with this natural cycle that surrounded them. It seemed to Thomas that all of these people went about their tasks as if they had been born for that very purpose. There were also small numbers of people, such as his father and uncle, whose roles seemed less evident, with them providing more oversight than actual physical labor. In all of this, Thomas was comforted by the partnership of the land and seasons with the inhabitants to provide a satisfactory life for all. The comfort of these early days filled with ample food, secure lodging, and a loving family, who seemed to be held in high regard by the many neighbors, confirmed to Thomas the wonderful bounty of life.

Later, however, he became aware of irregularities. He saw ill-kempt men and women, who often did not work, were often impolite, and did not seem to have a place in his comfortable world. For a precocious boy like Thomas, reconciling the habits of such people and the problems their behavior posed to his concept of an orderly and idyllic world would be the cause

15

for much thought. At first, it would be his mother, Helene, who would answer his many questions. Later, she would be helped by her younger brother Jean Marie, who, by virtue of his intellect, would later advance through the academic ranks, acquiring at a young age a prominent reputation at the same University of Paris where Thomas found himself today.

The irregularities that disturbed him in nearly medieval Provence would be far more disconcerting when he visited family in Paris. The first trips on the railroad, with its noise and clouds of smoke, served as a fit prelude to the grime and noise of a city in the middle stages of transformation into the capital of a modern industrial nation. The vast span of the Gare de Lyon, with its vaulted ceiling reaching over the numerous tracks that spread out into the vast reaches of his homeland, represented an architecture and technology unseen and undreamed of by his ancestors.

Outside the station, the hissing and screeching of the locomotives was replaced by the din of the surrounding quarter. Gone were the neat rows of homes common in Aix and the villages of Provence. In their place was often an irregular collection of buildings and shops, where large numbers of people often congregated. Merchants similar to those present in the South could be seen looming over their wares, but here, there was an ever-changing group of people altogether different in number and appearance from what he had previously experienced in Provence.

These people were often ill-dressed and ill-mannered, creating in Thomas an immediate sense of unease. On first appearance, it seemed that some spent the majority of their days in purposeless activity, loitering in the street and surrounding shops, smoking, drinking, and carrying on loud ill-mannered conversations. This aroused the same anxiety in him that he had felt in Provence when seeing people whose behavior seemed so incongruous with his perception of what was acceptable. It was only when he got to his grandparents' apartment on the Rue de Bac that he felt less threatened by this unsettling side of Paris.

There, in a more quiet and orderly environment, he felt more at ease and would often use these surroundings as a haven to better analyze the new and, at times, strange surroundings of this vast city. Here, his family would try to answer the many questions that came from his explorations of Paris. This eventually would lead to discussions of right and wrong and many other matters, ranging from the simple to the complex. Little did Thomas realize at the time how fortunate he was to have such able and caring family members, particularly his mother and her brother, whose patient counsel helped Thomas acquire a wisdom and maturity beyond his years.

His grandparents had provided both his mother and her brother with a rigorous education, beginning when they were quite young. Besides a solid grounding in Latin and literature, they were taught the major principles of logic, as well as mathematics, which helped to give structure to their reasoning. They came to appreciate and depend on this discipline to help guide their thinking about many questions and issues, both banal and large, that arose in the course of their lives. As they matured, however, they were taught theology, which considered those truths beyond human reason. From these studies came a deeper understanding of their true purpose in the world and a strengthening of their religious faith.

So it was that young Thomas was introduced to their methods and beliefs, and with experience he became proficient in applying these lessons to his daily life. He was taught that scientific findings should not be viewed with hostility but embraced as a means to gain a better understanding of the true nature of things. Yet even at a young age Thomas realized that many considerations were beyond the limits of science and reason. To address these problems, Thomas's mother and uncle also introduced him to the Holy Scriptures so that through God's revelations he might gain insight and wisdom that could not be gained by reason alone.

All of this led ultimately to Thomas's following the course of his uncle Jean Marie to Paris to study at the Sorbonne, where he had been for nearly three years now. There, the course work and all that comprised his life had continued to stimulate his many interests. The Paris that at first had caused him so much anxiety had become more familiar as he came to understand the circumstances and people of the many districts of the city. He had learned that in this mass of humanity, so different from his native Provence, there were many shared hopes and beliefs common to all, regardless of their position in society or of their privileges.

He continued to recognize, however, the darker elements of society in this urban locale, which seemed more evident than in the quiet order of Provence. Robbery, debauchery, physical violence, and other manifestations of evil were all too frequent in many areas of Paris. More subtle failings in fidelity, justice, and honesty abounded in even the most respectable quarters of society. That these failings were present was to be expected, as they had been a feature of humankind since the original sin. To Thomas, however, the consideration of evil was intriguing, if not frustrating, as he often felt his understanding of its origins was incomplete and wanting for corrective solutions. He also sensed that evil might be so deeply entrenched in some people as to be virtually impossible to eradicate.

This news from North Africa certainly was disconcerting

to Thomas, but as he thought more about it, the kaiser's actions posed a different threat than any with which he was already familiar. He had known of war only by his father's stories and by historical narratives. All of this had been related in the past tense. Now, the leader of a major country and neighbor, through a show of military force, was threatening France and the existing territorial order. To Thomas, this was not the usual failings that blighted every community but represented a potential threat on a vastly greater scale. In this case, one man, empowered by his position, was usurping the collective might of his homeland to extort change. The potential of such a threat, if ultimately realized, could bring a kind of misery long absent from the experience of most Europeans. Thomas viewed even raising the specter of suffering on such a large scale as particularly reprehensible.

War, from the earliest of times, was the ultimate breakdown in relationships between men, and these relationships were a great concern and interest of Thomas. Societies throughout the ages had suffered the loss of countless men, killed or wounded in war. And to what end? For those who were unfortunate enough to be on the losing side, the consequences were often much graver. At the very least there would be a significant disruption in the previous societal norms, with new laws and customs imposed by the conquerors. In the extreme, whole societies had been reduced by Mongolian hordes and Viking raiders, with cities destroyed and people killed or taken into slavery.

In more recent centuries, Europe had been spared many of the more severe consequences of warfare, which, until the early nineteenth century, was often fought by bands of professional soldiers who lent their services in return for the land and plunder that might reward their successes. In the aftermath of the revolution, however, France found itself surrounded by nations hostile to their republican form of government. To combat these forces, France enlisted the full breadth of its population in its army, bringing enormous numbers of soldiers to bear in great and historic battles during the first decades of the nineteenth century. The emperor's success ushered in a new age of warfare, where entire populations were involved in massive conscription, with wide swaths of the continent denigrated from the effects of war.

Now this kaiser, with his bluster and rhetoric, was reawakening a specter of destruction and suffering, where even the noblest were drawn into violence to protect their families and homeland. To Thomas, the stories that his father told about the Prussian War of 1870 gave a personal testimony to the horrors of modern warfare. Undone by an incompetent emperor and a strong enemy, the French army was routed at Sedan, and what resistance remained was concentrated around Paris, where, during a prolonged siege, the government fled to the southwest. Thomas heard stories from his father not only of death and injury from the war but severe societal breakdowns. Hunger, displacement, and the resulting stress served to bring out the worst types of behavior, with priests being shot, women raped, and ancient grudges leading to overt class warfare. Such behavior no doubt would return if the old enmity between France and Germany should be rekindled and lead to war.

Incensed by the kaiser's audacity Thomas, like his cousin, would spend the better part of his day carefully considering and then reconsidering the implications of the kaiser's actions and what potential consequences might come from them.

How could this kaiser act in such a manner? Modern Germany had been forged by the defeat of France in 1871, giving Lutheran Prussia control over the many previously independent German principalities, including Catholic states such as Bavaria in the south and large areas in the west of the country. In theory, Germany was a constitutional monarchy composed of a confederation of states, each with some autonomy and represented in a federal parliament in Berlin. From his discussions with various German students, Thomas had inferred that many regions such as Bavaria still had a great deal of autonomy. If the kaiser's actions were constrained by the laws of the German state, then he must have acted with the tacit consent of these constituent states, or else he believed his position to be so powerful that he could act without their explicit approval.

Germany, from the time of its unification, had undergone substantial demographic and economic change. In recent years industrial production had surged to the point where now Germany had surpassed Britain as the largest manufacturing economy in Europe. With this had come a substantial increase in population, with large urban working-class areas growing in Berlin and in the cities of the Ruhr and Rhine Valleys. If the kaiser, through his chancellor, had mollified the representatives of these forces in the Reichstag, it would mean that he had overcome the traditional resistance that the industrialists and the working classes had to the disruptions of war. It seemed unlikely to Thomas, from what he knew of these areas, that the kaiser could have such wide support for his actions.

Thomas had learned, however, from his conversations with students from all over Germany that one institution stood out above all others in terms of its power and influence. It was this group that most worried him. If the kaiser had gone forward without wide support, he would have done so only if he had the backing of the military and its professional officer corps. Prussia had always been a country that had given its military unusual prominence in the workings of the state. Indeed, under the chancellorship of Bismarck, it had become a significant means of diplomacy and had been instrumental in German unification. Even with the inclusion of the other German principalities into the military, with rare exceptions the brunt of the leadership and policymaking was concentrated in the hands of the Prussians. Thomas did not doubt that the kaiser's flamboyant show of force had been well vetted with his military command, and they must therefore be in full accord.

Yet Thomas could not disprove one other possibility: this entire episode had been far less planned than he had first imagined. This kaiser was capable of erratic behavior—that was well known. His friend Becker from Berlin had given Thomas much background on Wilhelm in many of their conversations. Thomas had learned that the kaiser had been injured from birth, leaving his left arm incapacitated, and this handicap, along with his diminutive size, may well have contributed to great insecurity in his early life. His mother, the eldest daughter of Queen Victoria, was domineering, outspoken, and headstrong. Her liberal British views, which her husband often shared, soon alienated her father-in-law. The young Wilhelm, increasingly at odds with his mother, came to identify himself more and more with his dour, conservative grandfather Kaiser Wilhelm I. His estrangement with his own parents, particularly his mother, would become complete in 1888.

In that year his elderly grandfather at long last died, and rule passed to his father. The reign of this unfortunate man was already doomed, as he suffered from advanced laryngeal carcinoma. By June he too had succumbed, and at the age of twenty-nine, Wilhelm assumed the throne as Wilhelm II. One of his first acts was to forcibly evict his mother from her previous residence, making it his own palace, and to confiscate as many of her and his father's documents as he could gather in the course of this eviction. Determined to show his independence, his estrangement from his mother only increased when he replaced many of the top advisers of the previous kaiser with those of his own choosing.

Thomas knew something of the kaiser's unstable nature and realized that it might be conceivable that his dramatic public appearance and subsequent speech might have been launched in a fit of pique, without benefit of appropriate consultation. Wishing to emulate the autocracy of his grandfather, what could be more natural than to show his displeasure with either France or Britain through a petulant act enhanced by the trappings and threat of his formidable military? If this spectacle in Morocco represented a spontaneous and undisciplined act by the young kaiser, then Thomas shuddered to think how much trouble Germany—and indeed all of Europe—might be in for in the future.

Whatever had motivated the kaiser to act, Thomas realized, was now less important than the implications that would inevitably follow. In the course of one speech, the kaiser had tossed aside the atmosphere of restraint that had moderated European diplomacy for decades and introduced a new bellicosity that demanded attention not only for its tone and manner but because of the military might behind it. The idea that German force was being employed to support German statesmanship was so unsettling it could not be easily forgotten.

All of this had ethical implications, a consideration that had long fascinated Thomas. His family background and subsequent studies had fostered a deep appreciation for the Greco-Roman and Judeo-Christian tenets of Western society. Now, in Europe a new idea was rising to challenge this ideal, based on the observations of modern biology. Influenced by his observations on a distant archipelago, the British naturalist

Charles Darwin had concluded that life as we know it is a process of continual change and evolution. Our present is not an exact mirror of our past but has been and will continue to be shaped by the struggles for survival. Biology teaches us the inherent inequality between and within species, an inequality that Thomas was well aware of from his simple observation of life around him. Unlike biology, however, his Christianity addressed the issue by exhorting those most fit to care for those less fortunate.

Others, however, had used these biologic observations to propose a new modern ethos, based on the notion of the evolution of the fittest. Some modern social philosophers believed that struggle would select the strongest, which would be the foundation of a better future. For some, war was viewed as the ultimate instrument to facilitate this sorting process. Seen from that perspective, the kaiser's actions could be construed as support for such an ethos. A world where strength served as the ultimate arbiter for the future of humankind was too unsettling for Thomas to dwell on.

As the afternoon passed, Thomas grew increasingly tired from attempts to understand the day's news from Africa, but he clearly understood that whatever the basis for it, the kaiser's actions had reawakened concerns familiar to generations of Europeans forced to suffer the consequences of their rulers' miscalculations.

At long last the dinner hour was close at hand. He, like Robert, looked forward to meeting with his friends, hoping that their conversations might give him further insight and even assurance for the coming days. As for news today from Africa, Thomas realized that the only thing left to him at present was to hope and pray that better spirits and wiser heads would prevail.

3

AT THE BIÈVRE

Robert d'Avillard had found the restaurant Bièvre during his first weeks as a student in Paris. Wandering the quarters around the Ecole Polytechnique, he often came across restaurants or cafes and in fact had passed the Bièvre at least once without noticing it. From the outside, it had no distinguishing features that would attract the eye of the casual passerby. It had a front composed almost entirely of windows framed with dark wood and a large door somewhat recessed from the street. What first attracted Robert's attention were the crowds of patrons that seemed to collect in the early evening in the passageway to the door. This crowd included not only proper bourgeois couples and businessmen, but also fair numbers of younger diners who almost certainly were students. Reassured by the presence of other students he had entered to find an atmosphere that he would come to welcome after a long day.

Robert quickly discovered the formula responsible for the crowds that would grace the tables from early in the day 'til late at night. The list of wines had been well chosen, with selections from many regions throughout France. They frequently had a complexity and bouquet that was uncommon for their often-modest price. Even the humble house Beaujolais was more complex and far easier to drink than the young fruity wines of some competitors. The meals included a large variety of standard fare, prepared in a manner to please the most demanding diners. The food was priced in such a manner as to give further satisfaction at the end of the evening. The sum of all of this contributed to an atmosphere of joviality that invariably increased as the night progressed.

The owners, Paul and Yvette Joliet, were the basis for the restaurant's success. Paul was thin and energetic and oversaw the dining area. In providing service that was both efficient and attentive, he succeeded in making nearly all of his customers satisfied. Yvette oversaw the kitchen in a reserved manner, quite the opposite of her husband, yet she was able to produce a cuisine of excellent quality and consistency. In their efforts, they were sometimes helped by their young nephew and a wait staff who demonstrated a maturity and discretion well beyond their years. For the first-time diner or regular, this mix of capable personalities and excellent dining created a welcome relief that was truly restorative after the stresses of a busy day.

Following his discovery, Robert came to dine frequently at the Bièvre and soon began bringing many of his acquaintances from school to share a drink or a meal as well as conversation. With the arrival of Thomas in Paris, the Bièvre became nearly a nightly dining hall for at least one of the cousins and their large group of friends. Soon their relationship with Paul and Yvette changed. No longer simply proprietor and proprietress, they counseled the gathered students about routine matters of daily life and in so doing increasingly took on the role of surrogate parents. The two cousins would rely on Yvette's studied, unrushed wisdom and Paul's enthusiastic encouragements to help their transition from their protected Provençal boyhood to early manhood in this most cosmopolitan of cities.

To accommodate the number of their evening gatherings, the cousins soon adopted the back area of the restaurant because it provided them greater privacy. As the circle of their dining companions increased, it was at first necessary to utilize more than one table. With the arrival of Thomas, this would soon prove inadequate. Thomas, with his quick smile, unthreatening manner, and formidable intellect, had a knack for attracting large numbers of acquaintances of diverse backgrounds and interests. Soon, a large table situated conveniently in the back of the restaurant would serve as the hub of their gatherings, where the often lively and at times weighty discussions could be more easily accommodated. The Joliets seemed nonplussed by such a crowd of students with the potential of bringing loud and unruly behavior. Instead, they seemed to adopt them much in the same manner as relatives, and in showing them a measure of respect accorded to more established patrons, they helped to create an expectancy of more mature and responsible behavior.

Dependent upon work, studies, and finances, the makeup of the group of diners might vary, but there soon would be a group of regulars who could be expected to show up on nearly a nightly basis. These regulars soon gravitated to certain spots around the large table, which, in their minds, gave them a certain de facto ownership of that location. The broad span of the oaken table surrounded by the regulars enjoying their companionship, food, and wine soon acquired the nickname of the Round Table. Indeed, Paris at this time was alive with a remarkable flourishing of the arts and, enriched by a flourishing economy, was, in the minds of the young people gathered, in many ways a new Camelot.

This group full of the optimism and energy of their youth must have felt some kinship with the ancient knights who also shared a fortunate position in their society. Of this group, it was clear that their modern-day Arthur was Thomas d'Avillard. Tall and thin and with a quick smile, he had an easy manner with people and rarely forgot a face or name once he had made even the most superficial acquaintance. He was an attentive listener, respected the views of others, even if they differed from his own, and rarely lost his patience or temper. What was most striking, however, was the ease with which he could grasp difficult arguments and concepts and the remarkable logic of his own thoughts. Such a compelling combination of personality and intelligence made him the natural center of many discussions.

The group that surrounded him was truly diverse, coming from different regions and from various disciplines of study. They all shared, however, an interest in discussing the ideas and concerns of the day, as they saw them. The majority of the students studied at the faculty of the University of Paris. Their interests were in a wide range of studies, from the law to economics, politics, philosophy, and theology. Another major division was the group of Polytech students that comprised many of Robert's friends. The natural reticence of these aspiring engineers and scientists balanced the verbosity of the law students and others. Students of economics and politics gave a more secular bias to the discussions than the aspiring theologians and philosophers. The dynamic engendered by such a group of bright and strongly opinionated people required, early on, that a set of guidelines for their conduct be accepted.

Such a group had the potential for noise and disruption that would be unwelcome to Paul and Yvette and harmful to their business. Thomas therefore proposed that it would be his duty (or that of another so designated) to insist upon conversation at a volume level that would be acceptable to any nearby diner. In part out of concern for Paul and Yvette's business but also to limit the size of the crowd, he insisted that anyone at the table had to be a paying diner. He also understood the passion that some topics elicited among his friends, particularly when differences arose, which they frequently did. Rather than avoid controversial subjects, he insisted that any discussants use restrained language and that they treat their fellow diners with appropriate respect. Anyone who broke these rules risked sanction or being ostracized altogether if his or her bad behavior became habitual. It was a testament to Thomas that rarely was the spirit of their unwritten agreement broken.

As Thomas entered the Bièvre, burdened by his thoughts about the day's events, he paused to allow his eyes to grow accustomed to the interior from the bright sunshine outside. Already a large crowd had gathered amid the tables decked in their red-and-white tablecloths, which contrasted nicely with the rich wood paneling. The large zinc-fronted bar was arranged along the length of a wall, which was flanked on one side by the door to the kitchen and on the other by a large passage to a backroom. This backroom was sunken a few feet below the front part of the restaurant and looked out on a small courtyard, which frequently hosted diners in the warm months. The backroom had several smaller tables and one very large round table at the very back. The location and design of the room, separated from the front of the restaurant, made it a natural gathering place for the many students of the quarter.

Already Thomas could see a large quorum of friends gathering in this area. The maître d' Paul quickly led him to the large table, where Alfred, the most senior of the waiters, was serving from a large carafe of house wine. Thomas was happy to see that Robert had already arrived, as his quiet presence always seemed to reassure him, and today this reassurance was certainly welcome.

"Thomas, where have you been?" Robert asked. "At last we can get some guidance in this German matter."

"So you may," he replied, "but I first need some of that red wine that Alfred is dispensing." Glass in hand, he took a long draught and with a sigh seemed to visibly relax. After a few more sips, he at last asked, "What does anyone know for a fact about this affair, beyond what is reported in the papers?"

Robert's friend Pelletier suggested that he had heard that ships of German troops had been assembled in Hamburg and were in the process of being dispatched to the Mediterranean.

"Who told you this? Someone of authority?" Thomas asked.

"It was an old family friend who is a major working on the staff of General Andre," Pelletier replied.

"Is this a fact or supposition?" asked Robert.

"I suppose it is just supposition, but the major says that planning for the present must consider this as a real possibility."

"Did you or anyone else observe any significant change in military activities along Rue Saint Dominique or anywhere else?" asked Thomas.

Aside from a general impression of an increased level of concern and intensity of action of the resident military, no one had seen indications of significant increases in the numbers of troops or weapons in the city or in transit through the train stations.

"Well, given the lack of an immediate tangible response on the part of the army, I suspect that the kaiser's actions were as much a surprise to them as they were to us," Thomas suggested. "The fact is that the kaiser has chosen a very public forum to deliberately challenge French colonial rule in North Africa, but where this will lead seems uncertain to me, at least as of now."

One of those sitting to the right of Thomas—a chunky, somewhat tall, sandy-haired youth named Jacques Painchaud— spoke out, unable to contain himself. "I am not convinced that there is any imminent military action behind this gesture. We had a long discussion with Professor Rolland today, and there were many German students present. I also spoke to several others afterward. Not one could honestly say that he had any notion that this would occur, and all seemed every bit as distressed by it as we French students. Most of the German students that I am most familiar with come from the south and west of Germany, where many have families actively involved in commerce. Such commerce in Germany is dependent on France to supply raw materials and to buy their goods, just as commerce in France is increasingly dependent on German participation. Many of the benefits that we enjoy from our present economic condition depend on the cooperation of the two countries, as well as others, such as Britain. We can no longer rely solely on ourselves to provide a modern standard of living.

"If the kaiser's threat is carried out and results in war, even a limited colonial war, what little that might be gained in territory would be offset by the severe economic losses that the disruption in trade and cooperation would cause in Europe. Modern Germany is no longer the play toy of the Prussian elector. My German friends see such a rash action as being every bit as destructive to German interests as to our own and seriously doubt that there would be any support for it among the commercial class or their representatives in the Reichstag. That is why I believe that this is nothing more than a glorified bluff, designed to bully concessions from us and the British. I know, Sarah, that you don't often agree with me, but I suspect we have similar views on this matter."

The Sarah in question, Sarah Morozovski, had made a habit of sitting directly across from Painchaud, either to stay far from him or to better confront him in their frequent disagreements. She had dark auburn hair that she frequently kept wrapped on top of her head, giving her an informal appearance that contrasted with her often-intense manner. When she became irritated or involved in arguing a point, her large brown eyes took on an increased intensity that was quite remarkable. She had a trim figure with an attractive bustline, all of which she took care to hide in the loose, drab fashion she usually wore, which was more in keeping with a working-class housewife than a student of the law. Those who knew her better, however, had come to recognize a young woman possessing strong beliefs and great intelligence, regardless of her appearance.

"Hopefully you are right, Painchaud, but do you really expect me to agree completely with anything you might say?" Sarah replied with a slight smile. "Any military adventure like this would be economic folly. Moreover, there are others more numerous than your beloved industrialists and capitalists who would strongly oppose such actions. The progress and wealth to which you allude has not fallen equally across our country. For every fine salon on Parc Monceau, there are thousands of squalid flats all through the northeast quarters of this city. Too many times the people living there have heard the empty promises of kings, emperors, and even revolutionary councils turn into ill-chosen adventures, primarily to enrich themselves and empower their followers. All too often the poor and the workers have borne the suffering and bloodshed that came with this stupidity, while sharing little if any gains that might have come from them. They have long memories.

"This is not simply the lot of the French worker," she continued. "Across Europe and especially in Germany, those who do the work are increasingly vigilant. No longer can it be taken for granted that the workers of France or Germany will cooperate with any plan to spill their blood and destroy their homes so that some illegitimate clique can cling to power, and some bankers and capitalists can make their profits. If this kaiser wants foreign military adventure, he will have to proceed not only without the workers but in spite of them."

"What you both say seems quite reasonable, and if the world operates by reason, then we can all rest more comfortably," Thomas added hopefully. "The history of humankind, unfortunately, is one of brief periods of constructive behavior interspersed with long epochs of destructive, irrational violence. We are living in the shadow of Darwin with his treatise on the biology of struggle and evolution, which has given some scientific credence to adventurers seeking to impose their will on others, no matter how irrational or immoral such actions may be. To such people, the destructive consequences of war might be justified as necessary collateral for the achievement of their ends."

"I see your point, Thomas, as frightening as it is," Sarah added.

"A rational person could take comfort from even Painchaud's arguments, but that conclusion may be a bit arrogant or at least naive. Who is it that says that the German government shares our beliefs or, more importantly, respects them? Without understanding their motives, it is impossible for us to draw appropriate conclusions. It is that uncertainty that is disconcerting."

"Exactly," said Thomas. "The more I thought about this today, the more concerned I became when I was unable to understand the true motives for the kaiser's actions. We all sense that they signal a very real change in our relations with Germany, but what is driving that change? Normally, I would not expect the Germans to act without a clear understanding of their actions, but with this kaiser, as erratic as he has shown himself to be, even that assumption is uncertain.

"I don't doubt what you say, Painchaud, about the beliefs of your German friends. It seems to me that in Germany there is a great diversity of opinion regarding the appropriate relationship of their government to the citizenry and to the rest of Europe. Your German friends, Painchaud, are what we at this table would call good Germans, since they share many of the liberal democratic views that we have become comfortable with here in France."

Paul Becker, another regular, whose interest was in the study of politics and government, quickly added, "What we often overlook is that the concern we have for individual rights in France is not shared or believed in by those in command of Germany. Our laws in this republic emphasize the rights of the common man to liberty and equality. Such ideals are held by some Germans as well, particularly in the more liberal western principalities where your friends are from, Painchaud. Unfortunately, Germany is shaped by Prussian ideals and institutions. From that perspective, the individual is important only in so far as he can advance the collective that is the nation. Any conflict between individual rights and those of the state invariably favors the collective over the individual."

"No doubt there are real differences between most of us here in this room and some powerful people in Germany," Thomas replied. "I am reminded of the number of influential writers there who believe it is time for Germany to take its rightful place in Europe. They draw their validation for these arguments in the aftermath of unification forged by Prussian military might. Some of these people view with disdain the traditional ethical values that we have relied on for centuries to provide law and order. A country such as Germany could be a formidable force with a powerful military aligned with such a new morality. I pray that what we are seeing in Morocco is not the first manifestation of such policy."

The animated discussion was interrupted by the arrival of a tall, well-dressed young man slowly entering the dining room. Although nearly the same age of the many assembled, his manner and dress made him appear older than he actually was. He had the appearance of a government functionary or of a diplomat from the Foreign Office, which, in fact, he was.

Upon seeing the young man approach their table, Thomas's face brightened perceptibly.

"Hervé, our most respected and able representative of the Foreign Office," he said in a tone of mock solemnity. "Please seat yourself among us, and give us a full appraisal of this change in world affairs."

The young man seated himself next to Robert with a self-satisfied smile, which seemed to acknowledge his importance in that moment. He first loosened his tie and sipped from a glass of wine that was offered him. Then, after a brief moment, he took up the challenge offered by Thomas's request.

4

THE GREAT GAME

Hervé DeLarmé was born for the Foreign Service. His father and grandfather had held prominent positions before him, and if the truth be known some relative must have served in some capacity back to at least the time of Hugh Capet. Unlike many, however, Hervé did not depend on nepotism for either his position or his advancement. He carefully cultivated his appearance with a tasteful, conservative wardrobe and a reserved manner, which gave him an air of gravitas more appropriate for someone older and more experienced. His somewhat imperious manner concealed a quick intellect with a deep knowledge of French history and its implications for foreign affairs. Though a few years older than Thomas, they had known each other since childhood, as their mothers had also been close childhood friends. Hervé at first treated Thomas with the tolerant attitude of an older, wiser sibling. When he later came to realize the intellect of his young friend, despite the differences in their ages and demeanor, he came to value his opinion and friendship ever more.

"What I'm going to tell you is not strictly confidential, but I know that some of you fancy yourselves journalists or journalists-to-be," Hervé began. "I would appreciate if you would use extreme discretion in how you use this information. Consider it off the record for the time being.

"We are now up to our necks in what the British call the great game. I believe that what we are seeing in Morocco has as much to do with our new relationship with them, the British, as it does with our own policy in the region. Our Foreign Office is now dominated by a generation that remembers, in vivid detail, the humiliation and anarchy that followed the disastrous war with Prussia in 1871. That it had much to do, initially, with an incompetent emperor mismatched against a shrewd Prussian statesman cannot be denied. What magnified this folly into the great tragedy it became was the lack of any ally or support for France from any country in Europe. Realizing our vulnerability, much time has been spent by our diplomats in trying to forge viable relationships with countries that might help balance German power.

"Russia was a logical first choice. Louis Napoleon had tried to engage them at the Great Exposition of 1867, but the Crimea was still too fresh in their minds at that time. Mutually shared fear, however, seems to facilitate accommodation, and as the Russians perceived the threat of a newly unified Germany, they began to negotiate with France in a more serious way. It has now been over ten years since DeClassé bound republican France to reactionary Russia in a mutual agreement to defend one another if attacked by an unnamed assailant; that is to say, Germany.

"At that time Germany was rather disengaged from the affairs of her neighbors, but for our senior diplomats this alliance, despite the great political difference of the two participants, was warmly welcomed, as it lessened the fear of being forced to fight alone against Germany, should she rouse from her quiet. Many at that time believed—and do even more so now—that a change to a more militant Germany was inevitable."

Hervé paused when his meal arrived, but after a few bites he soon resumed his monologue, interrupting it on occasion to make eye contact with his captive audience or to return briefly to his meal.

"Unfortunately for France, Bismarck was a truly historic figure. He made great plans and patiently focused all the economic, diplomatic, and military tools available to him to accomplish his ends. Chief among them was the unification of Germany. He fought wars with Austria and France, not so much for territory but to remove their resistance to the incorporation of the Catholic states into the greater German union. It is said he opposed the annexation of Alsace and Lorraine because he knew the poisonous effects that such actions would have on long-term relationships with France. It was probably one of the few times that the old Kaiser Wilhelm overruled him.

"After the French defeat in 1871, Germany was like a lion satiated after a large kill that withdrew to digest its meal. In the ensuing years Bismarck was much more concerned with the integration of the often quarrelsome liberal and Catholic German principalities into his new Reich than with the rest of Europe. This gave us in France valuable time to rebuild our cities and economy and to strengthen our army. In doing so we gained the strength and confidence to go forward with this Russian alliance, despite the great political differences between us.

"Once the alliance between France and Russia was made public, its implications were quickly recognized by Bismarck's successors. It may very well be that the policymakers in Germany dislike the French for a variety of reasons, but these pale in comparison to their emotions toward the Russians. Nothing gives the German aristocrat more fear than the image of Slavic hordes pouring across the flat plains of Prussia, burning his estates and raping his wife and daughters. They may dislike the French, but they loathe the Slavs."

Hervé paused to drink his wine, but before he could resume, Thomas interrupted.

"The Foreign Office had to know what effect a treaty pledging mutual support between Russia and France would have on Germany. At that time France was in a period of revival. Why then would they risk the relative peace and prosperity of these days by negotiating a treaty that would clearly provoke the Germans?"

"The defensible response is that our intelligence indicated a future change in German foreign policy. As the events of today prove, the present kaiser is a far different man than Bismarck. The opinion at the time of the Russian treaty was that the kaiser and his advisers were becoming restless with the limited role that Germany was playing in world affairs. They were becoming confident in the power of Germany after unification and their control over the country. Our Foreign Office believed that it would be only a matter of time before they would feel compelled to use their considerable assets to demand a leading role in Europe and throughout the world. What form these demands might take was unknown, but given the enormous German industrial capacity and the long Prussian military tradition it was a safe assumption that they would adopt a more confrontational foreign policy. If Britain and France were to benefit from vast and distant empires, why should they refrain from pursuing a similar expansive policy? If this led to conflicts with Germany, what country would want to face this threat alone?

"I will concede, however, that to suddenly be surrounded by two potentially hostile states was no doubt a shock to the Germans. Given their long-standing enmity for the Russians an alliance with Austria was a natural first step. This was quickly followed by accords with the Italians and Turks. This alignment of central European states may well have been sufficient to comfort their concerns were it not for the actions of one other, the most significant of all, our new friends the British."

At the mention of Britain the interest level of the table picked up, with even those far removed from Hervé leaning forward to better hear what he might have to say.

"Through such difficult lessons as the Thirty Years' War, the British long ago gave up trying to establish themselves as the dominant military power on the continent. Instead they have contented themselves with dominating the surrounding sea lanes and commerce. They have not ignored the continent, however. The very basis of their foreign policy is to ensure that no one continental power becomes dominant. To that end, they have used all their considerable guile, wealth, and—if necessary—military resources. It is due to our past position of prominence that we have been the focus of British enmity for centuries, as were the Spanish before us."

The assembled group, usually impatient with anyone dominating a conversation longer than two quaffs of wine, sat quietly, allowing Hervé to continue.

"For many years the ruling families of Britain were French. Now they are German and Protestant. This was reinforced during the last century when Victoria married the German prince Albert and her daughters various German aristocratic families, including the Hohenzollerns of Prussia. Such ties of blood and religion have made relations between many of the

German states and Britain naturally quite close. Suddenly last year, with great drama, there was announced a sweeping agreement between Britain and France, with each recognizing the other's territorial rights in Africa and suggesting that an even more remarkable agreement was being discussed for wider cooperation in other areas, including mutual defense. Many details, particularly with regard to a defense agreement, have not been completely spelled out, but the spirit of British cooperation in this Entente Cordiale is remarkable."

"My father swears that the British must be putting something over on us," Painchaud volunteered.

"It no doubt must strike many French and British odd that these old enemies can come to such a place in spite of history, religion, and family relationships," Hervé replied. "It is true that this present king is the greatest Francophile since the days of the Plantagenet, and his enthusiasm has served to warm the relationship for both governments. There is far more to this, however, than a playboy king's love of the good life of France. British policy is seldom fixed for a long time and is constantly being reevaluated. For years they were content with France, prostrate after Napoleon's fall, to disengage from continental affairs. They then concentrated on spreading their commercial interests worldwide in the form of their ever-growing empire. The dark clouds, however, began to form with our defeat by the Prussians and the consolidation of German power in the hands of the most conservative and militaristic of the German states: Prussia.

"Things were tolerable when Bismarck was concentrating on consolidating Prussian dominance of the new German Reich. This present ruling clique, however, is not beholden to Bismarck. Many there now believe that Germany is ready and deserving of its place as the dominant nation on the continent and the equal of Great Britain. To this end, increasing nationalism has been matched by increasing military expenditures and a more aggressive tone in their diplomacy. The change in German strength has been watched closely by the British. Such vigilance has most certainly led them to conclude that they can no longer ignore the continent."

Sarah objected plaintively. "As much as I hate to admit it, I am like Painchaud in not trusting the British. This whole thing strikes me as something out of Kipling, with the various Foreign Offices playing Europe like a chessboard and we the people of these countries forced simply to observe and accept the consequences."

"It is indeed the great game, Sarah. Believe me; I know from watching all the machinations in our offices this week," added Hervé. "To understand the game, however, it is helpful to know the players, especially the British.

"What followed from British alarm with the kaiser was our first substantive agreement with Britain in decades, which was remarkable in that by clarifying the spheres of British and French colonial interest, a major source of friction between the two countries was resolved. Even more remarkable than this first accord has been the rapid rate of progress that our two nations have made in drawing up terms of a mutual defense pact. The implication of all this is quite clear; the British have decided that German power and behavior has become so threatening as to require their intervention to balance its influence on the continent and elsewhere.

"If the Franco-Russian agreement was disturbing to the Germans, this accord with Britain has to have been a revelation. Wilhelm at first blamed it on the enmity of his uncle, King Edward, but regardless of its basis, he and his advisers must have understood full well the implications of British sea power added to that of the land power of France and Russia. Such an alliance must have caused long nights for the German general staff. Most importantly, it offers tangible proof to the German rulers that the English, a people to whom many are related, have forsaken the ties of blood for what must seem to them a treacherous alliance with those of far different backgrounds and beliefs.

"Now with Russia compromised by the failures in the war with Japan, and the incompetence of her military exposed, German anger has been given opportunity. This crisis in Morocco likely represents to the German government less of a colonial opportunity than a means to undermine the new Franco-British agreement on colonial rule. This military display and imperial bombast are a glove slap to the face of France and the alliance with Britain. It is not simply a rejection of the terms of a Moroccan agreement made without their consultation but more importantly a challenge to the French relationship with Britain itself. Now without a viable Russian ally, these two are much more vulnerable to the threat of German military power."

"Extortion on a national scale," added Thomas.

"If not extortion a very powerful challenge to the British and French alliance," Hervé replied. "If their challenge is accepted and war erupts, they no doubt have concluded that the present circumstances give them a distinct military advantage. If they are able to get significant diplomatic concessions, then that will undercut the strength of the Franco-British alliance. The unsettling implication is that the Germans seem willing to risk war at this time to obtain their ends. Is the threat real or simply extortion? At present no one can be sure, but nevertheless the kaiser's actions alone have transformed the thinking throughout our government."

As Hervé continued with his discourse, he was surprised

43

that the group around the table had remained quiet and intent on hearing what he had to say.

"Unfortunately, with this crisis, an attitude that I have observed with many senior foreign servicemen seems only to have gotten worse. German matters, no doubt influenced by their experiences relating to the Prussian War, seem to illicit intense reaction from them, which I sometimes worry may affect the way that we approach this problem."

Sarah interjected, "This whole affair makes me furious. How is it that the older generation can speak for me? What do they know of my concerns, or what do they care? Why is it that the people of our generation who will bear the brunt of any fighting have no spokesperson? I know that this has always been the fate of the young but does it make it right? Supposedly, in this republic the voters have some say-so in such matters, which might help restrain our own military aggression, but for me and the other women who make up half the adult population, even that option is closed.

"It now seems clear that our fate is to be determined by a ruling clique in Berlin who has no interest in any of us here tonight. All of this shows how naive we have been to think we have some control over our futures. It is as if we have been living in a dream world replaced now by a much meaner realty."

"I would not give up on the Foreign Office yet," replied Hervé, "even if you think they may be too old or too militant for your liking. Although many of them may be motivated by an intense dislike of the Germans, they are also quite intelligent and experienced. I feel confident that if we have the luxury of time, a solution can be shaped that will neutralize this crisis."

Eduard Laboteaux, an aspiring journalist who had just arrived from his new job at *Le Figaro*, broke in. "The real problem, Hervé, is that this crisis makes it essential that we clearly understand how far we are willing to go to oppose German threats. If we are not well prepared to face them this time, we must hope that we can escape a reckoning, but if not this time there will surely be a next in which the demands and risks become even greater. At some point, a time may come when we have to decide whether to acquiesce or resist. If we resist, our fate is uncertain. If we submit, our destiny is much clearer. Our way of life and what we hold dear will be made subservient to the needs and approval of the Germans. One has only to visit Strasbourg to see our future. Leadership will pass to the east, and we, as a people, will descend in importance, much like the Spanish before us."

"I believe there is a real alternative to this bleak vision that you propose, Laboteaux," answered Sarah. "It may be that if left to the nationalists, war might be a logical conclusion, but such wars will require every able-bodied man. What if vast numbers of men refuse to fight in such a war? Why should a worker in Lille or Paris go to war against his like in Berlin to enrich the industrialists and other capitalist overlords?

"I study legal theory and international jurisprudence but naively have given little thought to the mechanism by which that law can be upheld if conditions in Europe are radically changed. We enjoy our arguments and discussions with one another, deluding ourselves that we are actually deciding rather than simply discussing the questions that we debate. Now we see that the designs of men far away, with whom we share little, may disrupt our tidy little world. I am no longer in the mood for such naïveté. You are right, Laboteaux; we must choose to act or acquiesce. From now on, I plan to act in ways that might stop a mad progression to a senseless war."

"It is clear as of now that none of us has a clear understanding of what will come from these events," added Thomas. "We can only hope that it will be less serious than we imagine. Sarah, you may ultimately be right about our present impotence, but it seems to me that this marks a moment for us all to reevaluate our convictions and what we would be willing to do to support them. For now, I pray that God gives us all—and especially our leaders—the patience and wisdom to see this crisis through to a peaceful end."

As was often the case, Thomas's words served as a fitting coda, reflecting the thoughts of the many present. It only remained to see if they would be granted a reprieve that would give those inclined to action the opportunity to influence similar events in the future.

5

COLONEL FOCH

The following day, upon returning to the office in the afternoon, Robert was handed a note by Madame Broullard from Professor de Rochelle. It read, "Please bring your most recent work, if you can, to my home tonight after six o'clock. Afterward, I hope you may stay for dinner, as I have an old friend coming whom I think you will enjoy meeting."

Robert had often dined at Professor de Rochelle's and enjoyed the company and the informal discussions with him and his wife. Even more, he liked the chance to dine well in lovely surroundings. Armed with the work of the last several days, he arrived at the professor's home promptly at six and was shown into the library by Madame de Rochelle. "I am afraid that the professor will be a bit late, Robert. May I get you an aperitif while you are waiting?"

As the two talked about the recent events that had altered both of their daily routines, the professor at last arrived.

"Good evening, both of you. Once again I have to apologize

to you, Robert, for keeping you waiting. I trust that your day has been more productive than having to wait for me."

"I hope that is the case. I have what I believe to be nearly a final rendition of the plans that I have been working on, pending your approval."

In short order the aperitif was placed aside, and both were engaged in a contemplative discussion about the merits of various options and sites for two impending bridge constructions. Satisfied that his review was complete and a satisfactory plan was in place, the professor removed his jacket and joined Robert for a drink.

"I have an old friend that I mentioned in my note who will be joining us tonight," the professor said. "I expect him at any time, although he is even more involved with this German incident than I am, so he may well be late. He served with me in the Prussian War and knows your uncle as well. We both enrolled in the Ecole Polytechnique, but he would return to the military rather than to engineering. I am proud to say that he is a rising star in the army, and I am told on good authority that he will soon be promoted to an even higher position here in Paris."

At that moment Madame de Rochelle entered, accompanied by a short man with a quick and lively stride, bearing a prominent mustache that seemed to mask his face. He was dressed in the working uniform of a colonel, and upon seeing the professor, he quickly brightened into a wide smile. Robert could not help but notice how different the two seemed in size and temperament, but it was apparent from their response to each other that they were close friends.

"Here is your friend Henri, who has kept us all waiting for our dinner," Madame de Rochelle said with feigned indignity.

"Ah, Mathilde, you know that I would never keep you waiting if I could avoid it, if for no other reason than it would delay my eating a wonderful meal," replied the colonel. "If we must, we can eat when you wish, but I could use an aperitif if there is time. This day has seemed like a week."

Smiling as Madame de Rochelle brought him a kir, the colonel noted Robert, who had remained in the background until that time.

"Ah, Henri, this must be your young associate you mentioned today."

"Yes, this is Monsieur Robert d'Avillard, the young nephew of our old colleague Jean d'Avillard. Robert, I would like to introduce you to my old friend Colonel Ferdinand Foch."

As Robert shook the colonel's hand, his voice reflected his surprise at this unexpected meeting. "Colonel this is a great privilege to meet you. I have heard my uncle speak of you often and always with the greatest of respect."

"Thank you for your kind words. If you are anything like your uncle, then no doubt you will be a great asset to Henri. Your uncle is an old friend and a most honorable one at that."

As if in anticipation of a jealous hostess Foch continued.

"Henri, I always look forward to a visit to your home for the wonderful camaraderie and especially your wife's meals. Tonight, however, I fear that the events of the last days may dominate our conversation, but I refuse to let them dampen my appetite or affect my mood."

"Now, my distinguished colonel and the whole lot of you," interrupted Madame de Rochelle, "you must stop for a few precious moments and enjoy your dinner before you try to resolve all of your pressing issues, A good meal is your prerogative as Frenchmen, and what would be the use of all your efforts if you denied yourselves this privilege?"

"How lucky you are, Rochelle, to have such a wise and beautiful wife," Foch replied.

49

At that moment the maid entered, inviting all to the dining room.

Robert soon found himself seated across from Colonel Foch, while the professor and his wife sat at opposite ends of the table. Such seating arrangements were often as great a concern to a hostess as the meal itself, for great conversation, when paired with fine cuisine and wine, made a French dinner one of the great institutions of Western culture. As the first course was consumed, Madame Rochelle spoke of the new fashions for the coming season and her difficulty with the butcher's shop, where the proprietor, an old favorite, was away for the week. She worried aloud about the upcoming veal course but quietly expected it to be better than her concerns would suggest. When discussing her daily travails, her tone sometimes became quite somber, no doubt reflecting her anxieties related to maintaining a proper French household. What matter was a distant kaiser when your butcher was away?

By the time the veal course arrived, the colonel had gradually assumed command of the conversation. His description of his distant travels in western Africa and Algeria soon gave way to a most animated discussion of his trip to London, where he had met for a long series of planning sessions with his equivalent in the Royal Army, a Colonel Henry Wilson.

"I was surprised how much I enjoyed London and the countryside. I had expected the dreary weather, but the success of the meetings and the warmth of the British reception more than made up for that. It was remarkable, as if the centuries of past quarrels were no longer relevant. Wilson is a bit eccentric, as befits his English origins, but his energy and enthusiasm for my writings about tactics makes him seem to me something of an English kindred spirit. I would never have thought that I could become so friendly with an Englishman. As pleasant as my days were, however, there was still one significant detail of British life that seems unchanged—the abysmal nature of their incessantly fried and overcooked food. Jeannette, you don't know how much I appreciate your meal tonight as a reminder of what eating should be and as a welcome escape from that awful aspect of Britain."

"How incredible it is that we are actually discussing cooperating with the British," replied the professor. "It seems all of our history has us embroiled in one affair after another with them."

"Such are the times that we live in," said Foch. "The world has indeed changed profoundly. If we and the British are not able to adapt to these changes in a constructive way, then I am afraid that both of us will suffer the consequences from a new alignment of power."

"The German Empire," added the professor.

"No doubt," said Foch. "That is why I believe it so important to supplement the strength of our army with that of their small land forces and enormous navy. Such a formidable combination must give pause to any German idea of territorial expansion. We are only in the early stages of working out how such cooperation will proceed, but these talks have given me much optimism for the future, if only we can manage the crisis before us now. Enough of my monologue for now. I am more interested in asking Robert some questions. Henri tells me you are his star pupil. Do you really enjoy the work of an engineer, or is it simply easy for you?"

"A bit of both, I believe," Robert answered. "I enjoy mathematics and physics, which are my favorite subjects, but what I really enjoy is using some of these abstract principles in real-world applications. For example, we have been working on the design of several bridges to carry both rail and wheeled traffic. If one simply focuses on the mechanics of the structure itself, one loses sight of the more critical questions. We are in the midst of a transportation revolution. Rail and motor traffic have shrunk the scale of Europe to the traveler—or, in your case, an army.

"A bridge can be conceived as a resister in a circuit not of electrons but of traffic. A bridge must therefore be planned as part of a greater whole, which is the circuit of anticipated traffic. In any circuit design, it is important to know the potential magnitude of the current and to gauge the speed inherent in the circuit; in civil engineering terms, the current flow is how much traffic will be anticipated and how quickly it must move. Only by considering the entirety of the potential for a system can a bridge be designed to provide optimal function."

"An interesting concept, Robert, and one I hope we can explore later. You may know that I was a student with Henri at the Ecole Polytechnique years ago, but I was certainly not at the top of the class like he was."

"That is not completely true," interjected the professor. "You may not have been the best mathematician or designer, but you had a great sense of the feasibility and utility of a project. It is that talent that serves you and the army well today."

"You may be right in some way." Foch replied. "I have always valued the discipline in logic and problem solving that I acquired as an engineer, and I continue to use many of those principles today."

"I am curious, Colonel," Robert interjected, "why it is that you chose to go back into the military after your schooling?"

"For me, it was an easy decision. For a young man I had already experienced many things, including fighting in the Prussian War. Compared to the camaraderie and intense emotions that I experienced in the war, the predictable, planned life of engineering seemed tame. Young people unencumbered by other obligations naturally gravitate to excitement, and I was no different. What made my choice seem more rational, however, was my experience with the brothers Clerval, whom I knew from the army and who were students in Paris with me.

"Their family had held lands in Alsace, which they sold after the transfer of rule to Germany resulted in conditions that they could no longer tolerate. They moved to the Franche-Comté, close to the Alsatian border, where we would go frequently to fish and hunt when we had vacation time. Many times we would ride to the crest of the Vosges and peer toward their old village, now transformed by the German flag flying in the town square. That sight made a profound impression on me then, and the thought of it still does today. I knew from my experience with the Prussians that there might come a time when they would use this position to invade France once again. If and when that time came, I felt that I had an obligation to use what skills I had to oppose it. It was therefore a natural choice for me to return to the army."

Following dessert, the men retired with their brandy to the library, where the work of the evening soon began.

"Henri, have you had a chance to review the progress on the two bridges over the Meuse and Aisne that I asked about?" Foch asked.

"I have, and that is one reason I asked Robert to come tonight, as he has been updating the work on them over the last two days. I believe the changes to be sound and the plans ready to be implemented. Robert, please show us what you brought tonight."

As Robert laid out the plans, he began to explain the diagrams and the thinking behind them. "The professor told me that we would need to increase the capacity of these bridges for both rail and foot traffic. They have been widened in a fashion that will allow the possibility of two parallel rail lines, if needed. Flanking this is room for at least two lanes of motor or foot traffic, and more, if fewer rail lines are deployed. This can be done at little increase in cost or time by reconfiguring the support and reinforcing the pilings, if necessary. I believe that these structures will be able to efficiently support the volumes that were requested and can be built within the specified cost limits."

"How long will it take to build these?" Foch asked.

"If the usual permits, material acquisition practices, and labor are used, they will take at least a year. If extraordinary measures are employed, it might take anywhere from two to six months, depending upon the weather and number of workers."

"How long do you think we have?" the professor asked Foch. "Do you think that the Germans would really cross into France as a result of a fight over Moroccan rule?"

"I don't know anything for sure, but I do know the German way of thinking in these matters. They would not be so provocative unless they are ready with some military response. They are a people who will gamble only when the odds seem right to them. We are now very close to a formal military alliance with Britain, but it is not yet in place.

"I am also concerned about the ability of the Russians to fulfill their end of our alliance, should we be attacked by the Germans." Foch continued. "Their war with Japan has been a disaster, which has cost them enormously and has disclosed the many weaknesses of their military. There is much civil unrest in their large cities, which will require a great deal of attention from their government. The Germans know full well that if events get out of hand we are essentially isolated, since the present condition of the Russian army makes it unlikely that they could provide any relief to us.

"Fortunately, what information we can get from our agents in Berlin does not suggest a big military mobilization, which, in all likelihood, would be evident if any serious offensive into France was imminent. Based on this information, I suspect and hope that any military action, if it comes to pass, will be confined to Africa. Even if no conflict comes out of this, however, it serves as a reminder of how urgent it is that we increase our ability to deliver large numbers of troops as quickly as possible to the eastern frontier."

"If these bridges are completed as designed, what effect will it have on your planning?" Robert asked.

"If and when they are built, they will give us the means to quickly move troops to areas where they will be vitally needed. I have been concerned, as Henri can attest, that critical infrastructure such as this is developed. At present, I will do everything I can to help facilitate this project, as we do not have the time to get bogged down in the usual small niceties of less urgent times."

"In the worst case, can the army stand alone in Africa or here in Europe?" Rochelle asked.

"The army, as you know, Henri, has been at the center of a decade-long struggle between the conservative and radical politicians and their aligned constituencies. In the past, with the rise of the most liberal parties, we have suffered much political meddling in the command structure and have had difficulty in obtaining funds for existent programs and key future developments. This has affected both morale and readiness. I know that I have been slighted for promotion because my brother is a priest, and many like me, with family or political ties to more conservative groups, have suffered similar slights.

"The politicians in place now, however, seem to have a more pragmatic view of the army, and we can only hope that the present circumstances will bring rapid progress in improving funding and morale. Already it seems that changes in the command structure are being made, including even a possible promotion in my own position and rank."

"That is certainly both encouraging and overdue," Rochelle replied.

"The atmosphere around the high command is certainly improved," added Foch. "I am very optimistic that the army will be stronger with each passing year. I get a sense of reconciliation, both with the radical political elements and the country as a whole, which has been missing for some time. Despite this, I am afraid that we are likely still at a disadvantage to the Germans, certainly in population and possibly in readiness. It would be better for us that any fighting is limited to Africa or—even better—postponed indefinitely."

"So you think that war with Germany is inevitable?" Robert asked.

"Nothing is certain," Foch replied. "I have spent the greater part of my adult life planning for this possibility, and this affair now brings that probability closer than it has been in years. Their present leadership is untested in international affairs but seems increasingly inclined to seize influence in the world, commensurate with their power, by whatever means possible. Such a policy will inevitably bring them into further conflict with us and no doubt the British. The history of Prussia has been one that relies on military solutions to resolve conflicts. Nothing in the makeup of the present German leadership would suggest a change in that inclination. It is therefore imperative for us to be as prepared as we can be to face that challenge.

"I also believe, Robert, that for France to survive, the

country will need the services of its most capable men. The men of your generation will play a crucial role in the years ahead. Have you thought about this?"

"Until the last few days I have been too absorbed in the narrow focus of my life to think about the threat some outsider might pose. Now, after the kaiser's threats, I and many of my friends are aware, perhaps for the first time, of a real threat to much of what we value and have naively taken for granted. The question for my friends and me is how best to address such a threat."

"You know, my young friend," said Foch, "that you could have an enormous opportunity in the army to do just that in the years ahead. Someone of your skills and background would be able to work on many critical projects that would materially strengthen France and help to protect those values to which you allude."

"You make a compelling argument, Colonel, but I wonder if I might not be able to do the same as a civilian."

"You might be able to work on certain projects, and almost certainly you will make more money as a civilian. What you will not get is the very tangible involvement in the early planning and development of the most essential projects, nor the intangible feeling of working as an integral part of a group with a shared mission that is larger than the more narrow needs of any one isolated engineering project."

"I appreciate what you are saying, Colonel. I have always been intrigued by the thought of working on great and important projects. I have also learned from experience that impulsive behavior is the enemy of the prudent. I will need some time to think this through."

"I hope that we all will have time to reach considered decisions," Foch added. "If you do as I hope, Robert, and choose to join our cause, then Henri knows how to reach me. I would consider it my duty to see that you have the appropriate assignments and superiors to maximize the benefit to you and the army."

As the night was late and they all knew the next day's demands would be many, they drew their discussion to an end, but not before Robert had an opportunity to thank both the professor and the colonel one last time for the evening and the opportunities presented.

6

SARAH

For Sarah Morozovski. the events of the previous days had been a revelation that had forced her to rethink her present status. The kaiser and the threat represented in his actions, coupled with Hervé's account of the elaborate machinations of the French diplomatic corps, had alerted her to the danger that now hung over the continent. Even worse was the sense that she and her friends had virtually no influence over the process as it presently existed. Now she realized that the conflict she had sensed for the last several years between her desire to please her father and her desire to strike out on a more independent course would need resolution.

In the years immediately after the Prussian War, her father, Joseph, was sent to oversee the recently established French branches of an increasingly prosperous family banking business founded in Kiev. By the time that he and his two brothers had come of age, the business established by their grandfather had so prospered that it moved its headquarters to Moscow and began to spread westward into Central and

Western Europe. As a Jew and the youngest of three sons, were he to stay in Russia, it was likely he would be removed from the center of decision making in Moscow for some time. His father, recognizing in Joseph the requisite financial acumen and social skills necessary to be successful in the refined world of Paris, had recommended Joseph's appointment to oversee the branch when business opportunities in France became more compelling. Joseph, attracted by the prospect of autonomy and the challenge of increased responsibility, more than any particular affinity for France, welcomed the opportunity.

So in 1873, full of enthusiasm, self-confidence, and naïveté, Joseph arrived in Paris at the age of twenty-five as the formal director of the fledgling French offices of Morozovski et Fils in Paris. The city that he arrived in at that time still had large tracts of her northeastern sections in ruins from the bloody days of the Commune. Worse yet were the financial difficulties France confronted from the combined blows of Prussian occupation, civil war in Paris, and postwar reparation demands from the Prussians. The country had also been weakened by the annexation of large tracts of productive territory in Alsace by the conquerors. Fortunately for the directors of Morozovski and Fils, Joseph at this time proved an inspired choice for their French expansion.

With French capital depleted in the aftermath of the French defeat, he was able to provide money not otherwise readily available to finance the rebuilding of areas of prime Parisian real estate, which had been damaged or destroyed during the Communard uprising. This not only proved financially profitable but allowed him to forge strategic relationships that would prove profitable in the coming years. As the French economy recovered and the pace of industrialization quickened, these relationships allowed him to participate in the financing of many significant and strategic projects, resulting in increased profitability and influence for the bank.

When Joseph arrived from Russia, he came with some knowledge of French manners, acquired from winter escapes to Nice. Those experiences did little to prepare him, however, for the subtleties and intrigue of Paris. Ostensibly a republic, France, in general, and Paris, in particular, was still governed along lines of privilege. The government bureaucrats had usurped the role of the previous court and continued the strong hand of central management of the country from Paris. The monopoly of high society held by the aristocracy was gone but had been widened to include the entrepreneurial classes, enriched by the wealth of industrialization. To move in these circles required Joseph to learn the written and unwritten rules. He found this to be a natural extension of his business, requiring him to identify the men and women of power and the means to relate to them. For this he had a natural aptitude, and this synergy between business and leisure would not only provide him a social outlet but also a means to further enrich his business.

In his first years in Paris, Joseph had the energy and build of his youth. Of moderate height, he was thin, except for his chest and shoulders, which were prominent and gave him an athletic appearance. He had a full shock of curly dark hair and bright dark eyes, which often gave mirror to his moods. His eyes, dark hair, and rather olive skin set him apart from the Northern European merchants of the Ile de France. These differences he tried to minimize by adopting the manners and dress of his French clients. His interest in fashion and appearance became more refined with his improving financial circumstances, allowing him to dress in an increasingly fashionable and costly style. Not only did this appeal to his sense of vanity but seemed to facilitate his business relationships.

It was natural, then, that this young, handsome, and increasingly successful newcomer would draw the attention of the many available and suitable young ladies of the Parisian Jewish community. For a time, Joseph enjoyed a series of short but torrid relationships with various women. He did so for mere pleasure, assuming it to be the natural accompaniment of success, and gave little thought to a more serious long-term relationship. This stopped when he met Anne.

The youngest daughter of a successful jeweler, she was, in her own way, as cunning and focused in her ambition as was Joseph. Rather petite, she nevertheless had a stunning figure that she knew how to present in the most appealing manner. When cross or tired, she had a rather haggard appearance, but otherwise, especially when she had prepared herself, she had rather striking facial features, with thin lips, a well-proportioned nose, and light green eyes that she was capable of accentuating with great effect.

When she met Joseph at the party of a mutual friend, she was at once intrigued. Later, as she learned more of his status, she saw in him an object worthy of conquest and set about in a concerted manner to obtain her ends. Joseph was no match for her designs and soon became persuaded that Anne was not only desirable but also would be a strategic asset to his future plans. The mutual belief in the benefit of their partnership served to increase their interest in each other, and after a brief courtship, they became engaged.

After their wedding, they settled into a nice townhouse near the Place des Vosges, where Anne soon took charge of its furnishing, operations, and social calendar. Joseph, adapting quickly to his more structured existence, seemed to gain new focus in his work and many other aspects that made up his new lifestyle. This protracted honeymoon would exist for nearly three years, when suddenly the idyll was broken by Anne's unexpected pregnancy and the birth of Sarah.

Whether her pregnancy was an accident or a temporary surrender to the timeless allure of motherhood, few women have been more ill-suited for this task than Anne. She soon saw in the birth of her daughter tangible evidence that she had now passed into a more mature and responsible role, one for which she was not prepared and would come to detest. No longer could she think of herself as the young and desirable woman she had hoped to be forever. She would now have to devote some of her time to the many unwanted tasks of motherhood. As Sarah grew and developed, her mother sensed herself aging and perceived her sexuality fading. This was reinforced by Joseph, who lavished his attention and gifts on his young daughter, with whom he was clearly enchanted.

These were the circumstances of Sarah's childhood—a father who loved her and, by virtue of his success, was able to provide much material comfort, but due to the demands of his work was unable to share the time with his daughter that both would have preferred. This was balanced by a mother who disliked the responsibilities of motherhood and deeply resented the loss of her previous lifestyle, which she ascribed in great part to her daughter. As traumatic as this dynamic was to the young Sarah, it would fortunately be ameliorated by the arrival in her life of her governess, Lydia.

Lydia Rothstein came well recommended, despite her young age, as someone with great intelligence and a comforting manner, which would be ideal for nurturing a young high-strung girl. In many ways Lydia was the very opposite of Anne. Though younger, she had a maturity beyond her years that she had acquired as the eldest of several children. This experience, coupled with her own quiet yet assured manner, made her a natural for the difficult role of overseeing the development of young Sarah. Her position was further enhanced by being the niece of a governess well trusted by Anne's family. Anne herself felt even more comfortable with the younger woman, as Lydia's rather plump figure and bland attire represented no threat to Anne's relationship with her husband.

As young Sarah grew, her precocious intelligence and independent spirit would prove a challenge to even such an able person as Lydia. Her job was often made more difficult by the tension between mother and daughter. Sarah often reacted coolly to her mother's evident dislike of her maternal responsibilities, creating a dynamic that was a constant source of tension. Fortunately for Sarah, Lydia's presence helped to greatly alleviate many difficulties that came from this tension between mother and daughter.

Joseph soon realized that the quiet, unassuming, and somewhat dowdy young governess was becoming an indispensable fixture in the household. Not only was she able to oversee his stubborn and bright young daughter, but she was clearly giving her sound guidance that her mother was incapable of providing. Her own diplomatic manner reassured Anne and lessened the potential for conflict that might arise between the women. For this reason when Lydia announced her intent to marry Karl Gold, an Alsatian who had moved to Paris after the German occupation following the Prussian War, arrangements were made to allow her to continue her role as governess yet spend the majority of her evenings and weekends with her husband. Through the ensuing years, as the family became more familiar with Karl and as Sarah matured, Joseph even felt comfortable in letting his daughter pay visits to Lydia and Karl's home, particularly when he and Anne were away from the city.

During these early years of her marriage, it became apparent to Lydia that she and Karl would not be able to have children of their own. As much as this distressed her, it helped draw her ever closer to Sarah, and consequently she and Karl came to view Sarah as their surrogate daughter. As Sarah matured into her early teenage years and her visits to the Gold household became more frequent, she was introduced to people and lifestyles that she would not have experienced in the sheltered world as the daughter of a successful banker. In that realm, she was expected to attend social events where she could move among her social peers and hopefully emerge with a set of skills and contacts that would serve her well in the future. As much as Sarah enjoyed the attention that she received in these settings from an appreciative group of young men, her experiences with Lydia and Karl gave her a much deeper understanding as to the differences between this contrived world of bourgeois gaiety and the more somber reality of the working class.

On her first visits to Lydia's home, even though it was but a short distance to the northeast from her own home, Sarah was struck by how different the neighborhood was. The orderly streets of her quarter were replaced by often rundown apartments and commercial buildings. The streets were crowded and filled with often-disheveled locals moving in a noisy and seemingly purposeless manner. At first, she was both fascinated and somewhat frightened by the strangeness and novelty of this other part of Paris. Though Lydia and Karl would relocate throughout the years as their economic circumstances improved, they would always remain in the quarter. Sarah also became more comfortable with the neighborhood, acquiring, through her experiences with the Golds and their many friends, an insight into the personal stories of many of the residents and the forces that shaped their lives.

Lydia, with her calm and competent manner, soon became a counselor and confidant to the many friends and relatives who brought her their tales of difficulties. Such hardships seemed to be all too common in this quarter. Lydia would listen patiently and, if not able to provide an appropriate solution, would provide wise and reassuring advice. When Sarah was young, her presence during these conversations was ignored due to her age. Later, it was tolerated, as Lydia's confidants knew that Sarah could be trusted in much the same manner as Lydia.

It was Karl, however, who showed Sarah the true nature of the quarter when she became old enough to accompany him on the many jobs that comprised his business. Karl's family had been livestock merchants in Alsace, and with his move to Paris, he transplanted his knowledge of the business—along with some old contacts—to establish himself as a seller of cattle, swine, and sheep to both small and large enterprises. He was a natural salesman, with an easy understanding of the needs and desires of his clientele, which led him naturally into other ventures. Over time, the scope of these undertakings, nurtured by his mercantile skills, made him a most vital member of the neighborhood. Sarah, sometimes accompanying him in his work, acquired a sense of the commercial needs of the working class, just as her hours with Lydia gave her an understanding of their fears and hopes.

From all this she came to understand many things. The working class mob, so despised and feared by many of her family's friends, in reality was composed of many who had the same qualities widely shared with those more fortunate. It was true that there was much wanton behavior in this quarter and that violence was also a more common feature of life for some. It was also true that for most, the aspirations and hopes for family and loved ones were not significantly different from their French countrymen in the far-off provinces or the wealthier suburbs of Paris. Sarah recognized this and increasingly came to identify with these less fortunate members of society. In so doing, she began to seek ways to help them improve their lot. What she quickly realized was that the control that these people had over the forces that shaped their lives was often insignificant. Sickness, economic downturns, and a host of other unforeseen misfortunes kept them constantly at the border of destitution.

This had always been the fate of the laboring class, but now things were different. With the rise of the industrial economy, the worker was far more important in the production process. The coal needed for steel, which was needed for the rails and trains and engines, could not be gathered and assembled without the toil of the laborer. If Europe was to continue its rise from subsistence economies it could do so only with a large and skilled workforce. The wealth accrued to the holders of capital would continue to grow, just as it had for the landholders of a previous era, but now these fortunate owners and managers were more dependent than ever on the rising number of workers who were concentrated in the production areas of Paris and the coal- and iron-producing regions to the northeast. Without their numbers and cooperation, the industrialization so critical to the vitality and growth of a modern nation could be brought to a halt.

Few people came to understand the implications of this better than Sarah, with her widely varied upbringing and experiences. From her readings and the stories Lydia's friends told her, she had learned that in the anarchy that had come over Paris during the protracted siege by the Prussians in 1871, the working classes had seized control of the city for a brief moment. In the bloody aftermath of the Commune, the rebelling proletariat had been reduced in numbers by mass executions, when the more conservative forces, which would shape the new Third Republic, regained control of the capital. It would take years thereafter for them to gather the numbers and influence that their brethren in other industrialized states, such as Germany, had already obtained.

Now, however, Sarah believed that the workers had come to a point where they had the leverage to influence their daily lives more than in any time in history. In her conversations with her many acquaintances and friends that she had made through the years, she sensed an increased confidence in their power and a willingness to confront those individuals and institutions that they felt had opposed their best interests. She came to believe that, if properly organized, the workers could gain their rightful place of influence in the coming years and with it increased power and affluence.

In her schooling, Sarah's affinity for the working class had drawn her to study political philosophy and the law. In a modern republic such as France, Sarah saw the potential that organized political power gave for legislating protection against discrimination and arbitrary behavior so common under more autocratic rule. She was intrigued by the political dialogue pertaining to the working classes and especially in the writings of the social scientists and philosophers. This inevitably led to her interest in the various workers movements in the capital and ultimately in attending some select speeches and meetings. This process, along with her own youthful idealism, slowly shaped and influenced her thinking and led to the development of her beliefs regarding the relationships between those in possession of the means of economic production and the vast majority, whose lives were controlled by this powerful minority. She was also careful, however, not to be so imprudent or radical so as to disappoint her father.

In all the years, she had not lost her fondness and respect for her father or her need to please him. He had been proud as she matured not only in her physical attractiveness, which she acquired from her mother, but more importantly in her intelligence and independence, which he secretly ascribed to himself. Despite the limitations of her gender, he had hoped to nurture her involvement in the bank. As the years passed, he had expressed his hopes to her and had also taken actions to give Sarah various small roles in the bank that would provide not only experience but also greater visibility by various key people in the organization.

Now, with the present crisis, Sarah sensed that her concerns about the rising threat of German militarism might force her to act in a way that would disappoint her more conservative father. Yet, the thought of a small ruling clique in Berlin threatening war was repugnant to Sarah. Unfortunately, she had learned all too well from her schooling of the destructive aftermath of the Prussian War and Communard uprising on the lower classes, who had borne a disproportionate share of the suffering during those years of upheaval. She feared a future war would prove equally disastrous to the workers.

As her interest in the lower classes had increased, Sarah had come to appreciate the writings and speeches of Jean Jaurès, above all other prominent French socialists, on the destructive consequences of war for the working class. In recent years, she had attended various events in the city where Jaurès was present in order to hear him speak and for the chance to meet him. Also during that time, she had become reacquainted with Benjamin Schoen, a young man she had met in her younger years.

Such meetings were common, as both families moved in

some of the same social circles, where various well-organized events were held to introduce young people of similar backgrounds to one another. Sarah had paid little attention to him when they first had met, as he was several years older. Recently, however, after a socialist gathering that she had attended, he had reintroduced himself, recalling their previous meeting and how much he still remembered it. There was something about this more mature Schoen's manner that made Sarah uneasy, and afterward she tried to keep any of their future encounters limited and formal.

Recently, however, at a meeting that both had attended, Schoen had mentioned his position at the newspaper l'Humanité owned by Jaurès and several prominent socialists. He had even suggested to Sarah that for a person of her skills, if she ever had an interest in working for the paper or the political party, he felt certain that a significant opportunity would be available.

At that time she had shown little interest in his proposal, not yet being willing to make such a public break with what she felt her father would wish for her. Her present legal work, while not fully aligned with his interests, was such that it could not be construed as an overt repudiation of his life's work. Furthermore, she did not relish the thought of the complications that exploring such an opportunity might bring in having to deal with Schoen. Now, given the new concerns raised by the kaiser's actions, she realized that she was obligated to explore what options might be available.

Sarah knew of few, if any, groups who were more opposed and more outspoken about the threats of militarism than the French Socialists. Leaders of the Socialist movement throughout Europe were well aware of the disproportionate burden borne by the working class in the limited wars of the previous half century and were convinced that the workers' proportion of casualties would be even larger in future wars. Jaurès was outspoken in his belief that wide-scale destruction would come from modern industrial warfare and was adamant in his opposition to such wars, if it meant pitting worker against worker in order to advance the interests of the ruling classes and their capitalist allies.

Sarah sensed that if the threat of war was to increase based on the actions and interests of the ruling powers of Europe, then men like Jean Jaurès, with their allies and resources, represented one of the best means to oppose such a disaster. If only the majority could be made to understand how little was to be gained by their sacrifice and how, by uniting their great numbers into an effective voice of opposition, they could prevent this unnecessary slaughter.

Now, prompted by her anger and concerns about such a possibility, she had resolved to act. In so doing, she realized that any prospect of success would require strong allies, and recalling Schoen's previous offer, Sarah had made an appointment to speak with Schoen about opportunities with the French Socialist Political Union. As she approached the offices of l'Humanité, she paused in front of the building for one last moment of consideration. She realized full well the effect on her relations with her father if she were to cast her lot with France's most prominent Socialists, but convinced of the necessity of her visit she entered briskly, content to accept the consequences of what might follow.

7

L'HUMANITÉ

Benjamin Schoen was waiting for Sarah as she arrived promptly at their appointed time.

"Sarah, I'm so pleased to see you here, but when I mentioned your working at *l'Humanité*, I never thought that someone of your talents would seriously consider such an opportunity."

"And what would that opportunity be?" Sarah asked.

Schoen hesitated a moment then answered. "Before we discuss that perhaps I should give you some more background so that you can get a better understanding of our operation here."

Hearing no objection he continued.

"This paper is a relatively new enterprise, and despite the fact that it was founded by some of the leading socialist thinkers in France, it has taken some time to establish itself both in readership and profitability. In the last several months, the trends in our circulation and revenue have been quite encouraging. This has allowed us the luxury of hiring new personnel in areas that are not only critical for the readership but also will provide a more effective vehicle to communicate with different groups who represent the interests of the working class. Knowing this, I casually mentioned working here, never expecting you to take my offer seriously.

"I have seen you often at socialist meetings and have often wondered what motivated you to attend them. I have studied your work at the law school and have read your thesis regarding aspects of labor laws in Germany and Russia. We here in Paris believe it is past time that we have more formal relationships with other socialists and political parties throughout Europe and especially in Germany. When I learned of your background, I had little hope that someone as accomplished as you would have much interest in the rough-and-tumble world that often passes for present-day socialism. It would no doubt be far more lucrative and prestigious to work in more acceptable areas of polite society, such as your father's bank."

"You must remember, monsieur, I know that polite society that you speak of well. I was born into it, but my mother and her kind never drew me to its ways. I owe much that I believe important to my governess and her husband. Through my contact with them, I have learned far more of human dignity and the potential for good than I ever did in the salons of the wealthy. Much of what I learned and prepared for in school was to give me the necessary skills to help my friends and acquaintances who are simply honest and hardworking, rather than rich and connected."

"Even with such a passion for the worker's cause, why would someone with your talents seriously consider working at a new and struggling paper such as l'Humanité?"

"This Moroccan crisis has awakened me to the reality of a new and more dangerous time for us all. At present, we are dependent on the current leaders of Europe to settle this matter.

Unfortunately, there seems to be little input by the people most at risk. If we are fortunate and this crisis can be resolved, and if future ones are to be avoided, then control of this process must be influenced by the workers and those most imperiled from war. If the present German government insists on a course that raises the risk of a European war, then I feel compelled to do something to prevent it.

"When you first approached me about working here, I was marginally interested, but the present threat has forced me to reconsider. I have realized that it would be difficult for an individual, especially a woman, to affect the existing establishment without the help of others with great skills and resources. I am here because I know the makeup of the ownership and editorial board and respect their views. To work with such people under the right circumstances might provide a satisfactory means to enhance my own efforts."

Schoen gave a smug smile that suggested a certain dismissiveness of Sarah's idealism. "As you may know, I studied law as well and was hired to provide a legal consul to the paper in the period during its start-up. As is the case in many new organizations, I found that I was doing much more than simple legal work for *l'Humanité*. Much of my work, then and now, has to do not only with the paper but with the Socialist Party. What I am saying is that any job here might be modified by the needs of the moment, which around here has a habit of changing rather quickly.

"The scope of my work has increased immensely since we merged our party this year with the Socialist Party of France to form the SFIO. This was done to give new impetus to our commitment as representatives of the French worker. It has also provided more resources to reach out to other national parties and individuals in the international workers movement.

What has become evident is the need for our presence in other important neighboring countries, particularly Germany, to facilitate connections with our colleagues in these countries and to increase our influence internationally.

"For several reasons, we have concluded that this could best be done by establishing a bureau of the paper in Berlin. This will require the hiring of key full-time personnel to implement the start-up. From my own experience, I suggested someone to head this effort who is well versed in the peculiarities of the law in these countries, because the authorities there might well use their laws to help discourage our presence. It is important, therefore, that our bureau is established on a solid legal footing so as to keep it in good standing with the German authorities."

"Am I to understand that this position is to be a combination of lawyer and journalist?" Sarah asked.

"In reality, this position is to establish and manage a working bureau in Berlin. The scope of this job likely will be fluid. It certainly will involve, however, legal decisions as well as political analysis. To do it well will require that the person involved establish personal contact with many influential people in Berlin, particularly in the Socialist Party. It is therefore a position that will require someone with the ability to manage an evolving enterprise and who has the skill to meet new people and cultivate critical personal relationships."

"Why would you think that I would be qualified for such a job since I have little management experience and virtually none as a journalist?" she asked.

"Your legal ability is evident, and in the beginning that is the most critical aspect of the job. Furthermore, I know from my own schooling that your legal background gives you the analytic skills that are essential to a good manager or reporter. Your background in political philosophy and your presence at socialist gatherings testifies to your interest and commitment. What I know of you and have observed leads me to conclude that you have the intelligence and personal skills that will allow you to develop and prosper in these other aspects of the job.

"Besides, whoever is hired to manage the office will be accompanied by others with experience in managing the accounting and back-office procedures. As for the journalism, think of it as the preparation of a good brief, replete with the appropriate facts, ordered in a manner that is easily digested. In such a format any editorial embellishment is easily accomplished."

"It certainly would not be like a lecturer at the college or an associate in a law firm," she said.

"Indeed it is not," he replied. "This is not the job for someone with conventional aspirations or a low tolerance for risk or discomfort. On the other hand, if someone enjoys the challenge of starting something new and challenging, then this would be an opportunity to seriously consider. How many jobs would provide the possibility of active involvement with the people shaping policy throughout Europe in a time of great importance? For the right person, despite the uncertainty, the hours, the variable nature of the work, and the modest pay, this could be an extraordinary experience.

"As I said, I believe that you have the skills to succeed at this job and to have a significant influence. It is really dependent on what you want. If you like the comforts of Paris and the known routine of your present world, this is not an opportunity for you. If, however, you relish the chance to break new ground and possibly shape some part of the future of the socialist movement, then it could be a great opportunity. If you are interested, I would recommend your name to Monsieur Jaurès. Any further decisions would be up to the two of you."

"Whatever you may think of my experiences or my skills, you also know that I am a Jew and a female. Such a combination no doubt makes me a target for our detractors and might well limit my effectiveness."

"I know these detractors well," replied Schoen. "They claim that we are clannish, greedy, and opportunistic. We have a right to be clannish. We are the people of a proud culture, thousands of years old. Our ancestors built a great society founded on a desire for justice, a concern for those less well off, and on living a good and righteous life. We were building the splendors of the temple in Jerusalem while the Gauls and all the other tribes of Europe were living in mud hovels. Those who have been our persecutors through the ages have usurped our most sublime and noble ideals and have used them as their own to help transform their societies.

"As to the other slurs that are so often used against us, I would ask where, in all the great teachings of our religion, does it discourage initiative or encourage avarice and greed? Instead, these teachings admonish us to use our wealth and influence to look out for the less fortunate and seek a better justice for all."

"As a woman and a Jew, I have experienced my share of injustice, but it is something that I have learned to live with. My point is to make you aware of how this might hinder my effectiveness."

"It might—if you allow it to," added Schoen.

"I know the slights I might have endured are nothing compared to the daily disappointments experienced by many I have come to know as friends, living in the working-class areas of Paris. I will not allow myself to be discouraged by bigotry if it would weaken my advocacy for them."

"I believe," added Schoen, "that if you respect our traditions and draw strength from them, then in this job you will have a great advantage, even with those bigots who hold your gender and race against you."

After a moment Sarah replied, "There is much to think of here. I will need some time to consider it further."

"Of course, that is only natural and proper. Unless I hear any objections from you, I will mention your name to Monsieur Jaurès. If both of you are interested, a meeting could be set up that would allow you to gain much more information about his thoughts and your possible future as an employee."

"Yes, I think that would be all right," she said in a soft, reflective voice. "Please go ahead as you have suggested."

"Very good, then," he replied enthusiastically. "I certainly hope that we can come to an agreement with you in the near future, as I believe that you will be of great benefit to the paper and the movement it represents. Thank you so much for coming in to speak with me. I will get back with you as soon as I can arrange a meeting with Monsieur Jaurès."

————

Sarah was excited by what Schoen told her. A position centered in Berlin would remove her from Paris and away from her father's oversight. She also hoped that her father would secretly be pleased by his daughter's striking out on a more risky course than the comfortable world to which she had ready access in Paris. She had resolved, however, to wait until she had spoken with Monsieur Jaurès to ensure that she had a better understanding of what the job might entail before she gave further thought to the offer.

Sarah would not have long to wait, as the morning after her meeting with Schoen she received a request to meet with Monsieur Jean Jaurès the following afternoon. Dressed in a more conservative manner than on her first meeting, she set out with a mixture of curiosity about the potential job and a resolve to impress Monsieur Jaurès.

Upon being shown into his office, Jean Jaurès greeted her wearing a rather plain dark coat, gray pants, and a collarless shirt in the style of many common working men. Sarah had seen him speak on several occasions, but she thought that he appeared a bit older from this closer perspective. He was a large man, both in size and height, but his hair seemed grayer than she could remember, which seemed to give him an older appearance, albeit one of some gravitas.

"Mademoiselle, I must apologize before I begin, since I likely will ask you some of the same questions that Monsieur Schoen has already asked. I had a thorough discussion with him yesterday about your meeting, which made me curious to find out in my own way about certain aspects of your interview."

"I would expect you to ask whatever questions you might need to satisfy your concerns, monsieur, just as I would expect you to allow me the liberty to ask any questions that might arise in the course of our discussions."

"Very well, mademoiselle. The first question is one that I am sure Monsieur Schoen asked in some manner. Why is it that you would be interested in working for this paper and in this line of work? After all, you have, by virtue of your accomplishments, established yourself at the law faculty, and with your family connections you should have many other options that could prove far more lucrative than what we would be able to offer you."

"Monsieur, what you say is flattering and at least somewhat true. We live in remarkable times, however, and in a remarkable republic, which would allow me, a Jewess, to achieve a position in such a prominent faculty, even such a junior and insignificant one. I fear, however, that the scope of my future work may be limited by the need to confine my actions to ones acceptable to the institution. I have already sensed many occasions in which some anticipated action might or would be deemed unacceptable or awkward by the more senior, conservative majority that comprise the law faculty. I am aware of the unwritten codes of expected behavior that exists within the school and find myself increasingly uncomfortable with them. Such conflicts are to be expected when younger people try to claim a place of authority, but I am now unsure that I want to endure them for an esteemed place in the university or an established firm."

"I see that you have some familiarity with the workings of the family banking business," continued Jaurès. "You could no doubt find some position there where your skills could be used to good advantage."

"Possibly, but banks—especially banks like the one my family has started—don't function as a matriarchy. What authority I might ultimately obtain would come at the discretion of male seniors. For the present, that would, of course, be my father, for whom I have the greatest regard. It has been his wish for me to play a prominent role in his world, but it is a world that presently has little desire to open its doors to a woman. Besides, my greatest concern there is that my presence at the bank might complicate his normal business dealings. I detest nepotism, and to think that I might be judged in such a light is not appealing.

"As much as I love my father, however, I have come to respect my governess and her husband every bit as much as him. From her I have learned more important lessons than in school. She and her husband have shared their lives with me and, in doing so, have given me an understanding of how they and their many working-class friends live. From my experiences, I have often seen how fragile their lives are, with significant hardships from any economic downturn or other calamities being borne disproportionately by them.

"I don't need to remind you, of all people, Monsieur Jaurès, that we are living in exciting times that now provide new opportunities for that large class of people. With industrialization, the number of workers has increased dramatically in the cities, and these numbers can bring increasing influence. If the working class can be well organized, then there is a great potential to finally give them their fair place in society and, with it, the means to better support their families. I have been drawn to socialism as a means to increase their influence, and listening to you and others has given me reason to believe that I might very well accomplish far more engaged in the movement than in the sterile confines of the law college or the constraints of my father's bank."

"You must know that there are many other voices advocating change for the workers, some of whom have a much different view from me. What draws you so much to an old man many say is too timid for the task at hand?"

"Monsieur, as I said, I did not come from the working class but know of their lives through my friendships. I also know many people in more fortunate circumstances. They are far more similar than many people believe. There is much goodness and evil, pettiness and nobility, in both groups. Those advocating a sudden and radical change in the structure of society can ignore and cast aside the good qualities of those more fortunate than themselves, but if they do so, it will come at great cost. Sudden change promotes violence, with the risk of economic dislocation and a breakdown in morality. We have, in France, a glaring example of this for all to see in the horrible days of the Commune. Such change with anarchy, starvation, and genocide is not the basis for a better society.

"To me, it seems that change, whenever possible, needs to be more lawful and consensual. I understand that anyone in power is loath to give up his privileges, but ever larger numbers of enfranchised voters from the working classes cannot be ignored. If we are diligent in insisting that the laws of the republic be enforced, and if we continue to pressure legislatively and legally for reform, then the rise of the worker will be inevitable. To see this through will require both patience and steadfastness—virtues that I have clearly seen in you, Monsieur Jaurès."

"What you say, mademoiselle, is wise beyond your years. Too often people, especially young people, want immediate change, not fully understanding the many complications that come from a sudden reordering of society. I am pleased to see that your youthful optimism still sees room for the triumph of patience. Unfortunately, history is not kind to your vision. Revolutions are not made by patient people or by consensus. It is not human nature to defer to some distant utopia when they believe change can be forced to their ends more quickly. How would you propose to bring about this transformation that you speak of?" he asked, with a hint of a faint smile on his face.

Sarah was taken slightly aback by this question and paused for a time to compose her thoughts before she finally spoke. "What I believe is that the working class must recognize their strengths through legislation and the law. As I mentioned, their increasing numbers will lead to ever more power if they are allied with wise and appropriate policy. It is, therefore, necessary to define those areas most vulnerable and utilize our collective strength to change policy in any way possible."

"That is a rather bourgeois workers' utopia," he noted. "If the workers have this power, as you suggest, why should they be subservient to the present ruling classes?"

"It is a bourgeois vision because I have seen what

opportunity such a society gives to people like me, who might be of the wrong sex or religion. I believe a society that affords an opportunity for all is far preferable to one where relationships are forced by dictate or unnatural actions."

"Then do you believe that workers have the right to organize in some form of cooperative or union to achieve their goals?" he asked.

"In many cases it is already legal in France, as well as many parts of Europe," she said. "In areas where it is not legal, then this should be fought by all appropriate means. This should be the right of any worker to organize, as long as he is not coerced into doing so."

"Spoken like a true advocate of the law," he said. "If workers are organized, then do you believe they have the right to strike?"

"Speaking as a lawyer, there are many—if not most— instances in France where this may be forbidden or heavily regulated. I am not advocating for carte blanche work stoppage and strikes, as there may well be circumstances of national security or public welfare where this may be harmful. I do believe that in the absence of such circumstances, it should be the right of workers to withhold their work. Not only do I believe in this right, but I believe it to be one of the most powerful tools that the workers potentially possess."

"What if there are justifiable grievances, and striking is forbidden?"

"In that case, monsieur, a very serious judgment would have to be made as to the greater good. Such a decision would be difficult and could, in all likelihood, only be judged in hindsight as to whether it was right or effective. Nevertheless, such a decision might be necessary in some circumstances."

"What might those be?"

"I have heard you speak of the awful implications of a

modern industrial war, Monsieur Jaurès, and strongly agree with your assessment. I have to believe there are many in Germany, committed to the interests of the working class, who fear this threat as well. Any conflict between France and Germany in the immediate future will not be based on any enmity between the workers of our two countries, but in the final outcome the workers of both sides will be the biggest losers. We in France need to make common ground with the workers in Germany and indeed with all the great states of the continent to oppose those who want to use their armies as a means to advance their ends.

"The crisis in Morocco has alerted me to the threat of a war based on the usual imperialist greed for power and wealth. As much as I respect the law under normal circumstances, there may be times when extraordinary actions must be taken. If the present leadership in Europe brings us to the brink of war, then the workers of Europe will need to be mobilized to resist it. There could be no more powerful deterrent to the present ruling classes than a universal strike of the masses to oppose their own slaughter."

"Mademoiselle, I share your concerns, but I hope you exaggerate the present circumstances. Many people think that there is more bluster than threat in the kaiser's words."

"I can only hope that they are right, Monsieur Jaurès, but what if they are wrong? If not this month, what about next year or the next? I fear that the kaiser's actions serve as the opening notes of a new era of German policy in which they will no longer be content to simply coexist with their many neighbors. We cannot let a small clique of industrialists and Prussian militarists seize the initiative in continental relations. We must organize ourselves, along with those many people in Germany and throughout Europe who share our beliefs, to oppose these people.

"Despite my feelings on this matter, I also understand how futile it would be for me to act without a dedicated and competent organization. I know of no one who is more eloquent or committed in voicing opposition to war, Monsieur Jaurès. When Monsieur Schoen offered me a possible opportunity here, I was interested to explore it not only out of my respect for you but also to explore the potential that such an opportunity might have to further my aims."

"You are far too kind in your praise, mademoiselle. I fear that your enthusiasm may have blunted your ability to perceive the true reality of my own prowess. Nevertheless, such compliments from articulate women are one of the few pleasures left to us old men. I certainly share your aversion to any war that is based on the imperialist desire for acquisition and have a great distrust of professional armies, which are the facilitators of such schemes. You are right to be concerned about a rise in militarism, as now we have the means to make war a horrible conflagration.

"It would be naive and wrong to think that any modern state could exist without the means to defend itself. We must ensure that the army is controlled by the people and not a small clique of professionals interested in advancing their own perverted notions. We must have armies in the future drawn from every fabric of society and governed by legitimate representatives of all the people. I'm afraid, however, that I have deviated far from the purpose of our meeting. I am excited to see that a young person of your caliber shares some of the same passions with an old man like me. I can predict that whatever might come your way in the future may not always be pleasant, but it will certainly be interesting. I have asked all the questions that need

to be asked. Do you have any further questions that you wish
to ask me?"

"I cannot think of anything, based on our conversation.
Monsieur Schoen was quite thorough in our earlier interview,
and any questions that I might have in the future will depend
on more specific proposals."

"Mademoiselle, I fear I am already late for several
appointments and must interrupt this most enjoyable
conversation. I will talk with Benjamin this afternoon about
some ideas that have come from our conversation. Afterward,
I hope that one or both of us will be speaking with you in the
very near future."

Jean Jaurès accompanied Sarah through the length of the
office to the street outside. As she saw his large figure return
to the building, she could not help but wonder about a future
association with such a man.

8

STEIN

It was only a day and a half until Sarah received another request to meet with Schoen. By this time she had resolved to seriously pursue any reasonable offer from *l'Humanité*. As she sat down with Schoen, she had in mind a clear set of objectives that she wished to discuss if a job was offered.

"Well, Sarah, as I expected, you certainly made a good impression on Monsieur Jaurès. As I mentioned, we have realized the importance of expanding the paper outside of France. To do that well will require that the right people are in place to maximize our chances of success from the outset. I have argued—and Monsieur Jaurès has agreed—that it will be important to have someone in place with local legal expertise from the first days of operation. After talking with you, it is Monsieur Jaurès's opinion—and one that I share—that there are very few people who have both the legal knowledge and commitment to the workers that you do. He has therefore authorized me to offer you a position with us that will utilize your legal background fully."

"I am pleased to hear this, since my discussion with him was very interesting. Now I would like to hear much more about this position."

"You would be hired as a legal counsel responsible for issues that will impact the implementation and ongoing operations of any and all bureaus reporting outside of France. As such, you will be reporting to me as your immediate superior. I have spent some time in recent days developing early plans for an office in Berlin. In so doing, I have come to appreciate that I don't have the time or enough expertise to effectively implement the project in a timely manner. As a first step, if you accept our offer, I anticipate helping to transition the management of this project to you."

"What would that involve?" she asked. "I would be comfortable with the legal issues of Prussia and Germany and setting up a bureau to operate within these regulations. No doubt I would be capable of overseeing the day-to-day oversight of back-office management with regard to hiring and bookkeeping, but I suspect that such duties might be handled more effectively by someone else or even in Paris, whenever possible."

"What you say makes sense from the standpoint of effective management, but we are a company of limited resources, and as such any employee might be expected, from time to time, to perform duties beyond or beneath the job he or she is hired to do. The willingness to do what is necessary was instrumental in the early success of the paper and has helped to create a very strong workplace morale."

"It is not my intent to avoid work but simply to imply that, whenever possible, the most effective means should be used, regardless of the geographic location. I have virtually no experience in some matters pertaining to office management, and I doubt if it would be in the best interests of the paper if I learned on the job, with little oversight from Paris."

"Monsieur Jaurès certainly agrees with you on that point and has every intention of providing experienced personnel to address such matters when necessary. We both anticipate, however, that with some seasoning, you will be able to handle an ever-increasing list of responsibilities, including even reporting on some issues pertinent to our readership. He recognizes, of course, that you will have many concerns in starting up this Berlin bureau, and he wants you to concentrate at first on establishing our presence there on a strong legal foundation.

"To facilitate this start-up further, I have been speaking to a number of experienced journalists to find a person who has the writing and managing skills to act as bureau chief in Berlin. Your role would be as legal consul, acting in concert with whomever we might hire. I would also add that you would act independent of this other person's authority, essentially acting as codirector of the office. At first I would not anticipate your being asked to provide any significant copy, unless some specific matter might interest you."

"I am pleased to hear this," Sarah replied. "I was intrigued by my discussions with you and Monsieur Jaurès, but I was nevertheless concerned about the true nature of the job. It is rather late in my career to abandon my legal studies to become a journalist. What you are proposing, if I hear you correctly, is for me to primarily act as a lawyer on behalf of the paper and the party."

"That is essentially correct," he replied.

"Would I be employed by *l'Humanité* exclusively, or would I be used on an as-needed basis, allowing me to continue with other work?"

"From my experience, it is very likely that to do this work

well, you will have to devote the majority—if not all—of your working time to it. If it can be worked out, we would prefer for you to work for us full time. Furthermore, to demonstrate our interest in obtaining your services full time, we would be willing to match your present salary, based on full-time activity, and give you a 10 percent bonus. At the end of the first year, you would be eligible for further considerations if your work is, as I expect, at a suitable standard."

"Would I be required to live in Berlin?" she asked.

"I believe that in the beginning, though you may spend long days over many weeks in Berlin, you will find it best to maintain your residence here. Some of your work will require your presence here in the home office, and it is likely that you will be asked to travel to other cities to assess certain conditions there."

"I assume that there will be some stipend for travel and living expenses?"

"Although we have not had much occasion to use it, we have a standard policy covering such issues, which I would happy to show you."

"Fine. I would certainly like to review it at some time. One other question that naturally comes from this discussion pertains to the journalist you referred to for the Berlin office. Have you hired anyone for this position, or do you have anyone in mind for the job?"

"As a matter of fact, we are very interested in a Polish immigrant who has been living and working in Berlin for several years. He is about ten years your senior and has experience in managing as well as writing for papers in Poland and Germany. Of equal importance, he has, we are told, a large network of contacts within the labor organizations of Eastern Europe."

"Have you spoken with him about this position?" she asked.

"We have only communicated through intermediaries and by letter, but I am scheduled to meet him later this afternoon, if he is able to arrive from Berlin. An informal agreement has already been reached with him about this position if we find that he matches our expectations during our interviews."

"If he is hired, I would need to meet with him before I could make any final decision," Sarah replied.

"Certainly. What if I set up a meeting later this week after Herr Stein and I have had a chance to talk? Rather than the stuffy confines of this office, we could meet at a more congenial location. Do you have any recommendations?"

Sarah felt a natural reticence to agreeing to meet Schoen outside the formal framework of the office, but she realized that if she was going to work here, there would be no escaping such meetings. Subconsciously hoping to provide herself some outside support, if necessary, she suggested meeting at the Bièvre.

"I know the spot well," Schoen replied. "That would work out well. It is close and has an atmosphere where we could converse without much difficulty. Besides, the food is good. We could plan to meet at four o'clock in two days unless something changes. Would that be suitable?"

"I can think of no conflicts with that time at present," Sarah agreed. "Unless you hear from me otherwise, I will plan to meet you at the Bièvre, then."

With that, they adjourned to meet later at the appointed time.

———

Two days later, Sarah set out for the Bièvre, as scheduled. As she walked into the restaurant, she glanced toward the backroom to see if any of her cohorts had arrived earlier than usual. Seeing no one, she took a table at the far side where she could wait for Schoen, who arrived shortly afterward, accompanied by a short dark man attired in the rumpled, casual manner that one would expect of a journalist.

"Herr Max Stein, may I present Mademoiselle Sarah Morozovski," Schoen said with a sweeping gesture. The trio seated themselves, and Schoen ordered a carafe of wine, which was quickly placed before them. After a short introduction, which included a superficial résumé of both Stein's and Sarah's recent pasts, Schoen excused himself to attend to several other matters at his office.

Sarah, now left to converse with Stein alone, noted a rather bemused expression on his face.

Noticing her quizzical look, Stein quickly said, "I must confess, mademoiselle, that you appear much younger than I expected. I did not suspect someone with the accomplishments as described by Monsieur Schoen to have aged so little from such hard work."

"I take that as a compliment, monsieur, but what I might lack in age and experience I have tried to compensate for with hard work and by paying attention to the suggestions of those who are older and wiser than I am."

"I suspect that your intelligence doesn't hurt either, mademoiselle."

"You may call me Sarah. Such formality seems out of place here."

"I would be pleased to do so if you will call me Stein. It seems through the years that I have been addressed so much in that manner that I have almost forgotten my first name. You may call me Max, however, if you wish, but I might be slow to respond."

"Well, then, Max Stein," Sarah said, "how many years have you lived in Berlin?"

"I have been formally employed there at least seven years, but I have lived there off and on for much longer, having worked in a variety of jobs in and out of the newspaper business."

"How would you describe Berlin?" Sarah asked. "I have very little knowledge of the city, aside from what I have read."

"One is first struck by how large the city is. It is much more like London in that regard than Paris. It still retains its imperial center, aligned along the Unter den Linden, with the kaiser's palace at the one end and the Reichstag near the opposite. At that far end is the large Brandenburg Gate, near to which are many foreign embassies as well as the German Foreign Office, clustered around the Wilhelmstrasse. Beyond lies the old imperial hunting grounds, now built into an ornate series of gardens and pathways in the Tiergarten, which abuts the Reichstag. Along these axes is the center of power of the government, as well as the residences of many foreign diplomats.

"Like Paris and most other European capitals, the most desirable living areas are grouped close to the center of the city. What is new, however, is the rapidity with which the city is growing in all directions out from this center. All around there are many districts that increasingly reflect the wealth of the bourgeois, both in the scope and style of their homes and the affluence of the commercial areas. The rapid deployment of an efficient public transportation system has facilitated the growth of the city outward and has provided an effective means to link the center of the city with the rapidly enlarging industrial areas arranged to the east and along the river. In my years in Berlin it is here that the most growth has taken place, with working-class neighborhoods springing up in close proximity to the industrial areas. These areas are the province of steam and coal, with vast rail yards accumulating the necessary products to be fed to a forest of smokestacks that lie along the network of their tracks."

"Of the people, what percentage would be employed in these large factories?" she asked.

"It is difficult to say, as no formal census figures are available for the most recent years, but one senses that these areas are growing rapidly, with people drawn in from the surrounding countryside and even from more remote areas to work in the factories. I would guess at present that their numbers, while not a majority of the population, are significant."

"What do you think are the major reasons that keep this large a group from obtaining the influence and power that their numbers potentially could represent?" Sarah asked.

"The old Prussian ruling families are far more complex and shrewd than people realize. They are usually thought to be extremely disciplined, which is true, especially for the military, and frugal to the extreme. Their successes have rested on far more than that, however. Early on as a nation, their first great rulers appreciated that the country had few resources in terms of geography or natural wealth that could be used to advantage. To counter this, they welcomed the settlement of displaced people who possessed certain desirable qualifications from many areas of the continent. In so doing, not only did they increase the population of what was essentially a backward rural province but also provided an infusion of talent and sometimes even wealth. Some, such as wealthy French Protestants, quickly assimilated into the highest circles of society. Others, such as eastern Jews, brought with them a deep regard for intellectual matters and the skills necessary to facilitate the development of more advanced forms of commerce.

"One thing that the Prussian rulers, as well as many of their German contemporaries, have long insisted upon is order.

Progress and ideas would be tolerated only as long as they could be assimilated in the existing framework of law and custom. No single person embodied this better than Bismarck. The present German state is a codification of this natural distrust of uncontrolled change. To the degree that the workers can be assimilated without threat to the ruling class, then they will be accommodated. Bismarck initiated his landmark social security legislation more to pacify the workers than out of any sense of the moral necessity of such actions."

"Is it conceivable, given the present structure of German law and the long conservative tradition of the state, to expect that the working class can ultimately use their numbers to legally obtain their rightful share of power and influence?" Sarah asked.

"There is great hope that the justness of their arguments and the weight of their numbers will move this very conservative regime to increase the workers' share of prerogatives and power. Others believe, however, that given the nature of the Prussian ruling class that such an outcome is unlikely and that the workers will need to use more radical means to obtain what they believe to be justly theirs."

"How much do the laws and regulations limit your actions as a reporter?" she asked.

"That can vary, depending on the political climate and the events in question. The law, as I understand it, seldom prohibits the operation or establishment of newspapers. At times, however, much discretion is given to the state censors, which can affect what gets said or how it is worded. This can be overcome sometimes by a certain style that relies on symbolism. There are other times when publishing certain facts puts one at risk of some form of reprisal from those in power. It is sometimes necessary to find underground sources to publish delicate information."

"Have you yourself had experience with such publications?"

"I regretfully confess, Sarah, that from time to time I have felt it necessary to use such means to spread what I believed to be important information."

"Somehow that does not surprise me. It is what I would hope and expect from a true journalist. How experienced and how comfortable are you with this surreptitious style of work?"

"One is never comfortable, no matter how experienced, in breaking the law or flaunting authority in Germany. It can be tricky and as dangerous for your sources as it may be for you. That is why the services of a skilled attorney will make us all a bit more comfortable in our jobs." He smiled slyly.

"I can see, Max, even from this brief meeting, that working with you would certainly not be dull."

"I would hope not. Boredom is a sorry state of existence."

As the wine began to have its effect, the meeting began to change into a more relaxed and friendly conversation. Stein showed an impish, humorous side to his personality not appreciated by any casual acquaintance. Sarah slowly transformed her sharp businesslike manner into a warmer, more animated one. Even Schoen, upon his promised return after finishing his office duties, seemed less formal and more genuine.

As the afternoon lengthened, Stein said finally, "This has been a more enjoyable afternoon than I had anticipated. Sarah, it has been a pleasure meeting you. I had feared that you might be one of those passionless, inflexible ideologues all too common in our movement. I am happy to see that you are far from that. I have told Monsieur Schoen that I would consider his job offer only if I could be comfortable with my primary associate. I can say that you have relieved my concerns in that regard."

"I am happy to hear that," Sarah answered. "If the details can be finalized satisfactorily, I confess that I would look forward to working with you as well."

"Excellent," he said. "I must apologize, as the hour is getting a bit late, and I have a promised meeting with old friends that makes it necessary for me to leave. Monsieur Schoen, I will contact you in the morning to finish our conversation from today. Once again, Sarah, it has been a great pleasure to meet you."

As Stein left, Sarah once again sensed the awkwardness of being alone with Schoen. Try as she might, there was something that was both disingenuous and mildly threatening in his manner that she could not get over.

"Sarah—if I may call you by your first name—I hope that your meeting with Stein was productive. I certainly hope that you were as impressed with him as I was."

"It is hard not to be," she said.

"I hope that means you are willing to join us."

"I am even more interested in your earlier proposal after this meeting. As an attorney, I must, of course, insist upon a formal written agreement. I would expect the terms of the salary, range of expected duties, travel and expense allowance for foreign travel, and other issues that we have discussed or that you believe important to be included. If we can finalize an agreement on these points, I could be ready to start within the next six weeks."

"I will discuss the final details with Monsieur Jaurès and get back with you once we have a contract drawn up. Hopefully, that will be in the next two or three days. I will need to spend some time with Herr Stein over the next day, which may cause a slight delay in my attending to any final details."

Then changing his tone to a more familiar one, he added, "The night is young. I would be happy to continue our discussion over dinner, if you would care to join me."

Sarah hoped that her thoughts were not too evident as she stammered, "I appreciate the offer … but I'm afraid that I have a previous engagement and expect him to be here shortly."

As if on cue, she saw Robert enter and waved to him, hoping that her gesture would not look too frantic. She was relieved to see that he saw her, and as he turned toward their table he seemed to be pleased rather than befuddled by her greeting. As he approached, she quickly reached out to meet him, and while bussing him on the cheeks, she whispered, "Please play along with what I say."

"Monsieur Benjamin Schoen, this is my friend Robert d'Avillard. He is the person I spoke to you about."

Sarah was gratified to see the surprise in Schoen's face upon meeting Robert, an expression that gave no evidence of his being aware of the ruse being played on him.

After they exchanged greetings, Schoen said, "Well, I hate to leave, Sarah, but I suspect that Robert would likely tire of my presence here much longer. As I mentioned, I will try to finalize the documents in the next days and get back to you as soon as they are done. Until then, I wish you both a pleasant evening."

With that, he quickly gathered his things and left Sarah alone with a perplexed Robert, whose face now reflected some confusion.

9

NEW DISCOVERIES

Robert was puzzled, to say the least. Here was Sarah, a girl that always seemed so different from him in her interests and beliefs, who now, without warning, was showing an altogether different aspect of her personality. Not that he minded, as he had been intrigued by her for some time. He had met her as he had met many of his acquaintances—through Thomas. At first she had seemed like many of Thomas's friends, both literate and highly opinionated. Though he frequently disagreed with her, he had come to realize that her viewpoints were always well thought out. He had also been aware of her physical attractiveness, which, coupled with her other attributes, only added to her allure.

"What was that all about?" he asked.

"Oh, Robert," she replied with evident discomfort, "please forgive me. I had been discussing a job with Schoen when you arrived. I felt that he was using our interview and his position to his advantage and had asked me to dinner tonight. Your arrival was a godsend in helping me get rid of him."

"What did you mean by saying that I was the one you had talked to him about?" Robert asked with a coy smile.

"When he asked me to dinner, I did not want to go because I did not want to encourage a relationship that might cause complications if I decided to take a job offer with his company. Rather than tell him that and possibly jeopardize a job that interests me I told him that I already had plans for the night. Besides, I don't really like or trust him very much."

"How did you know that I would be here?" he asked.

"I didn't know for sure it would be you but hoped that you or one of the Round Table would arrive soon, and fortunately you did."

Feigning disappointment, Robert added, "You mean you could just have easily welcomed Painchaud? I must say I'm a little deflated."

"Robert, you of all people surprise me that you could be concerned by what I might think. If you must know, I was very pleased to see you. You or your cousin would be the members of our group I would have preferred to arrive in such a timely way."

"Very pleased," he teased, drawing the words out. "That makes me feel much better."

"Well, don't let it go to your head," she added. "I am surprised that you played your role so well. I didn't think a somber, scientific type like you could be so adept at acting. You did me a great favor."

"Then I would like to ask a favor from you in return."

"And what might that be? Nothing dangerous or disagreeable, I hope."

"I would hope not. Since you have been so forward as to invite yourself to dinner tonight," he said with a bright smile, "I hope that you would not think that I am taking unfair advantage of you by actually taking you up on the offer. I would hate to waste such a fortunate opportunity when presented to me."

Sarah looked at him for a moment, uncertain what to think. "Are you serious?" she asked.

"I couldn't be more serious. I feel some obligation to protect you from your deceptions if Schoen should ask you about your evening. Complying with your request, even if it was for deceptive purposes, would give you a clear conscience. More important, I would certainly enjoy the opportunity."

"Well, if you insist, then the only correct thing for me to do would be to agree," she replied with a feigned air of resignation. Then, smiling, she added, "I think that you have gotten off on the right foot, as I appreciate the honesty of my dinner companions. I think I might rather enjoy your proposal, as long as you behave yourself and if we can dine in an establishment without risking our health."

"Outstanding, mademoiselle," he said with enthusiasm. "I can assure you that you will not find a more perfect gentleman in all of Paris tonight. Besides, I am eager to hear of this new job you were speaking about. If you don't feel that you need to go home to change, we can go to a place that my family has known for years, which I think you will not only find quite hygienic but also quite special."

"Robert, you are really naive if you think that I can simply march off into the night without first stopping at home to refresh and change. There is an excellent café on the corner near my apartment where you can enjoy yourself while I get ready."

Extending his arm, he urged, "Shall we go, then? It seems that good fortune has increased my appetite."

———————

As they walked through the streets in the fading light of early evening, Sarah began to feel increasingly comfortable walking beside Robert. She felt a slight giddiness from the rapid change in her circumstances, having first avoided Schoen's uncomfortable proposal and now, surprisingly, accompanying this handsome man on a lovely Parisian evening, which promised excitement.

She began to understand how the many young Parisian women who seemed so enthralled in the company of their boyfriends must feel. The relationships she had had in the past were usually short-lived, as she soon tired of her companions. At no time did she have any sense of infatuation or interest, which seemed to be the case of so many women of her age. Perplexed when she would see young couples embracing, oblivious to their surroundings, she would often smile more out of derision rather than sympathy.

In the time that she had known Robert, she had come to appreciate that he might be different from the usual types, such as Painchaud, with whom she was familiar. He was certainly handsome, being tall with dark hair and features common to young men of the old aristocratic families. When she first met him, she was struck by how quiet he was in contrast to most of her other friends, especially at the law faculty. She at first ascribed this to an arrogance that was also common in young men of his class. Gradually, however, she had come to realize that his reticence was more a feature of his personality than any purposeful attempt at snobbery.

From their earliest conversations, he'd had an easy manner,

often seeming to poke fun at her ideas or actions, not in a malicious manner but in a friendly ingratiating way that seemed to underscore his quiet self-confidence. In conversations of more substance, his intelligence was apparent. He seldom spoke spontaneously, but when he did speak it would be to make a point in a succinct and logical manner, which was always worth noting. More often, his cousin Thomas would defer to him on questions of science and mathematics as they arose. His natural reticence, coupled with this obvious intellect, gave him an aura that she found interesting and appealing. They had known each other for some time but had only conversed in the company of the Round Table, with all its conventions. Though she had not thought of being alone with Robert, she now found herself enjoying the good fortune of the day's events.

When they reached her apartment building, she directed Robert to the small café across the street and went to change for the evening ahead.

For Robert, the evening's unexpected turn of events was proving to be quite pleasant as well. As they had walked to her home, he too had been keenly aware of Sarah's presence beside him. His interest was further heightened when she at last came down to meet him for the evening. At first he almost did not recognize her, as she had changed from the informal attire that he always saw her wear into a stylish outfit that gave full emphasis to her obvious femininity. Her hair, which was often tied in a bun atop her head, was now falling freely over her shoulders and gleamed with a luster that accentuated its dark auburn color. All of this seemed to intensify her natural beauty and caused him to smile broadly in appreciation of his good fortune.

"Have you decided on something to order?" she asked.

"Well, I did have a glass of wine, but I had another place in mind for this evening, if you don't mind? It helps sometimes to have a large family, as the husband of one of my mother's dearest cousins, Monsieur Tréssiet, owns a restaurant not far from here that I hope you will enjoy."

"I certainly hope that it's close because I am getting hungry."

"I hope your appetite is not so great that it will break my budget this month. You know I am just a poor student," he said, smiling as he led her on his arm toward the Seine.

Sarah said little in reply but her contentment was evident as she smiled and pressed herself against his arm while they navigated through the narrow streets near her apartment.

In short order they reached the riverside quay along the left bank, and as they neared the Pont Neuf, Robert paused in front of the door of the restaurant, Le Perroquet.

"You can't be serious!" she gasped, recognizing Robert's intent to enter one of the most well-known restaurants in the city. "This is way too expensive. How could you ever afford this?"

"I save my money for special occasions, and what could be a more special occasion than this? Besides, I usually get a family discount."

Sarah looked at him quizzically, but as they entered into the elaborate front reception area, the maître d' came forward with a broad smile. "Monsieur Robert, it is a pleasure to see you once again. Monsieur Tréssiet will be back shortly and will be happy to know that you are here."

"I'm glad to see you again, Henri. I was hoping that you might have some space for my friend and me for this evening."

"For you, of course there is space. Since you are not with that rascal cousin of yours, we can even put you in an area of public view." He smiled. "Please follow me." With that he led them to a small table in a quiet corner.

Sarah had been in restaurants of this special class before but always accompanied by her parents for formal family events. Looking at the large painting over Robert's shoulder, the freshly pressed tablecloth and napkins, the exquisite place setting, and the beautiful floral piece, she felt as if she had been transported to another world, a feeling that would only be enhanced with the formal routine that accompanied their meal. In short order, various members of the attentive but discreet staff appeared, offering water at first and then a selection of aperitifs. After careful study and consultation, great decisions were made. Wines were chosen with all the consideration due weighty decisions and further concentrated effort was spent in selecting the first and subsequent courses of the meal to follow.

Sarah was both amused and impressed with the serious manner in which Robert went about selecting an appropriate wine to match her dinner requests and also the attention he gave to ensure that she got the best of the evening's fare to match her tastes. To that end, he carefully listened to the waiter's suggestions before finalizing any selection. In short order these efforts were followed by the appearance of their aperitifs and then, with great formality, the first course of the evening arrived.

As the evening continued, the pleasure and wonder that Sarah experienced from the carefully choreographed meal seemed to increase by the minute. Each course was like a new act in a wonderful play, with the wait staff playing carefully cast roles. Amid such a richness of the senses, she quickly fell under the spell to which many other Parisian couples have easily succumbed.

Surprisingly, all of this was not lost on Robert. Highlighted by the soft light and fashionable setting of their table, he had become ever more aware of the beauty of his companion and other attributes he had never before appreciated. That she was intelligent and opinionated, he had long known. What he now appreciated was a very human quality and an alluring femininity that she had hidden so well in the male-dominated world where she was trying to establish herself. The effect of this transformation was intoxicating.

At last, Sarah could contain herself no longer and said, "Robert, I would never have believed you were like this."

"What do you mean?" he asked somewhat defensively.

"I never knew you could carry on a conversation so well."

"I apologize if that has spoiled your evening."

"Not in the least. What I mean is that I have rarely seen you so spontaneous in expressing yourself. You are usually much quieter, speaking only in succinct sentences laced with scientific jargon. I never knew that, given the right circumstances, you could be so charming."

"You must have had a little too much wine."

"I am perfectly sober. Although I must say that our present surroundings may have intoxicated me in other ways."

"It really is beautiful," he agreed.

"See? That's what I mean. I would have never have imagined you—or most men, for that matter—saying that something is beautiful."

"You must have lived a sheltered existence to have been spared the many modern Casanovas who undoubtedly would use such words to facilitate their conquests. I have little of their guile, however, and even less ability to use the language to such advantage. That does not mean, however, that I don't have opinions or emotions; they are simply well concealed. You have not seen me when I am excited by something. You might think differently about me then."

"I am definitely thinking differently about you, Robert.

Whatever it is, you seem far more outgoing this evening. Perhaps you have thought of a solution to one of those problems that you always seemed to be working on," she suggested with a teasing smile.

"No, I am by no means closer to the solution of some of my design dilemmas, although that would be nice. I am, however, reveling in a new discovery. Until tonight, I have thought of you only in terms that have been defined by our relationship at the Bièvre. There, you have always been articulate and passionate about your beliefs. There was something of the zealot about you which concerned me, however. It was as if there was something about you that I was missing, something that was sublimated to your beliefs. This evening at the Bièvre when you motioned to me, I saw you for the first time in a different way. No longer were you someone who was above the mundane matters of life, but instead you showed a bit of vulnerability, like the rest of us."

He paused a moment to savor his food before slowly continuing. "Tonight for the first time, I am discovering much more about you, which seems to have been hidden by your concerns for the plight of the oppressed and the inequalities of life. It is a discovery that is exciting, I will confess."

"How strange and wonderful this evening is," she added. "By some spell, the person I thought you were has been transformed to someone altogether different."

For the first time, he grasped her hand and, speaking slowly so as not to betray his emotions, he said, "The reason I seem different to you is that I am. How could I not be when I have been given this opportunity with you tonight?"

His touch and words caused her to gasp audibly. For a moment they were silent as they gazed into each other's eyes. Then, the owner, Pierre, appeared to greet his young relative, interrupting the emotion of the moment.

"Robert, I am so glad to see you. I must say that your companion tonight is a great improvement over Thomas."

"Sarah, may I present my mother's cousin Pierre Tréssiet. Pierre, Miss Sarah Morozovski."

"Enchanted, mademoiselle," replied Pierre as he took Sarah's hand. "Are you related to the banker Joseph Morozovski?"

"He is my father."

"I know him well. He has been a welcome guest here for many years. When you see him next, please give him my best wishes. Robert, I am even more envious of your good fortune tonight. I hope that everything has been to your expectations so far."

"It has been truly wonderful," Sarah replied. "I could not have hoped for better. Your staff is truly wonderful, and the meal has been exquisite."

"Such a compliment from such a lovely woman is greatly appreciated. Robert, I can see that you have more important things to do than talking to an envious old man. If there is anything I can do, let me know. Please wish your family my best, and tell Thomas it has been too long since we have seen him. I wish you both the best this evening."

As he left, they sat quietly for a moment, simply enjoying their presence together and the remarkable setting. Then Sarah broke the silence.

"I am the wordy one, and so it must be easy for you to sense how I feel about things. You are much more difficult to read. Now, seeing this other side of you, I am intrigued to find out what truly excites you."

"I was expecting you to ask something more romantic than my interests, unless you wanted me to say that it was you."

"That would be nice, no doubt, but rather predictable.

What I think romantic would be to find out more about you than what you appear to be."

"You are asking me to do something that is difficult. If you were someone I did not know or care for, I would graciously make some polite unrevealing statement or refuse to answer outright. Since that obviously is not the case, I will try to answer you, but you will have to excuse any clumsiness, as I am not used to talking about myself."

After a moment he started, hesitating at times to compose his thoughts. "Ever since I can remember, I have enjoyed things, particularly objects such as toys or tools, that serve a purpose. I like to study them to see how they work or to try to repair them when they are broken. While some people like to imagine things, I prefer dealing with the real and tangible. When I went to school I discovered that I had an aptitude for mathematics and science, which fortunately helps me to understand how things are built and how they work best. I soon found that combining these interests by applying my school lessons to building or repairing things around our properties gave me great enjoyment. To hold something that I have designed and then built is very exciting and satisfying."

"That is the side of you that is most evident and one with which I am already familiar," she said. "Tonight, though, I see that you can be more animated and expressive. Am I wrong to imagine that you are enjoying something besides the stuff of your sciences?"

"You may be surprised, Sarah, but I enjoy many things besides my work—this evening, for example."

"You seem a bit defensive when you say that, almost as if you feel that you shouldn't be enjoying yourself," she said in a perplexed tone.

"I suppose that is the result of trying to concentrate on what I would consider more important matters."

"Robert, I seem to remember that you accused me of a similar self-absorption earlier this evening."

"Touché," he answered somewhat sheepishly.

"You claim to be enjoying yourself this evening, so perhaps your notions of what might be important needs to be expanded."

"You are right, no doubt, but perhaps the same could be suggested for you."

"Perhaps we could both benefit from listening to each other more, Robert."

"I will make you a deal. In the future, I will try to act more like I am tonight, rather than a dull engineer, if it will give me another chance to see this other side of you."

"I am a better judge than you as to whether you are dull, Robert. I'm not interested in changing you or making you into something you are not. I am only interested in knowing more about this side of you that I have seen tonight. If you want to make a deal, Robert, here is what I propose. We should begin tonight taking nothing for granted with each other. Old assumptions and perceptions should be thrown out and replaced with being honest and straightforward with each other."

"I would very much like that, Sarah. What you propose, however, touches on something I have been thinking about at times this evening that is related to hearing you mention a possible new job opportunity. You see, I have been thinking about another opportunity as well."

"Now I am curious," Sarah replied.

"I've been thinking about how to bring this up throughout this evening but was reluctant to do so."

"Why?" she asked.

"On the surface it is an idea that might offend your own

idealism and beliefs. Given the time to discuss it more fully, I don't believe that you would find it so distasteful. I did not want to discuss it earlier, however, because I was being selfish. I wanted to avoid a discussion that at worst would have you think less of me and at the least would steal time from our evening."

"That is odd," she said. "I was hoping that you would not ask me about the new job I am considering for the very same reasons."

"Well, for the sake of what remains of this wonderful evening, let's suspend our honesty and consider other important issues, like what cheese and dessert to order."

"I will agree to that on the condition that we make the time to have this discussion we are avoiding. The decision that I have to make is important, and I would certainly value your opinion about it."

"That is a condition that I can easily accept," he said with a broad smile.

For the remainder of the evening, they avoided more serious matters, abandoning themselves to an intimate conversation about little trivialities that each, given their growing infatuation, thought wonderful or of the utmost importance. At long last they both sensed the need to call an end to the evening, with Robert settling the final bill, which, true to expectations, included a generous "family discount." As they left the restaurant, Monsieur Tréssiet was there to wish them off with a smile that betrayed his appreciation and envy of their blissful state.

On the walk home, Sarah impulsively asked, "How is it, Robert, that you don't have some attractive woman to whom you are close or even committed in some future relationship? On a scale of eligible men, you would be high on any woman's list."

Robert's warm smile hid his discomfort, but after a moment he answered. "Believe it or not, it is something that I have not spent much time thinking about. Perhaps it is because I have never found a woman who interested me enough to distract me. I think that, in some subconscious way, I have expected a day when I would be married and have a family, but my interests have made it convenient to keep that a more distant reality. Besides, I have always suspected that my family would arrange or facilitate a convenient marriage with a young woman that would benefit the families as much or more than it would please me. Such arrangements have been essential in preserving the lifestyle of our kind through the years. Tonight, however, seems to have brought some complications. I no doubt will sound like a poor poet, but from the time that you came down from your apartment dressed as you are, with your hair down and the sparkle in your eyes, I realized more than ever how beautiful you are."

Sarah gave a slight gasp and drew Robert closer to her, whispering, "Robert, hearing you say that is so lovely."

"This evening seems to have affected the independence that I took for granted only yesterday," Robert continued. "The new opportunity that I have been considering might require that I leave Paris for the next few years. It seems strange, but now, before I make a decision, I want to know how it might affect our relationship."

In hearing this, she turned to hold firmly to his arm. She was moved by his frankness and vulnerability. "That is important to me as well," she whispered. "I will be working late tomorrow, but I could meet you tomorrow night around seven at the Bièvre, or if not, the following day."

"I will be waiting for you tomorrow night," he said. Then, taking her in his arms, he paused and looked into the depths of her dark brown eyes. Overcome by that mysterious force that has long controlled young lovers in this most beautiful city, they shared, for the first time, a deep and passionate kiss.

10

DECISIONS

For Robert, the day at work had not been productive. The excitement of the previous evening had kept him awake long after he had gotten home. Consequently, his thinking had been affected not only by his lack of sleep but also by frequent lapses when his mind drifted to thoughts of Sarah. He was relieved when at last his workday ended and was excited at the prospect of their planned reunion that evening.

Upon arriving at the Bièvre, he was able to secure a table away from the usual gathering, trying to be inconspicuous to prevent any unwanted intrusion into what he hoped would be a private meeting with Sarah.

When at last Sarah appeared, he was pleased to see that both her hair and dress were in the more stylish manner of the previous evening and he was gratified by her smile when she recognized him.

"Robert, I should thank you once again for the wonderful evening last night, but the reality is that it made things more difficult for me today. When I should have been concentrating on my work or my reply to Schoen, I thought instead of how pleasant everything was last night. I have always felt a degree of contempt for the hedonists who are all too apparent in this city, but the experience of last night has softened my feelings for them."

"I had a similar day," Robert replied. "I constantly tried to regain my focus by telling myself how silly it was to allow one evening to so disturb my routine, but I confess that I was not very successful. All I could think about was meeting you tonight, even though what I might tell you may be unsettling."

"In what way?" Sarah asked with a note of concern.

Robert seemed to hesitate a moment before replying. "I know how much you are opposed to militarism and all the threats that it poses. This crisis with Germany has certainly sharpened this concern for both of us. I also remember, even as a boy, my father and uncle warning about the threat that a modern Germany could pose if it would revert to a reliance on its formidable army to obtain its objectives. Even if this present crisis can be resolved, it will be difficult to put this specter of a powerful and threatening Germany out of mind. I am afraid we are only at the beginning of a more dangerous time, making our future actions extremely important. If rising German militarism is left unchallenged then I fear that they will be only further emboldened in the future with ever-increasing risks to the peace of Europe.

"Several days ago I had dinner with Professor de Rochelle and an old friend of his and my uncle's. He and the professor were students together and then served in the military together during the Prussian War, but unlike the professor, he returned to the army. Through the years he has climbed through the ranks, and I am told he is now one of the chief strategists for the army."

As he spoke, Robert watched Sarah closely for any sign of approval or disappointment. He continued cautiously when it appeared that she was following his explanation closely.

"It is possible that his accomplishments might not impress you, and you might very well disagree with his viewpoint. From what I know of him, however, I believe that you would be wrong to prejudge him. I have found him to be a man with strongly held moral beliefs and a deep respect for the freedoms and benefits that we in modern France now have. I also found him to be very persuasive in his arguments. In talking to him, he cautioned about this change in German policy based on a deeply held belief that at some time they would inevitably turn to their military to threaten French sovereignty.

"As it now exists, they are the most advanced industrial economy on the continent and a leader in scientific and technologic innovation. These strengths give them many competitive advantages, especially when their advances are applied to their military. He believes that unless we take measures to improve our industrial output and couple it with ways to improve our national defense, we run the risk of falling further behind them, thereby increasing our vulnerability in the future. This gentleman, Colonel Foch by name, does not believe that it is the duty of the army to dictate foreign policy, but his firsthand experience with Prussian aggression has given him insight to the risks associated with a more belligerent Germany. He believes that the present crisis marks a turning point, since for the first time since German unification they have chosen overt military threat in their dealings with us and our allies."

"There is nothing in his assessment with which I would quarrel, Robert."

"Nor I, Sarah," Robert replied with some relief. "Foch also

believes that if we are to remain independent, all of us must make some individual sacrifices for the country. In the absence of a real German threat, it will no doubt be difficult to get many people to sublimate their own interests to this idea, especially if institutions they distrust are given more power. For someone like you, Sarah, I know it might be hard to imagine the army as anything other than an agent for obtaining and protecting imperial interests, but if France is to remain independent in the future, I believe that the military and all the citizenry will have to be more closely aligned."

"That is hard for me to accept without serious reservations, Robert. History, especially French history, makes it too hard to ignore generals and armies that have used their strength for exploitation."

"No one could argue with you about that, but I believe in the colonel's sincerity when he says that our army is fully under the control of the elected government, and its leaders understand that it exists to perform the tasks that the government dictates. That role today is clearly to develop the means to protect the security of the republic, not to gain power in Europe. Colonel Foch makes the argument that whatever one might presently think of the army, in the end it will be the institution that alone can save the freedoms we now enjoy, if we are forced to confront Germany."

"This colonel of yours must be as persuasive as you say because it appears that you have accepted many of his arguments."

"What I believe most about his arguments is the idea that if we, as a country, are to curb future German aggression, then the army—and indeed, France—will have to attract the country's best and most able citizens to strengthen us in relation to Germany."

After a slight pause, seemingly to formulate her thoughts, Sarah replied, "That is something that I did not expect from you. You know that I distrust the military, so I cannot honestly say that I am enthusiastic about what you have told me. I cannot completely disagree, however, about the risks Germany now poses to us all, and ideally, if the army was to act solely in defense of the republic, then I might grudgingly offer my support. You told me last night how important it is for you to use your skills in a meaningful way, and I have no doubt that you are sincere in your beliefs. I can't help but believe that you might have excellent opportunities outside of the army to contribute in a meaningful way, but you are in a better position than I am to decide what opportunities can match your expectations. Although I still have reservations, I now understand well enough to respect whatever you decide and sincerely hope that it will work out for you."

"That is a most diplomatic if not overt approval," Robert added cautiously.

"That is all that I am capable of giving at present. It is difficult for me to dismiss my concerns, even if I might respect your sincerity. My fear is that your hopes will be dashed by reality."

"Don't look so glum. I have not decided anything yet, and perhaps I may be able to accomplish many of these aims by working as a civilian, as you suggest."

"What options are available to you?" she asked.

"As you know, I have been working for Professor de Rochelle. He and his associates have been involved with military work for some time. I have been involved recently in some projects that are of great interest to the army. I could continue where I am and request more involvement with those projects that have military implications. At present, however, the brunt of the work in the office is far more concentrated in areas with little strategic military importance, so I would have to be content with what might become available.

"That evening when I met Colonel Foch, he made it clear that the military was in critical need of good engineering officers. This need has been magnified by the present crisis. He shrewdly pointed out the contributions of engineers in the past, including the elaborate fortifications of the great Vauban that helped pacify the German border. He was direct but honest when he told me that with my qualifications I would have an opportunity to participate in the planning and implementation of projects that might prove equally important.

"Coming from a man with his qualifications and responsibilities, that made me aware—perhaps for the first time—of the opportunity that the army might provide. If this were a year ago I would have had far less interest, but given the present circumstances, his proposal has been much more intriguing. My greatest hesitancy was giving up my present situation with good job prospects and all the advantages of living in Paris. After last night, those advantages seem even greater."

"I am smiling, Robert, because in many ways I see how similar my dilemma is to yours. It is ironic that these recent events, while appealing to our instincts to act, now are tempered by more practical and even selfish considerations. Before last night I was content to launch a new course radically different from anything that I have done. In would be funny if it weren't so unsettling, but now I am suddenly aware of what I might be giving up by leaving Paris and all of its possibilities."

"So what is this opportunity that is causing all this indecision?"

"You by now have heard my views many times at the Bièvre

and must know that I have strong feelings for the workers and their families."

"I have wondered where you acquired such a passion because I know that you come from a wealthy family."

"I do and a Jewish one at that. In many ways, however, my real family has been my governess and her husband. They are both wonderful people who, unlike the two of us, did not have the advantages of position and family to help them. They have succeeded by their skills and hard work, but despite their success, they remain involved in the same working quarter where they lived when they were first married. Through the years they introduced me to this world and gave me an understanding of the lives and struggles of the many people who made up their long list of friends and acquaintances. These people all too often have been marginalized by the more powerful and wealthy members of society. You may think that much of their misfortune can be blamed on their indolence, but I have come to know many of these people and have found them to be as worthy as the fortunate few of the upper classes. My concern for the conditions of their lives and my anger at the injustice of much of their misfortune influenced my decision to study the law. I believed that it was an area where a Jewish woman might be able to effect change for the benefit of large numbers of workers and peasants.

"Fortunately, we live in a time where there is now great potential for the workers to better their positions. Industrialization has transformed our society and all of Europe and has given the workers more influence than at any time in the past. Without their efforts, modern industrial output cannot be sustained, nor can the means to support the machinery of war. Recently I have begun to appreciate the limits that the present legal system imposes on my ability to influence change, and this present German threat has forced me to consider other opportunities that might increase my effectiveness. Schoen, the man you met at the Bièvre, suggested a possible opportunity with the paper *l'Humanité*, which is the principle news organ for the French Socialist Party, led by Monsieur Jean Jaurès. The result of several meetings has been interesting. I have been offered a chance to participate in forming a bureau in Berlin, which will cover the events of Germany and Central Europe, especially those pertinent to the socialist parties."

"Would you live in Berlin?" asked Robert.

"I would be expected to travel back to Paris frequently, but to facilitate the opening of this bureau I would no doubt spend most of my time in Berlin."

"What good would your legal training be if you become a journalist?"

"I would not be primarily a journalist. They already have a man selected to act in that capacity for the bureau. I would be responsible for negotiating all the regulations and legalities necessary to allow for a timely opening of the office and to ensure our compliance with their authorities afterward. I would also be expected to act as a liaison for the French Socialist Party, with the many elements of the socialist movement in Germany and Central Europe." Sarah seemed surprised to see Robert laugh softly as she finished her explanation. "What is so amusing?" she asked with mild irritation.

"Nothing to do with what you have said, I can assure you. I was laughing out of frustration with my poor timing. After last night, I realized that I had met a woman who truly intrigued me and one I would like to know much better. I spent the greater part of the day thinking how I might proceed with my plans, yet continue to see you. Unfortunately, the things that I find attractive about you are important to others as well, and no doubt our relationship in Paris, as of now, is poor competition against such intriguing opportunities."

"You're wrong about that, Robert. You have made my decision far more difficult. Part of me says that I should put off making any significant changes, hoping that all of our concerns will somehow work themselves out. In the short run, it would be the easiest thing to do and would offer the real opportunity of continuing to see you. Yet it is hard to ignore the opportunity with *l'Humanité*, which is unique and no doubt timely, if your colonel is right about the Germans."

Robert gave a wistful smile as he reached across the table and grasped Sarah's hand who quickly reciprocated by drawing their clasped hands toward her.

At that moment, Thomas, who was leaving the back room of the Bièvre, glimpsed his cousin with Sarah at their distant table and paused, seemingly fascinated by his discovery. As he watched, it was apparent that this was not a commonplace meeting, and seeing such an unlikely couple engaged in such intimate behavior surprised him greatly. His wonderment was further enhanced when he saw the couple embrace. Just as he was nearly out of their sight and heading toward the door, he heard Sarah.

"Thomas, where are sneaking off to without having the courtesy to say goodbye to us?"

Thomas approached rather slowly, hoping to hide any expression of his surprise discovery. "Well, this is certainly remarkable. Of all my acquaintances, I cannot think of two people with seemingly less in common than you two. Yet, unless I am mistaken, you are acting like a pair clearly enjoying each other's company. Life is truly enriched by the spice of surprise."

"It is a well-known fact of nature, Thomas," Robert replied, "that opposites attract."

"So I see."

"I am glad to see you, Thomas," Sarah said, "as you have come just in time to help us with a difficult matter."

"Why is it that I always seem to be the arbiter of difficult matters? What makes you think that my judgment is better than yours?"

"Thomas, you should know better than to ask such a question. People turn to you because you have a well-deserved reputation as a valuable counselor. You are one of the few people whose opinion I would value in such a matter."

"I could not have said it better myself, Sarah," Robert quickly added.

"Well, I appreciate you both saying that, but you should not place too much confidence in my infallibility. Nevertheless, having given me the opportunity to intrude on your conversation, I will try my best to help resolve your dilemmas."

And so in the course of the next hour, Thomas heard for the first time of his cousin's opportunity with the French army and of Sarah's with *l'Humanité*. After a short while, he abandoned his role as passive listener and gradually became more actively involved in the discussion.

As their conversation progressed, he became more aware of the full extent of their options and the various possibilities each might hold. With careful deliberation, he began to formulate an answer to help address the questions inherent in their choices.

"If what you want from me is some wise directive, telling you both that one decision is imminently more suitable than any other, then I must tell you in all honesty: that is something I cannot do. On the one hand, you each have an opportunity to contribute in new and possibly productive ways. In so doing, you will abandon the more conventional path that has already been productive and may also disrupt this relationship you both seem to care about.

"I have come to believe that an effective way to confront such difficult problems is to first acknowledge our own limitations. Recently I have been studying Aquinas, to the point where I can nearly feel his presence, like he was back roaming these very streets where we are tonight. Few, if any, before him or afterward could match his intellect, but despite his gifts he was keenly aware of the limitations of his own reasoning. He understood that true wisdom is different from reason alone, and it could only come through hard and conscientious effort, supplemented by the wondrous grace of God.

"God's gift to us is life itself with all of its uncertainties and complexities. To aid us, he has given us our greatest attribute— reason—but reason alone, due to our fallibility, is an unreliable gift. It can be used wisely for benefit or foolishly with ruinous consequences. Aquinas, therefore, turned to the holy texts to supplement reason with words engendered by the Holy Spirit to better understand God's purpose for our lives. I believe more than ever that if you can align your actions with his intent, you will have chosen the path that will give you the greatest chance of fulfillment and happiness.

"Sarah and Robert, I know you both well and consider you my dear friends. I know full well your capabilities. My only advice to you would be to act as God would want by searching your souls for that which you believe is right and proper, and settle for nothing less. Regardless of what comes from such a decision, I have no doubt that if it is made in such a manner that you will be satisfied, and your actions will be blessed. As Moses long ago reminded us, 'The Lord will honor those who honor him.'"

123

"So you are suggesting that we be bold in our choices?" asked Robert.

"I am only suggesting that your actions be guided by your best intentions, regardless of how impractical or inconvenient that might seem at the moment. Expediency all too often proves to be an illusion or, worse yet, lacks substance. If your acts are nobly guided, then you cannot fail." Then Thomas added, "Now I must make a confession to both of you. I too have reached a crossroads. For some time now I have been debating about continuing my studies or considering the priesthood. I have hesitated because I feel that the study and teaching of theology and philosophy is my great interest, and the new secularism in France would make it difficult for a priest to associate with our universities or at least have any meaningful influence."

"Perhaps it is time for the doctor to consider his own advice," urged Sarah.

"As I spoke to you and Robert, it became clear that I was speaking to myself as well, almost as if the Holy Spirit was shaping my thoughts."

"Then all that remains," Sarah added, "is for each of us to try to set aside the realities of the present, no matter how pleasant they might be"—she paused for a moment to grasp Robert's hand once more—"and to hope for that spirit of wisdom of which you speak."

"Amen," replied Thomas quietly.

BOOK 2
1911

11

HOME

As the train pulled from the station at Lyon, Robert leaned back and closed his eyes. The travel and excitement of the last days were catching up with him. For the past few weeks he had been in passage from Madagascar to Marseilles. Arriving in Marseilles, he had barely had a chance to take a hot bath and eat a hurried dinner before falling asleep, only to be forced to get up at an early hour to catch the train for Lyon, ultimately bound for Paris.

As the train progressed through the Rhone Valley, he became aware of the change in the intensity of the sunlight from that to which he had become so accustomed in the last year. The brilliant light of the African colonies and the French south was slowly softening as he neared Lyon. Gone too were the miles of arid landscape, replaced by the terraced hillsides of carefully cultivated vineyards. The transition became even more complete near Lyon, where the first vast fields covered with the shoots of young wheat spread like a vast green plain to the horizon. It was a reassuring sight. For all the new and strange places and cultures that he had come to know, it was good to see this reminder of the timeless fertility of this land, which for so long had nourished and enriched his countrymen.

The German crisis that had so disrupted his life several years before had taken more than a year to play out. During that year, the immediate threat of a European war had been averted, and a conference of the states of Europe had been convened that ultimately reached a diplomatic settlement of the matter. Robert had spent that time to further his training with Professor de Rochelle and to finish his degree. Despite the diplomatic resolution of the matter, tensions remained heightened among the great powers of Europe. It was the continued presence of a German threat coupled with the encouragement of the professor and even his father that had caused Robert to ultimately accept an army commission upon graduation. He set out with the hope of not only augmenting the defenses of France but also gaining valuable engineering experience while doing so.

Upon obtaining that commission, he experienced a gradual transition from the comfortable world of Paris that he had known in his student days. He was at first billeted near Saint Cyr, where he spent several weeks in indoctrination to the ways and customs of the modern French army. There, given the tension that existed between the conservative traditions of the army and the progressive views of the ruling government, he learned that an officer of even the highest rank had to guard his political opinions closely.

Having gained some insight as to the basics of military decorum and the more subtle aspects of military politics, Robert was soon passed on to the more pragmatic concerns of the engineering corps. Initially assigned a junior staff position near Paris, it soon became apparent to his superiors that he would be better employed in more responsible assignments.

For nearly two years he spent most of his time in the east of France, involved with the evaluation and strengthening of the crucial eastern frontier with Germany. These lands had been the concern of army engineers for centuries. In working here, he encountered many problems posed by the need to modify and improve existing fortifications to withstand the rigors of modern military tactics and armaments. Even more enjoyable had been the time he had spent on developing new designs for improving transportation into the areas deemed most critical in any future conflict with Germany.

Every senior staff officer in the French and German armies would come to know the topography of this terrain by heart. They also likely would know how that terrain had been modified in the past by the military engineers. Of that group, none had had a greater influence than Louis XIV's great engineer Vauban, who had designed intricate and formidable fortifications that had changed forever the face of France's eastern frontier. Vauban's ideas of defense and design had an influence so great that it had persisted to this very day. Robert knew well the French predilection to respect such genius, but he wondered if respect for the past would lead to future vulnerability.

These years provided valuable experience. His work often dealt with the design and construction of railway lines, road beds, bridges, and tunnels. Through his work not only did he gain a good appreciation of the geography and tactical importance of vast areas of eastern France but a much better understanding of how their defense could be strengthened by using modern communication and transportation methods. The quality of his work ultimately led to a new assignment in the colonies, where he was to be given increased responsibility over a wide array of projects.

His first assignment was in Algeria, where he was placed in charge of developing effective rail transportation into the vast interior as well as improving roadways and rail lines along the coastal plain. His work here was closely coordinated with military strategists, not only to improve the flow of commerce from the interior but also to increase the effectiveness of the colonial army. It was here also that he encountered for the first time the hostility of the native population.

French rule in Algeria, as he would come to learn, was based on the military. In a series of protracted battles during the latter half of the nineteenth century, countless Algerians had been slaughtered and their lands confiscated. Reduced to second-class citizenship, those who survived were often forced to watch as the lands of their ancestors were seized and subsequently distributed to waves of French and Spanish settlers who had resettled to the coastal plains. By the time Robert arrived, the brunt of the fighting was over, but he was always aware of tension that might be encountered at any time and in any place with the indigenous North Africans.

This hostility would be more evident in the northwest portions of the country on the Moroccan border and even more so in Morocco itself. The same Morocco that was at the center of the crisis in 1905 had been spared the feared war between France and Germany. Instead, in the following year, a peace had been brokered by the major European states that had granted effective control of the country to France in return for concessions to Germany for parts of French territory in the interior of the continent. Despite this accord, the Moroccans feared a similar fate to that of Algeria and were far from enthusiastic in their support for French protection.

Robert became more aware of the instability in Morocco when he was assigned to evaluate construction projects in that country. The demands of the military to quell revolts in various areas forced him to allocate his men and resources primarily to those areas most critical to the army. Projects that might improve the lot of the average citizen and subsequently strengthen their ties to France were given secondary importance. Consequently, he often found himself looking at Morocco and the vast contiguous Algerian coastline much in the same manner as his predecessors had looked at the eastern frontier of France.

He and his colleagues were told that the vast poverty and inequality of wealth evident in the native population could be overcome only by the imposition of European laws and customs. When the sunny coastal plains could mirror their French counterparts along the Mediterranean border in terms of law and the infrastructure necessary to facilitate commerce, then the miserable lots of the nomadic tribesmen of the interior and the crowded, impoverished city dwellers would all be considerably improved. Any attempt to resist this inevitable progress should be strongly resisted, not only to protect French interests but also to ultimately advance the condition of the native populace.

In recent months his role as an adjunct to the military command had been increased after his transfer to the French colonies of the Sudan and Madagascar, where the native populations were less pacified. Here, he and his staff were involved in constructing roads, bridges, and rail lines as part of the initial phase of a larger military buildup. As in Algeria, it would be necessary to coordinate the actions of the engineers with the commanding officers and the ground army, but here, he now was exposed to the hazards of working on construction projects in remote and often hostile environments. Here, he not only was responsible for the implementation of his designs but also for the safety of his men, which gave him a fuller recognition of how different his work was in comparison to the far safer demands of civilian engineers.

In this difficult environment he had been pleased to find that he was able to function quite well, in spite of the evident dangers. After a particularly risky job was completed, he would take even more satisfaction than usual in its final inspection. In Madagascar, with its thick jungles and often hostile populace, the risks associated with his work were such that he and his men were sometimes involved in overt military operations. It was the French plan to neutralize a central area of strategic territory and spread from there like an ink blot to incorporate and pacify even larger areas. As the scope of these areas increased, the supply and communication lines stretched from the safer zones. Often, the process would be limited by dense underbrush and nearly impassable jungle. The heavy equipment necessary to clear such foliage made their detection by hostile forces rather easy and required much care in scouting the area so as to deploy troops to minimize a surprise attack.

Despite these precautions, on more than one occasion his men came under fire. Most of the time this was a random sniper or a small band designed to disrupt and intimidate. On one particular afternoon, however, as the air was filled with smoke from burning underbrush, his men came under a more violent attack. Overriding the young lieutenant assigned to him that day by virtue of his rank, he drew up the heavy equipment to form a protective barricade. Behind this protective barricade, Robert soon determined the size and location of the attackers and was able to take successful countermeasures. The subsequent counterattack of his forces routed the attackers and resulted in the capture of two of their leaders, who subsequently proved to be a valuable source of information that helped limit future attacks.

Though he would return to Algeria and the north of Africa

at times, he found himself spending the majority of his time in the southeast regions of the continent. As his experience increased, he became more confident in not only his ability to design and build valuable infrastructure in difficult terrain but also in his military instincts.

The French army at that time was divided into the colonial and homeland forces. The primary battles that the army in France fought were political ones among themselves and the radical leaders who controlled the government. It was in the colonies that the real fighting occurred. Not only were these troops gaining experience in a wide range of combat conditions, but a whole generation of officers was being tested and trained.

After he had been in Madagascar for nearly six months, upon returning from an assignment in the field, he was summoned to his commander's office.

Colonel Pitcairn was an accomplished officer with the large girth that was common among the more senior officers in the colonies. He had spent his early career as an artillery officer, but now Robert had come to respect his understanding of engineering matters as well as his mastery of tactics.

He seemed unusually animated upon greeting Robert. "Well, Robert, I must compliment the pace and quality of your work in the last several weeks, particularly with all the rain we have had. It's too bad that you are such a damn good engineer, as you have it in you to be a superb field officer."

"Thank you, sir, but it seems easier to control construction projects than the messy variables of combat."

"That no doubt is true, but you have a first-class analytical mind that more than compensates for the uncertainties. You are flexible in the way you approach problems and have a reserve that allows you to stay calm in difficult situations. It seems that I am not the only one to appreciate your talents, which is somewhat unfortunate for us here in Madagascar. I have just received an order directing you to Paris to assume a position on the engineering staff in the bureau concerned with rails and transportation. It seems that you are being booted up the chain of command."

"When is this to take place?" Robert asked.

"As soon as your replacement arrives from Indochina, which I suspect will be in the next two weeks. You might as well get your things in order, as he may arrive even earlier than that. You should also know that you will be receiving excellent reviews from your superiors here and in Sudan. From Algeria through all of your postings in Africa, your superiors have all given you high marks, not only for your engineering accomplishments but also for your qualities as a real soldier."

"Thank you, sir, for your kind remarks," replied Robert.

"Oh, by the way," said the colonel as he handed Robert a small box, "you might want to take these with you, as they may help improve your trip."

Opening the box, Robert found two insignias designating the rank of captain.

"Congratulations, Captain, and good luck in Paris. You should be aware, however, that it can be every bit as dangerous for an officer there as it is here or in any other colonial outpost. Take care not to ignore the infernal politics that goes with the assignment around army headquarters."

After the colonel dismissed him, Robert took the evening to enjoy a leisurely dinner and then readied himself for his first return to France in over a year and a half.

———————

Now he was on the final leg back to Paris. As he awoke from a nap and peered out the window, he recognized features of the countryside near to the southeast of Paris. He was surprised by how little had changed. As the train neared Gare de Lyon, passing through some of the working-class neighborhoods, there appeared to be new construction here and there, but in general the whole city appeared much as he had left it.

As he left the station amid the usual commotion of assembled vendors and panhandlers, he noted the familiar smell of the city. Hailing a cab, he watched wide-eyed, taking in all his old familiar haunts until he arrived at his grandmother's apartment on Rue de Bac. She was not in Paris during this time of year, preferring the warmer sunshine to the south, so except for the housekeeper he would have the place to himself until he could get settled in a flat of his own. After taking a long and satisfying bath and then unpacking, he stretched out on the bed to take a nap. He only awoke when his hunger reminded him that he had had little to eat since his stop in Lyon.

Dressing quickly in his least wrinkled clothing, he headed out for the only place acceptable for a first night back—the Bièvre. Thomas would not be there, he knew. He too had taken the challenging and more uncertain path and had committed to the priesthood. He had been right in suspecting that the political climate would limit his opportunity at the Sorbonne, but fortunately, he had been welcomed in Strasbourg and its old and prestigious university, where there was far less anticlerical bias than in Paris. Robert had written to him on several occasions but had not seen him since his last time in France. His letters suggested that he was happy with his new situation, both in his more formal religious roles and in his teaching and writing.

As Robert reached the Bièvre, he paused to take in the old quarter before entering. The familiar surroundings came back to him instantly and seemed almost to blot out all the miles he had traveled and the adventures that he had been through since he had been there last. As he entered, he cast a furtive glance to the corner table that he and Sarah had shared in the past, hoping that by some outside chance she might be there. She was not, of course, and the table now was occupied by a middle-aged couple. Glancing toward the back, he saw that the round table was only partially occupied, and at this hour there were only a handful of people scattered around its perimeter, none of whom he recognized.

He did recognize Pierre behind the bar and made for an empty spot along the rail.

"Monsieur Robert!" Pierre exclaimed on seeing his old patron. "I can't believe it is you. What a surprise! Eh, you look well. Whatever you are doing must agree with you. I'm sure you didn't get that suntan here in Paris, but of course Thomas told us that you were in Africa. Did you see any lions or elephants or any other exotic creatures while you were there?"

"In fact I did, but they were in captivity, so they didn't worry me. It is good to see you, Pierre. How are things going for you and everyone here?"

"We are all surviving, Robert, which is all you can ask for, I suppose. The times are different from the old days when you and your crowd would take over the backroom. Money is a bit tighter after the financial panic, and everyone is a bit more cautious. The young crowd is different as well. They are more preoccupied and seem more somber than you and your friends. They often drink too much and, unlike you, they let their arguments get out of hand."

"I see one thing that hasn't changed is the beef steak, frites, and haricot verts," said Robert. He ordered his old favorite and helped himself to it when it arrived with the steak still sizzling. "It's as good as ever and a very pleasant welcome home."

"I'm glad you like it. It's good to see an old friend enjoy himself. It's too bad that there aren't many of your old gang still around. I miss all the vitality you and your friends brought to this place. I sure wish someone like Thomas was here to talk some sense into this present generation. They are always on fire about some new idea or politician. After a carafe of wine or two, any differences they have seem to grow, which can often make things interesting or uncomfortable."

"Well, you said you missed the vitality, but it's just that you have a different form of it now. Does any of the old crowd still come back?"

"Sure, some. Hervé and Mobillon and the others who still work and live near here come in often. They now have their girlfriends or business associates and have graduated to the more prestigious tables near the front. Some others, like you tonight, pop up at unexpected times."

"Has Sarah been back?"

A knowing smile came over Pierre's face. "I thought that you had moved past those days, Robert, to the dedicated service of the country."

"Pierre, I thought you were a Frenchman. You should know that one never really moves on from certain acquaintances."

"Well, if it will ease your curiosity, she has been in here several times in the last year. She apparently is spending most of her time in Germany and central Europe, but when she is back in Paris, she makes it a point to come in. Not that it is any business of mine, but when she has been accompanied by men, they seemed older than her, as if they are associates at work."

Robert tried to remain impassive. "I appreciate that interesting bit of information. If you ever need another job, I could recommend you for the army intelligence bureau. I hope to be in town for some months; here is my present address. If one of my old friends comes in and asks for me, you can give this address."

"The next time that she comes in, I'll do that," said Pierre, smiling.

As Robert walked home later that evening he felt the warm contentment that ample wine and a good meal can impart. His mind also kept coming back to Sarah. After their all-too-brief affair, she had chosen to pursue the opportunity in Berlin. Both had accepted her decision, knowing full well her absence would suspend or possibly end their relationship. He and Sarah had promised to keep in touch and had tried to do so, but with his assignments outside of Paris and hers in Berlin, it was nearly impossible for them to communicate in a timely manner. The long months in the most distant colonies only served to intensify his sense of lost opportunity.

In coming home, he looked forward to his new assignment, but the excitement of his new opportunity had been dampened somewhat by not seeing Sarah tonight. As he thought of what Pierre had said, however, he realized that by being here in Paris, he would now have the very real possibility of seeing her once again—and hopefully in the not-too-distant future. Thinking such pleasant thoughts helped him to fall into a long and welcome sleep in familiar and welcoming surroundings.

12

ÉLAN VITAL

After two glorious days, where he slept late and spent the rest of the day and much of the night revisiting his old haunts, Robert rose at a more proper time. He dressed in a freshly pressed uniform and set out to report for his new duty. Entering a large building on Rue Saint Dominique, he soon was directed to the Bureau of Transportation and the office of Colonel Henri Blanc.

Blanc, a tall, well-groomed officer, had the officious manner of one accustomed to staff work at a high level.

"Welcome, Captain d'Avillard. We have been expecting you. We usually have a full schedule here, but we have been even busier than usual lately, which makes your arrival very welcome. I trust that you will find your assignment here both challenging and worthwhile."

"I am looking forward to it, sir," Robert replied enthusiastically.

"We will have to share your duties for a while. It seems that you have been marked as one of the chosen who are to be given course work in the War College over the next few months as well. Apparently, you have demonstrated capabilities beyond your engineering responsibilities, and you have been recommended for more advanced training. I have here a packet of information and a syllabus of reading, along with a schedule of lectures. Tomorrow afternoon is the introductory lecture for your group, which will be given by General Foch, the former commandant of the War College. He is a formidable instructor; I am sure you will be impressed with him."

"I have had the great privilege of meeting him before, and I know that what you say is true."

"You will have today to familiarize yourself with our bureau and routine before your lecture tomorrow. I'll show you to your office and introduce you to Major Peltier, who at present is the head of the section where you will be assigned. He can give you a more detailed description of your duties and which projects you will be working on when your other training is finished."

After a round of introductions, Robert was shown to his office. He was pleased to find it both pleasantly lit and much more spacious than any of his previous offices. He took his place at his desk and laid out the curricular materials that he'd received for further study. The list of topics was inclusive, ranging from basic aspects of organization and discipline to more advanced topics in strategy and planning. General Foch would give the opening discussion and, from the looks of the materials, would serve as the coordinator of the remainder of presentations. Aside from a conference later that afternoon to discuss the status of current projects and one the following morning, where he received his first engineering assignment, Robert remained essentially free to study the materials provided prior to the first meeting of his class at the War College.

————

The following day, after a brief lunch, he set out through the pleasant tree-lined streets toward the gold dome of the Invalides and from there proceeded in the direction of Eiffel's imposing tower. In short order he reached the military school building aligned upon the long grassy plain facing the tower. On the second floor he found the lecture hall and took his place among the gathering group of officers to wait for the arrival of the general.

As he would come to expect from Foch, they did not have to wait long. The general arrived precisely at the scheduled time, walking through the door with a characteristically rapid gait. After a brief round of introductions and a discussion of the scope and intent of the future course work, Foch began his lecture.

"Gentleman, a great army is built on many layers of excellence. At the most basic level, it is built on discipline, which is essential for any army's success. Following discipline is an understanding of the principles needed for military success, which requires acquiring a broad range of knowledge. Knowledge alone is insufficient, however, unless it suffused with experience, either individually or from knowledgeable mentors. In this course we will deal with many important topics, hoping to improve your understanding of modern ordnance, transportation, logistics, communication, intelligence, and several other important subjects. For this army to excel, however, our leading officers must not only have discipline and knowledge but also important psychological attributes, which I will discuss later.

"The goal of this course is to provide a better understanding of the means to optimize your success on the battlefield through a study of best practices. As a young man I was trained in engineering and now better understand how that discipline has much in common with good soldiering. Both require acquiring facts and applying them in a precise and logical manner. As an example, we will turn to an old and vital problem that has confronted French officers for centuries—the geography of our frontiers and the implications for our own defense."

Foch pulled down a large map of France, along with much of the surrounding states of Western Europe. "This map is familiar to us all. It gives us much valuable information with regard to our border with our neighbors. This type of map, based on national boundaries, is aptly designated as a political map, but when supplemented with a map containing topographic information, it can provide numerous facts and inferences well beyond simple boundary lines. For a military strategist, therefore, consideration of geography is essential.

"For much of our past, the principle threat to France came from the northwest. For far too long, Norman dukes and their Saxon vassals kept this frontier in turmoil with numerous attempts to establish hegemony over the entire nation. It has been only in the brief span of our lifetimes that this threat has fortunately lessened. As our fate in 1871 reminds us, we now are confronted by a new and possibly greater threat to our east in the modern German Empire.

"If you were to compare this present map to that of a map of 1870, two major differences would be readily apparent. First, a large tract of what was eastern France, primarily in the province of Alsace, has been confiscated by Germany. I need not dwell on that reality further, but for me—and I dare say many of you here—that fact seldom escapes my thoughts. Second, the German Reich of the present includes many separate principalities and independent states, such as Saxony and Bavaria, which in 1870 were much more autonomous than now. The implications of both of these changes are significant."

He paused to take a sip of water and then drew down a second map, which showed the topography of the area. "This map gives a better topical representation of our situation in comparison to the simple two-dimensional representation of the political map. Study this map closely and those in the library so that you know by heart the rise and fall of the land along this territory reaching from Paris along the entire length of our eastern boundary. This is effectively the playing board on which any strategy for our defense will be formulated.

"If you look closely, you can see the Prussians acted wisely, from a strategic sense, by cleaving Alsace from our borders. Not only must we now contend with the buffer such lands provide to the German homeland, but in gaining these areas, they have also acquired an effective barricade provided by the Vosges Mountains in this region. As you study the German border further, you will see that there are other areas of great geographic and strategic importance that have been the sites of many bitter battles to control the region.

"We humans are most influenced by our most recent experience, and soldiers are certainly no different in that regard, with our modern concepts of warfare and tactics most influenced by recent history. Consequently, these crucial areas on our Eastern Frontier have been transformed by defenses shaped by past battles."

Foch then pointed to the map, beginning at the confluence of the French, German, and Belgian borders, emphasizing the line of fortifications stretching from Mauberges to Lille, then along the German border south through Belfort and Verdun, all the way to the Swiss border.

"Where nature has been lacking, we have enlisted our engineers for our defense. These forts and fortifications serve to complicate an enemy's passage through areas, forcing them to adopt tactics more advantageous to our defense. Now, if we supplement this geographic knowledge with intelligence information, our planning can be further refined. Our best intelligence estimates that the Germans have approximately twenty-five corps of regular troops that they can deploy on their western front. That is approximately one million troops, which is roughly equivalent to the troops we have available to oppose them. These numbers beg the question: what number of troops is sufficient to defend our borders?

"The estimate might be affected by the terrain and fortifications of any given area, as well as the disposition of the enemy. Given modern weaponry and tactics, however, it is safe to assume that to defend a well-fortified position will require fewer troops than initiating large-scale offensive actions. For an offense to be successful a certain critical mass of troops is required. We presently estimate it is necessary to have at least five to six men per meter to sustain an offensive to a successful conclusion. Everything that we know of German strategic thinking implies that if a war between Germany and France occurs, it will be vital that they attack to rapidly neutralize French forces in order to deal with a Russian threat on their eastern border.

"Now let's examine this map from the Germans' perspective. The Franco-German border is approximately 250 kilometers in length. Over this distance, however, they must maintain troops to guard against a French offensive, while maximizing their numbers in other areas for their offensive. Their choices for this offensive are not limited to our common boundary, however. To the south lies Switzerland, whose formidable mountains serve to strengthen their long-standing policy of neutrality, making this an unlikely route. To the north of our frontier, however, a different set of considerations exists, especially in Belgium above the Ardennes, where the terrain is flat and free of any natural troop impediments all the way to Paris.

"Fortunately, the continent's powers have recognized the potential attraction such lands have for aggression and put a treaty in place a century ago to guarantee Belgium neutrality. Any violation of this neutrality would be viewed harshly, not only by the remaining signatories but no doubt by the rest of the world as well. Such an act by Germany would represent a great gamble, as it would not only invite worldwide criticism but would virtually assure the enmity of Great Britain. The purpose of this discussion is to get you to think about military problems using many perspectives. Geography, mathematics, and politics impose potential limits."

Foch took another drink from his glass of water and then rolled up the maps that he had used. "In future discussions we will deal in much greater depth with many subjects that touch on this problem and others like it. You will be taught the most current thinking regarding both defensive and offensive tactics. We will revisit the topic of troop strength and will consider tactical questions that go beyond the static geometry of troop deployment and consider more significant considerations that come with changing battle conditions and fleeting instances of times when battles are decided. To command effectively it is essential that an officer appreciates the implications inherent in the dynamics of a battle, where speed and audacity can provide great advantages. A truly great officer has a sense that allows him to anticipate crucial events before they happen.

"The essence of all of our discussions that will follow will explore this question of effective leadership and the skills and traits that great officers possess. Much of what we will discuss will be tangible, like the issues of terrain and intelligence that are essential for sound analysis. What may be even more essential, however, are issues that are often more difficult to precisely define and deal with—the psychology and mental attributes of successful commanders.

"I am confident that when you graduate from your studies here you will have as good a foundation in theory and an appreciation of best practices as any group of officers in the world. As you go forward with your careers, you must, however, be constantly open to new ideas that might give you and your men further advantage in battles of the future. Yet, in spite of all your preparation and that of your colleagues, all will be in vain if you and your men don't have the most vital attribute for success.

"A great army, prepared in discipline, technique, and armament, can still succumb to a lesser foe if it lacks a crucial attribute—an unflinching will to conquer. We can master the details of terrain and strategy and know our enemies strengths and weaknesses—in short, be well prepared for battle—but without this resolve, this emotion, this unquantifiable desire for victory, we will be at a great disadvantage. We have seen this in our daily lives with the cyclist who persists in the most difficult hill-climb or the boxer who prevails, despite being knocked down and bloodied. At the critical time, when men are locked in struggle and all is in the balance, it is the one with the will to defy all, the one with the emotion to persist and to win, who will carry the day.

"For the army of France to be successful, it is not enough for its leaders to be well prepared and intelligent, which is an obvious necessity for victory. Beyond this they must infuse a spirit of confidence through bold and aggressive actions and an unbending will to prevail, regardless of the circumstances. It is this intangible emotion, this vital spirit, that will distinguish us from our enemies and restore us to the glory that has been the proud tradition of our armies from the earliest days.

"I believe that the time has come that we in the officer corps begin to reclaim the spirit of our ancestors. Housed at the Invalids we can see the many battle flags that give testimony to the spirit of a French army in full confidence of its power and skill. They give names to the battlefields where will and power combined to produce historic victories. Such glory is our inheritance if we are willing to recognize it.

"Gentlemen, we are now regaining the strength that is our birthright. Our weaponry is first-rate and getting better. Our men are well trained, and our officers are aware not only of our responsibility to the army but also to the nation. It only remains for us to infuse an indomitable spirit into this army so that it will refuse to be intimidated by the strength and numbers of our enemies. We must prepare ourselves to our utmost capacity so that we can defend what is rightfully ours. It is my duty and the duty of all your instructors in this course to prepare you for success when that day comes."

13

BERLIN

"Good morning, Boss," Stein quipped as he saw Sarah walk into the office. "You're a bit later than I expected. I thought I would see you at the first light of day, eager to get caught up on all the excitement you have missed around the asylum while you have been gone."

"Since when have I been the boss around here, Stein?" Sarah asked, knowing full well that the virtual boss was Stein, without whom the bureau would simply not exist. "If I'm the boss it must be that there is some particularly distasteful business brewing that you would rather not handle."

"Now, Sarah, you know full well that your title here is director of publications, so I did not feel free to speak for you when your old friend Herr Hahn came around asking about our relationship to various pacifist groups in the city. For someone so officious and arrogant, it is no doubt hard enough putting up with a socialist newspaper, but a foreign-based paper from France must tax his patience daily. Seeing us consorting with pacifists must have given him and his minions more ideas to further motivate their hostilities. As our director, you may well need all of your formidable legal skills in the coming days."

"That's a happy thought. Sometimes the machinations of working in this town are enough to outweigh all the many positives, like the weather and the friendly natives."

Since the Berlin bureau of *l'Humanité* had come into existence in early 1906 through the shared efforts of Sarah and Stein, satirical rhetoric had evolved as a primary means of communication.

In the beginning, Sarah had negotiated the tricky legal barriers to establishing a foreign-based paper in Berlin and had continued to monitor any and all regulations or laws that might threaten their continued operations. She had also acquired valuable skills in negotiating leases and other business arrangements that allowed for the bureau to operate in a smooth and economical manner. In those first years, she began to cultivate relationships with many of the leading socialists in the city and the Reichstag. This helped to not only gain a better understanding of the most significant socialist movement on the continent but also to provide the various German leaders a recognizable contact that might serve as a convenient liaison to the French movement.

Other groups soon attracted Sarah's interest as well, including the large German pacifist movement that shared an obvious antipathy to war with socialists throughout Europe. The pacifist movement in Germany was quite strong, with remarkable leaders who had helped to organize two large international protest meetings against war that had had a significant effect on the collective conscience of Europe. Her recent reports to the home office, detailing the German movement in general and its leaders more specifically, recently was published in a series of articles in Paris.

Stein, on the other hand, was the true journalist of the bureau. His past experiences in Berlin had given him not only knowledge of the territory but also an increasing list of sources from whom he could gain valuable information. Backed by Sarah's legal skills and the monetary support from the home office in Paris, his natural inquisitiveness and disdain for those in power had combined with his other skills to make him a journalist of the first rank. He was also a journalist both feared and respected by those who were frequently at odds with his views.

As the bureau began to prosper, new complications and challenges sprung from its increased success and the accompanying notoriety. By far the most complex was the surveillance that came from the various government agencies, especially the information ministry and even the interior ministry. This often forced Stein—as well as the other reporters working for the bureau—to use more caution in his reporting than he would otherwise be inclined. At the same time he had begun to cultivate an ever wider network of contacts and sources that gave him access to much valuable and timely information. In many ways, he was at the center of a network of information that those in the government could construe as hostile to their efforts. Through that perspective, the paper could readily be imagined as a ring of spies.

In follow-up to Stein's comments on the bureau's relationship to the city's many pacifist leaders, Sarah asked, "What does your little network say about a vendetta being threatened against us in relation to our pacifist friends?"

One of Stein's contacts was Herr Ernst Baldinger, who was employed at a senior level position in the interior ministry. Fortunately, Baldinger was not one bound by tenuous ties to the paper. He and Stein had a long relationship going back to their younger days that was cemented by the sharing of mutually beneficial information and many hours together in various beer halls. He also had an old-fashioned dislike for Hahn, with whom he came into frequent contact.

"Well, Herr B. has a theory that whenever the kaiser and his military friends are thinking about some new tactic or stratagem, they become increasingly worried about domestic opposition. The Social Democrats in parliament and the greater mass of the workers movement are always at the top of their list of concerns. It doesn't help their angst that the socialist parties are gaining strength nearly each election and the number of socialist affiliates is growing even faster. The main socialist groups and their leaders have been followed for years. In recent days, a call has gone out to intensify surveillance of other groups. One is the organized pacifist groups headed by some of your new acquaintances. As a consequence of your association with Bertha von Suttner, you too have become an object of their interest and should expect to be accorded all the trappings of that status."

"Given the people we represent and where we are headquartered, I frankly expected encountering this type of bother more frequently than we have," Sarah said. "That doesn't upset me as much as the thought of having to undergo a set of interviews with Hahn. Just imagining his arrogant little sneer and pompous manner is more than a bit depressing. It is no wonder that the population here is so dour, what with the gray weather and having to deal with legions of officious jackasses like him. Well, no one said the job would be easy, but I do so wish they could move him to another office. What other tidbits do you have for me?"

"Nothing too dramatic; The SPD is up to its usual infighting over various real and imagined threats and policy initiatives. No juicy scandals or shake-ups to report. The new Meistersinger at the Berlin opera is quite good, so I'm told. I could never stomach that bigoted bastard Wagner, however, so I cannot report to you firsthand on that.

"I have also sensed a bit more nervous energy than usual around the Wilhelmstrasse, and coupled with the suspicions of Herr B., I would suspect that the kaiser and his boy Bethmann-Hollweg are up to no good. If that is the case, I hope your visit to Switzerland was productive in organizing further resistance to any of their military adventures."

"In many ways it was more than I had hoped for," she replied. "The country is full of the most militant socialists in Europe, most of whom have been forced into exile there. They, of course, would bring commitment and organization to any planned large-scale demonstration or work stoppage. Beyond them, however, the greater part of the ruling and intellectual classes share a similar loathing for any widespread European conflict. Aside from the enormous destruction that a war might bring, it would threaten their sense of orderliness, to say nothing of their almighty banking system. Should the time arise, I dare say that the Swiss would prove good hosts to any international demonstration for peace."

"I have always thought Geneva beautiful and have liked the organization in the German cantons. Switzerland would be a nice place for a gathering, if only the beer was better and the women warmer," Stein added.

"By the way, while you were gone your articles on Bertha von Suttner and the German peace movement were selectively reprinted here in several papers of varying political leanings. Aside from provoking the interest of Herr Hahn, they have resulted in several requests to meet with you by others who are far more agreeable. The more routine ones we have handled in our established manner, but there are a couple of others that are very interesting and will require further attention."

"I was expecting to meet with Frau von Suttner upon my return to go over my conversations in Switzerland. Many of my meetings were with people she referred me to and were quite helpful in facilitating my visit. Besides, she is such an interesting person in her own right that I really enjoy visiting with her. Who were the others that you referred to?"

"For starters, there is General von Bernhardi. I doubt if you will be warmly received by him if your discussion turns to the topic of a peace demonstration in the Tiergarten."

"I had contacted his office before I left to request an interview in light of the impending publication of his new book. In a series on the German peace movement we would be remiss if we didn't afford an opposite opinion. Since old Treitschke is dead, he would seem to be his most likely successor. Besides, how can you not be enraptured by the title of his new book, *Germany and the Next War?*"

"He might be a good one to meet before you have your first stare-down with Hahn. I would certainly recommend that you have a chat with Hahn before meeting with another of your supplicants though—none other than Rosa the Red."

"That is curious," Sarah replied. "The few times we have met, dear Rosa has never seemed to take a liking to me. The last time we met she called me a spineless accommodator and a pseudosocialist. She can be rather undiplomatic, that one. Well, Stein, if there is nothing else, it's been nice gossiping with you, but I better get to my desk and start to dig out from the stack of papers that I'm sure is waiting for me."

14

THE BARONESS

The following afternoon, Sarah walked from the office to the Potsdammer Platz and caught a tram to meet with Frau von Suttner. As she passed through Charlottenburg to the northern parts of the city, she was struck once more by how little the urban development had encroached on these areas. Here, the true character of the land was more evident, with large tracts of flat sandy soil surrounded by clumps of aspen, birch, and evergreen trees, as well as numerous lakes. This was a land like Scandinavia, with little of the evident lush fertility that blessed great parts of France and Britain. The contrast between the bustling center as seen at the Potsdammer Platz and these sylvan suburbs was symbolic of the many contradictions and ironies that one encountered nearly every day in Berlin.

If one looked at the unpromising nature of the surrounding countryside, it would be hard to imagine how Berlin could grow into the modern dynamo that it had become. In the years when agriculture had been the major staple of European economies, Prussia had survived by the combination of extraordinary will and discipline. To this very day, the landed Junker class practiced a frugality that allowed them to profit from the limitations of their northern latitude and the mediocre quality of their lands. These practical traits were clearly evident in their many sons who comprised the highest echelons of the Prussian army, which now dominated the combined armies of united Germany. It was here that their Lutheran practicality, coupled with their fanatic devotion to discipline, would serve as the foundation for the development of the state. Indeed, to many of their neighbors it seemed that Prussia owed its existence to its cannons.

Yet it was apparent to Sarah from her earliest days that Prussia—and indeed the country that it had subjugated—was far more than a large armed camp. One of the most remarkable traits of the early ruling electors and subsequent ruling Hohenzollerns was their willingness to accept and cultivate outsiders into their society if their presence could benefit the country. The first great elector, Frederick, initiated this precedent by welcoming the mass of French Protestants being persecuted in the aftermath of the religious wars in France. The highest among them were soon welcomed and integrated into the upper stratum of Prussian society. More important, they brought an artistic sense that was to influence city life and the likes of Frederick the Great and helped to transform the dour cities of Potsdam and Berlin into major centers for the arts and architecture. Indeed, the neighborhood where she rented a flat near the bureau was located around the Gendarmer Platz, where the French descendants had concentrated and where their numbers and influence were still a presence.

Even more important and controversial had been the acceptance of the persecuted Jews of the Russian Empire, including Poland. Not only did their influx contribute a badly needed increase in population, which would serve as a stimulus for economic growth, but—most important—they would bring with them the many and considerable benefits of their people and their long culture. Accepted by the Prussians better than any area of Europe, these Jews would soon take root and flourish in countless fields, resulting in remarkable benefits to the emerging state. Soon, many aspects of commerce, ranging from agriculture to retail along with arcane advances in finance and more practical applications in the sciences and engineering, would be influenced by these eastern emigrants. In modern Berlin, the arts and intellectual life were increasingly influenced by their presence. So too was the large and increasingly powerful workers movement and their often-related allies, the pacifists.

As a Jew whose distant relatives had filled these very streets, Sarah sensed her kinship to many Berliners and therefore felt compelled to reach out to the pacifists among them to help spare them and her own French relatives the certain misery that would come from the old plague of war. Her efforts led to her meeting Baroness Bertha von Suttner, a woman whose life and background was vastly different from Sarah's.

Sarah had, of course, heard some of the most interesting details of the baroness's life that might read like a tale that Dickens would be proud of. Born into an old and respected Austrian noble family, she had been forced to move from Prague at a young age due to the severity of her mother's finances. When she was unable to sustain herself teaching music, she took up the role of private secretary to a prominent Viennese businessman Baron von Suttner. As fate would have it, she and the baron's son fell madly in love. Realizing the futility of their relationship, she fled to Paris, working for a brief time as a private secretary to a wealthy Swede, only to return and elope with her beloved Arthur when they could no longer remain separated.

There ensued twelve years of exile in distant Georgia, where Arthur, helped by old friends, gradually established a profitable business. At the same time, the couple had begun to overcome the resistance to their marriage from Arthur's family. During those years the Russo-Turkish War broke out, and large numbers of soldier and civilian casualties soon flooded into their town of Tiflis. The von Suttners turned their home into a makeshift hospital, and the shock of that experience would convert the baroness into an ardent antiwar activist thereafter.

They finally returned to Austria, and while there, she wrote the first of several books, a novel that reflected her experiences in the previous war and her revulsion with its effects on the family. The success of this book and others that followed propelled her to a leadership role in the pacifist movement, a role that was further enhanced in 1905 by the receipt of a peace prize from the foundation of her old employer and subsequent longtime friend, Alfred Noble.

Arriving at the baroness's home, Sarah paused for a moment to enjoy the quiet of the home's setting before proceeding to the main entrance, where, after a slight delay, she was shown to a sunlight parlor overlooking a small, decorative pond. Baroness von Suttner soon appeared dressed very stylishly in a patterned dress with a high ruffled collar, which only served to emphasize her stature and well-maintained posture. The entire effect was to give her a bearing consistent with her present esteemed status. To Sarah, she always seemed to embody the ideal of everyone's favorite aunt—reserved, stylish, wise, and supportive.

"I am so pleased to see you once again, my dear," the baroness said as she and Sarah gave each other a greeting buss. "I hope you had an enjoyable and productive visit to Switzerland. I trust that the contacts that I gave you proved beneficial."

"My visit was both exciting and productive," Sarah replied. "Between the names that you supplied and those that I had obtained from others, I was able to accomplish much that I had set out to do. As a bonus, the weather was unusually fine, and the countryside was even more beautiful than I remembered it. I had not been to Switzerland since I was a young student on a winter outing to Interlaken, so I very much enjoyed my visit to both Geneva and the German cantons. The response of many of the Swiss to my inquiries served to increase my enjoyment even further.

"They were quite receptive and warm to the idea of a European peace conference that we have discussed. In talking with many of their leaders, it is clear that they strongly oppose any European conflict for many reasons. It also seems that of all the Europeans, they seem to be the most tolerant of diverse political opinion. The number of foreign radical politicians and thinkers is quite large there, many of whom are sympathetic to any movement that would unite different factions and nationalities across Europe in opposition to war.

"I also communicated frequently with Monsieur Jean Jaurès, who was able to direct me to several people in the government who are sympathetic to our cause. As you may know, he is the head of the interparliamentary union of socialist ministers throughout Europe. With his backing, I was able to move forward with a plan designed to organize the structure of a meeting, whereby all such groups committed to peace throughout Europe could meet in Switzerland, should conditions warrant a massive rally to protest any threatened war. One of my first objectives upon returning to Berlin was to speak to you about this and get your input on what you think might need to be done further."

"What do you have in mind?" the baroness asked.

"After first agreeing on Switzerland as an ideal meeting site, we constructed a list of possible host cities to evaluate more fully."

"I couldn't agree more with regard to Switzerland's suitability as a host," the baroness replied. "Is there any one location that you favor more than another?"

"From my discussions in Basal, including meetings with the mayor and bishop, I was convinced that the city had both adequate facilities and a commitment from the authorities for support, if a crisis should prompt further action. I was even able to work out an agreement with the city to supply public space and security and reached terms upon a price for their services. It was agreed that at least seven days' and preferably two weeks' notice would be necessary for such an arrangement to be put into place. It was also agreed that the participants would avow any acts of violence or provocation in the course of assembly. Any failure to adhere to such a pledge could result in legal action and fines, which could be directed to the organizers as well as any participants. Most important, the bishop has a great interest in the project and under the right circumstances would provide the cathedral as a venue for a very large gathering. That insistence upon peaceful assembly was prudent on their part, and that is where leaders like you and your German Peace Society are essential to help in the planning to ensure a successful gathering. With a tentative meeting site in place, what remains is the hard work of organization."

"It appears that you accomplished a great deal in your visit," the baroness said. "What you are saying makes great sense. You have not lived in Berlin for as long as I have, so it is difficult to notice the changes that I believe have occurred in the last several years. Ever since the Moroccan affair in 1905, there has been ever more influence of those who believe it is time for Germany to demand her rightful place as the dominant power in Europe. Given the recent history of the country, it is no surprise that many people feel that the most effective means of realizing this end is through military coercion.

"As you know, I have lived in Germany for a small portion of my life. This has allowed me to see German society not only as one who lives in Berlin but also with the eyes of a foreigner. While it is true that the Germans have many strengths, it is also true that they have many failings. One is that their arrogance makes them oblivious to the feelings of others. In the case of their many European neighbors, this emerging militarism has not been lost and has increased their anxiety as well as their will to resist. From my perspective, I have no doubt that the greatest threat to peace rests with the very people of this city and their influence on the country. Prussian rule has always been conservative and shaped by the military. The more liberal German states to the west may not agree with this, but at present they are not in a position to argue with their Prussian masters.

"Yet despite these difficulties, I am thrilled by the number of people in Germany who share our peaceful viewpoint and by the fact that those numbers continue to increase at a rapid rate. Our numbers represent the single biggest counterbalance to Prussian militarism in Germany, but it is too much to expect that we alone can tame this mighty beast. That is why I am so thrilled to have you and your French associates on our side. We will need your strength to help combat the conservatives and their nationalist allies and their ideas of advancing German power.

"These groups have a deep suspicion that the other principle nations of Europe will contrive, by any means possible, to frustrate their rightful supremacy. Any movement that argues for peace solely from German organizations and does not include equally strong representation from the other potential belligerents will be perceived and represented by the present ruling class as a ploy to weaken Germany. As I said, I think a meeting in Switzerland seems very wise, and I would be honored to help in the planning in any way possible."

"I was hoping that you would offer to help and am thrilled that you have agreed to do so. We can continue our efforts at a time convenient to you, after I have a provisional agenda drawn up. That may take some time, as it will be necessary to reach out to other potential speakers and assess their willingness to participate."

At that moment the door opened, and a thin, well-postured gentleman, formally dressed in coat and tie, was admitted to their presence.

"Arthur, darling." The baroness smiled in greeting. "You're home a bit early, it seems."

"I had planned to go for a walk after my luncheon and meeting, but we were delayed in getting started, and afterward I stayed to talk with several others. By the time we were finished, I decided to come directly home."

"I would like to present my lovely young acquaintance. Arthur, this is Fraulein Sarah Morozovski."

"I am so glad to meet you, fraulein. I have heard my wife speak of you in recent weeks, so it is nice to put a most pleasant face with the name. If we are both home, we try to reserve the late afternoon so that we might share tea together. It is an old tradition we learned in Georgia. When you are done with your conversation, I hope that you will have the time to join us."

"Yes, that would be lovely," the baroness added. "Much of

what needs to be done has been accomplished. Tea would be a welcome coda to our visit."

"Yes, I believe it would," Sarah agreed. "I would be happy to stay, as long as I am not intruding on your privacy."

"Not at all," the baroness assured her. "It is good to have the voice of a visitor to add a different perspective."

As the tea cart arrived, accompanied by a handsome tray of accompaniments, Sarah felt transported by the surroundings and her companions to the aristocratic salons of Vienna. She had a small sense of discomfort, particularly in her knowledge of protocol in such a setting, that was promptly dispelled by the warmth and easy manner of the host and hostess.

The facts of her recent Swiss visit were explored further, with both host and hostess eager to hear details of their old acquaintances and to reminisce about past visits.

In a moment of quiet, the baron said, "Fraulein, I am curious how someone like you, who is so attractive and clearly intelligent, has such freedom to move around the continent unencumbered by the demands of a relationship with a young gentleman. I was always told that the French were so passionate about their women. What is wrong with this generation of Frenchmen that they have let someone like you escape?"

"You will have to excuse Arthur, my dear," the baroness said, with a mocking scold to her husband. "He is an unrequited nineteenth-century romantic who views much of this more modern world with distaste. Please don't take any offense, as I assure you he is harmless."

"On the contrary, I am flattered that someone would think me so beguiling as to be able to turn the head of one of nature's most vain and fickle creatures. I can testify from long experience about the juvenile behavior and marked insecurities of the average Frenchman."

"Alas, you must be an ardent man-hater then," Arthur jested. "That is a real tragedy."

Sarah replied with feigned indignation. "That is most certainly not true. I consider myself a romantic as well and harbor a secret hope that some Prince Charming exists for me, if only the time and circumstances could be right."

"Have you not had one fleeting moment of romance in your short life?" Arthur asked empathetically.

"I am hesitant to admit it, but I had an acquaintance who interested me very much. Unfortunately, our circumstances, in terms of our backgrounds and the subsequent course of our careers, made it virtually impossible to carry on a meaningful relationship."

The baroness looked up slightly from her tea, her interest clear on her face. "Did you care for the young man?" she asked.

"In our short time together I felt the strongest attraction that I have had for any man. At times, I was almost giddy, acting with little sense."

"Those are the worse symptoms," Arthur said with mock solemnity. "What tragedy befell you?"

"We were both forced to choose between major opportunities or to pass them up, remain in Paris, and be content with less promising alternatives. At that time, we had been involved for only a short time so that for either of us to abandon opportunity for the sake of a young and unproven relationship seemed imprudent. Besides, there were so many complicating factors that to imagine a fairy-tale ending seemed highly unlikely."

"This is all too intriguing for an old has-been romantic like me," said Arthur. "Please go on."

"Arthur, really," the baroness scolded. "You are like some silly old gossip."

"It's all right," replied Sarah. "It seems almost therapeutic to talk about it. Well, where to begin? First of all, not only was he not Jewish, but he came from an old aristocratic family from Provence. A young Jewess would not be kindly welcomed into such company. Where I am often extroverted, he is the opposite. He is, I must say, brilliant but in an altogether different way. He is adept in the occult world of higher mathematics and is a very accomplished young engineer. Oh, did I say that he is also very handsome?"

"My goodness," the baroness interjected, "it seems to me that you both have made a big sacrifice."

"At the time it seemed the only sensible thing to do. Both of us had been given the opportunity to pursue jobs that were challenging and well matched to our interests and aptitudes. The conflict in our social background was further complicated by his accepting a commission in the army, where he was promised the opportunity to develop key projects for the defense of France. The complications that such a relationship would necessarily bring made it easier to convince myself of the hopelessness of our situation and to go off to Berlin, where I find myself today."

"Oh, my dear," said the baroness. "Have you been in contact with him since that time?"

"We agreed to keep in touch, but he soon was sent to positions outside of Paris and eventually to North Africa, which made it virtually impossible for us to meet on my return visits to Paris. The last note I got from him was some time ago. He was limited in what he could say by security concerns, and he implied that he was quite busy and was no longer in his previous location where he had last written, which was Algiers. I could sense from some of his phrases that from wherever he was writing seemed to be a somewhat dangerous locale. I heard from some friends when I was last home that he is somewhere in the Indian Ocean and, thankfully, at last count, remains unhurt."

"Sarah, I have known you but a short time, but I see so much of myself in my younger days in you. I hope you won't be offended if I tell you a story."

"Of course not," replied Sarah.

"When I was your age, I had far less security and independence than I believe that you have now. Soon after I obtained what was a dream job complications set in. I fell very much in love with the son of my employer. Such a relationship would have been unacceptable to his father, and so in order to escape from the unbearable temptation, I moved to Paris, where I was fortunate to obtain a very good position. Despite this good fortune, I could not stand the separation; fortunately, neither could my lover. We soon eloped, leaving behind all that we knew, and moved to faraway Georgia. That wonderful man is sitting with us now. Arthur and I have shared much, some of it bad but most of it good. There is no doubt that my life—and I hope his as well—would not be so thrilling and/or as fulfilled without him.

"I am not trying to tell you that you should drop everything and chase after this soldier simply on the basis of my experience. What I am saying is that if, by some mysterious circumstance, you have a chance to renew your relationship with this young man, I would say that you should do everything that you can to grasp the opportunity. At this stage, you do not know whether the many obstacles you mention are enough to truly come between you. You owe it to yourself to find out, and in order to do so, you should not be hindered by conventional norms or by shyness. You may not be capable of the love or commitment that is necessary to make it work. If that is the case, all that you risk is some short-lived humiliation and heartache. That is a small price to pay to find out if he really is the one you are hoping for. If he is the one, from my experience, the rewards of finding a beloved companion are worth all the risk and hardship it takes to get him."

"I appreciate your frank and considerate advice very much. Coming from you, it gives me some hope that I am not destined to die an old maid. Watching how you and Arthur react to each other after all these years tells me what I can hope for, if I am fortunate enough to find that someone that you speak of."

"As an old romantic to a young one," Arthur said as he kissed his wife's hand, "persistence and patience only makes the prize more worthwhile."

15

MARIE

Robert had kept in touch with Professor de Rochelle as much as possible in the years after leaving Paris. At first, it was fairly easy to communicate with him, as his assignments were either in Paris or France, but when he was transferred to Africa, their communication was rare. After resettling in Paris, Robert now looked forward to reuniting with his old mentor in order to catch up on the work with which the professor and his associates were now involved. Unfortunately, Robert had been disappointed to learn that the professor was away inspecting several projects outside of Paris. Shortly afterward, however, he was pleased to receive an invitation from Madame de Rochelle for dinner the following week, noting it was a gathering of some friends and a few family members to welcome the professor home after several weeks' absence.

The evening of the dinner he wore a uniform appropriate for the occasion and arrived before the prescribed hour, hoping to catch the professor without a surrounding throng of well-wishers. Unfortunately, others had similar ideas. No sooner was he welcomed by the professor and his wife inside their large parlor than a group of several colleagues and their wives arrived. After a series of introductions, the professor turned to Robert, leading him toward a tray where he was offered an aperitif.

"Well, Robert, it is wonderful to see you. It makes a very good welcome-home present. Mathilde had told me that you returned to Paris on assignment, and both of us agreed to invite you for dinner as soon as I returned. I suppose in some way this gathering is as much a homecoming for you as it is for me."

"I am very happy to be here. I have been looking forward to this evening ever since I received the invitation."

"Well, from the looks of you, it appears as if the climate where you have been agrees with you. I feared that I would find you half wasted from improper army food and some type of tropical disease. Instead, you look as if you have filled out with some muscle on your bones, and you have a suntan that is seldom seen in this region."

"If you get hungry enough, even army food has certain charms. We also had an excellent wine cellar, which improved our appetites and helped keep the malaria away. In Madagascar we were often so far off the beaten track that the only way you could get a project done quickly enough to get back to civilization was to pitch in with the work detail yourself, which helped build up my strength."

As they sipped their drinks, more guests arrived, forcing the professor to break away and resume his duties as host. Robert stepped back from the center of the room and took in the arriving guests and the hubbub surrounding the hosting couple. He was pleased and surprised to see General Foch arrive, still in his less-formal working uniform. His wife, having arrived earlier, joined him and marked her territory by giving him a mild scolding for being late. Of the other guests, Robert was most intrigued by the arrival of a handsome middle-aged woman, accompanied by a very stunning younger woman, who appeared to be her daughter.

Robert quickly struck up a conversation with some of the engineers that he had known from his earlier days in the professor's office, trying to catch up on their activities and the state of affairs of the local engineering community. As he was listening to their stories, he saw Madame de Rochelle scanning the room, apparently looking for someone. As she saw Robert, her eyes seemed to focus, and much to his surprise, she began to walk his way, accompanied by the two women who had recently captured his attention.

"There you are, Robert," she said as she tugged lightly on his sleeve. "I have been looking for you. I would like to introduce you to two of the loveliest visitors that I know in Paris. Robert, this is my youngest sister, Margarite Bonneau, and her daughter, Marie. Ladies, may I present our old friend Monsieur Robert d'Avillard."

"It is a great pleasure," said Robert with obvious sincerity as he greeted the two women.

"We have heard so much about you from Henri and Mathilde, Robert, that I feel as if I already know you," the mother replied.

Robert could not help but take in the women with a critical and appreciative eye. From this closer perspective, they were even more attractive. The mother was very slim and appeared much younger than her sister. The daughter obviously favored her mother. She was of modest height with a trim and attractive figure. She had sparkling golden hair drawn back attractively, with long curls framing her well-proportioned face. Her thin lips and mouth were drawn in a manner so characteristic of attractive French women. All was enhanced by her blue eyes, which seemed to communicate an intelligence that added further to her attractiveness.

"Margarite is from Lyon, and she and Marie are staying here while Marie gets established with her studies at the music conservatory. I am proud to say that she is a pianist of great skill, which she no doubt inherited from our side of the family."

"How long have you been here in Paris?" Robert asked.

"We arrived last week, and the days seemed to have rushed by. We have barely had time to get settled, with Marie's auditions and grand occasions such as this taking up most of our days," replied Margarite.

"Fortunately, I have finished all of my necessary auditions and have been accepted as a student of Professor Frontenac," Marie added. "With a little luck, I hope to find a convenient place to stay that will take the burden of my presence off Aunt Mathilde."

"Nonsense, my dear, nothing gives us as much pleasure as having you and your mother staying with us. If I have anything to say about it, you are welcome to stay here as long as you wish."

"That might be too old-fashioned for this modern generation, Mathilde."

"Mother," replied Marie peevishly.

"If it is any consolation, mademoiselle, I can attest that my cousin and I lived with our aunt and grandmother while we were students. From my experience, I would say that our aunt was very old-fashioned compared to your family, and even with her old-school ways we were able to carry on quite independently."

"Well, thank you, Robert," replied Madame de Rochelle. "I feel so much younger and more chic now."

"Thank you, Captain, for your advice. My aunt tells us

that you have been living in North Africa and Madagascar during the last year. That must have been terribly exciting and frightening."

"I would prefer if you would call me Robert, as 'Captain' makes me think that I am back in my office instead of these lovely surroundings."

"Only if you will call me Marie," she replied.

"Come, Margarite, I want to introduce you to General Foch, who is an old friend of George's." said Madame de Rochelle as she pulled on her sister's sleeve. With a wry smile, she added, "It looks like these two can take care of themselves."

"Well, that was convenient," Robert noted after the sisters had taken their leave.

"A bit too convenient, I dare say," replied Marie. With a slight blush, she then said, "You still have not answered my question."

"Oh, you mean about my time in Madagascar? To be honest, I was so caught up in the strangeness and excitement of the place that I didn't have the time to be too frightened."

"No, honestly," she persisted, "how did you deal with all the threats to your safety that you must have encountered? At times I am worried even here in Paris. I cannot imagine how unsettling it must be to be surrounded by hostile people in the midst of some awful jungle."

"It is a strange type of phenomenon, at least for me. When something occurred that was extraordinary or threatening, I found myself concentrating so much on my responsibilities and looking out for my men that I felt little if any fear at the time. For me, it was not so much a matter of consciously being brave but of reflexively doing what I had been trained to do. Afterward, when I would have the time to reflect on what I had done, I confess that I was more often thrilled than frightened."

"How extraordinary," Marie replied. "Did you ever worry about how you would react if you came under fire or were in great danger?"

"I suppose all of us do to some degree, but I never worried about such threats as much as I prepared for them. My father told me once that rather than worry about something, I should try to prepare ahead of time to take control of the matter, should it arise. For me, that meant paying attention to even the smallest details so that I would have anticipated the best tactics to address the matter, if necessary."

"Not that my concerns are nearly as serious as what you have had to deal with, but I often wonder how I will react when performing in front of a large group that I do not know or how I will cope with the demands of new teachers with whom I have never worked."

"I cannot tell you how either of us might react to some future challenge, but I do know that for most things, we have the luxury of making mistakes and being able to learn from them. Making a mistake is a normal matter. What makes it bad is not some minor humiliation or embarrassment but becoming discouraged and giving up on something that might be of importance. Those failings are potent teachers, if we can only learn from them."

"You are very reassuring, Robert. I feel like one of your young recruits."

"You can be assured that I have never had a young or even old recruit anything like you."

"Well, they must be fortunate to have someone like you looking out for them."

Before Robert could reply, their conversation was interrupted by Madame de Rochelle, who informed the assembled guests that dinner was ready and that if all could gather, the maid would help everyone find their appointed places.

Robert soon found himself seated next to General Foch, with the professor sitting across from them. He was pleased to note that Marie sat just a short distance on the opposite side of the table from where he sat, and she quickly caught his eye as he was glancing at her and gave him a warm smile in return.

He was uneasy sitting next to Foch, but the general soon put him at ease by dropping any formality for the more relaxed setting they found themselves in.

"Robert, I am happy to be able to talk with you tonight since I have not had the opportunity to speak with you much in class. I am also pleased that your decision to obtain a commission in the engineering corps has worked out so well. I have followed your progress and have been greatly impressed with the quality of your work and the comments of your superiors. Already it seems that you have been a benefit to the army."

"That is kind of you to say, sir," Robert replied. "I have been surprised with how challenging and important the work often is. I have enjoyed it more than I would have believed when I first started."

"How are you finding Paris?" the general asked.

"Well, it is certainly a change from my recent routine. Some of the work is familiar, such as the planning and design, although the surroundings are much more comfortable than Madagascar. The structure and protocol of our office as well as the entire headquarters is obviously very different. It takes some time to learn the unwritten rules, and I'm afraid that I am slow to master many of them. In the field, the structure was far more transparent and streamlined."

"I would not get too concerned about making mistakes in that regard. I know of no man who is perfectly competent in negotiating the politics of the army. What is the accepted norm today may change with a new government and war minister.

"Changing the subject before I get too frustrated with the politicians, tell me your impressions of the German presence in North Africa."

"Well, to be honest I rarely encountered any significant German presence in Morocco or Algeria, aside from a few scattered merchants in the port cities and, of course, government officials. Why do you ask?"

"It seems that our intelligence in Berlin has revealed new interest in certain quarters of the German government in Africa once again. The Germans are many things, but persistence is certainly one of their many traits. In a world where colonies seem to be associated with national worth, it galls them that they are so behind the rest of the continent, and no doubt, despite the fiasco of 1905, they still harbor notions of an expanding colonial empire. That is why I am interested in your observations about their present situation in the north of the continent."

Robert could not help but notice Marie's evident interest in his conversation with Foch during their discussion, an interest that seemed to make her even more attractive in his eyes.

"Now, Robert, tell me as honestly as you can about your experience to date with the course, as I am always trying to get constructive feedback."

"It is, of course, early, so it is difficult to assess at this stage, but it already seems to provide an interesting synergy between theory and experience. I am already weighing what is suggested as best practices against my real-world experiences in Africa. I want to compliment you on your introductory lecture, not only for suggesting the importance of preparation and organization but also for emphasizing the critical component of psychological readiness. It is easy to lose sight of this facet of leadership when you are trying to master all the other material."

Just as Foch began his reply to Robert, he was interrupted by Madame Rochelle.

"Gentlemen, it would be a shame if you spent your entire evening going over the same matters that you deal with all day long. Take a break from all your worries and lofty responsibilities; they will be back soon enough."

"You are, of course, right, dear Mathilde," the general replied rather contritely. "I was so caught up in my conversation with Captain d'Avillard that I lost my perspective. Thank you for bringing my attention back to this wonderful meal and grand company, where it belongs."

"I have my selfish reasons for interrupting your conversation, aside from my own vanity as a hostess. My talented and beautiful young niece has all but volunteered to play the piano for us while we relax with our dessert. Her only fear is that it might interrupt more important matters, and she was therefore reluctant to proceed without assent from the other guests."

"I cannot answer for the others, but as for me, young lady, I can think of nothing more delightful than hearing you play," said Foch.

"Nor can I," Robert quickly added.

"Well, that settles it," said Madame de Rochelle. "Between the three of us we have the necessary force to command the field. Besides, I am sure she will be superb. I feel flattered because Marie usually is more hesitant to play before such a large gathering of people, so she must feel this is a special occasion."

"I do," replied Marie. "I have so enjoyed my stay here with you this week, and now that Uncle Henri has returned, his company and that of your kind friends has made this evening delightful. A sudden notion came over me to play some of my recent pieces, perhaps as my way to repay you for all your kindness. In listening to our distinguished military guests, I was so interested in the substance of their conversation that I feared that something as trivial as my playing would not be appropriate."

"When the time comes that I should ignore the talents of a beautiful woman for the soldier's routine, then I will no longer be fit to lead a French army and should be retired," Foch replied graciously.

Following cheese and port, the group retired to the salon and gathered around the piano. There, while they waited for their dessert, Marie took her seat at the piano.

At first she sat quite still, staring ahead at the piano as if to gather her thoughts. Her posture was true, with the straightness of her spine aligned perfectly with her neckline. Robert noted how composed she looked, which only served to highlight her natural beauty.

Her first piece was a Mozart sonata with an elegant, restrained phrasing, which seemed to Robert to complement Marie's appearance perfectly. He was impressed not only in the skill of her playing but also in her interpretation, which had the controlled pace and timing so characteristic of the Austrian master. She ended the movement with a subtle slowing and delay of the final notes, so as to further emphasize the sublime genius of the composer.

Flushed and encouraged by the warm reception she received from the gathered guests, she paused and then announced that she would attempt another piece that she had not intended to play.

Once again she sat in silence, as if in a slight trance. Then she started the slow first notes of a Chopin polonaise. Robert watched in amazement as Marie gradually transformed with the tempo and intensity of the piece. As she reached its climax with its rapid arpeggios, she cast aside the reserve of the Mozart piece with an intensity of playing that resulted in the locks of her blonde hair falling loosely over her forehead and left her pale complexion suffused with the coloring of her effort. At its ending, she looked to be nearly exhausted. For Robert, it was both remarkable and exciting to see this beautiful and proper young woman so transformed by her art.

Afterward, Robert waited patiently as the circle of guests gathered around the piano to share their admiration for Marie's performance. When nearly all the guests had moved away, he had the opportunity to speak to her privately.

"Marie, that was truly remarkable. What a perfect way to end a pleasant evening."

"I am so glad that you liked it, Robert, because I would not likely have been able to do so well without your encouragement. As I listened to your conversation with the general, I began to think of what you said about failure. I realized that if I did not challenge myself as you have done with your career in Africa, I could not expect to progress. The anxiety that I naturally felt was balanced by your perspective on failure. You helped me to understand that failure is something that should not paralyze one's thinking. Instead, I thought only of the opportunity to learn."

"Bravo," said Robert. "I wish I could be so effective with the men in my command. It is very gratifying to hear that I helped you, even in a small way. It is obvious that you clearly have great talent, which can only get better if you remember that success comes from persistence and confidence as much as it does from your obvious God-given ability."

At that time, Madame de Rochelle and her sister returned,

seemingly enjoying Marie's success as much as the performer herself did.

"Robert, what do you think of our entertainment tonight?" asked Madame de Rochelle.

"I did not think that anything could match the meal tonight, but I was delighted to find Mademoiselle Bonneau's performance even more remarkable."

"I just spoke to Henri, and he suggested that I speak to you about a future matter," continued Madame de Rochelle. "We have four tickets for a concert next Friday evening by Maurice Ravel, and Henri now tells me that he will not be able to attend. I was hoping that you might be able to join my sister and niece as our escort for the night."

Robert adapted a grave expression and then suddenly changed, flashing a broad smile. "Unless a major crisis breaks out in the interim, I can think of nothing that would prevent me from having the pleasure of your company for the evening."

All seemed to be pleased at the prospect.

16

A PRUSSIAN VIEWPOINT

Sarah had never met General Friedrich von Bernhardi, but she had been in contact with him through her office. Her request for an interview was at first rebuffed, but she had persisted until, overcome by either her arguments or weakened by her continued requests, he had at last agreed to a meeting. She had arrived early, hoping to demonstrate a sense of punctuality that he might not have expected from a French woman. His residence along the Wannsee was enclosed by an iron fence with a prominent gate, guarded by a large and dour guard. With little evident emotion, the guard consulted a roster and opened the gate, pointing her toward the rather dark and imposing entryway of the estate. There, she was met by a male domestic and led into a large library with a massive fireplace and large lead glass windows.

In due time the general appeared, wearing a stylish jacket, neatly pressed trousers, and well-polished boots.

"Good afternoon, fraulein." He greeted her with a voice more hospitable than she had anticipated. "I hope you did not have difficulty in finding your way here."

"No, as a matter of fact I was in this area on a different occasion for an afternoon of sailing, so I was well aware of how to get here. Berlin, it seems to me, is so unique in its proximity to such tranquil and rural surroundings. Looking through the woods toward the lake, it is difficult to imagine that such a large city is so close."

"We Germans have always had a fondness for our lakes and forests. It draws us closer to our ancient ancestors, I suppose. I must say, fraulein, that you are much younger and more attractive than I had anticipated."

"What did you anticipate, General?"

"I had imagined that you would be like so many women committed to a cause. So often they totally ignore or purposefully downplay their femininity, draping themselves in the most awful clothing and foregoing any pretense of social grace."

"Well, how do you know that I am different from that?"

"From your appearance, which shows an appreciation for fashion totally absent from those women to whom I referred, and also from the tenor of your letters, which demonstrated a degree of literacy often lacking by them as well."

"I appreciate the compliment about my literacy, as would my teachers at the Sorbonne who contributed to it greatly. As for my fashion sense, I can take no credit for that. I am French, and fashion comes to a Frenchwoman as naturally as breathing."

"Ah, it is a pity, given the glories of your country and especially the fairer sex, that the relations between our two nations have fallen into such a difficult state."

"I suppose that is one of the reasons why I am so interested in interviewing Germans of diverse views on that relationship, should it worsen."

"To be frank, fraulein, my first concern when you contacted me was that you were a journalist in name only, and what you really are doing is obtaining critical information to take back to your French colleagues in the intelligence bureau. The more I thought of this, however, I realized that all foreign journalists are essentially spies, regardless of who is paying their way. As I investigated you and read some of your writing, I realized that if you were a spy, your allegiance would be to the workers more than it would be to any bureau of the French government or its army."

"Well, let's assume for arguments sake, General, that your supposition is right, and I am simply gathering vital information to use for the international liberation of the working class. Why is it that you have graciously agreed to meet with me?"

"I believe that it is important that reasonable people understand one another, fraulein. You might think that an odd affectation for someone of my background, but it is a residue of my early education as well. It is impossible for any two people to agree fully about any topic, let alone the collective thinking of large groups or even nations. Unless we make some attempt to discuss our viewpoints in a mature and civil manner, then we, as people and nations, will increasingly isolate ourselves from one another, making any future progress more difficult."

"I must confess, General, I am surprised by you as well. I had expected to find you dressed in a military uniform of some type, with a demeanor less interested in discussion than in giving commands. What I find most interesting is trying to reconcile some of the ideas of your writing with your apparent civility today."

"What specific ideas are you referring to?" he asked.

"What interests me and compelled me to try to set up this interview was your stated belief in the inevitability and even the necessity of military conflict as a means to advance the fortunes of humankind. I must state from the outset that I am biased against this extraordinary position, as are the owners of my paper. Nevertheless, as you have reminded me, I too believe there is value in an open airing of divergent opinions."

"I suspect, fraulein, that much of our potential disagreement would center on a question of ethics. That question can be argued from different perspectives, but it is most important, I believe, that the ethical question itself be clearly formulated. My writings have not focused on the narrow prism of the individual or even the family. What I am most concerned with is the progress of humankind as a whole. It is that question of the general progress and betterment of the many, rather than the stagnation that comes from the protection of the few, that most interests me."

"So when you advocate for the necessity of war, you are advocating for an improvement in the human condition. I am interested in hearing how you believe this to be in the interests of all," Sarah said.

"Modern science continues to give us new and powerful insights into our condition, fraulein. The biologists have shown us that we are the product of a constant process of change. Look at some of the armor of the medieval knights and see just how small these men were. Through genetic selection and improved living standards, our present soldiers are vastly larger and stronger than the legendary warriors of old. All around us, every form of life is struggling to gain an advantage to survive in a world where there are limited resources. Through time, the effect of chance is lessened, and the advantage goes to the strongest, most adaptive, and most intelligent. In this manner, species evolve to better survive in a world of great uncertainty and danger. Those that are most successful survive and thrive, and those that do not evolve or adapt perish. In that regard, man is no different from any other living animal. In a competitive dangerous world, some will be favored by virtue of their attributes. Some would view this inequality as unfair or wrong, but in reality, it is necessary for any species to evolve and prosper.

"What can be said for animals or plants or individuals can be inferred for societies and countries as well. They are constantly undergoing change as well, with new developments in science and technology reshaping how we collectively relate to one another. Some countries, by virtue of their national character, resources, and governance, are better able to adapt and compete than others. Over time, this will lead inevitably to a competitive advantage that will ultimately allow them to prosper in relation to those people who are less fit. Such a process inevitably results in those that are most advantaged, individually and collectively, dominating. That is the law of biology."

"So what role does warfare have in this process? Can't humankind manage its progress without resorting to old ways with so much senseless destruction? Can't we rise above the rest of the animals?" asked Sarah.

"Ah, if only it were as simple as the tribes of the earth gathering around a table and agreeing upon a leader and the distribution of power and wealth. History teaches us that our own frailties prevent us from obtaining such a utopia. The reality is that there is a limited amount of wealth and power. At any given time, there are some individuals and countries that are at an advantage. Inevitably, they will use this advantage to ensure their favored status. This is how empires are born, as our British cousins can attest. The problem inevitably comes from change."

"Surely not all change is bad or problematic. We have all

been the beneficiaries of new technology and knowledge," replied Sarah.

"Exactly, fraulein, but some have clearly benefited more than others. In so doing, they have gained an advantage, which inevitably brings them into conflict with those who hold power based on the conditions of an earlier era. You know full well how that conflict will play out. Influence and power are not easy to give up. The old order will resist by any means they have available. The only recourse for the newly enfranchised is to counter with all the resources at their disposal. This has been the history of humankind, with those that have trying to resist those that want. When those that want become strong enough by virtue of their accumulated advantages, they prevail. It is not an easy or by any means a certain process. The resources available to those in power provide a formidable advantage. It is axiomatic that the rise of a newly advantaged individual or country will lead to conflict with the existing status quo."

"Why must this process lead to war?" Sarah asked. "There are examples of progress where the old, graciously or by wise planning, gave way to the new."

"Unfortunately, history has far too few examples of such wisdom. What you suggest requires that those presently with power be willing to share or relinquish their position. Such behavior rarely exists in the animal kingdom. For a man to act that way requires wisdom and strength beyond the capacity of all but the rarest individuals. All too often, our dark impulses outweigh the thin veil of civility, and the process is reduced to a struggle no different from two beasts struggling on an African plain."

"Let us accept the inevitability of conflict," replied Sarah. "I am not convinced that it must or will lead to war or violent confrontation."

"It is all a matter of timing and circumstances," replied Bernhardi. "If the ascent of one group is relatively slow, as compared to the decline of another, then the transfer of dominance will be slower and likely be more incremental. If, on the other hand, one group ascends very quickly, they will be far more impatient in claiming their rightful place of dominance. Change is always a difficult process and made more unsettling and difficult if it is forced or comes on rapidly. This inevitably leads to much more resistance from those presently advantaged and increases the risk of violent confrontation significantly."

"What kind of progress is it when men are killed, families displaced, and wide-scale destruction occurs?" Sarah countered. "This is not progress but an apocalypse."

"This brings us back to the question of ethics," replied the general. "Seen from the perspective of the weak and those victimized, this is an unfair and terrifying process. That perspective is characteristic of one who values the individual over the whole. The laws of biology refute this time and time again. When a herd is attacked, it is the weak that are lost. Does the herd stop to protect its least fit, or does it move on and, in so doing, inevitably strengthen the remaining group? When there is a forest fire, the dead and decaying, along with those less fit, are sacrificed, and the forest is much fitter. The laws of biology demand that those most fit survive and dominate. It is in this manner that the whole improves. Progress in biology is a constant struggle, and the fate of those less suited to survive is like that of a decaying tree in a conflagration. Seen from the narrow sensibilities of individual ethics, any loss of life seems cruel or senseless, but from the perspective of biology, it is necessary."

"This ceaseless struggle that you envision seems to me a call to a rule of brute force, where the outcome justifies the means," Sarah countered.

"That may be the case with lesser forms of life, but humankind is a more sublime organism. Advantage is most often gained by intellect, rather than force. Any dominant culture must have strength of will as well as muscle, but such attributes alone don't ensure success. Strength must be coupled with an intellect that produces sound ideas that lead to better governance and scientific and economic progress. Those most dominant will protect their position not by brute force but by the power of their intellect and ideas. Absent that, their superiority will rapidly wane."

"Utopia through conflict," Sarah replied, "a new paradigm for the new century. I have read your new book on the next war. You argue that Germany not only has the right but the necessity to fight wars. What would necessitate such actions?"

"Since unification, Germany has consolidated the resources that were wasted for centuries by rivalries and through divisions into petty states, based on geography and religion. Our common strengths now are more apparent than ever, and with their widespread recognition, the people of the German Reich are further inspired and strengthened. For centuries our poets, musicians, and philosophers have been the leading figures of Europe. Our major universities are the centers of development in the sciences and medicine as well. German engineers and chemists are the best in the world, and the application of their work has led us to become the world's most productive and strongest economy. In aggregate, our people and our country have a dominant place in the modern world.

"That is not enough, however. To be great, countries must grow their various strengths. To flourish, great nations must continually expand and grow, not only in their homeland but into wider geographic areas. Such an expansion provides markets and influence over populations that will facilitate further growth and well-being for the fatherland. Such a process requires the establishment of a dominant position over such areas of influence, often requiring acquisition of whole nations or territories. Already the nations of Europe have laid claim to their share of that territory. It is now our time to do the same. It is naive to think that such an expansion will go unopposed. Conflict will inevitably arise, which is a natural consequence of our growing confidence in our rightful place in the world. As difficult as that conflict may be for some people to accept, it is a normal and necessary process of evolution. Like all forms of natural selection, it will lead to an improved future for humankind, achieved at the expense of those presently less advantaged."

"What if the Germany you extol is unsuited for such a challenge?" Sarah asked. "What will come from your conflict then?"

"If I am wrong, which in this case I doubt, then our people and culture will be swept aside by those who have marshaled the forces to prevail. Such are the laws of biology."

"Well, General Bernhardi, you make a case for a very unsettling future."

"Since our fall from grace in the garden, the lot of humankind has been unsettled, fraulein."

As if on a prearranged signal, their conversation was interrupted by the arrival of a stern-faced maid bringing tea and small cakes. This brought about a notable change in the general, who assumed the manners of a gracious host, and in so doing, without saying anything further, Sarah sensed that their more substantive conversation was at an end. After a short conversation that touched on opera and the stretch of pleasant weather they had been experiencing, Sarah took her leave.

As she walked to catch the train to the central city, Sarah could not help but feel uneasy with all the general had said, despite his gracious manner. Perhaps it was only here in Prussia where one could encounter such a seemingly cultured man espousing such beliefs, rife with potential for destructive violence, in such a cold, scientific way. Such behavior no doubt had some of its origin in the very different concept in Germany and Eastern Europe of the relationship between the state and its citizens.

Here in Germany, she witnessed daily a society in which the collective sense of morality and what was acceptable held immense power to shape behavior. Such a sense compelled elderly women to publically scold children for some breach of etiquette, some disruption of the normal order so prized by the great mass of its citizenry. Here, order and compliant behavior were revered, while spontaneity and individuality were scorned.

How different this was from her Jewish tradition, which encouraged independent thinking and valued the worth of an individual's work. In France as well, since the revolution, it was the spirit of liberty that was to inspire brotherhood and justice based on the worth of the citizen, rather than the rights of the state or a privileged few. As Sarah reached her office, she realized more than ever how important it was for the workers of Germany to resist the notions of men like Bernhardi, who would coldly sacrifice their lives to advance the notion of a greater Germany. Such a stark reality, rather than discouraging Sarah, only served to give her greater energy and resolve to do what was necessary to oppose such a perverted future.

17

MINISTRY OF THE INTERIOR

The following morning Sarah set out for an appointment with Herr Ernst Hahn at his office in the Interior Ministry along the Wilhelmstrasse. Arriving at the reception desk, she was directed to a different area from where they had previously met. From the appearance of the new location, Hahn must have had a promotion, as his allocated space was larger, and he had more evident secretarial help nearby. Without an undue wait, she was shown into his office.

His appearance had changed little since her last visit, despite the change in his apparent status. He still was as plump as ever, with the red nose and thick neck of one who drank a bit too much beer and ate too much sausage. His dull eyes merged with a countenance seen so often in German bureaucrats, reflecting at once indifference and arrogance.

"I am pleased that you came by for this visit, fraulein," Hahn greeted her. "I had told your man Stein that it was important that we update our information on your activities. It is only a matter of routine, of course."

"Well, Herr Hahn, little has changed from our last visit, but I see that the same cannot be said for you. It looks as if you have moved up in your world."

"As a matter of fact, I have. I have been advanced a class and am now dealing exclusively with foreign workers, such as you. I hope that what you say is true, fraulein, about your activities. Unfortunately, on questioning we often find that what might seem innocuous to you is of concern to us."

"I can state that since our last visit, my activities have been the same," Sarah replied. "I am in charge of coordinating the management of the office, along with ensuring compliance with all pertinent regulations from your office and the state and city."

"What interests us, fraulein, is a series of articles that were published in the domestic issues of your paper pertaining not only to workers issues but to the peace movement in Germany. These actions are those of a journalist and not simply a manager."

"I see nothing illegal in my writing about my experiences for my home country, Herr Hahn."

"It is certainly not illegal, fraulein, in France, but it places your activities here in a new context. For the purposes of our work, our interest in journalists is altogether different from that of office management."

"I would be interested in knowing why."

"Of course I cannot tell you our exact reasoning, but suffice it to say that journalists are professional snoops. In the course of their activities, they cultivate many relationships to gain information. It is one thing to have someone like your Herr Stein involved in such activities. He is German, and as such we have clear-cut laws and regulations to govern his behavior. You, on the other hand, are not a German citizen, which makes our relationship with you much more ambiguous."

"I am an attorney, Herr Hahn, and am fully aware of my legal standing and responsibilities as a French alien."

"Sometimes the line between what is legal and illegal, fraulein, is very indistinct and may be subject to interpretation. What you might believe to be right might be viewed by my superiors in a different light. It is my responsibility to ensure that what you believe to be right is also what the German Reich believes to be legal."

"What is it that so concerns you about my articles in *l'Humanité?*" she asked.

"As I stated, it is in part related to your new status, in our eyes, as a journalist. Among many of my peers, a foreign correspondent is a spy until proven otherwise."

"As you know, Herr Hahn, the workers movement has, from its earliest days, opposed war, believing it to be the cruelest means by which the capitalist class exploits the workers. It is even meaner than the worst of labor abuses, in that it not only robs a worker of his dignity and rights but risks his life. In these unsettled times, it is of great interest to our French readers to know who in Germany stands on our side in this matter."

"That may be, but many of the people that you interviewed, such as Frau von Suttner, have no relationship to the Socialist Party or the workers movement."

"In such times as these, Herr Hahn, there are many throughout society who share our resistance to warfare and are worthy of our friendship and support."

"Friendship may be one thing, but if you organize to undermine the will of the German people and their legitimate government, then it becomes a matter of great interest to our office."

"In that case, you might be interested as well in my conversation with General Bernhardi," Sarah replied. "No doubt his views and those of his followers are of interest as well. It is absurd to think that my conversing with him or any other person is a pretext for conspiracy."

"Fraulein, it is not my position to know what your intention might be at any given moment. My job is to gather as much information as possible so that when events occur that might subsequently lead to consequences for the state, we will have the necessary information to respond accordingly. No doubt you and General Bernhardi had a most interesting conversation. I wish I could have been there myself, but for the moment, your relationship with the general is of little interest to us."

"What does interest you and your government, Herr Hahn?"

"Fraulein, we live in increasingly dangerous times. It seems that with each day, some new group or movement emerges that poses a threat to our country and way of life. We have long expected the enmity of France and have taken measures to protect ourselves. Now, we find ourselves surrounded by hostile states, with the Russian Empire pledging mutual support to this same France. Why the czar could rebuff the hand of friendship offered by his relative and instead turn to ally with republican France is of great concern to all Germans. Why should our success not serve as a bridge to a more peaceful relationship among the ruling houses of Europe? Emperor Franz Joseph sees the merit of such cooperation. In a time when the monarchies should be cooperating to advance the future of our peoples, we see only a senseless defection by the Russians, which has brought greater tension between our two countries. Now, each day seems to bring more unsettling news regarding the apparent hostility on the part of the British, whose rulers are more German than English.

"What are we to make of this? What do we, as a people,

get from our fellow Europeans? Instead of admiration and cooperation, we are confronted by jealousy and hostility. For many, it seems better to resist our successes to maintain their former prominence than to cooperate with us and advance the lot of us all. In such a perverse world, it is my lot and that of my colleagues to be vigilant to the threat posed by those who resent our achievements to better protect our homeland and way of life."

"At what point does your paranoia move beyond the stage of simply acquiring information?" Sarah asked. "Your actions generate a certain momentum that at some time may well compel someone to act upon all the supposed facts and half truths that you have amassed in your dossiers. When that is done, you will have crossed into more dangerous territory, in which individual rights will be at the discretion of policemen and members of the interior ministry."

"I am nothing more than a bureaucrat of the state," Hahn replied. "It is not my responsibility to decide what to do with the information but simply to acquire and organize it. What becomes of it then is at the discretion of others more senior than I."

"That is a convenient rationalization," Sarah replied. "I hope someday that you don't have to use it to ease your conscience."

"That would only be necessary, fraulein, if I was convinced that I had done something wrong. I can assure you that I sleep as soundly as a baby. I hope that I have made my position clear today. My interest in matters and people is in direct proportion to the perceived risk that they pose to the security of the Reich. If your association with such groups is as inconsequential as you say, then in the future you and I will have less and less cause for conversation. For both of our sakes, I hope that will be the case."

"That is something on which we can both agree, Herr Hahn."

With the meeting at an end, Sarah excused herself, leaving Hahn and the Interior Ministry as quickly as possible. It was not until much later, however, that she was able to get beyond the implications of the meeting and think of other matters.

18

MESSIMY

Adolphe Messimy was not happy. This was not an unusual state of mind since his appointment as war minister. At that time he had become the fourth war minister in four months, but his knowledge of the workings of the army and his zeal for reform made him far different from his predecessors. Bull-necked, pugnacious, and loud, his mercurial personality and enthusiasm contrasted with the staid manners of high-ranking officers and often led to conflicts over long-standing traditions and the guarded prerogatives of the top command.

The history of the French army since the French Revolution and its relationship to the various ruling governments was one of tumultuous change and often bitter division. Forced to defend the borders of the new republic against the collective ire of the entirety of Europe, the army had amassed virtually all the country's able-bodied men and, under the rising star of Napoleon, had shattered the smaller professional armies of its combined enemies. This was truly a national army, with its soldiers drawn from all regions and all social and economic classes. For many, the army gave tangible proof of the new equality and ideals of France, and in all its collective might, it became the principle guardian of that new order.

Many of its leaders however, were drawn from families used to the traditions and practices of the past. These men believed the army was the principle institution that France could rely on for protection. They were conservative and Catholic by birth and background, making them natural enemies to the various progressive politicians that dominated the government in the closing decades of the nineteenth century.

This new order that had emerged in the Third Republic in the aftermath of the Prussian War often distrusted the military, seeing it as a powerful remnant of a discredited age. The future for them would be shaped by enlightenment and science, which would guide the rule of future governments for the betterment of all. The antipathy of these groups for one another, the conservative elements of the old order and the proponents of the new, climaxed with the arrest of Alfred Dreyfus, a Jewish officer of liberal political leanings, for purportedly supplying critical French military intelligence to German operatives.

Passions on both sides were quickly inflamed in the aftermath. For many in the army, Dreyfus represented all the elements of change that had brought decadence and, with it, defeat at the hands of the Prussians. Their opposites saw Dreyfus as an outsider from the conservative ruling clique of the army and suspected from the very beginning something sinister about his arrest and the subsequent handling of his prosecution. Their suspicions were subsequently proven correct, as evidence accumulated to suggest not only the accused's innocence but also an elaborate deception on the part of the army to cover up the errors made by his unfounded arrest. For many, the willingness of the army to perpetrate an injustice against an innocent man in order to protect their own reputation confirmed their worst suspicions about the character of the army leadership and the integrity of the institution itself.

This entire affair had been a revelation to Messimy, who at the time was a captain in the army. As advocates for Dreyfus accumulated damning evidence about the means of his conviction, a petition began to circulate among the officer corps, urging that the case not be reopened, fearing the damage new revelations would have on the future effectiveness of the army. Refusing to be pressured into signing such a petition, Messimy resigned his commission, resolving on a career in politics, which would allow him to reform the army to more closely represent the nation, while at the same time improving its capabilities. Now, some eleven years later, by much effort he had finally reached a position where he could exert his influence.

He soon realized, however, that the power of his position was no guarantee that he, like so many of his predecessors, would be successful in reforming the army, and now after three months, the enormity of the job was becoming more evident. Much of the leadership in the War Office and the army itself was composed of the most senior generals. This had provided continuity in the face of revolving war ministers but had also brought much inertia and inflexibility, producing a widening gap between their practices and those of the rising leaders of the younger generation. Such a condition was intolerable to someone with the impatience of Messimy.

Nowhere was his frustration greater than it was with General Michel, who was the ranking general on the War Council, a position that would grant him commanding status of the entire army in the event of war. In many ways, General Michel was the opposite of what Messimy had expected or wanted as commander of the army. Michel brought years of experience in policy making to the War Council, as well as knowledge of the politics and intrigue among the general staff in Paris. He was no doubt intelligent, but Messimy had the feeling that his intelligence often served him poorly. To him, it seemed that Michel was hesitant and indecisive, unwilling to proceed until he could be certain of the circumstances.

As concerns with Germany increased, so did Messimy's worry about the readiness of the French army. After much prodding and delay, he had gotten from Michel his recommendations of necessary measures to counter rising German military power. The document was lengthy, and the more that Messimy read, the more dissatisfied he became. He saw in the document's many pages a codification of the thinking that had dominated French military planning since the Prussian War. Such thinking only served to stir Messimy's antipathy to that older generation that he held responsible for the excesses of the Dreyfus affair as well as for the failure of the army in defending the country against the previous Prussian invasion. Instead, he had come to embrace the more vibrant and aggressive thinking that was gaining influence, even before he had resigned his commission.

The logic of General Michel's plan seemed well outlined. He could not necessarily quarrel with its conclusions about a well-planned German offensive against France in the first weeks of any future war, but to Messimy, his tactical response was unacceptable. In place of aggression, his emphasis was on committing the army to a large-scale defensive strategy. Such a position virtually conceded the initiative to the invaders and, in so doing, gave them the crucial psychological advantage that Messimy and many others now believed so essential to the outcome of any great battle. Messimy was unwilling to concede such an advantage without a struggle.

———

The first stage of that struggle had occurred in a subsequent meeting with General Michel. That meeting had not gone well—the differences the two men had in philosophy and the logistical plans, as outlined by Michel, was only heightened by the differences in their personalities. Michel's staid, aristocratic bearing only served to further alienate Messimy as the meeting progressed. Unable to reach an agreement on details of a plan of defense to counter a rising German threat and other related matters, such as increasing the terms of enlistment to three years, the matter was referred to the entire War Council for final resolution.

The War Council was the second step in Messimy's resistance to Michel's plans. As war minister, he did not have the authority alone to override Michel but was dependent on the consensus of the entire body of the War Council to finalize the matter.

Including General Michel, the council was composed of some of the foremost generals of the army. One notable omission from its ranks was General Foch, who was felt to be the leading proponent of the offensive mind-set that had so influenced Messimy's thinking. He was distrusted by some of his seniors not only for his ideas but also for his outspoken criticism of those who disagreed with him. He was further compromised by a brother who was a priest, thereby alienating him to a large and powerful faction of anticlerical politicians. General Gallieni was the most senior member, having served with distinction throughout the colonies. He was responsible for much of the organization and tactical planning of the colonial troops and had brought stability and progress in the areas where he had commanded in Africa—most notably in Madagascar. General Pau was next in seniority. He had served heroically in the Prussian War, where he had lost an arm in combat. General Dubail, although younger, dressed in the style of the Second Empire. His dress coupled with his manner gave him an appearance of an officer from a different time, more elegant and refined than was common in the contemporary officer corps. The youngest was General Joffre. He had served under General Gallieni in Africa before his own command, primarily in the colonial arena.

Messimy did not know for certain which position each of these men might take with respect to General Michel's proposal. He suspected that at least two were much more in line with his thinking than that of the general. He was determined, nevertheless, to make an active case for his view on the matter.

As was customary, General Michel introduced the topic and proceeded with a rather formal presentation of his plan. It contained all the elements that he had presented to Messimy but with much more detail as to troop strength and topography.

"Gentlemen, the current assessment of our intelligence bureau gives very strong evidence that in the event of war, Germany is likely to address the threat posed by our alliance with Russia by launching a rapid and overwhelming offensive to quickly neutralize one of their frontiers. We have long suspected that that offensive will be directed toward the west, but information that we have recently acquired from several sources in their government and army has provided compelling information about their intentions. Our intelligence confirms the German intent of a massive invasion to their west. What is now believed is that this offensive will be launched not through France but through Belgium, north of the Ardennes. I have reviewed this information and am convinced that our intelligence personnel are right in this conclusion.

"Conventional wisdom suggests that such an attack would prove fatal to the Germans by significantly diluting their troop strength along the totality of their lines, thereby making them vulnerable to a French offensive against their interior. Our most recent and most surprising intelligence, however, suggests that the Germans have been employing reserve units in training exercises. If that is the case, it is the solution to the manpower shortage that would be needed for a more northern attack through Belgium. If they are successful in incorporating their reserves into regular units, they can launch a massive attack at the northern extreme of their lines, while providing adequate reserves along their lines to the south.

"One thing that we have learned, time and time again, that the German general staff is extremely thorough and persistent. Our intelligence has reported coordinated maneuvers between regular and reserve units for more than a year. More ominously, these sightings have increased significantly this year. This would suggest that their experience to date has not shaken their confidence in the use of these reserves. If they succeed in integrating them with only a minor drop-off in effectiveness, the implications for our own troops are profound.

"Given the necessity for a rapid and decisive offensive, the most compelling option for the German command would be an attack through Belgium, leading into France where we are most vulnerable. Such an attack would be feasible with much larger numbers, if the reserves can be effectively merged into the regular army. As difficult as it is for all of us to accept, I must conclude, given their persistence, that they are concentrating their efforts upon improving the capabilities of their reserves to the point that they will provide an effective presence in the great offensive they are planning.

"To address this situation, I propose several options. The first is to increase the enlistment period for the army from two years to three, thereby effectively increasing our numbers to meet the threat of a potentially larger German army. Mr. Messimy suggests that this may be a difficult proposition at present, from a political perspective. In order to address this political reality, I therefore believe it essential that we use our existing manpower in the most effective way possible to counteract this German offensive. I am convinced that modern weaponry gives well-positioned defenses a great advantage over attacking forces. The experiences of the American Civil War and the Russian war with Japan bear that out. Large-scale offensives against well-prepared defensive positions are extremely costly in terms of casualties and require marked superiority in manpower and weaponry to be successful. If the enemy is willing to gamble all on a massive first strike, it is my judgment that our best chance of success is to concentrate in newly fortified positions in northern France to stop that assault before it can penetrate across that flat and strategic countryside. Thereafter, the advantage will quickly pass to us and our allies to exploit more fully."

As General Michel paused in his presentation, General Pau asked a question. "What information was used to conclude that the German invasion route would be through Flanders? I am deeply suspicious that many key elements that would be necessary for such an extension of their lines are not in place."

Michel replied, "We have been alerted of such a plan dating back to information obtained at some cost from a German operative in 1904. As you may remember, our predecessor, General Pendezac, evaluated this information thoroughly and concluded that it was very plausible, given the German tendency for large enveloping offensive operations. Since that time I have tried to find evidence that would corroborate that strategy further. As my report delineates, the intelligence bureau has been noting increasing numbers of reserve units participating in training exercises throughout the country. Such numbers suggest to me that these troops will be used to extend the line of attack to the north at great risk to our present strategy and deployment."

"If you are right," said Dubail, "it is a significant gamble by their general staff. They are no doubt thorough in what they do, but the Prussian army was never one to put much stock in any but the most disciplined of troops. I have a hard time believing that the whole mind-set of their unified forces would have changed so much as to risk such a massive undertaking so greatly dependent on reserves."

"It seems likely that it could be nothing more than a grand ruse to divert our thinking into deploying our troops to oppose a phantom strike," replied Joffre. "The risk of this plan is enormous from the perspective of the Germans. As General Dubail implies, it depends on large numbers of inferiorly trained troops for its success. More important, it would compel Britain to enter the war. At present, Great Britain is our elusive ally. She is motivated by one concern only: the security of her empire. There is one absolute that will motivate them to actively commit troops to a continental war: the invasion of Belgium. The guarantee of neutrality, from their standpoint, is less a multipower document than it is a guarantee of the safety of the English Channel and their own southeastern borders. A German invasion through Flanders assures their active alliance with us and Russia."

Gallieni, who had sat impassively through the discussion,

spoke at last. "The lengthy discussions we have had with the Russians and even the British have underscored the advantage of attacking a German enemy simultaneously. To dwell in a defensive position and allow the enemy to choose his time and place of engagement is to sacrifice the key advantage of our alliance with Russia. Only by a coordinated attack, bringing the full might of both armies to bear on both German frontiers, can the enemy be most imperiled. To sit by passively, while our ally launches an offensive, weakens our combined strength and makes it easier for them to divide and conquer. If we are stretched across this extended northern frontier, we will not have sufficient strength to succeed in breaking the German lines. Berlin lies for us not on the Flanders frontier but through Mainz. With such tactics as proposed by General Michel, we confine ourselves to the defensive when our best hopes lie in coordinated attacks with the Russians. For that reason and many of the others suggested here today, I cannot support the wholesale weakening of a vital offensive that General Michel's plan will produce."

Messimy, who had listened to the debate, now felt the time right to speak. "Gentlemen, we have had a thorough presentation by General Michel of his plan, which all of us have had the time to review before today. The questions that have been raised today are similar to my own. I am in agreement with General Gallieni. I believe that our best option is in boldness and attack. This plan, by its emphasis on the defensive, forces us away from our best means for success. For that reason, I am prepared to vote against its adoption. I would move, therefore, unless there is further discussion, that we proceed to vote on the adoption of this plan."

General Dubail said, "Much of the concerns about a Flanders invasion have been raised in the past and should not be dismissed without some reasonable contingency to address this possibility. I would suggest that we consider in our planning this option. It seems more vital than ever that we get some commitment from the British for troop support, as their interests would be best protected by their presence along this frontier."

"No doubt you are right, General Dubail," replied Messimy, "but such planning is the subject for another time. Now, we are considering adopting the proposal before us."

"I would second your original motion," said Joffre.

"Before this vote, I would like to add a final note of caution," General Michel said. "If the war minister is right in his opinion, then all will be well. If our offensive fails, however, consider the risks. By concentrating our troops elsewhere, we will expose our left flank to the full force of the invading enemy, thereby risking large losses of vital French territory, including Paris. Of the two proposals, I believe the risks are far greater in initiating an attack without first checking the main intent of the enemy. Having first secured French territory, we can then concentrate our counterattack."

With that, there was no further discussion. The motion was considered, and the plan of General Michel rejected. From that moment, France would be committed to a large-scale offensive as a first response, should war break out with Germany. For Messimy, all his years of struggle to gain the power to shape the future of the French army now seemed realized. What remained, however, was vindication of this gamble, the risks of which General Michel had clearly foreseen.

19

THOMAS RETURNS

As Robert stood on the queue, he could hardly contain his excitement. Since he had received Thomas's letter several weeks ago, announcing his return visit to Paris, he had been looking forward to his arrival. This afternoon he had difficulty in concentrating during a particularly long and unproductive staff meeting. Now, amid the sounds of arriving trains and surrounded by the frantic pace of passengers hurrying to make their connections, his anticipation had only increased.

He had not seen Thomas since the Christmas holidays two years ago. Even prior to that time, much had changed in both of their lives. As Robert had taken up the challenge of his military career, Thomas had chosen a commitment to the priesthood. His ordination in many ways was a culmination of his previous studies and beliefs, and rather than leading to a significant change in his lifestyle, it had served to enrich it. Even prior to his ordination, his interest in philosophy had been broadened by turning his focus to questions of theology. After completing the rigorous demands of the faculty of the venerable

Sorbonne, he was awarded his doctoral degree, which in other times would have qualified him as a master and would have ensured a respected position in the university.

In modern France, the relationship between the clerical scholar and the University of Paris, as well as the entire country, had been radically changed, however. Political turmoil had served to increasingly alienate the secular and progressive political class from the institutions of the old order. Chief among their targets were the prerogatives and power of the Catholic Church. At the height of the revolution, much property had been seized, monastic orders scattered, and priceless artifacts and buildings defaced. In the ensuing years, clerical authority and influence would rise or fall with the ruling powers. Now, in the aftermath of the Dreyfus affair those elements shaping political policy had once again turned their ire toward the church and its authority in society.

The major focus of their efforts was directed toward the central role that the church had held for centuries as the arbiter of public education. In a series of sweeping reforms, support—both fiscally and legally—for the oversight and participation by the clerical bodies in the nation's education was removed. At first these reforms were designed primarily for secondary education, but soon after they were extended to the universities. Even Paris, the very greatness of which was founded on the genius of men such as Peter Abelard and Thomas Aquinas, was not spared. Clerical faculty soon experienced both tacit and overt discrimination within the administration of the university. Authority and influence were stripped from them, placing their positions at the whims of the ever-changing educational ministers. Such hostility would inevitably have its consequences.

Of these, the most significant was the flight of some

of the university's most gifted thinkers. Confronted by an increasingly hostile work environment, the most able among the clerical faculty found that they were able to relocate to more accommodating locations outside of the country. One of the first to make such a move was Thomas's uncle, who quickly relocated to a much more hospitable location at Strasbourg. He was quickly followed by many others until what was left, in many cases, was the most junior or least accomplished of their peers.

His uncle had been frank with Thomas as he considered his commitment to the priesthood. He had told him that such actions would no doubt stigmatize his academic career in France. Perhaps inspired by the boldness of Robert's actions—or more likely by the depths of his own commitment—Thomas was undaunted by such risks. In the end, once he had decided to pursue the challenges of the priesthood, Thomas's faith in the justness of his actions gave him the resolve to press on and to endure what challenges that might follow.

Even before his final dissertation and its defense, the quality of his writing had made him a desirable applicant for many scholarly positions. Thanks to the experience of his uncle, whose work had been widely recognized in Strasbourg, Thomas was viewed with great interest by many there. Perhaps as a reward for his competence and faith, an invitation subsequently came to join the learned community of scholars at the long-renowned Alsatian university. Now, after more than a year there, he had his first opportunity to return to Paris.

At long last, Robert saw his cousin striding toward him along the queue. As Thomas recognized Robert, he broke out in a broad smile and quickened his pace. To Robert, his appearance seemed little changed from their last visit, and his casual wear, distinguished only by his cleric's collar, was in keeping with his old habits.

"You look well, my dear cousin," Thomas said as he grasped Robert's hand, "although I must say that uniform gives you a rather serious appearance. Here I am, bursting with the enthusiasm of a schoolboy on holiday, ill-kempt and proud of it, only to be humbled by my cousin's proper bearing and dress."

"You of all people should know how little appearances matter in things of worth," Robert replied. "I didn't have the time to change into something more suited to this occasion, so rather than miss your arrival. I came more properly dressed, as you say."

"I hope you are hungry because I am starved," Thomas said. "I knew what time I would be arriving, so I only had a small snack on the train."

"I know an excellent brasserie close by that ought to make you feel back at home in Alsace."

Within a matter of a few blocks, they arrived at Brasserie Vosges, a large, sprawling establishment with the usual festive air of restaurants that combine the elements of a German beer hall with French sensibilities and taste. At Robert's request, they were placed at a more distant and quiet site and soon had large steins of beer before them.

"How strange it is to be back in Paris with so much of Strasbourg around me. I have to admit I have acquired a taste for good beer while I have been gone," Thomas said happily as he took a large quaff from his tall stein. "Now tell me what wonderful things you have been doing since we last spoke."

"Well, my life has certainly been more structured than my time in the colonies. Aside from a crash course in military strategy and leadership, I have been involved in routine engineering work, designing several critical additions to our rail network.

This has required a fair amount of planning, since some of the lines are made up of older construction, but when done right, the end results can be excellent. We have built bridges spanning gorges and ravines that would put the Romans to shame. The availability of dynamite and other explosives has allowed us to tunnel into bedrock and open up areas previously impassable. Even if I do say so, it is quite dramatic, and it is gratifying to see the design of these structures come to completion."

"You are very fortunate to have such tangible proof of the worth of your work," Thomas said.

"I have never thought of it in that way, but it is very true. Seeing a train travel toward the horizon to a region that was previously poorly accessible, over a bridge I was responsible for building, gives me a thrill that I never tire of. Such enjoyment might amuse a philosopher like you, concerned with weighty and sublime questions, but it is very real to me."

"I am not one to quibble with what gives you pleasure, but I am happy to know that your work seems so rewarding," Thomas said.

"You look quite well yourself, Thomas. What have you been doing, nestled among the Germans, that appears to have served you so well?"

"I have come to appreciate how location can improve a person's attitude. In my case, a few hundred kilometers has made a great difference in my outlook. In Paris, the political intolerance of the ruling government for the church and the cultural struggles precipitated by their hostility has greatly poisoned the atmosphere for the productive participation of young priests in their secular society. In Strasbourg, however, since their forced separation from France, there has been a great nostalgia for all things that remind them of the old order. Consequently, the church is welcomed in the school system by the Alsatians, as well as in many other aspects of society. Much attention is paid to the bishop and leading members of the church with regard to their views on a wide range of subjects beyond the usual boundaries of theology.

"No doubt some of this is political, since such adherence to the old ways by the native Alsatians is a very real form of resistance to their German overlords. Nevertheless, it is a pleasant contrast from Paris, and this sense of relevancy certainly makes the days there more pleasant. You no doubt will be pleased and probably a bit surprised to learn that I have taken up with a group of physicists and mathematicians. Part of this is professional, in order to gain a better understanding of the new and, I must say, revolutionary ideas in the natural sciences, but part of it comes simply from the pleasure of their company.

"My colleagues were at first confused why any priest would be interested in the world as perceived by their methods. Since the renaissance of science, many believe there is a distinct separation from what Aristotle would call physics and metaphysics. Certainly since the time of Newton, men have given great importance to the information we can obtain with our senses and instruments and what we can deduce with our intellect as to the realities of our universe. With each great discovery, many make these scientists into prophets, spreading insight about a world order built on a foundation of science and rationality.

"This type of thinking has the great risk of marginalizing what Aquinas called the greatest of the sciences—theology. Such a study, devoid of hard empiricism, is difficult for many skeptics to accept; they believe that truth can only come from human reason and inquiry. For them, theology is a foolish remnant of medieval times and religious faith, something to which only the ignorant or naive still cling. Such beliefs are shaped by misperceptions and prejudice. By excluding religious inquiry into the nature of our universe, there is a real risk of losing perspective, not only of the very omnipotence of God in creating such wondrous complexity but also in gaining a better understanding of its workings.

"I enjoy thinking about modern science because it often reveals, in its marvelous findings, the true genius of God. Its discoveries also often reveal the fallibility of human reason. Now, the world and universe, which my physicist friends felt they knew so well only twenty years ago, is a huge blob of uncertainty. The physicist Michelson, smug in his certainty of the infallibility of the knowledge of his time, said in the closing days of the last century that the most fundamental laws and facts of physics have all been discovered. Those laws that applied to Michelson and all of humanity were the same laws that held for the entire universe, regardless of location or any other conditions, such as speed or mass."

"Galilean invariance," added Robert.

"Invariance, indeed," replied Thomas. "It was the last century's way of placing man once more at the center of the universe. An arrogant lot, we humans. Like most arrogance, it is often based on false perceptions. If the laws exist, as Michelson believed, then as we swing on the earth around the sun in an elliptical orbit, our speed should change. As we proceed toward the sun, light should have a different speed than when our orbital path carries us away from this light source. One theoretically could measure the speed of earth in the ether of the cosmos by comparing the variations in the speed of light.

"Unfortunately for Michelson, the more he and his associates measured, the more perplexed they became. Through many variables there remained one constant—the speed of light. Wisdom and truth, however, come not from what we think is true or what we want to be true but from God, who has crafted all in his omnipotent plan. True insight, which is wisdom, sometimes comes in odd places through God's grace to even the humble or unknown."

"I think I know where this is going," Robert said. "An unknown patent officer in Switzerland, perhaps?"

"Don't ruin my sermon, Robert. I am only getting started. Oh, what's the use? You know the ending better than I do."

"Master Inspector Third Class Einstein," continued Robert, "was struck by the constant nature of the speed of light in these measurements. He concluded that it was not the time or distance a mass moved that was constant but the speed of light, which remained fixed while all other entities changed. Thus, time and space, as we know them, are not separate entities but wrap around each other in relationship to the speed of light. The mass of a ball or any other object is not distinct from its potential energy but is directly related by this same constant of light speed."

"It is truly remarkable and sublime," added Thomas. "You are as well versed as anyone, Robert, in the application of the old rules of mathematics and physics. Your passion for the products of their application gives meaning to your work, and through such efforts, we, as a people, have enjoyed historic progress. Yet this new physics shows how parochial our knowledge really is, constrained by the norms of our everyday experience. This is the fallacy of relying on the material of our senses and the reality that they define. By excluding the potential of reality beyond what we can readily sense, we are limiting ourselves from a greater understanding of the truth.

"I have been challenged countless times to explain the discrepancy in our modern understanding of science and the many biblical descriptions, such as the creation of the universe in six days, as described in Genesis. How can divine revelation of the primacy of God be so incompatible with our science? As Herr Albert Einstein has shown, we should not be too impressed or influenced by our flawed understandings and the conclusions that such imperfect knowledge may bring. We, in our nonrelativistic world, find it impossible to believe that such a creation could be achieved in merely six days. Where does it say that the Almighty moves with human speed? If he moved with the speed of light, then our conventional day would be infinitely slower than what we might measure at the clock tower in Zurich."

"I understand what you are saying and have often been thrilled by sublime complexity that you describe," added Robert. "In mathematics one must dwell on the infinite and minute, concepts far removed from our real-world experiences. I am often amazed at the relationships between numbers across such a breadth. When I stumbled upon the intersection of the differential and integral in the fundamental theorem of calculus, there was a real sense of wonderment. With a formula that relates two variables, we can know where we are at present, where we will be in the future, and the sum of our experiences in the past. Such sublime power from something as abstract as the calculus can only be the product of God. It is as if the mathematics is his chosen *lingua franca*, allowing us to explain the world more powerfully than our own words."

"It is unfortunate that we are all too often blinded by habit and experience," Thomas replied. "Only in going beyond the common, as Einstein did, can we more fully understand the truth. The price of conformity is equilibrium with the norms and ideas that define the present. Progress comes from those who are uncomfortable with what is accepted and are willing to challenge those norms."

"That talk would have branded you as a heretic in the church in the past, Thomas. What you say is no doubt correct, but such people will likely have to suffer much hostility. Change is a frightening thing that brings not only anxiety but resistance. The greater the change, the greater is the uncertainty and the more it will be resisted."

"There is also the unsettling possibility that the future might not belong to reason and restraint. You and I, Robert, were raised to hold reason in high regard, and men's passions were tempered by an expectation that their actions should conform to norms of civilized societies. Instead, we must face the awful possibility where the impulsive and irrational shape the behavior of humankind, for better or worse. In Strasbourg, there is much more awareness of German and Central European thought than in Paris. Much of the talk centers on the theories of another Semite, Dr. Freud of Vienna. Freud has spent much of his life in the study of the anxieties and neurosis that accompany modern society. It seems that Dr. Freud has a new perception of our personalities and what might shape our behavior and our mental health. He argues that we are not simply the product of rational thinking based on our experience and societal norms. Instead, the human condition is defined by the struggle between the external standards of accepted behavior, standards often based on rational beliefs, and accepted morals and the desires in the depths of our unconscious, irrational minds. For him, humankind does not conform to the ideals of Kant, but instead we are torn by carnal desires and sexual tension, arising from our earliest days of existence."

"I have tried to understand some of his writing," replied Robert, "and can only conclude that the world where he is living in Vienna is far different and much stranger than Paris, with all its bawdy pleasures. I have never been to Vienna, but from his writings I've lost what desire I might have had to go there. There is little doubt that for a person of conscience, breaking the law or committing a grave sin might well be the cause of much mental distress. To blame it on suppressed sexual desires and failed gratifications seems a bit extreme."

"Some of his writings may be simply a reflection of his own neurosis and insecurity," added Thomas, "but they still are widely discussed and have gained a substantial following in many parts of Europe. The portrait that he paints of modern man, trapped by the conflict between his conscious expectations and the unmet demands of his unconscious self, is unsettling and offers a vision of our collective future that is far from comforting. If his influence grows, I cannot help but believe that this image of humankind, driven by primitive desires and sordid relationships, will adversely affect our general well-being."

"It seems to me, Thomas, that his beliefs have already had a negative effect on you. I thought you looked quite upbeat earlier, but being around the influence of these Central Europeans seems to have compromised your usual optimism. Take up your sword, and crusade against what you dislike and distrust about this concept of humankind. Your actions will be a good tonic to combat the creeping pessimism that naturally comes from such ideas."

"You can dismiss my sobriety as travel fatigue, Robert, but our contemporary world, it seems to me, is filled with much less certainty and optimism than I had known when I lived in Paris. There seems to be a sense among people of diverse views that something is lacking in our old beliefs, and they are not quite sure what better to replace them with. This contributes to uncertainty that can be manifest in many ways. What will come from all of this is unclear, but we can no longer assume that people will behave as in the recent past.

"Now, on a more optimistic note, it seems that Strasbourg is much more cosmopolitan than I remembered. Much of this, no doubt, has to do with the university. It really is quite excellent and deserves its reputation, which has been burnished, no doubt, by such students as Goethe, Metternich, and even Bonaparte. Its openness and tolerance of me, as a cleric and theologian, as I have said, is a welcome relief from Paris. My spiritual and scholarly lives both have flourished there, for which I am truly grateful. I am even acquiring a taste for the innumerable variations of sausage and pork that seem to be at the center of all of their meals, along with the beer to accompany it.

"There is a dark side there, however, that is based on the hostility of the native Alsatians to the German authorities and the growing number of Germans migrating into the area. There is always some tension between the two camps, but the bishop seems optimistic that even that is easing in recent years."

"Well, that is an optimistic note to end on. We have too much to catch up with and to celebrate to become caught up in Central European malaise. I feel that a good dessert is more appropriate for our present situation and a remedy certain to brighten your spirits."

"Well, I can certainly agree with that," replied Thomas. Then, raising his glass, he toasted. "To our futures—may they be as we hope and deserve."

The pair then settled back to study the potential of the dessert menu before them.

20

NEW CHALLENGES

As Robert returned to his office after a first meeting with General Joseph Gallieni, he could not help but reflect on how much the pace and quality of his life had changed since returning to Paris. Just two days ago he had received a request to meet with the general, who was viewed by many as being the most accomplished and competent general in the French army. Such a request to a junior engineering officer had been both intriguing and unsettling. Now, after nearly an hour-long interview with the general, Robert felt more at ease.

Robert's impression of General Gallieni before their meeting had been shaped by his experience in Madagascar, where the influence of Gallieni's command there several years before had profoundly strengthened the French presence in the region. Upon meeting the general that afternoon, Robert first was struck by the man's age and apparent frailty. He was thin and maintained a perfect military posture and bearing, despite showing evidence of pain when he moved too quickly. Soon, however, Robert appreciated the depth of Gallieni's intellect in the details of their conversation, which was amplified by the intensity of his eyes.

He had called Robert in to discuss a project that related to his position as commander of the French Fifth Army, responsible for defending the vast plains of northeastern France from German invasion. Concerns had continued to come to him from various citizens and political figures, indications and rumors of a German preference for this region as the primary target for a future invasion. Gallieni knew full well the arguments for and against such an invasion, but as the man responsible for defense of the region, he did not have the luxury of dismissing them without considering the breadth of contingencies available to him to counteract such a move.

Even a cursory survey of the area revealed how woefully unprepared the region was in comparison to those areas abutting the German border. A thorough survey of the existing defenses and a list prioritizing the necessary upgrades and new construction was needed as soon as possible. After a search of possible qualified officers, Gallieni had called Robert in to see if he would be suitable to lead such a project. To Robert's surprise and gratification, he was offered the assignment that very afternoon.

What little time he had to reflect on his triumph was cut short by the need to finalize his work for the afternoon so that he could meet with Thomas and Marie Bonneau for an early dinner. Even in their brief acquaintance, Marie was proving to be as much a focus for contemplation as many of Robert's engineering projects.

From their first meeting, much had attracted Robert to her. Her beauty, poise, and social standing were compelling and seemed like an all-too-natural fit for someone in his position. In the days that followed, as he and Marie saw more of each other, their relationship seemed to take on new meaning for their many family members and friends, giving Robert an uncomfortable sense of their increasing interest and expectations. He had expected such a relationship to come forward at some time, as arrangements of this kind had long supported the future lineage of the old families of France. It was the implications of such a relationship as much as Marie that had given Robert pause for thought in recent days.

Yet Robert was not yet willing to yield to those forces drawing the couple together until he had a much better understanding of the young woman in question. It was true that of all the women his wide circle of family and friends had introduced to him, Marie was by far the most attractive to him. Aside from her obvious beauty and stylish manners, perhaps it was her aptitude in music, which was so different from his own background, that most appealed to him, but for whatever reason, he found himself increasingly comfortable in her presence.

Still, there was much of the unknown about Marie that made Robert uneasy. Perhaps that unknown and its allure was a prerogative of femininity. For someone who valued knowing the full scope of a problem, however, Robert's very makeup made it difficult to accept a future with anyone without more knowledge of what such a relationship would entail.

For all of Marie's beauty, charm, and cultivated manners, she seemed to have a well-constructed façade at times, designed to hide her true feelings and personality. No doubt she had many causes for anxiety that could contribute to this, given their differences in age and worldly experience. Still, Robert was hesitant to march boldly forward without a better understanding of Marie's true personality. Fortunately, in recent days Marie had become more relaxed and open, giving Robert further insight into her true character.

Their meetings had gradually evolved from formal oversight to periods of more relaxed and less supervised liaisons. It was there that Robert appreciated the vast difference in their worldly experiences. It was not what Marie had done as much as the constraining effects of her age and her social position on her experiences. She would listen intently as Robert described his days in Africa, often questioning him more about his emotions and reactions than the details of the events. Robert often felt as if he was of a different generation than Marie, yet her evident curiosity and manner only increased his attraction to her.

Robert welcomed Thomas's return to Paris for the summer because he saw in his cousin someone who could provide valuable insight into his relationship with Marie. To further facilitate Thomas's help, Robert set out to make Thomas and Marie comfortable with each other.

At their first meeting, Thomas, in his usual disarming way, quickly put Marie at ease. Thomas seemed attracted to Marie as well, perhaps captivated by her youthful naïveté and her natural beauty. It was her musical skill, however, that seemed to fascinate him most. After first hearing her play a series of pieces by Chopin, he seemed to view her in a different light. Soon, he had taken up her cause with his many friends, becoming an unofficial agent and impresario dedicated to facilitating the progress of his new and talented friend. Unfortunately for Robert, any hope of an objective appraisal of his relationship with Marie was soon lost in his cousin's infatuation.

———

After finishing his work, Robert set out for the Bièvre, looking forward to meeting both Thomas and Marie for dinner. With Thomas's return to Paris, the two cousins began to frequent their old haunt whenever circumstances allowed. Now, with a priest acting as a very suitable chaperone, Marie came to dine with them often as well. As Robert entered the restaurant, he saw that both of them had already arrived and were engaged in animated conversation.

"Robert!" Marie exclaimed as she saw him enter. "You won't believe what this cousin of yours has been up to."

"I have long given up trying to guess what he might be doing."

"He has succeeded in getting me an invitation to play a concert after the Wednesday evening mass at Saint Sulpice next month."

"That is quite an accomplishment," Robert replied with enthusiasm, knowing quite well the quality of musicians who had performed at the great church, which had long served the parish around the Fauburg Saint Germaine. Its giant organ had nurtured the works of Cesar Frank and led to a high quality of music being performed in many other disciplines. He knew that a performance in such a venue would be a real accomplishment for someone as young and inexperienced as Marie.

"We were just going over a possible program when you arrived. Fortunately, Thomas has good ideas that emphasize pieces that I know well and am comfortable with."

"Thomas, does your uncle's old friend the bishop still hold sway at Saint Sulpice?" asked Robert.

"Well, as a matter of fact, he does," Thomas replied with a twinkle in his eye. "He is well and has asked of you. He is such a lover of music that it took little more than my enthusiastic recommendation to help him decide to use Marie's considerable talents to fill an opening made by a Scottish choir, who had unexpected difficulty with arriving in Paris as expected. I was able to outline a potential program that impressed him and that is well within the capabilities of our young friend here."

"Thomas, you are simply an angel," Marie said. "How can I ever thank you for all you have done."

"Simply to play as well as I know that you can," he answered.

After several minutes of excited conversation between the artist and her newfound impresario, the waiter arrived with a carafe of wine.

The subsequent pause allowed Robert to steer the conversation away from Marie's engagement at Saint Sulpice. "I had a rather interesting meeting with General Gallieni today," he began.

Thomas looked rather intrigued. "I understand that he may be in line as chief of the general staff."

Robert smiled. "Your contacts are usually better than my own, so this might well be the case, but his concerns were primarily over matters of his present command, the Fifth Army. His assessment of the situation in his sector has raised several concerns about the region he now oversees. He had come to the conclusion that I might be able to help him develop a plan to improve the readiness in the area and to shore up its defenses."

"If he asked you for help, I am impressed with his judgment," Thomas said.

"What did he want you to do?" asked Marie.

"Basically, he requested that I review the existing fortifications and the road and rail networks. This will be used to better understand existing deficiencies and to design a plan to correct them."

"When will you start this work?" asked Thomas.

"I will start as soon as possible, but I doubt if I will leave for the Northeast for several weeks, unless circumstances dictate otherwise."

"How long will you be gone?" asked Marie, with some concern in her voice.

"I don't know. It depends on many factors that are hard to know without actually seeing the terrain and the facilities. Of course, some of that can be done by studying information that already exists here in Paris, but so much information is lost in two dimensional representations of structure and terrain that it is usually much more efficient to study the subject firsthand."

"Just as I am getting settled into my surroundings, you will be off, and Thomas, no doubt, will return to Strasbourg, leaving me to fend for myself," Marie said somewhat wistfully.

"You are not giving yourself enough credit, Marie," Thomas told her. "Already you have the skills to excel, if you have the confidence to do so."

"It is hard to learn confidence because we all have these little demons that seem all too eager to spread self-doubt at the most inopportune moments."

"The trick," Robert replied, "is how we manage those demons. Success often owes more to your skill in managing your doubts than it does to your own aptitudes."

"That may be right, Robert," Marie said, "but it is one thing to say something, and quite another to do it. With you and Thomas, I have people I trust, and that gives me confidence. I sometimes feel like a yearling trying to walk on my own. Just knowing that you are around makes it so much easier."

"Well, if it's any consolation I will be able to return to Paris frequently," Robert assured her, "unlike when I was in Africa. I also have a time deadline that limits the project to several weeks away at the most."

"That does make me feel better," Marie answered with a broad smile. "Let's dispense with all of this serious talk of fortifications and invasions. I want to simply enjoy our meal and give thanks for the day's good news."

"And to think about what you should wear for the concert," Thomas added with a twinkle in his eye.

21

KAISER STORM

Kaiser Wilhelm II was the head of the most powerful state on the continent. He had inherited a government that his grandfather and his great chancellor Bismarck had carefully constructed to jealously guard the prerogatives of the Prussian ruling classes, even as the country developed increasing wealth in regions to the west and south. Bismarck was careful to ensure that power would not be unjustly influenced by popular will or unpredictable democratic ideals. The state that the kaiser oversaw was autocratic and gave limited power to the people's representatives populating the Reichstag. It was to be the Reich's great misfortune that the young Kaiser Wilhelm was ill suited for heredity autocracy.

His early years had been influenced by the conflict between his strong-willed mother, the eldest daughter of Queen Victoria, and his strong-willed German grandfather, Kaiser Wilhelm I. The old kaiser was one of the most conservative rulers on the continent and looked with disfavor on the more liberal beliefs of his daughter-in-law and her many German relatives, who had been rulers of more minor yet liberal principalities in western Germany before the unification.

Young Wilhelm, upon assuming the throne, immediately adopted the manners of his grandfather, only to relent at unpredictable times to the more conciliatory and inclusive ideals of his deceased father and often-estranged mother. Nowhere was this more evident than on his state visits to Great Britain. He would insist on being the first among equals in dealing with his mother's large extended family, including most of the principle rulers of Europe, but then, overcome by the pomp and power of the British ruling family, he would make a great show of his affection for this, his other nation, by virtue of his maternal inheritance.

It was the ambivalence of his relationship with Great Britain that would cause many of his worst public mistakes. Anxious to prove Germany's legitimacy as a power of the first rank, he looked at British naval power as a potent threat to German control of the continent. Egged on by an ambitious naval chief, Admiral Turpitz, he had launched a program to extensively increase the size and power of the German navy.

This program was instrumental in alienating the British, who were fanatic in their determination to ensure the unquestioned supremacy of their fleet. Consequently, the emerging German naval threat brought about a naval arms race that saw the development of massive British dreadnaughts, which, by virtue of their size and power, superseded much of the efforts of the German building program. Recognizing the futility of continuing such a costly and ill-advised policy, the kaiser subsequently agreed to a treaty with Britain, permanently fixing the relative size of the two navies and consigning the Germans to a position of inferiority that virtually assured British dominance of the seas.

Such a humiliation was difficult to accept for the kaiser and his many allies in the high command of the navy, who saw Britain's naval superiority as a continued means to frustrate their own imperial ambitions. This frustration was further heightened by Wilhelm's intense dislike of his uncle Edward, the oldest son of Victoria, who became the British king following her death. The dislike was shared by Edward, who came to view his nephew as irresponsible and dangerous. Edward was quick to show up Wilhelm whenever he made one of his social blunders, which were the natural consequence of his impetuosity. This would only increase the tension between the two rulers and lead to further deterioration in the relationship between their countries.

During the early summer, the kaiser had seen his racing yacht defeated by the British and Edward in the annual regatta off the British coast. One particularly galling loss came when his boat, having crossed the finish line well ahead of his British rivals, was disqualified for unsportsmanlike tactics. His subsequent foul mood may have made him more amenable to an idea hatched in the naval department to reassert German power and influence in the Mediterranean. Once again it would be centered on Morocco, where a civil war was threatening the safety of the European population throughout the country. France had been assigned protectorate status of the area as a result of the diplomatic solution of the first Moroccan crisis of 1905, and had already intervened in Fez, sending troops into the ostensibly independent state for the protection of their own nationals.

Now urged on by his own admirals, the kaiser decided it was time to protect the German nationals in Morocco by sailing a gunboat into Agadir. Despite the previous provisions granting France protectorate status for the region, orders were given, and on July 1, 1911, the German gunboat seized the port with the intention of establishing a base of protection for her citizens in the country.

How well the kaiser understood the implications of his actions was unclear. What soon became evident, however, was that the governments in Paris and London would see them from a much different perspective than Berlin. The French, no doubt, would view this as simply another brazen attempt to wrest influence from them in North Africa using German military power. In Great Britain, already sensitive to previous German naval threats, this attempt to establish a major base in the Mediterranean, potentially threatening Gibraltar as well as their access to the Suez Canal, no doubt would raise grave concerns. These concerns had the potential to easily lead to another Moroccan crisis, amplified by a climate of suspicion that had only increased in the subsequent years. Once again the continent would awake to the prospect of real hostility between its major powers, provoked by the sudden German presence in a distant North African port.

In the weeks that followed, Agadir would loom ever larger over the continent. Like waves promulgated from a sudden shock, its effects would be far-reaching and marked by a cyclicality of pessimism and optimism. They would be powerful waves, however, and of such a magnitude that they threatened the continent's many citizens, be they king or pauper.

22

SOLDIERS OF PEACE

On the morning of July 2, the news of the actual landing of the German gunboat seemed anticlimactic for Sarah, in that it only confirmed what she had sensed as imminent, not only from Stein's warnings but from concerns that Rosa Luxembourg had shared with her the previous day. For Rosa Luxembourg to seek Sarah was confirmation beyond doubt that something unusual was in the winds.

Of all Sarah's contacts in the German workers movement, her relationship with Rosa Luxembourg had been the most strained. Nowhere was the philosophic split among socialists more extreme than in Germany. At one pole was the Social Democratic Party, which had amassed influence by pursuing a course designed to accrue power through the existing structure of the state and the ballot box. Their chief proponents believed themselves philosophically aligned with Marx, who saw the revolution coming with the incremental rise in power of the proletariat by virtue of the weight of their numbers. To date, they had had success with several measures, including social security and education reform. Bismarck had taken care, however, through his carefully crafted constitution, to give the autocratic rulers many checks to the power of this class, regardless of their numbers. The frustrations inherent in working within such a system had confirmed the beliefs of the more radical elements, who believed a true revolution could come only from the proletariat and refused to participate in existing institutions and legislative governance. Of this group, perhaps no one was as outspoken as Rosa Luxembourg.

On the surface, there were apparent similarities between Sarah and Rosa, as both were women and Jewish and had training in the law. In reality, there were significant differences between the two. In many ways, Rosa was the ultimate outsider. She had come to Germany from Poland, where she had already suffered from the arbitrary and corrupt practices of those in power. She had also borne the stigma of severe scoliosis, resulting in a deformity that greatly detracted from her appearance. A life of disappointments gave impetus to her native brilliance, energizing her in a crusade against those who held the power to frustrate her aspirations and support for the great mass of the proletariat to which she felt instinctively close.

Their meeting the previous day had started out with a cautious reserve based on past encounters, where Rosa had accused Sarah of being an incremental socialist. It was only when Rosa disclosed her concerns about an aggressive German outreach in North Africa that their mutual antipathy to such an overt military adventure helped animate their conversation. Rosa had heard from the baroness of Sarah's recent trip to Switzerland and had come to inquire more about the details and outcome of that visit. When Rosa had learned of her actions, Sarah had been surprised to see how appreciative she was for her efforts and had been gratified to hear that Rosa was interested in helping support any peace demonstrations in Switzerland. At the time, Sarah had filed that information for future use, but now, with the sudden news from Morocco, that future had drawn much closer.

The news from North Africa had been shaped by the state-run media and touted the heroic landing of the *Panther* in Morocco to establish a base of protection for German expatriates living in the area. In the first communications, no mention was made of the Moroccan government, except to say that the actions were made necessary by the failure of the government to provide adequate protection to the German nationals due to an ongoing civil war. This was said to be necessary, as the French, burdened with protecting their own nationals, had been unable to provide similar protection for the German citizens in Morocco. The account, as it was written, made the German actions seem straightforward and easy to defend from criticism.

The average German, when appraised of these actions, had little concern for French and English sensibilities, as it appeared that this was an act necessitated by the unstable circumstances of the region. Indeed, even Spain had sent a rescue force to the region for similar purposes. Both Sarah and Stein suspected that the news would be received differently in France and Britain, however.

"I don't like the looks of this, Stein. It looks all too convenient and far too well planned. I know a little about the region and know of no significant group of German immigrants in the whole of North Africa. Even if there were large numbers present, I doubt any rebel group or government would risk the wrath of Berlin by some foolish, hostile act against them. Unless I am badly mistaken, this will not sit well with the French and likely not with the British. If that is the case, there is just enough ill will to go around to lead to some very dangerous circumstances. I am going to telegram Paris the German account and get some idea of what is happening there right now. Perhaps it would be wise to gather with Frau von Suttner and others here as soon as possible to make appropriate storm plans."

"My contacts have felt that something like this has been in the works for some time," Stein replied. "It seems that this government and its chief constituency in the military cannot be content with simple social and economic progress. They are too impatient with seeing that Germany be given its rightful spoils of land and territory needed to increase the nation's wealth and influence. They are envious of their neighbors who have already enriched themselves by establishing extensive colonies in Africa and Asia and are reluctant to share their spoils. A powerful military is difficult to ignore, however, and can be easily frustrated and impatient with diplomacy and minor concessions. Might and threat, it seems, are being substituted for patience and diplomacy, with the outcome far from certain."

"What a strange people, these Germans—and frightening," Sarah added. "Here in Berlin, we see the tangible proof of their success everywhere. Great buildings of state and monumental architecture, great universities, and sprawling industries all attest to their power. Yet all of this is not enough. There are many who are enamored by a mythical past, hearing the siren call of their ancient Hun ancestors, barbarians content only with forcing their will on those around them. To them, diplomacy, treaties, and even Western ethics are simply a means by which the weak and corrupt can deny those most deserving their spoils. Which will it be—the Germany of Beethoven and Goethe or that of the neobarbarians Bernhardi and Treitschke?"

"Let's hope that the poets prevail over the barbarians, for all our sakes," Stein replied.

"If that is to be, then we need to get busy," Sarah said. She made her way to her office, resolved to mobilize all the resources she could muster for this new battle.

———

Within the week, a meeting had been scheduled at Baroness von Suttner's to bring as many people of the antiwar faction in Germany together to plan measures to help defuse the situation. Sarah arrived after a large number had already gathered. She recognized some present and knew others by the names that identified their places at a large table assembled for the occasion in the dining area of the home. Though not yet present, Sarah noted that Rosa Luxembourg was assigned to the seat to her right.

As the meeting was called to order, Rosa still had not arrived, but as Frau von Suttner began to discuss the nature of threat that the recent events posed, Rosa entered and hurriedly took her place next to Sarah.

"Welcome, Fraulein Luxembourg," Frau von Suttner said in greeting. "I am pleased to see that you could come after all."

"I apologize for being late," Rosa replied somewhat breathlessly. "The interior secretary's men seemed intent on delaying my arrival. I was grilled by two men from their security department for well over two hours. It seems that our meeting today is not without notice on their part. It is my suspicion that they have someone in this room today or at least someone with access to the discussion of today because they certainly were aware of this meeting and its intent."

Rosa's assertion brought an immediate silence to the room, where more than a dozen invited guests were seated around the table.

"What makes you suspect that someone here is working as an agent for the interior secretary?" asked Frau von Suttner.

"Just a hunch and a bit of paranoia," Rosa answered. "They were very knowledgeable about the time and place of this meeting and were able to infer from its location the nature of the discussion. What they seemed most interested in was who the participants were to be. Since I had no exact knowledge of that, I proved of little benefit, at least in that line of questioning. They apparently did not have enough information at this time to simply have deduced this on their own."

"Under the present circumstances, we are simply assembling to discuss our common ideas and grievances about the nature and implications of the kaiser's actions," said Frau von Suttner. "There is nothing illegal with that in Germany."

"At present it may not be illegal, but it is certainly of interest to the security agents," added Rosa. "They made it clear that the day might come in the near future when any attempt to interfere with the government would not likely be treated in a restrained manner, if such actions were judged to be injurious to the Reich or to abet the cause of a potential enemy."

"The laws of the Reich presently have a mechanism that allows for the declaration of martial law, should a state of imminent danger exist to the stability of the nation," added Sarah. "That option has not been evoked, but unfortunately, that does not mean that each of us in this room may not be subjected to increased scrutiny and possible harassment, especially if our actions might adversely impact their policies."

"Those are the risks that we have always had to consider," stated the baroness. "If any of you here today fear for your own safety or that of others by your association with us, then I would urge you to leave now, before you could be further associated with our actions."

No one budged from her place.

"Then if we are in accord, we can proceed. If at any time in the future your concern for your personal safety overrides the comfort you can draw from acting on your beliefs, I will certainly not fault you for withdrawing your active support. In the end, I believe that our cause will justify our actions."

"I'm afraid it is not enough to simply be right," Rosa said. "We may be right and just in our beliefs but fail. We must have more. Our effectiveness—and ultimately, our safety—will come from persuading the mass of the citizenry to oppose any war that will benefit only a few imperialists, while subjecting them to slaughter and hardship."

"You are no doubt correct, fraulein," replied the baroness, "but persuasion will require different means for different people. That is one reason why we are here today, to discuss those means. I believe that all of our work can be readily justified by pointing out the horrible cost to the disenfranchised, especially the working class that you are concerned with, fraulein, while showing the more affluent how disruptive war is to their commerce."

"I understand the need to justify our actions in principle, but such arguments, I fear, will not be enough," Rosa argued. "The reality is that this battle for the peace will ultimately not be won by appealing solely to polite society. If modern warfare is to be waged, it will be necessary to use all the resources of a modern state. The entire populace will be needed to fill the ranks of the army and manufacture its weaponry. The majority of that requisite population comes from the working class. If we can shape their will, we will have the means to veto the more sinister aims of any ruler, general, or government."

"I am perhaps the only foreign representative at this gathering," Sarah said. "Baroness von Suttner asked me here not to suggest specifics to any German initiatives, which would be presumptuous on my part, but to share with you the thoughts of the many French who are sympathetic to your views. I was also asked to discuss some plans that we have made to have an international gathering of workers and others committed to peace to demonstrate our resolve to oppose any war among the nations of Europe. In France, we in the workers movement share a deep desire to avoid the disaster that any wide-scale outbreak of war would produce. Consequently, we have developed plans to have large antiwar demonstrations in Paris and other cities if the threat of an armed conflict becomes serious. The initial plans are to limit these demonstrations to large public gatherings without resorting to more protracted work stoppages or strikes.

"We also share Rosa Luxembourg's belief in the critical role the workers will have in any decision to go to war. If they oppose an armed conflict, then the prospects for a successful prosecution of a war will be severely if not completely damaged. A large demonstration throughout critical areas of the country will have the effect, we believe, of persuading many to seek a more peaceful solution to the crisis at hand. Failing that, however, we have no hesitation in urging a general strike among our supporters as a more dramatic measure to emphasize our opposition to war.

"Unfortunately, it would be difficult for us in France to act alone. If we or any other national group should act unilaterally, it would be all too easy for those who oppose our view to characterize our opposition as traitorous. The tenor of the press and some of the citizenry, along with the threats Rosa Luxembourg has already encountered, are an indication of what we could expect if we acted without coordination with like-minded groups in other countries similarly threatened by the crisis. I believe it is essential, therefore, that we coordinate our actions in those key countries, most certainly to include France, Germany, Great Britain, and Russia. Part of my reason for being here is to offer my assistance in any way to coordinate your future actions with our own. To that end, I will await the outcome of your deliberations. I also want to make you aware that I recently made a trip to Switzerland to explore possible sites where a large peace gathering could be held, allowing the participation of groups and individuals from throughout Europe. I have discussed my findings with Jean Jaurès and Frau von Suttner, who asked that I share them with you.

"Many here know of the tradition of tolerance that the Swiss have shown in the past to both the workers movement and the cause of peace. I am pleased to report that they still harbor strong support for the cause of peace and were warm to the outline of our plan, should conditions warrant the calling of such a large international gathering. Upon further discussion, we were able to persuade the authorities in Basal to host such a rally, to be held over two to three days. They have asked that they be informed of the intention to hold such an assembly at least ten days in advance and that, prior to the arrival of the attendees, they receive ten thousand francs to help cover the expenses associated with providing space, security, and upkeep in the large park near the cathedral.

"I would like to inform you that the French Socialist Party has approved the funds to support this request, if needed, and would be willing to underwrite the cost alone, if that is necessary. While I am speaking to you in Germany, others of our group are conferencing like-minded groups in the most crucial countries of Europe to participate, if necessary, in such a gathering. What I hope can also be accomplished at this meeting or in the days ahead is to get some sense of the support that is present for such an international gathering from each of you and the constituencies for which you speak. If many of you agree with us, I would hope that you can select a steering committee to work with Baroness von Suttner to help shape the agenda for the meetings. It is not necessary to tell you how important that we in France believe active participation by our German colleagues will be to the success of our efforts. It is essential.

"I feel I have spoken too much already, but I want you to know that those of us in France share a deep concern for this cause, just as I believe you do. I will now defer to Frau von Suttner, who may wish to expand on our previous discussions."

Following a few words congratulating Sarah on her efforts and encouraging further discussion of the Basal meeting, it was moved that the group take a short break before resuming their activities. During that time, Sarah was quickly surrounded by the attendees, questioning her in more detail about the particulars of French plans. She carefully noted the names of those she did not know and the others she did and promised to arrange individual follow-up in the following days. As the crowd thinned, she noted Rosa Luxembourg waiting patiently on the side, slightly removed from the rest of the participants.

"I must congratulate you on your work to date, fraulein," Rosa started, upon finding a convenient opening to approach Sarah. "What can you tell me of your plans that you did not know the last time we met?"

"As I briefly mentioned last time, we have had very successful negotiations with the Swiss. They want assurances from the organizers that the crowds will not be disorderly and that any increase in municipal costs to oversee the gatherings will be borne by the organizers. Based on the estimate presented to me, those costs would be reasonable and well within the budget of the French Socialist Union. As to the matter of controlling crowd violence, much will ultimately depend on the organizations involved and the final program chosen. That is where much work will need to be done in the days ahead."

"Will this be a rally limited to socialist unions?"

"I should think not. The baroness has been active in the preliminary planning in order to ensure that her large group of supporters will be involved. Many are clearly not from working-class backgrounds. From our discussions, I understand that her intent is to demonstrate—by the size of the crowd—that there is widespread opposition to war and that this is not just an issue for a particular group."

"It would be a shame to waste such an opportunity without addressing the concerns of the workers in more concrete language," Rosa replied.

"No doubt this can and will happen. Our idea is to have a group of influential speakers from diverse backgrounds. This will convey the universality of the opposition. My plan was to group the key socialist speakers in a block that is strategically positioned at a time when the crowds will be the largest."

"How will these speakers be chosen?" asked Rosa.

"Monsieur Jaurès has already drawn up a list of people I should contact, which includes you and some of your associates. This is a large inclusive list and is drawn primarily from his experience at the First and Second International. The final format of the rally will no doubt be determined by those who wish to be involved and by the extent of their involvement in terms of the number of participants and the revenues contributed. There is little doubt that those most influential in shaping the size of the gathering will have the most influence in determining its ultimate makeup."

"That is well and good," Rosa added, "but such a policy will give great influence to those factions who are largest, such as the SPD, but the most likely to compromise with the militarists."

"Your point is well taken. I would hope that you, Herr Liebnicht, and your other associates would be actively involved, regardless of whether the SPD is present or influential. Frau von Suttner is concerned that we not get consumed in factionalism but focus on the single overriding threat of war and its disastrous consequences. At the same time, I understand that it is difficult for you to isolate your antiwar views from your concern for workers' rights. It would be impossible to insist, therefore, that such matters not be argued, as it is the working class that will be most severely affected by the consequences of war.

"As to the final nature of the program, it is well beyond my authority to guarantee or even imply what the final format will be. We have only negotiated a convenient neutral site that is willing to provide a forum for our gathering on short notice. Its final form, if it comes to pass, will be shaped by those most committed to our goals and to helping in the planning and implementation necessary to see those goals realized. For that reason, if you are interested, knowing your passion and the influence that you have, I feel certain that your viewpoint will be well represented, in spite of any size disadvantage that you might have.

"Rosa—if I may call you that—I am not sure what will come of this meeting today, but I would be happy to meet with you at any time in the coming days to do what is necessary to enlist your help."

"I would welcome the opportunity to speak more about this, Sarah. I must warn you, however, that such actions risk alienating you with the authorities. I am not certain who their contact is among us, but what has been discussed and by whom will soon be known. My suspicion is that it is Ebert's chief deputy, but regardless, by proceeding further today we have already likely alerted the interior agents of our purpose."

"Now is not the time to be frightened or bullied," added Sarah. "I'll plan on meeting with you briefly after these meetings to discuss a future time when we can get together."

The rest of the day passed quickly. Perhaps motivated by their common concerns or the example of their French colleague, the participants resolved the issue of organizing for possible protests across Germany and participation in the international rally in Switzerland. Committees were formed to oversee these matters, and an executive committee was selected that would help coordinate all activities. Sarah was pleased to note that Baroness von Suttner was selected as chairman of the committee, and Rosa was also included.

Sarah could only hope that the specter of a war they all dreaded would be enough to expedite their efforts to oppose it.

23

TRIBULATIONS
OLD AND NEW

Thomas first heard of the German excursion into Morocco en route to conduct the evening mass at Notre Dame. He had agreed to conduct mass during the summer in various locations, in part to help his fellow priests who often were shorthanded due to summer holidays. In reality, he had confined his efforts to a few locations, such as Saint Sulpice and Notre Dame, whose grandeur enhanced the beauty and mystery of holy sacraments and inspired his messages.

His thoughts that early July evening were quickly disrupted by the news from North Africa. His mind was drawn immediately back to the time six years previously when German actions in the area had jolted him and his friends from their innocence, introducing them for the first time to the potential of a more frightening future. His mind retraced his thoughts of that time, which seemed as relevant now as then. Only when he arrived in front of Notre Dame did his mind return to the evening service at hand.

In the glow of the evening sun, the pale golden warmth of the stone seemed to shine forth from the darkened layer covering its outer surface, bringing to life the statuary around and above the main western portals. The stories that these statues told to the illiterate masses of the Middle Ages gave testimony to not only the magnificence of this edifice but also to the spirit that had moved men to such a creation so many years ago. Thomas believed that only divine grace could explain such an edifice. That a man in the very backwater of ancient Rome, reared not by emperors but by a lowly carpenter and his wife, could so move men in a distant future and a distant land to such deeds gave ample testimony to his enduring spirit. The very stones of the building wrested from the ground and still bearing the marks of their masons' work spoke with eloquence through seven centuries distant of the genius of humankind when moved by such transcendent power.

As he entered the long nave, the light shone down through the massive rose windows in ethereal coloration. At the distant altar, the light focused on a large gold crucifix and the pale white marble sculpture of that holy mother embracing the lifeless body of her slain son. Thomas loved the mass in this cathedral because it embodied all that had been passed down of the traditions and teachings of that man, doomed by the fear and intolerance of those in power. Here one could see tangible evidence of humankind at its finest in the moving surroundings and the haunting music of the mass. The story was that of a God, undaunted by the weakness and folly of his flock and who was determined to show them a way to redeem themselves from the original sin and the many that inevitably followed. The mystery of the human condition, which had inspired the ancient masons and architects, also seemed to Thomas most easily approached here in this place, with its beauty and the spirit that inhabited it.

How sad it was to stand here and to sense what a man should do for his salvation and what men should do for the betterment of all, yet hear the old tired story of the powerful pressing their advantage for their betterment alone. He feared that now, like children fighting for a trinket, Frenchmen and others would be forced to act in an all-too-familiar manner, bringing humankind once again to the specter of warfare and destruction. For what end such folly? So that one tribe of men might gain rule over its neighbor? Are we moderns so ignorant as to ignore the inglorious history of such behavior or the hollowness of such victories? Here in this sanctuary, he could see clearly an alternative to such a world. In such a kingdom, men were moved to more noble and sublime ends.

The first reading for the night's service was from Deuteronomy, in which Moses spoke to the Israelites about the Promised Land, which was within reach after forty years of tribulations in the wilderness. Their happiness was assured, Moses reminded them, if only the Israelites would honor the covenants made with God and their ancestors. Moses feared that his people, caught up in their own wealth, would soon forget the real source of their good fortune and would turn their backs on God and their responsibilities. Moses knew the consequences of such behavior.

As Thomas read this, he knew too well the subsequent fate of Israel when its leaders turned away from God to false idols and fruitless pleasures. How often had men followed such folly in the centuries since, assuming they alone were responsible for their good fortune, and blindly elevating those most successful to nobility. As he thought of Moses's great parting sermon to the Israelites, Thomas could not help but wonder if a day of retribution was soon to come to Europe.

Here in Notre Dame, surrounded by much that he loved, it was easy to sense the Promised Land through Christ's kingdom of God. He feared that man's own arrogance and pride, the belief in his own primacy, the same faults that led the Israelites to fall from grace, would cause many to turn from this even greater covenant to their ruin as well. He saw in Germany's leaders people emboldened by their power and fully capable of drawing the continent into calamity if their actions were not tempered. As he closed the service, he spoke of such concerns to those gathered. In closing, he prayed for the wisdom to see the folly of such arrogance and to remember the great covenant God made with all of humankind through the sacrifice of his Son. If not, he feared a modern exile in Sinai for the present generation.

In the ensuing days, as tensions spawned by the German aggression in Morocco increased, Thomas was forced to deal with far more tangible matters relating to his earthly flock than simply concerning himself with conflicts between his clerical ideals and state actions.

Word had come from the bishop in Strasbourg, expressing his concern over the effects that the new crisis was having on the already divided loyalties of the city and region. The relationship with the indigenous French population and German usurpers had never been easy, but, as the bishop related, it was rapidly deteriorating to a level that he had seldom seen. Of great concern to Thomas was the account of affairs at the university, where tensions were now running high and seemingly increasing,

SOME DAMN FOOL THING

despite the fact that many students were away for the summer. The tone of the letter was obvious to Thomas, who saw in the bishop's letter the first notes of an appeal for him to return to Strasbourg. As such, Thomas began to make plans for an earlier return to Alsace than planned.

Even closer to home was the disruption that the demands were placing on Robert and his evolving relationship with Marie. Early on, Robert had given indications of his interest in Marie, which was an admission Thomas had seldom heard from Robert with regard to any previous female acquaintances. He had voiced some concerns about the differences in their life experiences more than their ages, and he feared rushing into any relationship, regardless of the feelings of others, until he could be more certain of his compatibility with Marie. Given Thomas's relationship to Robert and his increasing concern for Marie's well-being, Thomas had taken more than his usual interest in trying to facilitate their relationship.

He had few concerns for Robert in this regard. He was more mature in age and experience, but he also possessed a temperament that allowed him to deal even with romantic matters with a remarkable sense of objectivity and restraint. For someone with such an empiric orientation, knowing more about what truly motivated Marie's feelings and hopes was central to any future relationship with her.

Marie, on the other hand, was a far different matter. Thomas quickly learned that some of Robert's early concerns were unfounded. While it was true that Marie at times appeared naive, it was a naïveté that was not feigned but came from a lack of real-world experience. The more Thomas had come to know her, the more he appreciated Marie's inherent warmth and good will. He also was coming to realize that despite any anxieties she might have, she was fully able to overcome them through her stubborn resolve to do what was best or necessary. It was almost a misfortune that many of her most remarkable characteristics were hidden by her beauty.

Yet despite all of these gifts, Thomas recognized that Marie would require careful handling. Though determined to meet the goals she had set for herself, her inexperience often posed obstacles to her success that were often more mental than physical. Marie was clearly a very social person and as such derived a great deal of support from the interaction and acceptance by others. Her struggles to succeed with her music seemed at times to need some outside measure of support and recognition to encourage her efforts and lift her confidence. That her confidence could be lacking at times, for someone as gifted as Marie, was a testament to the frailty of the human ego. Yet Thomas and Robert both had chosen to provide support that was grounded in frank but measured criticism and practicality, rather than empty rhetoric, to strengthen Marie in the face of new challenges.

Thomas arrived at the Closerie des Lilas on a remarkably beautiful evening to meet with Robert and Marie, only to find that they had already arrived and were engaged in a serious discussion.

"Thomas, at last!" Marie blurted out when she saw Thomas arrive. "Please join us, as already we have been forced to consider matters far more serious than this lovely surrounding warrants, and I, for one, would welcome your thoughts on such matters."

"That must be serious stuff to draw both of you away from an appreciation of this beautiful evening."

"I don't know how serious it is at this time, Thomas," Robert said, "but I was simply updating Marie on the effect this German threat was having on my work. As much as either of us may dislike it, it is something beyond our control."

"If I'm to contribute to this conversation, please bring me up to speed, Robert."

"As I was telling Marie, the concern about the worsening relationship with Germany has forced a reappraisal of many of the army's plans, which certainly includes the project I have been working on in evaluating the readiness of our defenses to the northeast. Their condition and potential vulnerability is of far greater concern now than it was only weeks ago, when I first learned of the project."

"What he is trying to say, Thomas," Marie interjected, "is that it is necessary for him to leave Paris to attend to matters, and he likely will not be able to attend my concert. I know these matters are beyond our control, but it doesn't mean that I have to like accepting it. Robert, you don't know how deflating this is to me. I have been working so hard to impress you and make you proud of me. Now, no matter what happens, if you are not there, it will be far less important or rewarding."

Robert nodded with an expression that showed his discomfort. "I know how important this performance is to you, and that is why I dreaded telling you that I might miss it. If only the kaiser had had the sense to wait for two weeks to launch his adventure."

"If you are to be gone, there is little that can be done except to press on like a good soldier. It would not be possible to change the date at this late hour, unless the concert was canceled. How frustrating to have spent so much time and emotion in preparing for this, only to have some madman turn our world upside down. What is Morocco to me? I would gladly give up ten such places to prevent such stupidity from ruining our lives."

"I only hope that those who are responsible in France and Germany will have a similar perspective," Thomas added.

"To me, Thomas, it seems preposterous to think that rational men would go to war over such trivial matters on the basis of old scores and prejudices."

Robert was unable to easily reply to Marie's concerns and could only weakly second Thomas by saying, "I trust such rationality will prevail."

"It simply must," she exclaimed. "It is difficult enough for people to manage the responsibilities and challenges that they have already without worrying that those that they care for will be swept up in some terrible war. How have we gotten into this crisis, Robert? I can see no good coming from this if it gets out of control. What benefit will there be for the women and children of all the countries? What will become of the beauty and progress that we now enjoy? Can't the men of the world understand how much misery they will create if they can't avoid another senseless war over a meaningless slight or old grievance? I am coming to think that the world would be much better off ruled by poets and artists than by kings and generals. Maybe then we would forsake these juvenile notions that cause men to grasp for more power at the risk of widespread destruction and misery. What good is it to rule if the country is ravaged in the process?"

"No doubt your feelings are shared by most of us, Marie," Robert said, "but that does not dismiss the risk if those in charge of this crisis fail to act in such a reasonable manner. Unfortunately, history is not encouraging, as men have all too often fought over similar senseless slights."

"What a terrible vision that is, Robert," replied Marie. Her resolve surprised Robert. "How can such men be trusted who fail to consider the consequences of their plans on the women and children they are supposed to protect? I know of the consequences of their actions from my reading of the history of

Napoleon's wars. After all the glory had been proclaimed and then vanished in the humiliation of defeat, what remained were countless widows and orphaned children. Even today, one can see the maimed who suffered from the Prussian War. Don't the men of this world recognize how selfish they are to get caught up in these old follies? Why must our lives be held hostage by bullies and fools?"

"It may be foolish, as you say," Robert replied, "but men have learned painful lessons by ignoring such bullies and madmen. The behavior of many powerful men has shown little regard for your concerns, Marie. There comes a time when if their worst is not confronted, they will be emboldened to do more. The challenge is knowing when enough is enough. Acting prematurely—perhaps needlessly—exposes everyone to the risks that you fear, but acting too late virtually ensures trouble on an even larger scale."

"That seems like too stark a choice to me," replied Marie. "Can't we demand more from our so-called leaders and come to a more adult resolution of these crises?"

"That is a fine goal, Marie, but the paradox is that the dialogue that you hope for is most effective when an aggressor's actions are tempered by strength that commands respect."

"That tactic is full of danger, Robert. By strengthening ourselves, we only make our adversaries more wary and insecure, leading to cycles of crisis fueled by the paranoia of the militarists. That is the danger of the monopoly of the rule of arrogant men. In all of Europe, women have no voice in this matter. We have to stand by idly, accepting the unacceptable, while our wishes have no champions in our government or any in Europe. Our lives are led, trying to secure our futures by whatever means God has given us, but all too often we are simply at the mercy of men, be it our husbands, boyfriends, or leaders. Our lot is to accept this without recourse, hoping for the best yet always preparing for the worst. We are entrusted with the most important elements of a normal society to maintain the home and rear our young, but we have no say in shaping the most vital conditions that frame our lives."

Robert was moved by the intensity of Marie's arguments. This was a side of her that both cousins had rarely seen. Yet this outburst was testimony to Marie's increasing maturity and gave evidence that she would be able to handle much harsher affairs than he had previously imagined.

Hoping to ease her concerns, Robert added, "Well, there is little that any of us can do at this stage, Marie, except to focus on our obligations. When I am gone, I want you to carry on as usual, without any consideration of whether I will be at your recital or not. It will be good training for teaching you that good preparation can free you from dependence on others. If you do that, I'll do everything that I can to get back at least for the evening of your recital."

"Sound advice," Thomas said with an appreciative smile. "If followed to the letter, Marie, I am sure it will show how little either Robert or I mean to your success. Now let's not waste the rest of this beautiful evening with matters we have so little control over. Let's resolve to enjoy our meal and company together."

"I don't want to prolong any argument, Thomas, but you are wrong to think that either of you are not important to me, regardless of how I might do in my concert." After a pause, she added impulsively, "Oh, Robert, I so hope that you can get back because it would mean so much to me."

Thomas, recognizing the discomfort the discussion was causing Robert, gave a subtle nod to the waiter whose appearance provided a timely interruption of the ongoing discussion. With a refill of their wine and the subsequent appearance of their meal, Thomas was gratified that Marie seemed more relaxed and conciliatory in her manners.

The remainder of the early evening progressed as was befitting such lovely weather and surroundings. Afterward, as the trio rose to leave, Marie leaned over and gave Robert a kiss on his cheek. Then, in further confirmation of her attraction to the cousins, she took them by the hand, drawing them closer to her as they set out on their walk home.

24

WAR LORDS

With the first reports coming out of Agadir, few were under more pressure than the war minister, Adolphe Messimy. He had dithered in replacing General Michel as Army Chief of Staff after the War Council had rejected his defensive plans, and now the urgency brought about by the German presence in Morocco was a bitter reminder of the need for a decision on the matter. At first word of the German action, he had contacted General Gallieni to discuss offering him General Michel's position.

Gallieni was the natural choice. His seniority and proven competence made him widely respected by the general staff and throughout the army. More important, he was the general with whom Messimy felt the most comfortable.

Gallieni had arrived at the scheduled hour, dressed in his field uniform.

"Good evening, General. I appreciate your meeting on such short notice. I'll forgo the pleasantries and get to the point. What do you make of the German actions?"

"It is difficult to know, with as little information as we have at present, but my first impression is that this is the action of a bully looking for attention. Matters have been quiet lately, and no doubt the kaiser and some of his advisers have decided that the time was right to reexert their efforts to expand their colonial presence. If we are fortunate, that is all the further it will go. Our best course is to make the best preparation we can for any eventuality and then hope that the diplomats can diffuse this nonsense."

"Why do you say that?" the minister asked.

"As you know, Monsieur Minister, I have been assigned the command over the Fifth Army, responsible for our most northeast borders. Unfortunately, I am afraid that what General Michel has said about the preparedness of the area is true. If the Germans launched an attack through this region, it could be a difficult situation. At present, I have detailed one of our best engineers to provide me with plans to upgrade the defenses in the area, but such work will take several months at best."

"What about the French offensive that we discussed in repudiating Michel's plan?" Messimy asked.

"At present, it is more in theory than in actuality. Any large offensive requires thorough planning with regard to logistics. We have plans in place for troop deployment in the event of a national mobilization, but the detailed plans for a massive and coordinated offensive are incomplete. In my opinion, the best present alternative, in the event of a war with Germany, would be to rely on defensive tactics to confront their attack and then to counterattack at the first opportunity. Only with time will we have the resources and preparation needed to optimize a first-strike offensive."

"Well, General, whatever comes from this crisis, it is apparent to me that the army desperately needs to find a replacement for General Michel as early as possible. That is one of the main reasons that I have called you here tonight. Of all the general staff, I have the most confidence in you to lead the army in whatever course is most appropriate. You have the combination of experience and wisdom that will be invaluable in the days ahead."

"I appreciate your vote of confidence, Monsieur Minister, but if it is your intent to offer me General Michel's position, I must make you aware of several considerations. As you may know, I am of an age where it is customary to retire by the end of next year. If we are fortunate enough to survive this affair without a major engagement, you will need someone with a longer-term perspective than what this window of time allows. I should also make you aware that for the last several months I have been undergoing treatment for a prostate condition, which likely will limit my effectiveness, even if I choose to stay past my customary time."

"What are you trying to say, General?" Messimy asked.

"I am saying, sir, that if I am needed in a leadership capacity for the immediate future, I would, of course, accept such an offer of command out of a sense of duty. I believe, however, that given the limits of my age and health, the army would be best served by selecting a younger man. From a more personal perspective, I also feel uncomfortable replacing a man whom I had some role in bringing down by openly disagreeing with his positions. I am too old to be perceived as an opportunist and want simply to be judged on my actions."

"Who would you recommend for the job of chief of staff, then, General?"

"The army is a very tradition-bound institution. Someone like me, who has served the greater part of his career in the colonial services, would not be as well received as someone from the home forces. There are several members of the senior staff with excellent qualifications. General Pau is a logical consideration."

"I have considered Pau," replied Messimy, "but he is too inflexible in his demands and is far too reactionary for the taste of many in the government. We are only now getting the battles of the Dreyfus years behind us. I am afraid General Pau would be an unpleasant reminder of those ugly days past."

"Castlenaugh is both experienced in the field and in staff work and has a first-rate mind," added Gallieni.

"He is even worse than Pau. He wears his religiosity on his sleeve. He is half general and half priest. If he were named chief of staff, he would have every radical politician in the city beating my door down."

"Speaking frankly," replied Gallieni, "if I were looking for a good man for such a job I would carefully consider General Joffre. He was my chief engineering officer in Madagascar, and I have worked with him enough to know his strengths very well. He has a strong analytical mind and is not easily given to impetuous decisions or rattled by unsettling circumstances. His quiet manner masks a resolute, almost stubborn, character, but he is capable of seeking assistance from others when he deems it necessary without affecting his own confidence, which is considerable. In my experience that confidence is justified, as he is solidly qualified as an engineer and has an excellent record of command in many hostile areas in the colonies."

"What are his weaknesses, as you see them?" asked Messimy.

"He has an aloof and laconic manner that is difficult to get used to. That is less of concern in a commander where such a bearing may be favorable, but it is difficult to deal with at times when he is your subordinate. He also, at times, is very stubborn and finds it difficult to change his position.

Having worked through a problem to reach a conclusion in his own manner, he is hesitant to change his thinking. In an unstable and rapidly evolving situation, that may prove a hindrance in developing flexible and effective tactics to address changing circumstances. This, however, is mere conjecture. He has never been placed in such a situation, so it is difficult to extrapolate his tendency to a larger, more complex condition.

"He also has spent the greater part of his career in the colonial services, which makes him less well known to the metropolitan and home leadership. These weaknesses, in my opinion, are outweighed by his strengths, which I believe would serve the army quite well going forward."

"It seems he has virtually no experience in staff work and planning at the highest level of the command structure in Paris," Messimy commented.

"If we are granted the time to prepare and avoid any major conflict during this present crisis, there are many senior officers available who could guide his hand in this matter. Castlenaugh would be ideal in this capacity and would be less of a political lightning rod in this more subordinate position. The present crisis makes all such planning uncertain, but no doubt creates an urgency to resolve the new command structure going forward. As I said, I would help in any way possible in the immediate days ahead, but for more stable long-term leadership, I would recommend another man, such as Joffre."

"I appreciate your candor, General. I will keep our conversation well in mind in the days ahead. I value your service and the advice you may have going forward."

"You may be assured, Monsieur Minister, that I will do my best to provide the help I can in the days ahead."

It seemed to Messimy that each passing day brought new tensions to his attention, relating to the landing of the German ship *Panther*. Consequently, he had wasted little time in arranging a meeting with General Joffre, who, after some further diligence, seemed to be as Gallieni had suggested—a serious candidate for chief of staff.

As Joffre entered his office, he was struck by the physical size of the man. In contrast to Gallieni, Foch, and nearly all the younger general staff, he had a large frame, made even more noticeable by an amply filled girth. Messimy was mildly amused to think the early afternoon hour of their meeting must have interrupted Joffre's lunch, something that, by reputation, was most sacrosanct to the general.

After a few brief pleasantries, Messimy got to the point. "General, I have asked you here for your assessment of the present situation and how the army should proceed in event of an outbreak of hostilities with the Germans."

"Monsieur Minister, I need not belabor the point that at present our options are limited by the nature of the planning that is in place. As you are aware from our review of General Michel's formal plans, much of our planning has focused on our army adopting positions behind strong fortifications and using these, along with defensive tactics, to neutralize any German attack. If successful in repulsing their offensive, then it can be hoped that an appropriate opportunity for a counterattack can be realized."

"From our past discussion, I gathered you have some reservations with such a strategy, General."

"I have several, Monsieur Minister."

"What might they be?"

"My first concern is with the tactics themselves. I believe that modern weaponry, with its firepower and mobility, gives a distinct advantage to an attacking army. If such an army can mobilize and deploy its troops rapidly, they can choose the most advantageous locations for engaging their enemy and can better seize the opportunities that might arise in the course of any given battle. By waiting in defensive positions, we are ceding the initiative to the Germans and, with it, the distinct advantage that goes with allowing them to choose the time and place of the battle. Their army is one that has traditionally relied on elaborate planning, and to let them unfold their plans without the threat of a French offensive only strengthens their advantage."

"So the advantage is to the attacking force, and by limiting our initial options to a defensive posture, we are limiting our best chance for success?"

"That is right, Monsieur Minister. Unfortunately, whereas we now are at relatively equal strength with the Germans, our emphasis has been such that we have been content to achieve that parity before we have developed any significant alternative to the defensive tactics that were formerly necessary."

"General, how do you assess the risks of such a conflict at present?"

"From a purely military point of view, the German position in Morocco is untenable. The French have the support of the present government, many more troops in the area, and the advantage of diplomatic precedents based on the last crisis in the area, which ceded protectorate status to France. At its base,

I believe this to be nothing more than a threat designed to gain concessions from the Entente for some territory in the region.

"I am not, however, a politician or a diplomat. My job is to carry out the orders that my own superiors in the army and government give me, to the best of my ability. At present, I would prefer that this incident not accelerate into a large-scale confrontation. Any limited confrontation in Africa is potentially treacherous, since the Germans will not be willing to accept their almost certain defeat in Morocco without some form of retribution, if for nothing more than to save face. Therefore, if a more widespread conflict is to be avoided, it is entirely up to the will of the politicians and the diplomats. We in the army must stand on alert."

"Do you believe that a diplomatic solution is best at the present?" Messimy asked.

"A diplomatic solution that is advantageous is always preferred, Monsieur Minister. Only failing that should we accept the enormous collateral damage that will come from a war with Germany, even if prosecuted successfully. I would prefer to avoid that option at present."

"Why is that?"

"Monsieur Minister, I am of the school that believes in the primacy of the offensive. Any war with Germany, by necessity, will have to be short-lived or the economies and the very fabric of the countries involved will be destroyed. The only way to conduct a war for rapid victory is by seizing the initiative offensively. At present, we do not have the planning or resources that would allow us to launch a successful attack into Germany. The time is not far away, however, when that will be possible. If the time comes when we must fight the Germans, it will be a fierce and likely short-lived conflict. When that time comes, we should have our best options available to us."

"What more would it take?"

"More thorough planning will be necessary, with the development of actual plans for deployment of troops and a schedule and routes by which any attack would proceed. This will require more extensive staff work to devise these plans and coordination with the engineers to ensure adequate means to rapidly deploy the troops to where they are needed. In all likelihood it will require more trained regular troops. The best way of achieving that objective is to extend the period of conscription from two to three years."

"That third year will be no small task, politically," Messimy observed.

"Nor will be defeating the Germans," replied Joffre.

"I will be honest with you, General. One of the reasons I asked you here was to evaluate you as a possible replacement for General Michel as chief of staff. I had considered General Gallieni, but for various reasons he has deferred. He has recommended that I consider you for the position. Do you have any objections to such a consideration?"

"I have never really thought about it, Monsieur Minister. It is an interesting proposal, however, and one that would require serious consideration on my part. I should remind you that my past experience leaves me at somewhat of a disadvantage with regard to certain aspects of that role, which would be of some importance."

"What do you mean?"

"My background is in engineering, and so I have spent the brunt of my career in the field, working on problems of logistics and troop deployment. I am confident in my ability to coordinate various armies in their deployment in the most advantageous manner. What I am lacking is extensive staff work, doing the preparation for potential contingencies and finalizing plans to meet those needs. Of all your candidates, I likely have the least experience in that area."

"I appreciate your candor, General. What you lack in such experience others lack in the experiences you've had in the field. At this point, before I proceed further, I would like to know if you are opposed to the idea of assuming the role of chief of staff. If you are, there is no point in pursuing it further."

"I am not opposed to the idea at this time, but as I said, I would have to give it more thought."

"Very well, then, General Joffre. I appreciate both your candor and your insight. You will be hearing more from me in the future."

After the meeting finished, each man seemed struck by the implications of their relatively brief discussion.

For Joffre, the proposed offer confirmed a premonition that he had long held and strongly believed—that he was destined to lead France in a battle for her very survival.

For Messimy, he sensed that he had found a man who was not only acceptable politically but would strike out at France's enemies, rather than concede any first-move advantage to them.

They next met within the week, and shortly thereafter, Joffre was named as the new chief of the army. This selection would commit France to the audacious notion of a full-scale attack as the basis for survival against their ancient enemy to the east. It was a bold doctrine, perhaps fitting the spirit of the times, but as appealing as the notion might have been for many, it had not yet been tested by a trial of fire.

25

TRIUMPH

The evening of Marie's concert at Saint Sulpice had finally arrived. Much to Thomas's chagrin, he had been forced to tell Marie earlier that afternoon that Robert's duties would keep him away from Paris for the evening. Marie's disappointment had been evident, which only caused Thomas further concern. He tried desperately to provide some comfort to her, just hours away from the biggest concert of her career.

"I know from Robert's message how truly disappointed he is, Marie. He wanted me to tell you how much he had wanted to be here tonight, but just yesterday, he and the men assigned him were ordered to reevaluate an area that, from recent information, was causing great concern in the Military Intelligence Bureau. I know how important this must be as I am sure Robert would have been here otherwise."

"I know that is true, Thomas, but it still is very disappointing, as his last messages were so encouraging."

"It no doubt has something to do with this crisis, as I have sensed more tension around the military quarter along Saint

264

Dominique going to Saint Sulpice to hear you practice these last few days."

"Father came to town last night, and he says the same thing. He has heard that Premier Caillaux has become concerned to the point that he is carrying out discussions with various German contacts independent of the Foreign Office."

"Whatever may be going on, it is out of our control at the present. Robert wanted me to reassure you that he is not at risk and that you should not worry about him but concentrate on your performance."

"That certainly sounds like Robert, and I appreciate both of you trying to reassure me. I once told Robert that I sometimes feel like one of his men, and so the best thing for me to do is to act the part and do what he says."

"That will only make it easier for you to perform like both of us expect, Marie; that is, superbly. Now, if you will excuse me, you have your preparations to attend to, and I have to get ready to thoroughly enjoy your performance this evening."

"Thank goodness one of you will be here tonight."

"Even a papal encyclical couldn't keep me away, Marie. I look forward to seeing you later this evening."

———

That evening, the crowd assembled included more than the usual gathering of parishioners and other music devotees who habitually gathered on Wednesday evening in Saint Sulpice to hear the great organ or other selected performances. Connections to some of the prominent families of the quarter had transformed the evening into a social affair as much as a concert. Thomas and Robert's grandmother, who was ailing with her arthritis, would be unable to attend, since she had returned to the more hospitable climate of Provence, but she had used her considerable connections in the quarter to ensure an appropriate turnout for the occasion. The same efforts were exerted by Marie's aunt, with the result that nearly thirty minutes before the start of the performance, many of the most chic members of one of Paris's most fashionable quarters had gathered in anticipation of an evening not only of music but also to bask in each other's presence. Adding to the mix were many clerical associates of Thomas's, as well as the countless others he had befriended from his days in Paris. Some of the attendees were indeed knowledgeable and passionate about music, but many others saw the evening more as an interesting gathering than a cultural experience.

Upon entering the church, Thomas was promptly greeted by Marie's mother, who brightened perceptibly on seeing him. She led him to seats at the front of the prospective audience, where he was quickly introduced to members of Marie's family that he had not previously met, including no less a figure than Marie's father, who had come to Paris from Lyon for the occasion.

"Thomas, I am very pleased to meet you. I have heard so much about you and your cousin Robert. I am sorry he was unable to attend the concert this evening, but I certainly understand the circumstances of his absence."

"I am sure he truly regrets his absence tonight as well."

"At least we have the good fortune of your company tonight, Thomas. I certainly want to thank you for getting this opportunity for Marie to play here tonight and all you have done to encourage her."

"It has been more than a pleasure to do anything I can to help, as she has such remarkable talent."

"I hope we can talk later this evening. I'd like to hear your impression of her work."

"I look forward to it, Monsieur Bonneau."

At that moment the crowd quieted, following the ring of a bell that served to announce the anticipated arrival of Marie.

While the crowd was gathering, Marie was preparing, quietly out of sight. She had had many small recitals among friends and family, as well as in her teacher's salon, but this was her first large public performance since being in Paris. Consequently, the nerves that she commonly felt before any performance seemed more intense and difficult to control on this occasion. As her mother oversaw the final preparation of her hair and gown, Marie tried to block out all but her most essential thoughts and focus her mind on the music she had chosen to play.

At long last a young priest arrived and escorted her to the front of the large gathered assembly. As Marie looked over the audience, she was struck by the size of the crowd—far larger than any she had ever played before. She was thrilled to see her family and a large number of acquaintances, but it was Thomas's presence that seemed to settle her and renew her confidence. As she sat before the piano, her gaze fell upon the large Delacroix painting of Jacob wrestling with the angel, situated nearly above her. She could not help but relax a bit, imagining that somehow Thomas had contrived its presence to make light of her present situation. Taking a deep breath, she struck the first notes of her program.

For most assembled that night, both the music and the performance were certainly up to the standards set by the many great musicians who had performed on the great organ that Marie could see directly over her shoulder. The evening began with a Mozart piece, demanding in its classical elegance an interpretation both restrained yet attuned to realizing the genius built upon each successive note. One could play this music technically correct without missing a note, yet fail to move an audience if the sublime nature built within its almost perfect construction was not conveyed. Such was not the case this evening. Whatever small technical flaws Marie made were overcome by an interpretation that gave both grace and majesty to the master's work.

After the Mozart piece, Marie selected a sonata by Beethoven. Here too the music demanded more than a high level of technical excellence to reach its fullest expression. This was a piece that held in its tight classical construct an unfolding of evident emotion and passion that marked the genius of the composer, a genius that had ushered in a new age. In her rendition, Marie did not fail the master. As the piece unfolded, the listener was taken from the controlled and elegant opening passages to the noble and dramatic finale.

As Thomas watched from his vantage point close to Marie, he had difficulty in concentrating on the music, however well it was performed. Instead, he was wrestling with the many emotions he was experiencing in seeing this young woman, to whom he had grown close, expose some of her private being in this most public venue.

She looked stunning, with her beauty carefully enhanced by the embellishments of a knowing mother. Her gown and hair seemed to take on even more elegance when bathed in the late evening light that filtered through the stained glass. Her appearance was made even more remarkable by her movements around the keyboard in bringing the inanimate notes to realization. These movements, which seemed in complete harmony with the music, seemed much like those of a great dancer choreographed to reveal in movement the inner meaning of the score.

Thomas could only marvel as he watched Marie's performance not only in the skill of her playing but also her remarkable stage presence. She seemed both composed and remarkably mature for someone of her age. How much she had changed in the short time he had known her. This very performance seemingly added even more grace and maturity to her bearing before his eyes.

Marie now came to her finale, a collection of short pieces by the beloved Polish expatriate Chopin. Now her naturally ebullient personality was clearly evident as she went from impromptu to etude to polonaise. The subtle constraints of the previous masters were relaxed as she played this more intimate and expressive music. Once again, Thomas marveled not only in how well she played but in the relationship between her and the music. As the mood of the pieces changed, it was as if Marie, by her interpretation, was shaping that sense as much as the master's notes. Evident were passages that elicited melancholy, pathos, defiance, and triumph, all of which were rendered in a manner that seemed shaped by the inner feelings of the young interpreter.

With the final bars of her spirited and moving interpretation of the polonaise, the concert ended with great triumphant applause from all gathered. For a moment the crowd was one in their shared admiration for the performer and the emotions that her playing had evoked. Thomas was lost in the crowd of admirers gathering around Marie, all of whom seemed to share a mutual admiration for her performance. It seemed a bit odd to him to see her in this manner, surrounded by a large and animated group of people, many of whom she did not know, and he silently commended the manner in which she was handling what would be an ordeal for most.

Marie's mother appeared at his side, radiant with pride in the evident success of her daughter.

"I am biased," she said, "but I have to say that she was magnificent."

"I am biased myself," Thomas replied, "but I would most certainly agree. She exceeded even my highest expectations."

"We are so grateful, Thomas, for what you have done in helping prepare her for this evening. Your help and encouragement has meant so much to her. We are having a gathering at our home this evening, and of course you are invited."

"That is very kind of you and your husband, and I would like nothing better than being there to share Marie's triumph with all of you."

"We'll see you shortly, then. I must go and help finish the preparations."

After some time, Thomas was able to get into the smaller circle of people surrounding Marie, and on seeing him she gave a broad triumphant smile. As the crowd thinned she was able to pull away long enough to talk with him.

"You were magnificent, Marie. I knew you would do well, but this was a triumph. I am truly in awe. I just wish Robert had been here to see it firsthand, because my description could never do your performance justice."

"Thomas, I owe you so much for this night. Not only did you arrange the performance, but without your help and encouragement, I know I would have had enormous difficulties. Your very presence here tonight seemed to dispel my anxiety, making it seem almost as if I was back practicing in the studio with you alone."

"Thank you, Marie, but what you accomplished owed far more to your hard work and God-given talents than anything that I might have done. As a teacher, that is the lesson I want to leave with you tonight. You still have many admirers to talk to, Marie, so I don't want to hold you up any longer. Your mother has invited me to your home later this evening, where I hope to have the time to flatter you in the manner you deserve."

"That will be the best part of the evening, Thomas. I can hardly wait to see you there."

With that, she turned to the still large crowd of well-wishers with a confident stride that Thomas thought gave her an aura befitting such an inspired performance.

At the reception afterward, everyone was in a state of excitement, sharing their feelings in seeing Marie succeed so spectacularly. Even for those not in her family, there was still much to enjoy in the shared experience of such a successful performance.

Thomas quickly busied himself, focusing on two men he knew were influential critics, trying to impart his own impression of the performance in the hope that it might further influence any opinion that they might have formed about Marie.

At last the conquering heroine arrived, and the gathering was shepherded to their assigned places for dinner. A place had been reserved for Thomas and Robert at the family table, and in the latter's absence, Thomas found himself seated next to Marie, with her parents seated directly across from them.

Her mother had an air of pride in her daughter's performance that helped justify her own role in nurturing Marie's talents. Her father, on the other hand, had a perplexed look that reflected his discomfort in the novel position in which he now found himself.

Monsieur Bonneau seemed uneasy at the attention that his daughter was receiving. His feelings seemed to be split between the pleasure of seeing his daughter's success and his reservations about such a public triumph. He had been gracious in his praise and loving in his embrace following the completion of her performance, but there was also hesitancy in his comments that suggested ambivalence about the evening.

"Marie, your mother and I are so pleased to see you so happy," he said as he watched her infectious enthusiasm in the aftermath of her performance. "You should enjoy this evening and remember it well. We are given only a few such days in our lives, and for me, it is a joy to share it with you."

"I am happy to hear you say that, Poppa. I feared that you would not approve of such a public performance."

"When your mother first made me aware of it, I admit I was not enthused with the idea. I was then told that this was not so much a first step in a career as a means by which you could gain valuable experience and confidence. I can see clearly that your mother was right in that assessment."

"Is it wrong to be a career performer, as you suggest?"

"It is not wrong to use your God-given talents to their fullest. What I am most worried about, however, is the notion that your worth depends on popular opinion and the judgment of so-called critics. In the world of a performer, it is all too easy to get caught up in trying to please others for personal vanity and to lose sight of more important matters."

"Poppa quit being so serious for once, and enjoy the evening. There is time enough to worry about such matters in the future. At least give me some credit that I might have enough sense to think for myself. I am not so foolish as to do something important without giving it serious consideration and listening to the counsel of those I love and respect."

Her father seemed to ease with that. Smiling, he loosened his tie and turned his attention to Thomas. "What can a father do with such a daughter, Thomas, since I can no longer bring her to bear with a stern gaze and frown?"

"Yours must be the plight of every other caring father," replied Thomas. "In your case, however, it is much more agreeable than most. You have such a remarkable daughter that your greatest concern will be how best to enjoy her success, rather than worrying about any indiscretion or lack of judgment."

"So there you have it, Father," replied Marie. "You can stop worrying. Thomas is a very wise man whose opinion I trust nearly as much as yours."

"I know what you are saying is true, Thomas, but it is a father's plight to worry about his daughter, even one as rare as Marie."

"We have far more important things to worry about these days," asserted Marie's mother.

"No doubt you are right, dear. I spent much of the day talking with clients who told me how destructive this crisis has been for their businesses here in France, as well as for their associates in Germany. Like it or not, our prosperity here in Western Europe is dependent on the peaceful exchange of trade with our neighbors and most certainly with Germany. I say give the Germans what they want in Africa in return for increased trade with Alsace and the Western German provinces. What little we would lose in profits from ceding some distant African colonies would be more than compensated for by the increased revenues at home."

"Premier Caillaux seems to have the same disposition as you," Thomas said.

"Caillaux is a businessman, which puts him in an awkward spot. He can do what is right from an economic sense and alienate these groups calling for some inane war with Germany, or he can concede to their demands, like many other amoral politicians, placing us at risk of destroying the future of the whole continent."

"Dear, this night is too special to talk politics and business," Madame Bonneau reproached.

"You are right, madame," replied Thomas. "If anything, Marie's performance shows how much good we stand to lose if more reasonable men don't prevail. It has also made me more optimistic. I am a religious man, and how could God's presence not be felt tonight among us. His spirit aligned with the likes of Marie is more powerful than the lot of agitators on all sides."

"Thomas, I can see that Marie is correct in her assessment of you. I wish I only had the sense to listen more to her music and less to grumblings of my friends and clients."

"Well, Father, as Thomas might say, that is a lesson for us all."

For the remainder of the evening, the conversation was far lighter, with the question of impending war shoved far from everyone's discussions, if not their consciousness. As the gathering began to disperse, Monsieur Bonneau excused himself in order to attend to some affairs that he had neglected, and his wife busied herself in the tasks of a hostess, which she performed with the expertise of someone well versed in such behavior.

At an opportune moment, when they were separated from the crowds of people leaving for the evening, Marie drew Thomas aside.

"Thomas, you were so wonderful with Father tonight. You must be my guardian angel. I can't begin to thank you for all you have done for me since we met."

"I have looked out for Robert all these years, and now, because of him, it seems even more natural that I look after you."

"You may not want to hear this, Thomas, but as much as I care for Robert, you are the one person on whom I can truly rely."

"You should not underestimate Robert, Marie. He is the practical one and certainly one on whom you can depend."

"All that may be true, Thomas, but you were here for me tonight, and it seems you are always with me, even if only in spirit."

Thomas was stunned by the sincerity and passion of Marie's words. For a moment he felt he could not breathe and could scarcely move. Before he could reply, Marie's mother called to her, requesting that she come to see off her many well-wishers.

As she turned to leave, Marie added one last thought. "Thomas, you don't know how important it was to me for you to be here tonight. I will never forget it."

Thomas would not forget the night or Marie's sincerity either.

26

A CALL TO ACTION

As the train pulled out of the station in Berlin, Sarah looked out on the passing city with a wave of relief as she set out on a return trip to Paris. The demands of the last days had been hectic and nearly incessant, given the unresolved Moroccan crisis and the effect that the stuttering efforts by leaders on both sides was having on the psychology of the populace. One day there would be suggestions of progress, only to receive news the following days to the contrary. Such contradictions, with their inevitable delays, seemed to contribute to a general sense of pessimism and worry that was plainly evident in the many Berliners Sarah encountered.

This apprehension had served to energize the efforts of those committed to organizing peace rallies throughout the country for the proposed gathering in Basal that Sarah had been working on. It was with a sense of pleasure, if not relief, that most of the decisions regarding German participation had been made, and a great part of her return to Paris would be to finalize their coordination with French planners. Sarah had also noted, despite Rosa Luxembourg's concerns, that she had been given a prominent speaker's role, if details could be finalized.

To further complicate matters, on her last afternoon in Berlin, as she was rushing to finalize loose ends, Hahn had made an unwelcome visit to the office to pointedly declare that unless matters improved, there was a very good chance that all aliens would be forced to deal with harsher measures within the next week, including, among other provisions, a requirement to register their locations each evening with a local magistrate or at the hotel where they might be staying. It was not the provisions that worried Sarah as much as the threatening zeal with which Hahn pointedly presented them to her. Despite her happiness in getting out of Berlin, Sarah did not feel full relief from Hahn's threats until she crossed the German border.

She had been both pleased and excited to see the cooperation and progress that was rapidly taking shape in Germany among the many different groups opposed to German militarism. The plans that she had worked on for a large peace rally in Switzerland would benefit greatly from these efforts, where already demonstrations had been held in Berlin and Dresden to protest the possibility of a coming war. She was also pleased to be able to report to her French colleagues the status of these actions, knowing that it would motivate them further to carry out similar demonstrations throughout France.

As her train reached the eastern outskirts of Paris, the weather became sunnier, as did her disposition. In the distance, she caught sight of the dome of Sacre Coeur, and soon other familiar landmarks came into view. At the station she stopped for a brief coffee; then catching a cab, she proceeded directly home. She was not expected into the office until the following afternoon so she looked forward to using the time to become reacquainted with her family and to simply unwind from the trip and her hectic schedule of the last weeks.

As expected, her father was not yet home from his office, but her mother was home and seemed genuinely glad to see her. Sarah excused herself in order to refresh from her long journey and then joined her mother for tea. Free from the concerns and demands of motherhood for which she was ill suited, her mother had grown much closer to Sarah through the years and now seemed genuinely pleased to hear of Sarah's recent accomplishments. At times it was if she was living vicariously through her daughter's adventures, relishing a life of excitement and nonconformity that she had not experienced in the sheltered world of her own making. Soon, Sarah's father arrived from work to join them.

As always, a special feeling came over Sarah in the presence of her father, and he also seemed transformed by her visit. Seldom had she seen her parents so animated. Sarah relished the warmth of this reunion, only wishing that such occasions had been more frequent when she had been younger. After a delightful leisurely dinner, Sarah excused herself to attend to some final matters before the day ended. Sarah was pleased to note that Lydia had sent her a note indicating her availability in the days ahead and stating that she looked forward to their meeting.

The following morning, after an early breakfast, Sarah set out to report back to the home office. Each time she returned, it seemed the paper had changed. An ever larger number of workers were employed in bigger and more dispersed quarters. Schoen had moved on to a position in the party more suitable,

Sarah thought, to his propensity for meddling and his fondness for scheming. She now reported directly to the managing editor, Felix Placard, and often to the chief ownership, including Jean Jaurès. She had arrived early that morning to meet with Placard at a time more convenient for him.

As their meeting progressed, they were joined by others, including one of the principle owners Aristide Briand. Collectively, they were pleased with the progress that the Berlin bureau had made, not only in providing vital information concerning events in Berlin and Germany but also in meeting some economic goals that helped to ease the cost of supporting the expense of a foreign bureau. What most excited everyone, however, was Sarah's news about the actions of the German socialists and their various allies, particularly with regard to their antiwar activities. Word of their coordinated efforts, which already were being put into place with active demonstrations, seemed to visibly lift the spirits of all present. Her work in coordinating the rally in Switzerland was well known, and a meeting was scheduled for the following morning with several key participants, including Jean Jaurès, to finalize their own plans for the event.

As the meeting neared its end, Placard requested that Sarah stay for a few minutes while he updated her on the activities that were planned in Paris and around France. Events, such as the rallies that had been held in Berlin, were to take place at several locations in France during the next days. Indeed, a rally near a large Renault plant in the eastern suburbs was scheduled for this very afternoon. Placard had passed on the request of Jean Jaurès that if Sarah was able to attend he would appreciate her presence at the gathering. Not knowing the area where the meeting was to be held, she left promptly in order not to miss the beginning of the ceremonies.

After a longer than usual trip, necessitating changing metro lines, Sarah emerged from the final station and could see in the distance that a crowd had already gathered around the open park that abutted the south edge of the Renault plant. In the distance she could hear the noise of the crowd and the high pitched sound of a speaker's voice coming over an amplifier system.

As she neared the assembly, she could hear the speaker more clearly and could see that the crowd that had gathered already was quite large. She estimated that at least five hundred people were there, even before the day shift had ended.

She knew the speaker only by name, as he had originally come from Lille and only recently had become more active in socialist circles in Paris. At that time, a cheer arose as the crowd recognized the arrival of several key speakers on the dais, including Aristide Briand, who, after a short but passionate speech, introduced Jean Jaurès to the assembly.

She had heard Jean Jaurès speak on many occasions in the past, but it had been some time since she had been able to see him speak in person. He seemed larger this time, perhaps due to the significance of the meeting. Already he was perspiring in the afternoon heat and had removed his jacket and cap, speaking only in his white linen shirt with the sleeves rolled up. It seemed to her that he had aged, even from her last visit with him several months ago, and he certainly was much older than the man that she remembered having first seen and heard when she was a young student.

By the time he began to speak, the crowd had grown considerably, with the arrival of many of the workers from the day shift of the Renault plant. As was his custom, Jaurès started speaking in a slow and almost subdued manner.

"Workers of Paris and those of you who share their

concerns, it is my great pleasure to be able to speak to you of my own feelings about the present crisis involving Germany. You no doubt have heard much discussion about the German actions in North Africa and may have drawn some conclusions for yourselves. As for me, I would have no qualms in ceding all of Morocco to the Germans if it would spare a larger and more lethal conflict. To that end, those that would lose in such a solution are not the workers that are here today and for whom we have the greatest concern. No, it will be the imperialists who use the power of the state and the military to acquire the land and labor of those far from our shores for their profit, with little benefit flowing back to the citizenry of France and even less to the working classes.

"The riches of this plunder are intoxicating for those that benefit. A closer look shows a more unsettling reality. For all the splendor acquired by the few, there are countless native working men and their families who suffer unimaginable indignities and hardship. They labor so that the wealth of their lands can be mined and their soil exhausted to provide a handful of investors and well-connected insiders with unimaginable profit. Many of your ancestors suffered similar exploitation by the privileged classes in centuries past. Even that may pale in comparison to the stories that have emerged from the Belgian Congo and Dutch Indonesia in recent years.

"You say that is disgraceful and sympathize with these poor people, but realistically, you ask what can we do? I say that these actions are nothing more than a symptom of a much larger condition of imperialism, which views the lives of others less privileged or weaker than their own as a basis for exploitation. The same mentality that allows the imperialist to enslave and abuse Africans and others allows for the exploitation of the worker and his family in our modern industrialized Europe.

"I have heard it said that by opposing war with Germany, I am being a traitor to my country. Let me say that if the time comes that the republic is threatened by the invasion of a German army or any other, I will be one of the first to take up arms in her defense. The situation that we presently face is different, however, in that it is not the German worker or indeed the vast majority of peaceful German people who are threatening France but a small cadre of German militarists and industrialists. It is this group that has usurped this process for reasons that will ensure their grasp on power and increase their wealth and influence.

"You men working for Renault know well what modern industrial production can accomplish. Make no mistake; if war comes to the continent, it will be on a scale unimagined in times past. It will utilize all the modern production capacity of the nations involved, resulting in weapons so numerous and awful in their lethality that the destruction and death will be horrific.

"Despite this, some will benefit from such a war. The generals who oversee this great tragedy will grow in power and influence, with the possibility of gaining glory and immortal fame if fortune smiles upon them. For the industrialists such as Renault and his many colleagues, both here and in the enemy camp, huge profits will flow their way from the enormous production that will be required to fuel the incessant demands of warfare on this scale. For the winning rulers, it goes without saying that they will stand to gain wealth and much more from their conquered foe.

"Such prizes are too great a temptation for many to ignore. And you, the workers, who make these factories function with the skill of your labor, how will you benefit from all of this? If you are too old or too infirm to fight, then you will no doubt have more work than you want or can reasonably do. Unfortunately, such demands will destroy the balance of a normal economy, making many goods scarce and prices inflated. To combat this, rationing and price controls will be imposed so that your increased work will not be compensated by increased purchasing opportunities or real wealth.

"For the rest of you who are of an age to fight, your fate will be vastly different. The old days when wars were fought by professional armies are no more. A modern war will require all able-bodied men. You may be assured that the generals on both sides have planned for armies far larger than they have enlisted at present. If the awful day comes when we are forced once more to fight, then the lot of you and all of those like you in the factories, shops, and farms of France will be the same. You will be enlisted and sent to animate the plans of the generals and admirals, but unlike them and their staffs, who will be sheltered far from the storm of battle, you will face its terrible reality."

Sarah noted that as he spoke, Jaurès became more animated, even though his tone had grown more somber. The large crowd became quieter and more attentive to a message that seemed directed to them.

"So who are these enemies in Germany that we are constantly reminded of?" Jaurès continued. "I know many Germans well and can speak to you frankly and honestly about them. Many I know have been leaders in the socialist movement, pioneering thinking and actions that have led to major improvements in the quality of the lives and the influence of workers throughout Germany. These men and women are not our enemies. Their concern is not the enrichment of the favored or the glory of the army but the welfare of their own class. Like me, they view with alarm and distrust a kaiser who seeks to profit by gambling the welfare of his citizens for the sake of his own misguided view of his country's destiny.

"I know the working men and women throughout Germany as well. If they spoke French and were living in Lille or Nancy or any other town in France, their lives, with all their hopes and stresses, would be indistinguishable from your own. They worship the same God and have wives and children and hopes and fears that are virtually the same as yours. What good can come from their sacrificing their lives—or you yours—attacking workers whose only difference is the random chance of the location of their birth?

"No, I tell you the real enemy is the people who agitate for conflict, telling us that we must defend our pride or reassert our rightful place of authority and retrieve our lost lands and honor. Look closely at such advocates, and you will see few who are in harm's way. You will see few who are forced to leave the comfort of their homes and family in order to implement their grandiose plans. You will see those, however, who profit enormously in terms of wealth and influence by the destruction and violence that will come from such actions.

"If you are one who feels compelled by passion to take up arms and kill your like kind in Germany for such empty causes, then I am not speaking to you. If, however, you see the greater nobility in peace and protecting and expanding our rights as honest workers and farmers, then my cause is yours, and my message is directed to you.

"Many have asked me and my many friends, what can be done to stop such a calamity? In France, there are many who are rallying to our banner. Your presence today at this rally is testimony to that spirit. In the next days, my friends and I will meet with many groups like you to sound a message of opposition to a war driven by interests that are destructive to our own lives. More important, we are not alone in this undertaking. With us today is a young associate who has been involved in organizing similar resistance in Germany."

With that, Jaurès identified Sarah in the crowd. "She can attest to the spirit of resistance there to an unjust war among the workers and other groups committed to peace and verify it is as strong as here in France. With her help, a great protest rally has been organized in the coming days in Switzerland, where the workers of Europe and all others committed to a peaceful solution to this crisis will meet. Such an international gathering will defy our critics who say that our actions are designed to weaken France to the benefit of our enemies. Our actions know no national boundary but share a common concern for the safety of the worker and the common man. Our intent is to weaken not France but the militarists in all countries, who are dragging us to the precipice of a calamity such as the world has never known."

Now the crowd had become increasingly enthusiastic and animated. Many came and shook Sarah's hand out of appreciation and support for her efforts.

"It may take more than rallies, however, to stop this madness," Jaurès continued. "These rallies are important, however, in many ways. One of the most important is the reminder they give us of our power if we act collectively to achieve our ends. Make no mistake that that power is considerable and is vital to the plans of those who today are preparing for war. Such a war will depend on the products of your factories and the fruits of our farms. The ranks of the armies will depend for much of their strength on the effort of workers and farmers. Without a full accounting of this potential, they will be critically handicapped and their adventures doomed to failure.

"You men here today control this process like no time in history. You must think of your own interests and that of

your families. Ignore the empty call of the nationalists and
warmongers. Your lives will be squandered for their criminal
ends. Now is a time to seize your historic destiny and stand up
for that which is right and in your best interests.

"In the coming days, you will have the opportunity to be
soldiers in an army of opposition to war. Assert your power and
demand that you are never again taken for granted. Now is the
time to join with us and rally around the Red Flag in defiance
of those who would steal your future."

Sarah had seldom seen Jaurès speak with such power, and
the effect was electric among the vast crowd assembled.

"If you are willing to join our fight, the men who are with me
here today on the podium and representing you in the Socialist
Party will circulate among you to sign you up to volunteer for
future rallies and events. They will also be available to you in
the days ahead to answer any other questions or address other
needs.

"Open your eyes, and you will see the vision of a new day,
when the workers will lead their old masters to a time of greater
peace and progress, a world where your power and numbers
will be fairly represented. I urge you to join with us and make
history, which is our destiny."

With that, he bowed and exited behind the large curtain at
the back of the stage to the roar of a crowd moved not only the
by power of his message but also the hope it engendered.

Sarah herself was not spared from such emotion. The
afternoon had filled her with an optimism that she had seldom
had in Berlin. With such leaders and such a worthy cause, how
could they not be successful?

27

REUNION

Robert at last had reached the point where his field work was essentially finished, and he welcomed a return to Paris to finalize the incorporation of his findings into a report that would meet the needs of General Gallieni. Upon his return, he had found enough time to meet with Marie and her family, who, following her concert, were planning to depart for Lyon and then to the south of France. That meeting was filled with stories from the evening of Marie's triumph, but despite her enthusiasm, Robert sensed her disappointment as she contrasted his absence to the many glowing accounts of Thomas's supportive presence. Their conversation only served to frustrate Robert further, since Marie knew that it had been impossible for him to be at her concert that evening. Nevertheless, he showed great interest in conversing with her father and answering his many questions. It was evident from his responses that he appreciated the necessity of Robert's absence, even if Marie might not.

Robert had subsequently learned from Thomas that he was returning to Strasbourg at the request of the bishop to help counsel the students and others he had previously ministered to in a region that was increasingly divided with the tensions of the Moroccan crisis. Robert knew from his recent experiences that Strasbourg might be a very dangerous place if war broke out. His respect for his cousin only increased, given his willingness to accept such a call. In response to Robert's concern for his safety, Thomas had dismissed any threat to his safety as insignificant to the necessity of his relating Christ's gospel of love and reconciliation.

Robert was pleased to learn that Thomas would not be departing until later in the week, and furthermore a going-away party was scheduled at the Bièvre before his departure. As fortune would have it, the demands of his work had abated enough to allow Robert to find some time to attend.

———

On entering the Bièvre that evening, Robert had no difficulty locating those gathered to wish Thomas off. They had been given their old customary place at the great table in the backroom where Alfred, their old and trusted waiter, was attending to the gathering. Already many people had gathered, some of whom Robert had not seen since his student days. Robert was enthusiastically greeted by the group as a long-lost friend.

Although Robert did not recognize some who were present, most of the faces were familiar to him. Some of his old friends from the Ecole Polytechnique were there, and he quickly gravitated to their area of the room. Jacques Painchaud, who was now serving in the government of Joseph Caillaux was sitting near Hervé DeLarmé, who, as expected, had progressed up the ranks of the diplomatic corps. Opposite them was a group, many of whom Robert did not recognize, except for

Pierre Poinselle who was becoming known for his nationalistic opinions written in *Figaro*, where he was a journalist. Robert assumed that those surrounding Poinselle were fellow writers, given the similarity of their dress and behavior.

As introductions and reunions took place, the group continued to slowly grow, and Alfred expertly delivered to the gathering their requests for wine and hors d'oeuvres. In short order, the excitement of the reunion, coupled with the wine, had transformed the gathering into a mild celebration. For the moment their concerns were eased, and the memories of a time less threatening were fondly rekindled.

Just as Alfred began the serious business of taking down the diners' requests for their meals, to the astonishment of Robert and all the others, Sarah Morozovski entered through the wide door leading to the backroom. Thomas was the first to recognize Sarah, calling her name in a manner that betrayed his excitement in seeing her. Robert was at first so surprised to see her that he could do little more than stare with his mouth slightly agape.

The years since he had last seen her had been kind to her. She had matured in a way that enhanced her sexuality, which she had taken care to accentuate this evening by the tasteful manner in which she was dressed. He had seldom known her to be so careful with her appearance, which she previously seemed to purposefully neglect for matters she deemed more important. Whatever the reason for this transformation, he could not help but approve the result.

Her arrival was a mild sensation, with even old adversaries like Painchaud greeting her warmly. As she passed through the group, Robert was excited to catch her eye and see her broad smile as she made her way toward him. He was excited by her warm presence and the faint note of perfume in her hair as she kissed his cheeks warmly and took a seat at his side.

Before she could catch her breath, Alfred had expertly arrived with a glass of red wine, which no doubt he had selected for her. Robert smiled knowingly, as he had long suspected that Sarah was Alfred's favorite of the group.

"Welcome back, Mademoiselle Sarah. It is so good to see you again. Please enjoy the wine while I attend to the orders of the others. Then I will return to find out what you might like."

"Thank you so much, Alfred. It is so good to see you and everyone again. I will have to think for a moment to decide which of my many favorites to choose tonight."

"The sole is quite excellent," Alfred added.

"I'll try to keep that in mind," said Sarah.

"I hope it's just not the staff of the Bièvre that you are happy to see," Robert said plaintively.

"Of course not, Robert. I am excited to see you all once more—and certainly some more than others." She smiled as she squeezed his arm with enthusiasm.

"How did you find out about this gathering?" he asked.

"I got back in town two days ago. Yesterday was a very busy, productive, and exciting day. On my way home I had a sudden urge to revisit the Bièvre to rekindle my memories and to see who of the old group might possibly be around. I was thrilled to see Yvette again and even more excited when she told me that Thomas was in town and was having this going-away gathering tonight. I knew that I would have a long day today, but there would be no amount of work or obligations that could keep me away from here tonight."

In spite of himself, Robert could not help but confess, "As exciting as it is to see so many of our old friends, it is nothing compared to the surprise in seeing you."

Once again she grasped his arm fondly at his genuine and heartfelt response. For much of the meal that followed, they spent the time frantically trying to catch up on their lives since their last meeting several years before. At times others would break in to reintroduce themselves, but they soon became so caught up in their own conversation that the noise of the large and animated crowd around them seemed to dissolve into the background.

For Robert, seeing Sarah so unexpectedly was at once exciting and yet somewhat disquieting. He had a mild sense of guilt at the intensity of his reaction in light of his relationship with Marie. He had come to believe that his feelings for Marie were truly genuine and not simply a subconscious act to please the expectations of their families. Yet here in an unexpected instant, Sarah's actual presence had rekindled emotions that he had relegated to romantic memories. Whatever his feelings might be for Marie, however, he would not put off Sarah, now that she was so close after these many years apart.

Just when the effect of the wine and their presence next to each other was exerting a powerful effect on Robert and Sarah, the mood of the evening was interrupted by the outbreak of a fierce discussion between Painchaud and Poinselle about the present German crisis, which had been blessedly forgotten until that moment by most everyone present.

"You are close to the president, Painchaud," Poinselle could clearly be heard to demand. "We understand that he is carrying on his own negotiations with the Germans in order to resolve this matter."

"He has had conversations with high officials in their government, which is only appropriate given his position and responsibilities."

"There is a great deal of concern that Caillaux will overstep his authority in this matter," replied Poinselle. "Many fear that he will place the interests of commerce over that of France."

"Commerce is vital to the interests of France," replied Painchaud. "We no longer can prosper relying on our own production supplemented by that of our colonies. Progress demands an ever-increasing commercial interdependency between nations, including France and Germany. They buy our coal and iron ore, and we buy the products that they subsequently produce. If you suggest a war with Germany is in the best interests of France, you are gravely mistaken. Such an event would so disrupt the critical interdependence of European commerce that it would set us back for years, if not generations."

"That is precisely why a war that you speak of cannot last long," replied Poinselle. "None of the nations involved can sustain a long conflict, and so by necessity it must be brief. Many, including me, fear that Caillaux, in his desire to preserve his commercial interests, will make significant concessions to the German militarists in the hope that this will sustain a peace necessary to maintain his business profits."

By now the entire group had been drawn into the conversation. Thomas abandoned his role as the celebrant of the gathering to take part in the discussion, hoping to mitigate the increasing tension that it was causing.

"Tell me, Hervé, how are things going at the Foreign Office?" he asked, directing his question to the only guest who was involved in those discussions.

"Of course I cannot disclose specifics, but I can tell you of the general trends in the discussions. Whatever prompted the German landing on Moroccan soil, it is clear that the reaction from the major European countries, particularly Britain, was not what they had expected or hoped for. I believe that the greatest surprise came in the strength of the British protest and their clear alignment with France. It gave them enough concern that in the weeks immediately following, there were many initiatives from Berlin seeking a negotiated way out of the dilemma.

"Unfortunately, the dynamic began to change at this first sign of German vacillation, with some in France and Britain seeing an opportunity to impose on the Germans a humiliation that might serve to lessen future adventures of this sort. This has proven ill advised, in my view, as it has strengthened the hands of the German military, and it is now unclear whether they or the accommodators control the process."

"What do you think will happen?" asked Thomas.

"As of yet there are too many unknowns for me to be certain about anything. This much I know. This kaiser is impetuous and far less self-assured than is good for a man who has so much power at his disposal. I am afraid we are in for some dangerous days ahead."

"It is a calculus that you seem to concede solely to the Germans," continued Poinselle. "Why shouldn't we make the same calculation ourselves?"

"Of course we have and will continue to assess our position, as events dictate," added Hervé.

"Ultimately," continued Poinselle, "we have to decide at what point we will not defer to German demands. What good is this economic prosperity that you speak of, Painchaud, if we become a vassal of the Germans? Since our humiliation during the Prussian War, we have adopted a policy of survival in which, by necessity, we have been servile to German power. We have to decide if we are willing to continue with such a policy or stand up for our own rights and autonomy."

"So you would be willing to go to war at this time?" asked Painchaud.

"I believe that we are now more capable of fighting the Germans than at any time in our recent history, and we have allies on whom we can rely to aid our cause. We must be willing to accept their challenges, or we will lose any future credibility and, with it, our prestige and the hope of regaining our lost lands."

"So to regain the myth of our prestige and some lands in the east that have not always been French, you would condone pushing the Germans to war?" asked Thomas.

"It is far more than that, Thomas. That prestige rests on the strength of our beliefs and historic traditions. I believe that it is essential that we in France be willing to accept the risks necessary to ensure the autonomy of our people and protect our culture from usurpation by Germany or any other country."

Sarah could no longer refrain from the discussion. "What you may believe most vital to France may not be the same for a miner in Lens or a factory worker in Paris. What do they care if some landholder or factory owner is forced to obey new rules from outsiders when they have never been justly treated under the present system? For the housewife who worries at the inequities of her life and has no franchise to vote, what does she care if her life is controlled from here or in Berlin? Yet if we are forced to fight against the Germans for our sacred honor, these will be the people who will bear most of the costs and will suffer the most sorrow—and for what? I can assure you that there are far fewer willing to spill their blood in such a conflict than you may think."

"If the day comes that the small farmer no longer fights for the land of his ancestors or the worker won't protect the city where he lives and works, then France, as a country, has no reason to exist and will become irrelevant," Poinselle replied. "I have seen how many respond to the sight of the tricolor and the sound of 'The Marseillaise,' and I strongly believe despite what you might say or think, Sarah, that we are not at that point yet."

"I have heard these arguments here and in Strasbourg for some time now," Thomas replied. "They are not arguments that are easily resolved because they are based on tradition and emotion.

"I know many whose passion for France has nurtured a deep and long-smoldering hatred for the Germans due to humiliation of the Prussian War." Thomas continued with increased intensity. "I also know many Germans who feel that those events confirm their rightful place of dominance in the affairs of Europe. At one extreme, some see war as a means to adjudicate these differences, while most understand and fear its consequences. Most of the people I believe to be earnest and sincere in their beliefs. The honest German burgher of the Rhineland, who sees the debauchery and decadence that characterizes parts of Parisian life, cannot help but suspect the moral fiber and strength of France. The Frenchman who sees the humorless automatons that comprise much of German society senses a country more concerned with conforming to an expected norm than recognizing the worth of nonconformity and creativity.

"How can it be that well-meaning people on both sides can feel vindicated by opinions that are often built on prejudice and half truths? It is an old curse that makes us think we are somehow different and superior to others. We pay little heed to history, instead believing, by virtue of our own unique talents and reason, that we are wiser and above repeating folly. Such thinking can bring disaster. When the serpent tempted Eve, he was subtle and gave her only a taste of the tree imparting to mankind only an incomplete knowledge of good and evil. We have reached this crisis because we, as individuals and our collective nations, too often fail to understand that our insight lacks wisdom. In comparison to God, even the best among us are hopeless.

"Until we recognize the primacy of God and sublimate ourselves to his purposes, the great wisdom that comes from his infinite grace will elude us. It is not in our power to know what is best in this present crisis or any other of great significance without it. If our leaders proceed on their own, deluded by their own competence, then we all will lose a powerful check against our worst actions, bringing us ever closer to the threat of a new descent into barbarism that has plagued humankind far too often."

Thomas's words sounded a powerful coda to all the previous arguments, for a moment bringing a hush to the gathering. Then, slowly, they regained their voices and resumed the celebration, although perhaps chastened by the realization of their own frailties. Each also realized how much they would miss Thomas's presence in the coming days.

28

LYDIA AND KARL

Shortly after Thomas spoke, the group began to break up, with the various members paying their final wishes to him before parting. Robert was unwilling to leave, however, as long as Sarah stayed. To his relief, she seemed in no hurry to leave and seemed more eager than even earlier in the evening to continue their conversation. As the crowd thinned, Thomas wound his way at last in their direction.

"I'm afraid I dampened the spirit of the night," he said. "As Poinselle kept going, I could not help myself from speaking out."

"I was equally guilty, Thomas. If anyone is responsible, it was me and that moron Poinselle. For a moment, at least you seemed to get through his thick skull, which is no small achievement. I wonder if what you said will register with him tomorrow?"

"Well, we can only hope. What about you, Cousin? You seem awfully quiet."

"You know me, Thomas. I'm an engineer. I make few comments on those things that I cannot readily reduce to a calculation or equation. I live in a world of probabilities. We build a bridge to withstand the limits of its probable maximum stress. I can speak to that. If this crisis could be reduced to a mere calculation of probability, I would be far more comfortable than with the subtle notions you speak of or the wild speculation of some of the others."

"An honest man you are, Robert, which unfortunately seems increasingly rare these days. Sarah, I wanted to tell you how much I enjoyed seeing you once more. It seems like forever since we last met. If you will both excuse me, I must get home and finish my packing, as my train leaves at seven tomorrow morning. Would you care to accompany me, Cousin?"

"I am afraid I must finish some work even tonight, as I promised to have a report available to the general staff by the morning. I will try to see you off before you leave."

As Thomas left, Robert looked at Sarah, hesitating to leave without ending their reunion in a meaningful way. As he stumbled for the words he wanted to say, she spared him by speaking first.

"Robert, I must leave for Switzerland in two days, which makes my time here in Paris even more valuable. When I heard of this gathering tonight, I hoped to see you even more than Thomas. It has been a long time since we last met, and much has happened in that time. I have caught myself, from time to time, wondering what you might be doing. What little time we had together tonight only made me more interested to see you again before I leave."

"Sarah, it was one of the best surprises that I have had in some time to see you come through the door tonight. It is strange how the mind works, but I have often thought of you as well, sometimes in the most unlikely places."

"What do you mean?" she asked.

"I have thought of you, of course, whenever I pass one of our old haunts, but my memories of you have often been the strongest in places far from Paris. One night that I still remember—we were on maneuvers in Madagascar, and I could picture you as if you were there. I swear I could even smell the light scent of the perfume you used to wear."

Sarah smiled at his recollection. "I remember that perfume. How funny; it was called Tropical Night. I also remember that I paid a lot for it at the time, but now I see that I got my money's worth. The Bièvre is far less exotic than your own tropical nights, but seeing you here has brought back good memories for me too. I'm wondering if you would consider what may seem like an unusual request."

"I would be happy to try."

"I was hoping that you would not think it too forward of me to ask you to dinner tomorrow night, if nothing else but for old times' sake," she said with a note of hesitancy in her voice.

"This German business makes my life uncertain from hour to hour. Were it not for that, I would jump at the opportunity, but I'm in no position right now to guarantee that I can keep an appointment, even one as appealing as yours."

"I understand, Robert."

"I don't know if you do. I was not trying to use my job as an excuse. Unless circumstances make it virtually impossible, I will try everything that I can to free up time for dinner together."

"Robert, please excuse my insecurity, but I hope you mean what you say and are not just trying to soothe the feelings of an old friend."

"Sarah, I had hoped that you would remember me well enough to realize that though I have many failings, dishonesty, especially with those for whom I care, is not one of them. Unless

I am forced to do otherwise, you can expect a most willing and excited dinner companion for tomorrow night."

"Well, if that is the case," she added quickly, scrawling an address on a notepad she had in her purse, "I will be at this address after seven o'clock tomorrow evening."

Robert looked at the address that she had written and seemed perplexed. "I was expecting that you would be at your home."

"I will be visiting one of my dearest and oldest friends tomorrow. As my governess, she has been a true mother to me for most of my life. She and her husband have been a great source of support and inspiration for me during all of these years."

"I would very much like to meet them, then," Robert said.

"I had hoped that you would. I know that you have work to do, so I don't want to hold you up anymore. Now that I have a hope of seeing you once more before I leave, I can see you off tonight without any regrets." She then drew him near to her and gave him a passionate hug and a loving buss on both cheeks before they departed, each befuddled but thrilled by the unexpected turn of events.

———

Fortunately for both Robert and Sarah, the events of the following day proved uneventful, making it possible for them to keep their rendezvous. As the morning wore on, both seemed to realize their good fortune, which only served to increase their anticipation for the evening ahead.

Sarah had spent the morning at the office of *l'Humanité*, preparing for the events of the coming rally. In the afternoon she returned home, where, after a brief lunch with her mother, she left to visit with Lydia and Karl.

Lydia's home and surroundings had changed greatly during those years, reflecting the success of Karl's many business ventures and also her own status as one of the most respected women of the quarter. With their increasing affluence, Lydia had been able to retire from her duties as tutor and guardian when Sarah left home during the latter years of her schooling. She had used her time to pursue other worthwhile ends, using the skills that had so endeared her to Sarah to provide counsel and comfort to the many young women and mothers in the neighborhood where she lived.

Upon her arrival, Lydia greeted Sarah with a warmth that conveyed the pride and love she had for this young woman that she had done so much to nurture through the years.

"You certainly look well, Lydia, and I am impressed with some of the changes you have made since I was here last."

"We have been so fortunate in recent months that I am almost embarrassed by it. It is hard for me to imagine that the Karl I knew when we were first married has now become so successful. I knew that he was intelligent and had a keen nose for business, but I never dreamed that it would come to this. Fortunately, neither of us has any great desire to move from here simply to buy some new place to show off our success. The real blessing is that neither of us has changed much in our needs. We have more than enough to be satisfied, so that we now have the luxury of using the money to help people and causes that we care about. You are well dressed for a visit to our quarter," Lydia noted.

"I am meeting an old friend for dinner and asked that he stop here to meet me," Sarah replied.

"From the way that you look, I would guess that whoever you are meeting is not one of your usual associates."

"Why do you say that?"

"I would be very surprised if the person you meet is a real socialist. He would not appreciate such fashion."

"You are right, I will admit. If my socialist friends saw me with my companion tonight, they might have doubts about my sanity."

"Now I am intrigued. Who is this mysterious person?"

"He is someone that I have spoken to you about. We met when I was still at the law college."

"A nice respectable Jewish lawyer, then; your mother will be proud."

"Far from it, Lydia, and he likely would cause my mother something other than pride."

"Goodness, can you tell me who he is?"

"Since he is coming here to pick me up, you will find out soon enough, but his name is Robert d'Avillard. He is the cousin of Thomas, whom you have met, and was a part of the group that I often had dinner with."

"Thomas—is he the likeable young man who is now a priest?"

"That would be the one."

"Oh my, you are seeing a young man from the old order. I doubt if he has ever been in a humble workers quarter like ours. You may not see him at all tonight, as he may get lost trying to find you."

"I am confident that he will not get lost, Lydia. He is a man of immense practicality. He is a very skilled engineer."

"Does he have his own firm, or does he work for someone else?"

"He once worked closely with Professor de Rochelle, but

in the last years, while I have been gone, he has been in the military and is now stationed here in Paris."

"I have known so much about your work that I was going to urge you to be more like a normal young person and try to find a bit more time for yourself in your life. I see you are ahead of me on that, which doesn't surprise me, but if you and this Robert are serious about each other, it will give your mother a heart attack."

"What makes you think that we are serious? He is just an old friend," Sarah interjected.

"Child, give me some credit. I have watched you grow up for many years, and I can read your thoughts by your mannerisms and what you say as plainly as I can read a book. If you did not care for this young officer, I cannot imagine your saying anything remotely civil about him. Instead, I see that you voice not the slightest protest at his present position and are far more excited than you ever are when visiting your old governess. So I must conclude this must be serious with this Robert."

"I don't know anything for sure, Lydia. That is why I asked him to come by here tonight. I wanted you to meet him so that I could get your opinion. You know that there is no one that I trust more."

"Sarah, even Solomon would have difficulty in counseling you in such matters. It is difficult to encourage a relationship between two people of such different backgrounds, beliefs, and occupations. I know you, Sarah, very well and know that your life will not be fulfilling if it is too mundane. No one except you can know your true feelings for this man. That can only be determined by that mysterious and often painful process that evolves with the two of you being together. Of course I will be delighted to meet him and even share my opinion of him, for what it is worth. I would say to you, however, that whatever becomes of this affair should be determined by your own hearts. If your feelings are strong, then you should pay little attention to the concerns of others and be willing to defy convention and accept the risk to see things through. That may sound too romantic and impractical, but hope and romance are the greatest blessings that life bestows on young people."

"Lydia, I do love your optimism."

"If it wasn't for optimism, our lives would be far more difficult to deal with, my dear. It can be a very potent antidote to help combat the meanness and mediocrity that often surrounds us. Who knows? If you believe hard enough, you might just find that charming prince who seems so elusive to you. Sarah, knowing you as I do, I am sure God has a plan for you. I certainly can't say what that might be, but I suspect it will be important and challenging."

Sarah gave Lydia a spontaneous hug, and the two women spent what was left of their afternoon in conversation, lifted by the notion of blissful possibilities, only to be interrupted by Karl's return from work. For the next half hour, Sarah was regaled with tales of Karl's new ventures in supplying parts for the ever-enlarging manufacturing enterprises in the city and, most recently, a partnership in a newly formed taxi company. Karl's excitement gave testimony to his success, and Sarah could not help but admire the spirit of the man to have risked taking on projects far from his initial expertise in trading livestock.

Midway through Karl's description of how taxi cabs were dispatched, Lydia caught sight of a lone man dressed in a military uniform coming in their direction and gave Sarah an appropriate warning. As he neared her building, he stopped, as if to assure himself of his location, and then proceeded to cross the street.

Shortly thereafter, she answered the knock at her door and

was greeted by a tall, well-proportioned officer she could not help but think quite handsome.

"Excuse me, madam, I have been told that Mademoiselle Sarah Morozovski might be at this address."

"You must be Robert. I am her former governess, Lydia. Sarah is here, but you must be content to wait until she finishes her preparations. You know that no self-respecting woman can be expected to be ready at the first sign of her beau."

"You are the Lydia I have heard Sarah mention. It is a pleasure to meet you. From what Sarah has told me, you are one of the wisest women in Paris."

"You would be unwise yourself to believe such claims, although I am flattered by them nevertheless."

"Robert, this is my husband, Karl." Lydia added as her husband, intrigued by the uniqueness of their visitor, appeared at her side.

As the pair shook hands they were interrupted by Sarah's entry from a side hallway.

"Hello, Robert. I hope that I haven't kept you waiting too long?"

In the brief time since Lydia's warning, Sarah had taken pains to ensure that she was properly presentable, relying on the innate sense of style inherent to all Frenchwomen.

Robert could not escape the spell, as Sarah seemed even more striking than she had been on that evening, now several years ago, when they had first dined together.

"Good evening, Sarah. Lydia, Karl, and I were just getting acquainted." With a deeply appreciative smile, he added, "If all the socialist leaders could look like you, your cause would be virtually assured of success."

"Thank you, Robert, for such a compliment, even such a backhanded one."

Lydia grimaced slightly at Sarah's willingness to defy accepted norms, even in the expected rituals of courtship. Hoping to change the topic, Lydia asked, "Robert, would you or Sarah care for an aperitif before you leave?"

"I would like that very much, if that would be agreeable with Sarah. I have had a long day and could use a moment to unwind."

"I would like a kir, Lydia, now that you are offering," Sarah said.

"That would be fine with me also," Robert said.

With drinks in hand, along with a tray of almonds, Lydia felt more at ease in questioning her young male guest.

"Tell me, if you can, Robert, how this crisis has affected your work."

"It goes without saying that it has intensified all of our work and planning, meaning more hours in the bureau and, in my own case, much more time in the field."

"Away from Paris?" asked Lydia.

"I'm afraid so. I have spent much of the last month in the north along the Belgium border, surveying and cataloguing our facilities in the area."

"I thought it was the Germans who are causing the trouble, not Belgium," questioned Karl.

"It is never quite as simple as one would hope for. Our worry is that Germany will choose to invade France, not directly as in the past but an indirect route through Belgium in the case of war."

"Isn't Belgium a neutral country, protected by mutual guarantees of both France and Germany?"

"If a war ever comes, it is likely that all previous political agreements will be subjected to a new, more urgent military expediency rendering such understandings immediately obsolete."

"Karl knows that area well," added Sarah.

Before Karl could reply, Lydia said, "Tell me, Captain, how is a handsome young man like you not married?"

"Lydia, please give Robert the courtesy of his privacy as our guest," Sarah said with obvious embarrassment.

"I am very sorry, Captain, but my old instincts as a governess are hard to suppress."

"I accept your apology," Robert replied with a laugh. "Somehow I would expect nothing less from someone who cares so much for her responsibilities. You can rest assured that I am not married."

"How does the present woman in your life feel about your absence and the risk of your work?"

"Lydia, really!" protested Sarah.

"I have been seeing a young woman over the summer, and she fears that my absence confirms her worst fears of a coming war."

"She sounds like a very reasonable woman," added Lydia.

At that moment, much to Sarah's relief, Robert chose to divert the conversation to Karl, who had just reentered the room after refreshing his drink.

"Your wife says that you know quite a bit about the north of France and Belgium."

"It is true that at one time I spent a great deal of time in those areas, but in recent days I have been confined by my business interests, for the most part, in Paris. Why do you ask?"

"I have just spent a great deal of time in the area on military matters, so I am interested in knowing more about the people there and their views on this German crisis."

"I am a simple peddler and trader, Captain, not a politician, so I see life from a different perspective than the high and mighty who make up the ruling ranks of the army and government. I know these cities and villages from the perspective of those who buy and sell to subsist, rather than to speculate. I no longer have as much time to visit these areas as frequently as in the past, but I have young associates I trust who act as my eyes. From our businesses, we know what the people are buying and what their mood is.

"I have good customers in Belgium and Germany as well as France. A peasant in France is closer in spirit to a peasant in Germany than he is to some haughty government minister. They have little use for a war with their neighbors because they understand instinctively that, for them, there will be little gain and much danger and hardship. If the army is looking for the French peasants to rise up in support of a war of revenge against their German neighbors, I can tell you, from my knowledge of these people, that is not likely to happen."

"Would they oppose such a war?"

"They will do what it takes to survive. That is true for the French and Germans that I know. Almost all the people that I deal with are fearful of the consequences, should the peace break down. What they will do afterward I cannot say. I do know, however, that if their lives are severely disrupted, they will judge those they believe responsible harshly and will look to extract a just payment in return."

"Thank you for the information, Karl. When time permits I would like to talk with you again. It seems to me that you have more practical knowledge than an entire bureau of our best intelligence officers."

"Be mindful of his time, Karl," Lydia interrupted. "I know how you love to talk. These young people have far more important things on their minds tonight than talking to a couple of old folks."

"Under most circumstances I would disagree with you about that, Lydia," replied Robert. "I can easily see why Sarah has such a high opinion of both of you. Tonight, however, I have a dinner reservation that makes it necessary that we leave here shortly. That is no reflection on you or your husband's excellent company but more out of my responsibility to see that your young friend here is well fed tonight."

"Well, off with you two, then, and quit wasting your valuable time with us," commanded Lydia in a tone of mock authority.

After finishing their drinks, Robert helped Sarah into her coat and warmly thanked the Golds for their hospitality.

"Lydia, thank you for the afternoon visit," she said. "I promise to stop by tomorrow before I leave."

"Worry about that tomorrow. You and Robert take care to worry about yourselves tonight."

"I give you my word on that," replied Robert as he led Sarah to the door. "Karl, I was serious when I said I would like to talk with you again in the near future."

"I would consider it an honor," he replied.

With that, the young couple offered their final goodbyes and left with what promised to be an exciting evening still ahead of them.

29

ECSTASY

For several moments after leaving Lydia and Karl, Sarah and Robert scarcely said a word. Instead, they were content to simply walk almost aimlessly, happy to simply be with each other. Their journey began to retrace, almost subconsciously, the paths that they had often followed in the past when they had first discovered their attraction for each other. Slowly, the late pale azure of the western sky began to give way to the darkness of early summer. The pleasant warmth and mild breeze made for the kind of evening that was welcomed by a populace forced to bear the short days and cold nights that often were their lot during much of the year. Such a night, coupled with the remarkable beauty of the city, served as a potent catalyst in forming the spell that is so often cast over young lovers in Paris. A casual observer would no doubt smile in seeing Sarah entwined in Robert's arms, demonstrating all the symptoms of being under such a spell.

He would laugh at her slightest comment, and she in turn would dwell on his reply as if it were a pronouncement from above. For no apparent reason, she would draw him closer to her, and he would acknowledge her by drawing his head down toward her, brushing against her neck to inhale the fragrance of her hair. So it was they would walk, often silently; then sudden bursts of conversation would erupt, carried out with a seeming urgency so as to catch up on so much that they had missed in the years of their separation. Then, as if momentarily exhausted, they would revert to blissful silence, drawing closer to each other again. It was the familiar ballet so common to young lovers in Paris now being danced by such an uncommon pair. At last Robert could resist no longer. Caught up in the spell of Sarah's presence, he drew her through the small gate into a quiet park in the shadow of Notre Dame, whose presence loomed above them only a short distance across the Seine. There, on a stone bench, he pulled her to him and kissed her with a passion that had been pent up during those years of separation.

The spell of the moment was broken by an old woman and her dog leaving from the nearby building, setting out to find relief for his needs. Smelling intently along his path, he suddenly stopped a few meters from Robert and Sarah, lifted his leg, and issued a loud and lengthy spray. What annoyance they might have had by this strange intrusion into their privacy was quickly replaced by laughter in recognition of the absurdity of the moment. Then, with their bliss not in the least diminished, they drew themselves up and once again resumed their walk.

After a brief moment, Robert broke the silence.

"I know this may not sound very romantic, but we should really consider getting something to eat. That kir is starting to wear off, and although I hate to admit it, I'm starting to get hungry."

"I'm open to suggestions," Sarah replied encouragingly.

"Well, I was thinking about this evening all day long, and

it was only natural that I remembered your friendship with my mother's cousin."

Sarah looked perplexed; then quickly changed to a smile of recognition. "Do you mean that pleasant gentleman at Le Perroquet?"

"That would be the one. I remembered how fond you were of him and thought it only fitting that you have a chance to become reacquainted while in town. I sent my orderly to make inquiries earlier today, mentioning that I was not sure when we would arrive but wondered if a table might be available for some time tonight."

"Was there a table available?"

"No doubt if it was only me there would possibly be some difficulty, but when I specifically instructed my orderly to mention the name of Sarah Morozovski, he was told that there would be no trouble in accommodating us, regardless of the time."

Sarah drew a short gasp of excitement and squeezed Robert's arm in anticipation.

"It just so happens that by some odd circumstance, we are not far from there right now, so if you are willing, I suggest we make our way there as quickly as possible."

"Let's hurry, then, Robert, as now that I am away from the pleasant distractions of that little park, I am hungry as well."

Now, walking with more purpose and direction, it was but a short time until they reached the art deco entrance to Le Perroquet. Upon seeing Robert, the maître d' recognized the couple and, as if greeting long absent royalty, quickly whisked them to a small private dining room already laid out with fresh linen and decorated with a stunning centerpiece of freshly cut flowers.

"I hope that this will be satisfactory, sir."

"More than satisfactory. Please tell Monsieur Tréssiet how appreciative I am for his finding a table for us at such late notice and how indebted I am to him for his kindness."

"I am sure Monsieur Tréssiet will be by to see you later, and you can thank him yourself. I suspect that just seeing the two of you here and knowing that you thought especially of our establishment will be pleasure enough for him, however. Now, if you will excuse me, please relax, and I will send Henri to take an order for an aperitif."

With that he left the couple alone to marvel at the beauty of their surroundings and their remarkable fortune in being able to share it with each other once again. They soon were sipping exquisite champagne, with accompanying toast points and caviar, which only added to their pleasure.

In no time, they were enveloped in the routine that they once found so remarkable on their first visit years ago. A seemingly choreographed procession of servers appeared as almost by intuition to meet their needs or present a new course, with all the flare and drama of trained showmen. Monsieur Tréssiet appeared, smiling as if he had rediscovered two long-lost dear friends, and seemed to take great pains in making their reunion memorable. In short, all their previous concerns of the recent days were simply lost, replaced by the power of this remarkable present. For some time, they were simply content to take it all in without feeling any need to do anything but revel in each other's presence. Then, after some time, Robert spoke.

"How remarkable this is tonight. It's as if we have never been gone, and all the years since we were here last have simply disappeared. How young and naive we were the first time we were here. It was little wonder that we were so affected by it all."

"Being young and naive, Robert, has nothing to do with what I felt at that time. I hope you don't dismiss those times as simply a juvenile fling, because I know that my feelings were very real and not in any way trivial."

"I am not trying to dismiss them at all, Sarah. What I was trying to say was how little we knew of the world at that time, despite our foolish sense of self-importance and good intentions. Off we went, looking for some great opportunity, while tossing away possibly greater ones under our noses. Sitting here now, I can't help but wonder what might have been."

"I have learned from experience that thinking too much about what might have been is not wise, Robert. At the time, we both did what we thought was best."

"That may be true, but being here tonight makes it impossible for me not to think about it."

Sarah suddenly asked with a note of concern, "Are you unhappy, Robert?"

"Far from it; when I think about my decision back then, I seldom have had any regrets. I have had opportunities and experiences that I would not have had if I had stayed in Paris, and I believe that I have been able to make real contributions in the way I had hoped."

"I heard many of your stories the other night, but even in those exotic tales from Africa I didn't hear any details of your personal life."

"Until recently, before coming back to Paris, I did not have the time or opportunity to have any kind of reasonable personal life."

"What has gone on since then?" she asked persistently.

"I have found that it is difficult for family and friends to let someone my age, who is unattached, escape without repeated attempts to arrange my affairs in a way that they think will fulfill my expectations and make me deliriously happy."

Sarah smiled. "It sounds all too much like a Jewish family to me."

"It seems well-meaning meddling knows no religious bounds. As soon as I was back in Paris, I was introduced to many eligible young women by numerous people looking out for my best interests."

"Well, have they succeeded in finding you a suitable match, or are you trying to persist in leading a life of a highly eligible bachelor."

"A little of both, I'm afraid."

Sarah could not help herself from blurting out, "Robert, I hope that you are not becoming like so many of the men of your class who insist on having things both ways, with a conventional marriage and convenient liaisons on the side. I had never imagined you to be one of them."

"It is not like that at all, Sarah. I actually have become involved with a younger woman. At first I found her a little too conventional and immature, but with time I have come to appreciate many attractive qualities about her. She would, of course, make an ideal match from my family's standpoint, which has made our relationship as important to them as it might be to the two of us."

"So you are engaged, then?" asked Sarah, somewhat hesitantly.

"No, not yet, as there are several matters that need to be resolved before we take that step. I know you might want to know what those might be, but while some of those are straightforward, there is at least one that is more difficult to resolve. You seem to want to know about my personal life, but I have heard nothing of yours. Has your Jewish family that you talk about arranged a marriage for you yet?"

Sarah blushed slightly, as if caught off guard by his

question. "One of the great benefits of being in Berlin is being out of their sight and certainly their influence to arrange such matters. My mother has become far more interested in my affairs now than in all the years of my childhood combined. She would like nothing better, for her own peace of mind, to see me married to someone with good connections and from a wealthy background. I have been able to avoid many of her machinations by simply being in Berlin, although that has not lessened her interest or her matchmaking instincts. Fortunately, my dear father is becoming more unconventional the older he gets. He has often cautioned me about certain suitors, preferring to see me die an old spinster than be ensnared in one of my mother's schemes."

"I think that I would like your father," Robert added.

"I am sure that he would like you too, Robert, although you might give my mother a real start if she knew we were friends."

"Then I would have to avoid her, because I would like to believe that we will be friends for a long time."

"Robert, I would like to believe, regardless of what others may think, that will always be true."

"In Berlin, I can't believe that you don't have someone, even without your mother's efforts."

"My social circle is largely determined by my work. Most socialists that I have known are too caught up in the cause or their own importance to be attractive to me, and most of the others that I associate with are either women or older married men."

"Well, then, it seems that despite all the efforts of others, we have been able to remain free to set our own courses," Robert added. "I have little reason to regret that status, except on rare occasions like tonight."

"I sometimes imagine that I might have a chance to go back

and pick out things that I might do differently, but then I realize our lives would lose their interest and challenge," Sarah added wistfully.

"You have always been a realist, Sarah, which spares you from romantic fantasies."

"I would like to be swept up in such fantasies more than you can imagine, Robert, but one thing that the years have taught me is how much more serious life is than I first imagined. This crisis in Morocco has only complicated matters further, making everything seem even more uncertain and treacherous."

"It seems you needed a trip to Paris and a night on the town even more than I imagined. Your confidence and resolve always attracted me to you. I would be concerned if you lost some of that belief in yourself and your ideals."

"Robert, I think that you have become even more of a romantic than I can remember. It took me a while after we first met to see that side of you, but ultimately I recognized that there were many attractive things hidden behind your quiet manner."

"It may be simple naïveté, Sarah, but I have always been an optimist and romantic. I refuse to change simply because the times might be darker or more challenging."

"If things get even darker, as you say, Robert, don't you see how irrelevant and frivolous such a place as this might be?"

"Why would you think that?"

"Because if, for some reason, we get into a war with Germany, then it will be true. Then all the suffering and sacrifice people will be forced to bear will make an evening like this seem extravagant, if not obscene. Then there will be little place for such beauty and happiness."

"There must always be room for beauty and grand ideas, regardless of the circumstances, Sarah. How else can we hope to endure all the misery that you worry about, let alone to change it for the better? It may be that as we get older, our experience will make us more cynical, but if we lose our decency and optimism, what will we have gained from living?"

"Robert, maybe it is the wine and these beautiful surroundings, but I would desperately like to believe that what you are saying is possible."

"If we are ever to achieve some smidgeon of wisdom and happiness in our lives, it has to be, Sarah. I have always admired your determination and courage, and I can only hope that the future you are so worried about will not weaken what makes you so special."

Sarah drew him closer to her, but for a long moment she remained silent. "All of this seems so impossible, Robert. Here I am, sitting next to a man who is so remarkable in so many ways that it seems as if I am in a dream. Being with you here tonight is causing bittersweet confusion. When I returned to Paris, I hoped that I might be able to see you, Robert, but I never imagined a reunion like this. All that I have done and have been committed to seems far less important than it was merely days ago. Now, I realize that everything that I do will be influenced when I think of you."

With that, Robert was astounded to see tears forming, ruining forever his notion of Sarah's vulnerability.

"Sarah, if I had known how painful this meeting would be …"

"It is not this wonderful meeting, Robert, but some realizations that have come from it that are painful."

"Sarah, when I said that I have always been drawn to your passion, I was being sincere. It is at the core of your being. When I met you again, I was hoping to see evidence of that person I once knew, and I have not been disappointed. I said

SOME DAMN FOOL THING

earlier tonight, when I mentioned the younger woman, that there were things that were still unclear in our relationship, but what I did not say was that one reason for my hesitancy was my memory of you. We cannot undo the years that we have lost to our past, but in seeing you, I am even more aware of how much I have lost being away and how important it is not to lose contact with you again."

"Oh, Robert, how can we do that as things exist now? I must go to Switzerland and then return to Berlin, and you will be assigned to who knows where."

"I'm not saying it will be easy, Sarah, but I intend to do what is necessary to see you once more."

"Hearing you say that, Robert, is all I need to know. Whatever else that might be ahead in the coming days will be easier for me to deal with by remembering this moment."

Having reached such an understanding, Robert and Sarah seemed to visibly relax for the remainder of the evening, content simply to be near to each other. By the time Monsieur Tréssiet greeted them good night, it was clear to both what a remarkable evening it had been.

As they finished their last sips of cognac and settled their bill, Robert, sensing the end of their evening, suggested, "It is later than I expected, so it is time to think about getting you home."

"Robert, being with you tonight has made me realize all that I have lost since we were last here and has given me another idea." Robert seemed perplexed but before he could answer, Sarah suggested, "Instead of taking me home, I would prefer to spend the rest of the night with you."

Robert, caught unaware, stuttered, "Are y-you sure th-that is what you really want, Sarah?"

"Robert, I have never been more certain of anything in

my life. I appreciate your noble gesture to save me from my passions, but my feelings are so strong for you that I don't want to run away from them again."

The look in Robert's eyes confirmed his feelings for her proposal.

"I remember the wise counsel of a remarkable German acquaintance who sacrificed and endured much to be with the man she loved. In the end, they were able to endure many hardships, and their love remains stronger than ever. I am not asking anything more from you, Robert, than the chance to be with you. Neither of us can predict the future and what will become of us. I am in no position to demand a commitment from you, nor do I really expect one. God forbid, but this might be our only chance to be with each other for a very long time. I could not bear the thought of wasting such an opportunity once more."

Robert could resist no longer and drew her to him, and they embraced with an ever rising passion. Hand in hand, they quietly made their exit from the gracious staff at the restaurant, walking with an ever quickening pace to his old quarters in his grandmother's house, where his room was still kept for him, with a convenient side entrance that allowed him to come and go relatively undisturbed. By the time they reached that door, his anticipation was so great that his shaking hands made it difficult to open the lock. Sarah quietly placed her hand on his, steadying his effort, and soon they were both inside.

Alone at last, they came together with a kiss that unlocked the passion of the night and all the years of their separation. Slowly undressing each other in the gray light, the lovers marveled in the sensations of their nakedness for the first time. Sarah's brown hair fell over her pale shoulders, the sight of which was further enhanced by the smell of her soap and perfume. Her large breasts and dark areolae accentuated her nipples drawn tight with desire. As they fell into bed, drawn by the momentum of their embrace, the bright plane of her abdomen outlined in sharp contrast her luxuriant pubic hair and glorious womanhood. Robert's muscular torso narrowed to reveal the full effect that all of this was having on him.

Sarah spoke with a voice restrained by her excitement. "Robert, this is my first time with a man."

Seeing his evident passion, she relaxed even before he caressed her face in a gesture that spoke of his tenderness. As he drew her closer, his presence so close and strong made the pain of that first entry seem bearable in its confirmation of their love. In short order, the pain was transformed by the rhythm of their motion into an ecstasy that neither had previously experienced. In the next hour, they would experience this ecstasy several times until they climaxed one last time, collapsing into each other's arms in exhaustion.

In those moments it mattered not at all that they were from different backgrounds with different beliefs and even less that they were not married or even engaged. All that mattered was the power of this moment that they were sharing together.

They awakened to the first early morning light, both keenly aware the previous hours had changed their relationship forever. Whatever complications might come from the expectations of their families and friends now seemed far less important or insurmountable.

"Sarah, I will not let you slip away again without knowing where you are and what you are doing."

"I will leave you my address in Berlin, Robert, but if there is any question where I might be, then Lydia will know as well as anyone. She keeps close track of me and has a sixth sense of where I might be. That is one reason why I wanted you to meet her. Robert, you should also know that I am a very persistent person when I set my mind to it."

"So am I, Sarah. So am I."

Overcome by the moment, they fell into each other's arms, sharing their passion one last time. Then, slowly and with great reluctance, when they could no longer prolong the inevitable, they embraced one last time before going their separate ways.

BOOK 3
SPRING 1914

30

GLORIOUS SUMMER

The spring of 1914 was proving to be unusually glorious throughout much of Western Europe, with prolonged periods of sunshine interrupted only by occasional rains in amounts just adequate to ensure the farmers a bountiful growing season. The weather seemed to mirror the optimism that was on the rise throughout much of the continent. Two severe crises in the last decade had been confronted, and through a combination of balanced alliances, concerted diplomacy, and continent-wide protests, the threat of war had passed without incident. Now there was once again the sense that the balance and restraint of power that had been essential to ensuring the long peace after Napoleon's defeat was once again in place.

As Thomas made his final preparations for his afternoon departure to Paris, his mood became ever brighter. He had been preparing for this summer sabbatical for several days, but he had been thinking of it for much longer. Paris always seemed to energize him, perhaps with all its happy memories and the fruitful years of study, and he was eager to return, as this would be the first time in three years that he would be able to spend a protracted period of time in the city.

His many years living in Strasbourg had been rewarding in many ways, but there was always a tension, sometimes subliminal and often more overt, that had long detracted from the quality of life in this old and lovely city. Those tensions had been greatly exacerbated at the height of the recent Moroccan crisis. Only in recent months had Thomas and the Bishop of Strasbourg felt that enough progress had been made to allow him to spend the summer in Paris. Thomas valued the time he had spent helping to mediate the conflicts between many Alsatians and their German masters, but it also gave him an appreciation for the opportunity that a summer devoted to his own studies and writings might afford.

Those studies, shaped by his early training in Paris, focused on reconciling the most contemporary findings of science with the chief tenets of Christian theology. Such work, by necessity, required that he become conversant in many aspects of science to burnish his expertise in logic in order to lend validity to his work. He had spent many hours wrestling with the complex concepts of modern physics, with its frame of reference well beyond the comfortable parameters of commonplace experience. He could not help but smile to think of his cousin Robert's approval when, with patience and persistence, he would come to understand the implications of some difficult yet profound new finding. Yet for Thomas the real joy of his work was the confirmation of God's omnipotence and grace that came with this understanding.

It was the process of disciplined reason that fascinated him almost as much as the products of such inquiry. He began to realize during this time however that true wisdom could not be obtained by process alone. Reason, sacrifice, and diligence were not enough to guarantee success even when abetted with money. There was something of the miraculous about it. As such, Thomas began to suspect that a sense of humility and a recognition of God's omnipotence were more important requisites than cerebration, regardless of its efficiency.

He readily conceded that his work in Strasbourg, outside of his studies, had provided him many benefits as well. His knowledge, enriched by his daily personal experience, when coupled with his natural enthusiasm made him a wildly popular instructor with many students of the university. It was not long before he had acquired a substantial following of young devotees attracted by the substance of his teachings and his personal charisma.

The sum of all of this should have been fulfilling, but often, during the short gray days of winter, he found himself gripped by melancholy that he attributed to the strains of living in Strasbourg and trying to mediate the many conflicts that came from the tensions between the students and native Alsatians with their German masters. As his departure to Paris neared, his spirits had risen. When he finally boarded the train for France, with each passing mile, he seemed to regain the spirit of his younger student days. The beauty of the passing fields of wheat and the infinite shades of green unfolding in this lush corner of the world made it easy to dream of a brighter future for the area and its inhabitants and to overlook the history of conflict between covetous rulers of the region that had frequently besmirched these borderlands.

As the train neared the outskirts of Paris, Thomas's anticipation for his arrival increased. He had written to Robert about the date of his return, as well as to his grandmother, who, although she was by now back in Provence, would no doubt make arrangements for him to occupy her residence while he was in Paris. Thomas hoped that Robert would be at the station to greet him, as Robert's presence always seemed to make his return even more special, but he knew that the demands of his cousin's work were unpredictable; he was fully prepared for the possibility of Robert's absence for his arrival.

As he stepped onto the platform amid the busy crowds, he searched in vain for the tall silhouette of his cousin. Instead, he was surprised to see the smiling countenance of Marie, waving frantically to him, half hidden by the milling crowd around her. Her presence seemed a perfect beginning to this visit to Paris.

Thomas had been enchanted by Marie from the time they had first met. Some of this was due to her beauty, but Thomas had sensed there was much more to Marie than her comeliness. Early on, it seemed that he had earned her confidence, which had led Marie to readily share her true feelings and concerns in the months and years that followed. By now, Marie seemed to Thomas essentially without guile, and he had come to recognize her as a most special member of his flock.

When Thomas watched his cousin Robert's interest in Marie grow, he had been amused to hear him describe her as someone different from the other women he had met, reciting a list of attributes that Thomas had long realized. Their relationship, however, had been complicated by the Moroccan crisis, which had necessitated that Robert be out of Paris for protracted periods of time in the ensuing years.

During this time Marie had been fully engaged in mastering the difficult challenges of her musical training. In her first important public concert in Paris, it had been left to Thomas, in the absence of his cousin, to help Marie through the anxieties in the days leading up to her performances.

From that time onward, in the brief times Thomas had been in town or far more often through written communication,

Marie would turn to him as a trusted confidant and mentor. Despite their separation, in these years their relationship had endured and strengthened. Now seeing Marie unexpectedly, Thomas grasped her with a vigorous hug, bussing her on both cheeks.

"Marie, I am thrilled to see you. I was expecting Robert to emerge from the crowd, but instead I am rewarded with your presence. Where is he, by the way? Off on some adventure with the army, I assume?"

"He apparently has been involved in some advanced planning with the English regarding the Belgium border, which is a subject in which he seems to be an expert. It is all hush-hush, apparently, as he is even more closemouthed than usual when talking about it. All he said was that he would be away in England for the next few days. He asked if I would be able to meet you at the station."

"Very mysterious," Thomas said.

"You know Robert. If you did not know his tendency to get caught up in the countless things that occupy his mind at any given moment, you would think him mysterious or the most arrogant man on earth."

"I have known him too long to think of him in any other way than Robert," Thomas said. "I have always attributed his mannerisms to the eccentricity of genius. I dare say that he will be a great hit with the British, as they are a race of eccentrics and will gravitate to one of their own kind instinctively."

"Well, Thomas, you are not so eccentric, and seeing you lifts my spirits."

"This lovely weather certainly helps all of our moods as well. It is a wonderful tonic for all those interminably long, gray winter days."

"I hope that all this sunshine is a harbinger of good fortune as well," added Marie. "Since you were here last, I have made progress on a number of issues, especially with my music, and have taken on some new challenges that I am eager to tell you about."

"I am looking forward to hearing all about it as soon as I can get home, unpack, and possibly take a long nap or get a good night of sleep. My brain is boggy from the stress of packing and rushing to tie up all the loose ends necessary to leave town for the summer. All I can think of is to take off my shoes and put up my feet on one of those large stools in my grandmother's apartment and think of nothing more substantial than what I will order for lunch tomorrow."

"I know how you must feel."

Thomas exposed his face to the south and took a deep breath. "This sunshine is remarkable. I hope you are right, Marie, about its being a harbinger of better times. Even in Strasbourg, things seem to be changing for the better. For the first time since I have been living there, the German authorities seem to be making concessions to the French population. Maybe all the anxiety that we lived through in the Moroccan crisis is behind us."

"Well, judging from things here in Paris there is certainly reason for optimism. It seems to me that the economy has never been better and that the mood of the city has seldom been gayer. The other day I even heard an Englishman, of all people, comment on how lovely Paris looked and how it seemed to reflect his own optimism in the future of French and British relations."

"That is truly a testament to the bounty of the times," Thomas added.

After gathering up his possessions, they were progressing to the line of cabs waiting outside the station when Thomas spied the headlines from the evening paper: "Henriette to Testify; Day in Court Imminent."

"Who is this Henriette to deserve such bold headlines?" asked Thomas.

"You must really be living in a monastery, Thomas. Haven't you heard of the murder of Gaston Calmette, the editor of *Le Figaro*?"

"I did read something about it, but the Germans suppress sensational news, especially from France, if it doesn't meet their needs."

"Henriette is the woman who murdered Calmette. She is no less than the wife of the former prime minister Joseph Caillaux."

"That is the Caillaux of whom Painchaud was so fond. He is some sort of financier, is he not?"

"He is, and that may be why he was attacked in *Le Figaro*. Now, unfortunately, his wife has been caught up in the politics and even worse."

"How so?" Thomas asked.

"There are many in the country who cannot warm to the idea of any reconciliation with Germany. They have always been suspicious of Caillaux, whom they view as far too friendly to Germany, especially German business interests. The Right has often suspected that he values the interest of French commerce, particularly as it applies to his businesses, above the welfare of the country. In short they have accused him of selling out the country to protect his own commercial contacts in Germany."

"In what way?"

"Well, you will recall that during the Agadir crisis three years ago, there were many tense days when it seemed that war might be inevitable. Caillaux was the prime minister at the time, and those who oppose him politically have uncovered some evidence that he was carrying on secret negotiations with the Germans to avoid the outbreak of war."

"If he was responsible for the peaceful settlement," Thomas said, "then he should be commended rather than made out as an enemy. The only thing of merit the Germans got was some fairly useless African marshland, well away from Morocco and the coast."

"That is not what some of his opponents think. They believe that the deal he negotiated demonstrated our weakness and lack of resolve to the Germans once more. Due to these efforts and his long-standing belief that cooperation with Germany is vital to the economic success of France, he has become a symbol of treachery to some. Now, with the election of Poincaré as president, all of their considerable vitriol was turned once more against Caillaux when he was named finance minister."

"So what did the unfortunate Henriette have to do with all of this?"

"Nothing, but she proved an irresistible means by which to undo her husband."

"Now I remember—there is a juicy scandal involved in all of this. That explains those banner headlines."

"Your logic is quite good, as usual, Thomas. She is at the center of one of the most dramatic scandals that our city, well known for scandals, has experienced in some time."

"Please go on," Thomas urged.

"It seems during the years leading up to his becoming prime minister, he was married to another woman. Subsequently, his marriage to her helped his political prospects, as she is a much more sociable and likable figure than he is. Unfortunately for their reputation, he was carrying on a liaison while he was still married to his first wife. The fury of this spurned wife, as you can imagine, was considerable, so when she came into possession of certain intimate letters linking her then-husband to Henriette, she resolved to use them to destroy him politically."

She paused a moment to enter the cab while Thomas deposited his bags with the driver. After they were comfortably seated, she resumed.

"She could not have found a better ally than Gaston Calmette. His hatred for Caillaux was nearly as great as that of the aggrieved wife. Within days after being apprised of the letters and their content, he launched a smear campaign in *Le Figaro* that was to include nearly daily diatribes against the finance minister, as well as biting political cartoons and, of course, published excerpts of the letters. I have not read all the articles, but they have apparently been well orchestrated to underscore Caillaux's political ambition, his alleged treachery in the negotiations with Germany, and slowly and inexorably, the sordid details of his infidelity and relationship with Henriette.

"As the details of her private life became increasingly public, the strain apparently became too much for the present Madame Caillaux. One day, dressed stylishly in a manner befitting her position, she waited patiently at the office of Monsieur Calmette for his return, and then, in the privacy of his office, after a few words, she withdrew a pistol from her fur hand muff and proceeded to shoot him four times."

"I knew that I have missed Paris, but until your story, Marie, I did not realize how much. There is nothing quite as compelling as a good old-fashioned scandal to make public all of human folly and weakness. This is a real dandy. I'll bet the newspapers are in heaven with this."

"Every day the headlines are of nothing else. It is beginning to get tiring and a bit absurd."

"Human frailty of this sort is an old story, dating back well before this unfortunate example. Lust, infidelity, hatred, greed, and so many other failings destroy reputations and lives. Perhaps this beautiful weather has made me too optimistic about the human condition after all. All this may force me to reconsider my opinion."

"Thomas, I hardly expected to hear such cynicism from you."

"I didn't mean to disappoint you, Marie, but this reminded me that we have a long way to go as a society to being a city of God. Let's think of something more worthwhile than this spectacle."

"Before we were diverted by the fate of Madame Caillaux," Marie said, "I was about to report to you the status of my current studies outside the realm of my music. I suspect that you might find that interesting."

Thomas could not but smile at this, recalling how he had urged Marie to broaden her studies early after they had first met. Through the years he had suggested some readings for her in literature, religion, and philosophy. Robert had also been involved in this project, but unfortunately, he had been forced by circumstances to be reassigned out of Paris, returning only the first of this year. Now it seemed that through Marie's urgings, he had reenlisted to help further her studies.

"Since Robert has been back, I have been trying to gain a better understanding of mathematics, which so intrigues him and for which he clearly has a facility. At first it seemed like an imposing task to try to go beyond my knowledge of algebra and geometry that I learned in school. Robert, though, is a surprisingly good teacher in something as complex as this. He has patience and a way of explaining the essential elements in a manner that I can understand. Now he believes that I have reached a point that a better understanding of certain basic concepts of logic would not only help me better understand mathematics but also train my mind to think about other problems as well."

"There is much to what Robert has recommended. I have found using such methods very helpful through the years," Thomas volunteered.

"We have only recently started, but already I can see that it will be challenging."

"It will be challenging, but that's what makes it exciting and rewarding when you master it."

"I have heard Robert refer to Aristotle and his discussions on logic. Out of curiosity and to prove to myself that I can master a difficult challenge, I have been trying to read his writings on logic."

"This is not the stuff of easy reading, especially for someone new to the subject. You are to be applauded for undertaking such a major task, but it might be more enjoyable as an exercise to read instead the English book about the young woman who falls into an underground wonderland."

"You mean *Alice in Wonderland?*" Marie asked quizzically.

"That is it. Lewis Carroll, as I believe he called himself, was really a man named Charles Dodgson, who was not only a writer but a well-known mathematician and logician. In that odd book, there is much logic to peruse, and it might be more amusing at first than reading Aristotle."

As the cab pulled onto Rue de Bac, Thomas smiled in anticipation of his arrival at his grandmother's. "Fortunately we are home," he said as the cab pulled up before her building. "I am far too tired today to think of old Aristotle, or Alice, or any other thing. In the next day or two, I expect I will be thoroughly rejuvenated and will be more than happy to act as your guide in your study of logic and that formidable Greek."

"I was hoping you would say that. Robert says that you are a master of this subject."

"Robert often exaggerates my prowess, but you can be sure that between the two of us, we will make a good effort. Now all I care to think of is a good meal, which I hope will not be long in coming. Would you care to join me?"

After paying the driver, Thomas grabbed his belongings from the cab and, with Marie accompanying him, set out to enjoy a shared meal and conversation that no doubt would be even more enjoyable than the food, no matter how well prepared.

Indeed, for them both, the prospects of a very promising summer seemed bright.

31

REMARKABLE TIMES

Upon returning to her office, Sarah seemed in unusually good spirits. Stein even thought he heard her whistling on the sidewalk as she approached.

"You seem in a good mood," he noted in greeting her.

"In what way?" she asked.

"You seem unusually cheerful, and if I didn't know you better, I'd think for an instant that I even caught a glimpse of you smiling as you came through the door."

"I know that is surely something that you would never condone, Stein, so please pardon my indiscretion."

"I would like to be more warm and sunny, Sarah, but somehow the circumstances of the day always seem to get in my way. Given my line of work, it is better to be cynical and irascible. It makes it easier to cope with the inevitable disappointments I uncover when investigating our great leaders."

"Well, do your worst; it will not detract from how I feel this afternoon."

"Are you on some new diet or therapy?" he asked with a sly smile.

"If you must know, I have just been to a wonderful lunch with Frau von Suttner. The afternoon weather couldn't have been more perfect, and the lunch itself was superb."

"A good meal is always a good tonic for what ails you," Stein said.

"It was much more than the meal or even the glorious day that made the day so pleasant. In the course of our visit, we had the occasion, as we most always do, to reflect on present times, and with little hesitation she volunteered that for the first time in years, it seemed that those in power here in Germany have stepped back from martial threat as a means of increasing German influence."

"Maybe they learned from the humiliation they received— from their attempts to extort a colonial empire in North Africa—that such tactics were not terribly fruitful."

"Baroness von Suttner believes that German economic progress has been so great that it is difficult for all but the most ardent militarists to argue that some military adventure will improve our well-being."

"It is the oldest of truths," Stein said, "that a full belly dulls even the most zealous of revolutionaries. What good is some risky and bloody war somewhere if everyone has enough to eat, a job, and a safe place to sleep?"

"Exactly. In many ways I have to agree with some of my old antagonists in Paris. It now seems that the economic benefit of expanding commerce through mutual cooperation with the French and others makes a war that would upset this balance not only prohibitively expensive but absurd. At lunch we both marveled at the continued expansion of the factories all around Berlin and the employment related to the work there. Much of this has been built on recent discoveries made in modern science and engineering, many of which have come from here at Berlin University.

"The baroness related a story of her meeting with Professor Albert Einstein, who she says is quite charming and very mild-mannered. He fervently shares her pacifist beliefs, which is why they first met. I told her of the time when I went to a lecture by Max Planck at the Kaiser Wilhelm Institute, where I saw Einstein surrounded by a large gathering. I had gone to get some information for a colleague in Paris who was working on a story on some aspects of modern physics. In short order, I was lost by the complexity of the information, but afterward, talking to Professor Planck, I sensed that he and his colleagues were at the center of an explosion of knowledge that would have immense implications for our future. The longer we talked this afternoon, the more optimistic both of us became. It is marvelous that our affluence is such that only a series of extreme events or a very unstable leader could disrupt the interdependence of our countries."

"If both of you are right," Stein replied, "then we are entering a rare time in history when the lamb might be able to lie next to the lion."

"Well, nothing as melodramatic as that, but at least there is hope that we can concentrate on other issues far more important and constructive than some senseless and destructive European war."

"There certainly is tangible evidence to support your theory. In the last several months we have heard virtually nothing from Hahn and his stooges at the Interior Ministry. Either they have become bored with their harassment of us, or they have found other uses for their time. Either way, it argues that the powers that be are less concerned with critics of the policies that may not have a high priority now."

"So you see, Stein, there is a reason why I am in such a good mood this afternoon. You should really try to see things with more optimism; it might be a revelation to you."

"I fear that I am beyond ever achieving such a happy state, Sarah. If all is as you describe it, however, now might be an appropriate time for you to lighten your self-imposed crusade as guardian of the working poor and defender of the peace and try to take time out for yourself."

"And just what do you mean by that?" she asked.

"Given the times as you describe them, it might just be that those struggling with the injustices of modern capitalism can afford to be without your constant oversight long enough for you to acquire a personal life. Before you reject what I have to say out of hand, just listen to me for a moment."

"So what are you suggesting, Stein?" she asked, somewhat impatient with his line of conversation.

"What I am suggesting is that it might be time for you to look out for yourself a little more than you have in the time that I have known you. If you were a man, I would tell you to go out and have an affair; make an attempt to find someone to share your bed with. Since you are not, accepted social conventions prevent me from suggesting such a thing."

"This is quite extraordinary. I could never imagine you, of all people, Stein, to be a matchmaker or counselor in the affairs of the heart, especially with your past history."

"I will readily admit I have had more than my share of bad luck with women. That, however, does not detract from my effort to try to find a kindred spirit to warm my house and lighten my days. It seems at heart I am an incurable romantic. Besides, as you should know well by now, there is no better teacher than failure to help you realize your mistakes and what opportunities they may have cost you."

"The years must have softened you a bit, Stein, and turned you into a philosopher."

"Maybe so, but it has also given me a perspective on how others that I care for can avoid the same mistakes that I have made. I am afraid that someday you may end up too much like me, cynical from lost opportunities and unfulfilled expectations."

"So what is your prescription for avoiding such a fate?"

"Now that you ask, my sources have conveyed to me very interesting accounts of your meetings with someone who, on the surface, is far from the usual crowd of revolutionaries and pacifists with whom you normally associate."

"You and your damn sources. There is not a secret in the world safe from such a combination."

"Aha! So it is true, then, that you are seeing an officer—and an aristocratic officer at that. No wonder you have to sneak off to Switzerland for such an affair."

"It is not what you think, Stein. He is an old friend from my days in Paris who happened to be in Switzerland when I was there, and we arranged a meeting to catch up on each other's affairs."

"On the record, I will accept that, but off the record, my sources have told me too much to make an old skeptic like me believe such a story."

"So what business is it of yours or your precious sources?"

"Only this: you are not only my associate but also someone I consider a dear friend. Friends don't like to see friends live their own lives without the benefit of our counsel because even if it doesn't amount to much, it gives us a small measure of self-worth."

"You have spent the better part of fifteen minutes hinting at what you want to tell me, Stein, so for the sake of us both, get to the point."

"When I heard of your affair, my first reaction was disbelief. I then realized that the person who told me this was completely trustworthy, and therefore I could only conclude that it was true. If it were true, I wondered how such a practical person like you could get involved in such an impossible situation. The answer was obvious to someone as knowledgeable in the human condition as I am. It could only be explained by one compelling reason: you must be in love."

He raised his hand to prevent the protest he sensed that she was about to make. "There is one great benefit that you have achieved by the lifestyle that you have chosen over the last few years. You have broken with all the bourgeois expectations that you and your family may have had for you. You are already viewed as a nonconformist, and so anything that you do that is unusual will be viewed as usual to them. I doubt that the same can be said for him, but that is far less relevant to our discussion."

"Your point is?" she asked in feigned impatience.

"My point is that your past has made it possible for you to escape from many of the conventions of polite society. No one can predict the course of an affair, much less me, but I can tell you by experience that you should not let others dictate the terms of your relationship. Everything and everyone else be damned."

"You sound like another dear friend of mine."

"As I said, what are good friends for if they can't offer unsolicited advice?"

"Stein, if only it were as easy as that."

"Sarah, I have never known you to be frustrated by

difficulties in this job, and so it should be with your personal life. If it were easy, it wouldn't be worth anything."

She reached over and gave him an affectionate kiss on the cheek. "You are a cantankerous, impossible old busybody, but I cannot help but love you dearly. I am truly grateful for your advice and will hold it dear if I get a chance to apply it in the future. Now I suppose we need to get back to work. What is on the schedule for tomorrow morning that needs doing?"

"Only a meeting of the Socialist Council of Berlin, where you will no doubt be asked to mediate the irresolvable differences for the hundredth time between the accommodators and the revolutionaries."

"Well, that promises to be a fruitful day."

"Less fruitful, I hope, than your relationship with that mysterious young officer."

"I certainly hope so as well," she said as she gathered up a stack of communications and turned toward her office.

———

The following afternoon the meeting Sarah was attending quickly reached a point where each consideration raised seemed impossible to resolve with any form of consensus. At that point, the differences between the participants were so great as to produce a discussion where the opposite sides were carrying on virtually parallel conversations. Out of boredom, she began to think back to her conversation with Stein from the previous afternoon.

How he knew of her affair with Robert was less of a surprise than the timing and manner in which he had related it to her. Stein was an impatient and impetuous person, traits that had served him well in some aspects of his life and had failed him miserably in others. One side of Sarah was sympathetic to the notion he'd raised to defy all convention and expectations in her relationship with Robert. Another side, however, shaped by her years of struggle to achieve a position of relevance, urged a more measured and conventional course. She realized the irony of the similarity of her dilemma to the battle for the soul of socialism between the more radical and moderate factions.

One thing was certain, however: she desperately wanted to continue seeing Robert, regardless of the conflicts or consequences. For the last two years, when time and circumstances allowed, they had continued to meet, usually in locations such as Switzerland, conveniently far from the prying eyes of their family and friends in Paris. These meetings had been bittersweet, with their attraction for each other unsettled by the realities and difficulties that their relationship presented. At times they had quarreled, either by letter or in their brief times together, in great part due to the frustrations of their unconventional relationship. These disagreements quickly disappeared, dissipated by their feelings for each other.

As her mind drifted back to the present meeting, she realized many aspects of her life involved people in this room and the ideas they stood for. Since her earliest days in Berlin, much of her time had been spent in cultivating relationships with various factions that represented the workers' interests in the city and the country as a whole. At first viewed with suspicion as an outsider and an unknown, she had gained credibility and the trust that came with it through many actions that demonstrated her commitment to the cause they all believed in. This trust was not easily earned, given the broad differences among the German socialists, and had required much diplomacy to maintain through the years.

Among these socialists at one extreme were those who

sought change by an involvement in the existing structures of the country, including participating in the popularly elected Reichstag. At the opposite end of the spectrum were the most radical proponents who favored the overthrow of capitalist society in favor of a community run by the workers. To them, any participation in the structures of the existing society only served to perpetuate an evil that needed to be abolished.

Sarah had tried to be impartial in her dealings with all of these factions. Though she had been criticized at times by both sides for partiality, she was never accused of being arbitrary or unfair. Consequently, she had gained a role as an arbitrator in the many attempts that were made to mediate the differences between the various groups. Today's meeting was one of many that she had participated in with the influential Berlin Workers Council. Now, as one seemingly petty quarrel was punctuated by the outbreak of another, it was becoming harder to believe that any good would come of such efforts.

Perhaps Stein was right. If things had shown so much improvement, why did she need to tie herself up in such endless and nonproductive meetings? Today's gathering only seemed to reinforce her increasing disenchantment with the whole process, drawing her back once more to her last meeting with Robert. The allure of recklessly abandoning all of this to be with him tempted her more with each passing minute.

She had often felt the pull of this impulse in the past, but then thoughts of the many possible complications would snap her from her reverie.

In their all-too-brief liaisons, Sarah had come to know more about Robert than his aptitude for science and the enjoyment of its application. He was a man who held high regard for his duty and the responsibilities that entailed, as well as his family and their traditions and lifestyle. With such a man, how could such an untraditional relationship have any chance of succeeding?

It was the realization of this likely futility that haunted Sarah when she was alone in Berlin. It was made all the more painful after a day's visit with Bertha von Suttner and her seemingly idyllic relationship with her beloved husband. Then, Sarah would remember some small moment with him so lovely and exciting, and she would realize how much she must love him to persist in such a hopeless pursuit. Around and around her mind would go, tempted at times to risk all that she now had for a relationship that was likely doomed to fail, not from lack of love or passion but from a society unwilling or unable to condone such a behavior.

In their first liaison in Switzerland, they had both had insisted on an honest dialogue about their feelings. On one of those early meetings, Sarah had learned more about the other woman she had heard Robert mention in the past. Sarah had never met Marie, but she could easily picture her, believing that she was likely everything that she, Sarah, was not. She could imagine her natural beauty, enhanced by the instinctual and cultivated manners of her class. Such attributes no doubt would make it easy to be accepted in the circles that Robert was accustomed to. Yet as Robert reluctantly described Marie, struggling to master her art and at the same time trying to meet the expectations of her family, Sarah also realized instinctively that there must be more to her imagined rival than beauty and convenience. When she would think of Marie afterward, the image that Sarah conjured up in her mind would only depress her further.

Despite these thoughts, Sarah would later take comfort in the fact that Robert had earnestly kept in touch with her. Despite much inconvenience and possibly some risk to his status, he had made several trips to be with her for those short but unforgettable meetings, where her apprehensions disappeared in his presence. The passion of those meetings and her sense of Robert's sincerity made her willing to endure the painful ambiguity of their relationship until a time came when they could be together or choose to end it. Despite Stein's admonitions, until now she had neither the time nor courage to force this day by some more assertive action.

Her thoughts were interrupted by someone's making a motion and actions that served to bring the meeting to a close. Little protest was made when it was announced that the group would not meet again until the routine date scheduled for six weeks.

———

As Sarah was leaving, she fell into step with Rosa Luxembourg, who nodded to her and said, "You looked disinterested in the meeting today, Sarah."

"I didn't know it was that obvious, but it gets rather boring when we seem to go over the same ground each time with little evident progress or agreement."

"It is a difficult time to be a revolutionary," Rosa countered. "The masters have fed the workers a few crumbs, and they have lost their appetite for change, at least for the time being."

"It may take a while to change that appetite," Sarah suggested.

"You overestimate the present masters and the corruptness of their world. There will be a day when they overreach and bring disaster down on their heads. We who believe in the justice of a world where the workers control their own destinies must bide our time until that happens."

"And what then?" asked Sarah.

"Then we must be ready to seize power from the corrupt and illegitimate hands of those in power. These meetings are nonproductive, as you would say, because there are so many irreconcilable differences from those who want a revolutionary realignment of the means of production with the producers and those who think we can get there by those in power willingly ceding their prerogatives."

"If that time does come, seizing power will be difficult and dangerous," added Sarah.

"No doubt it will be; those now in control are addicted to their property and the wealth and power it gives them. To take this from them will not be easy. It can only happen when, through their greed and stupidity, they create such a state of waste and injustice that the masses will regain their appetite for change and use whatever means necessary to achieve their rightful justice. When that day comes, I will come looking for you, Sarah, and your support."

Sarah could only smile and nod affirmatively, hoping to postpone a commitment to such a radical course.

They had reached the street and exchanged one last glance before separating to go their own ways.

For Sarah, the images provoked by Rosa Luxembourg's revolution were unsettling, all the more so for the risk such a solution would pose to her relationship with Robert. She now began to better understand that her feelings for Robert had become such that they had the power to trump the ideals that she had invested so many years in supporting. Perhaps Stein was right, she conceded to herself, smiling as she reconsidered once more the beguiling aspects of his advice.

32

A NEW CHALLENGE

As Robert stared at the ceiling, he realized how unlikely a peaceful sleep would be in light of the many conflicting thoughts racing through his mind. This had been the last night of a combined conference in England between French and British planners, designed to discuss planning of joint continental actions in light of a possible German invasion of Belgium or France. Robert had been chosen by General Foch, who had headed the French contingent as a representative due to his knowledge of the terrain of the territory at risk and of its existing fortifications. By any objective measurement, Robert believed the conference had been a great success, and he was further gratified by the prominent role that he had played in the French delegation.

Just hours before, at the final reception and dinner, Foch had drawn Robert aside to thank him for his participation and to offer him a promotion and a new job as chief engineering officer of the XX Corps, of which Foch was assuming command. This corps would be a vital element of the French Second Army, located in Lorraine, should hostilities with Germany break out in the future. For any rising officer, such an offer would normally be regarded with elation, not only as a concrete confirmation of his present worth but also as an optimistic indication for his future. Unfortunately for Robert, it was becoming ever clearer to him that he was not the usual aspiring officer.

This realization had less to do with his army career than it did with the complicated status of his personal life. Indeed, he had seldom had any significant regrets with his military career, enjoying increasing opportunities to apply his engineering and design skills in large worthwhile projects that clearly enhanced the defense capability of the country. His talents had been recognized not only with promotion but—more important— with increasing responsibilities beyond his years and rank. For Robert, the army was the least of his concerns.

Robert had realized the cause for his present dilemma long ago but had seemed powerless to address it. He appreciated the irony for someone who placed a high premium on objective reason and considered action to be caught up in a web of emotion, but caught up he was. Foch's offer, instead of a confirmation of his worth, now seemed to Robert only another dilemma in the complex web that had become his personal life.

He had not intended it to be that way, nor did he have any previous predilection for deceit and duplicity. He had been brought up to value structure, hard work, and integrity and still held these notions dear. The problem was how to reconcile those inner beliefs with an inability to resolve a substantial conflict that had only grown in recent months, brought on by his relationship with two remarkable women.

When he had returned to France from a colonial posting more than two years ago, his life was blessedly free of such worries. Nature abhors the freedom of a highly eligible young man, especially in Paris, and shortly after resettling in the French capital, Robert was introduced to a number of the city's most desirable potential matches by well-meaning family members and friends. Of that number, the one who had most attracted his attention was Marie Bonneau. By the most exacting standards, she possessed beauty, talent, and breeding. One could hardly imagine a better match for a young aspiring officer of the old order.

Yet from those early days, there seemed to Robert something almost too perfect about Marie, and that notion caused him at first to view her with some degree of skepticism. Such an attitude made it easy for him to appreciate the differences not only in their ages but more importantly in her worldly experiences. The world that she viewed was shaped by her sheltered upbringing and by the upper class mores of a prominent banking family from Lyon. She had been greatly free of the harsher realities evident not only in Paris but certainly in North Africa, where Robert had spent nearly a year filled with tumult and danger.

Despite his misgivings, however, Robert had come to appreciate, with the pointed guidance of his cousin Thomas, Marie's talents, enhanced by her drive to succeed in Paris on her own merits and beliefs. Robert had watched Marie's maturation unfold quickly in Paris, enhanced by the vitality of the city and her own desire to master the demands of her art. Within a short time, she had experienced increasing confirmation of that mastery, including a well-received recital at Saint Sulpice nearly two years ago.

The flowering of their relationship had been complicated by two significant events. The first was the intensification of the Moroccan crisis with Germany, necessitating Robert to suspend his previous social life for the demands of the risk posed by the German threat. This at first had necessitated his being absent from Marie's first great public concert, an absence that had a noticeable effect on Marie. For much of the next two years he had been stationed near Lille, overseeing a major upgrade in defenses in that area. His chances to see Marie were, therefore, intermittent and served only to maintain a relationship rather than to nurture it. Earlier this year he had returned to Paris on a full-time basis and had found Marie not only more mature but eager to make up for the deficiencies of their protracted absence from each other.

During the span of those two brief years, Marie had visibly matured, giving even more allure to her beauty, but from Robert's perspective, she had also grown more confident in her art and in her judgment of matters that she viewed important for her future. How could one not be entranced by such a woman? Yet despite all of this, their relationship had been complicated by the other woman, Sarah Morozovski.

In many ways, Sarah was the very opposite of Marie. Bright and opinionated, her passion for defending the less affluent and oppressed often led to passionate outbursts that contrasted sharply with Marie's poise and reserve. Unlike Marie's instinctual understanding of polite French society, Sarah, despite her privileged background, viewed French societal expectations through the ancient skepticism of her Jewish kindred. Yet it was Sarah's passion that seemed to unlock her inner being, giving Robert a glimpse of her beauty and vulnerability. Their very relationship had been almost serendipitous from the beginning and had, at one time, faded to no more than pleasant memories. Then, with a sudden dramatic reappearance, she had reentered Robert's life in such a way that made it impossible to ever forget her again.

Now here, he was drawn ever deeper into some type of commitment to Marie, all the while refusing to abandon Sarah. It would be an easy manner for many of his status to simply have the one legally and the other on the side. Yet for Robert, such a solution was unthinkable, as it ultimately would cause him to hurt both of these women. He had too much feeling and respect for each of them to play the cad. It was like some ancient Greek comedy, where his life was made miserable by a surfeit of riches that others could only dream about. He had wrestled with this dilemma to no avail. Now ensconced in a too-soft bed in distant England, the machinations of his mind made it virtually impossible to soothe his concerns with blessed sleep.

———

The following day, Robert dozed fitfully throughout his train ride to Dover and on the ferry to Calais. Only on the train to Paris did his mind seemed refreshed enough to deal with the uncertainties that waited for him in Paris, especially in the person of Marie Bonneau.

Since his return to Paris earlier this spring, it had been apparent that the resumption of his relationship with Marie was an item of much importance to their families and friends. As the weeks passed, there was an increasing air of expectancy regarding an announcement of some formal engagement. Robert had been pleased to note that there was some reluctance on Marie's part for such a commitment until she could be, as she stated, more certain of Robert's future plans. It was apparent from many things that Marie's concerns were primarily centered on Robert's future commitment to the army. Now, returning home from supposedly a triumphant visit to England, only to announce an immediate reassignment out of Paris, would be a set of circumstances, Robert realized, that might certainly affect Marie's perception of their relationship.

As Robert thought more about this, he came to accept the

consequences of his acceptance of Foch's offer as a possible means to help resolve his dilemma. He was obligated for another year of service, regardless of his ultimate career decision, and Robert now believed that that year would be most productively spent on Foch's staff. If such a hardship would be too much for Marie to accept, then so be it. If Robert was unable to make a difficult choice on his own, perhaps the choice might be determined by the demands of the moment. As the train arrived at the station, Robert saw Marie waiting for him. As he stepped from the train, she rushed up and gave him an enthusiastic hug and kiss.

"Now this is some welcome, Marie. I was thinking about you all the way home and hoped that you would be waiting."

"Thomas told me when your train was to arrive, and he suggested that I meet you, as he seemed to have some mysterious commitment at the last minute. I am so happy to see you, Robert. It seems like you have been in England for the entire spring."

"It does seem like a long time. How good it feels to be back in Paris."

"Tell me about your trip."

"Well, the trip home was really uneventful; that is, until I saw you waiting for me."

"No, I meant the whole trip. What did you do in England? Nothing you would be ashamed of, I hope."

"Scandal in proper old England, Marie? Hardly. Seriously, I cannot comment on some of what I did, not that it was so scandalous but because it dealt with classified military matters. What I can tell you is that I could not live very long in England without missing Paris and all that makes Paris what it is for me."

"What are you saying?" Marie asked with feigned innocence.

"If you must hear it more plainly, I enjoyed my time in Britain, but all the pleasant company and surroundings were soon overcome by homesickness and thoughts of my friends, especially you."

"That is the most lovely music I have heard since you have been gone, Robert. Let me help you with your bags. I must leave early this evening, as I have a previous obligation that I made before I knew of your arrival."

"Let's go, then," he replied. "I doubt if I have enough energy to stay up much past nine tonight anyway."

As they waited for a cab, Robert was startled to read the newspaper headlines and the details of the impending trial of Madame Caillaux.

"I cannot believe Henriette Caillaux's trial has not started. Even in England, we have been hearing a great deal about this for some time."

"What did the English think of all the news?" Marie asked.

"They are drawn by a good scandal as much as anyone, but the people that I was with, for the most part, had a positive opinion of her husband. Were it not for Joseph Caillaux's actions in 1911, I heard it said on several occasions, France might have gone to war with Germany. Many felt that his wife was simply innocent collateral to the nasty business that is politics in France."

"What are they like, the English? I have never been there."

"I cannot say for certain, as I was, for the most part, surrounded by military officers, government officials, and at times, their wives. The people that I was with are clearly the product of a successful empire. They exuded an air that showed their familiarity with responsibility and influence. Much of their speech and mannerisms, as well as their dress, were designed to show their evident status and their difference from the countless others over whom they hold authority.

"To me, they were unfailingly polite. At first their politeness masked a certain social aloofness, but when they found out my background, it was if I was one of them. I heard many times how happy they were to know that the French Army still had members from the traditional class and had not been completely taken over by the radical politicians. They seemed further gratified with my assurances that there were still many who came from families with long traditions of military service.

"I was pleased by their interest in my knowledge of the terrain and fortifications of the areas abutting Belgium, as this area would be central to any British force, should it be sent to the continent to fight. Despite that, I got the impression from many of their government officials and even some of the officers that there was a great deal of ambivalence in sending their army to the continent in the event of war, unless Belgium neutrality was violated.

Though their entire empire is administered from London, and the men that I met were used to life in the city, they all seemed to have a deep affection for their countryside, which in the south of England, where we stayed, is every bit as lush and fertile as France. The entire setting at the estate where we were based was quite magnificent, with large manicured lawns set off by magnificent gardens and large stands of old oak and maple. I was invited to several outings at nearby estates, which were quite enjoyable, and even once to a fox hunt, which I was able to avoid by claiming the need to attend to several pressing chores."

"You have not told me the most important thing about them," Marie interrupted teasingly.

"Which is?"

"What were their women like, of course, and what seemed fashionable to them?"

"Well, I only had exposure to them during some formal meals during the conference and during weekend visits to their estates."

"You can't tell me that you were oblivious to half of their population for the entire time you were there."

"The women that I met were quite formal and reserved, for the most part. Only after some time did a few of them seem to relax and show a less formal side to their manners and conversation. I never got past the sense that I was constantly being assessed by one and all of them to see if I met their notions of what a Frenchman should be."

"I trust that you did not disappoint them," Marie added.

"You would have to ask them that. I have no idea what those rather inscrutable women were thinking for the most part. My impression of them is limited, given their formality and reserve."

"What impression did you form, if any?" Marie asked with obvious interest.

"On the whole, they are not a terribly attractive lot and are very clumsy in enhancing what femininity they might have through the style of their dresses and mannerisms. For most of the occasions when I met them, even during weekends in the country, it was if they had all been schooled to behave with a formality that was more in keeping with an ambassador than a woman. They seem to be very much caught up in conforming to a behavior expected of them, at least in public. There seemed to be little that would appeal to an average Frenchman—or at least to this Frenchman. All of that made my seeing you today even more pleasurable."

As the cab passed through the city, Robert gazed intently at all the many sights of Paris that he had missed while away.

"What have you been doing while I have been gone?" Robert asked.

"Now that you asked, I am pleased to report that I have made good progress in my studies with some Chopin pieces. Even more exciting to me, however, is that I have also made progress in my understanding of some principles of logic that I have been studying with Thomas, who, as you know, is a wonderful teacher. He not only is an expert on the subject, but he is able to teach even some of the more complex concepts to someone like me. His enthusiasm is contagious, and he makes learning fun, even if the subject is not easy."

"Thomas has a unique ability to sense what you are thinking or what may be causing confusion. I have never met anyone with as much intuition as him. It is often as if he knows what you are going to ask before you do. He is uncanny in that regard, and as you no doubt have experienced, he can use that talent to explain or answer your questions in a manner that meshes perfectly with your thinking. This is one reason why he is able to clarify complexities in logic—and in many other areas—as well as anyone I have ever known."

"That's exactly right. In the few sessions that we had, I learned as much about other matters as I did about logic. He takes those abstract principles that order logical thinking and extends them to the mundane of the real world, making it seem much more coherent and manageable."

"Be careful," Robert cautioned with a smile. "He is a captivating rogue." Sensing Marie's relaxed manner, Robert took the opportunity to broach the issue of Foch's recent request. "I had another issue come up while I was working with General Foch at the conference, which is quite important."

"That sounds intriguing, to say the least."

"During our meetings, I spent a great deal of time with the general, who is highly regarded by the British and therefore was chosen to lead our delegation. During one of our private discussions, he made me aware of his new position in charge of the Twentieth Corps of the Second Army. It is the principal corps of that army, which is positioned in the critical area around Nancy, guarding Lorraine and facing toward Alsace. From my earliest days in the army, I have had the utmost respect for General Foch, and he is one of the main reasons that I took up a commission in the army in the first place. Near the end of the conference, he offered me a post on his staff as chief engineering officer."

"What does that involve?" Marie asked cautiously.

"It involves several things, which I have been anxious to talk with you about. The most tangible is a promotion to major. More important, the nature of my work will change substantially. I will now be in charge of not only the key transportation infrastructure and fortifications in our sector but coordinating their usage in event of any military engagement in the area. Consequently, my future role may well be involved with military planning and operations as much as with engineering. This would be a new type of challenge, somewhat like some of my activities in Madagascar."

"Will you be based in Paris as you are now?"

"The Second Army is based in and around Nancy. Though no doubt there may be many occasions when I will be in Paris, my station would be in Nancy and Lorraine."

"I have been expecting some change in our good fortune for some time," replied Marie. "We have been very lucky to have had the time together in Paris this year without so much separation. If you accept this position, all of that will change."

"That is why I wanted to speak with you before I accepted his offer."

"Robert, while you were gone I had time to reflect more about our future. Perhaps it was the effect of my logic studies, but I began to compile a list of possibilities and priorities in my head. When I thought of our situation in that way, I realized that most of my thoughts revolved around one concern. I know you well enough, Robert, to understand how important your work is to you. I could not insist that you compromise that aspect of your life to please me. What I do believe, however, is that in the years ahead, you could have a very fulfilling and rewarding career here in Paris, without the obligations and—to be frank—the frightening possibilities that a career in the army poses. I have spoken with my uncle, who assures me that with your experience and skills, you could have your pick of any prominent engineering firm here in Paris."

"Until I met you, Marie, these types of opportunities were less of a concern to me than my army assignments. In these last few months, I too have begun to weigh the differences between what I might expect in the next few years in the military versus in civilian life. Both jobs, to be done well, will require a large commitment of time and dedication. Both would likely require protracted periods away from Paris. The major difference, of course, is the added hazard that is inherent in the army. This new position certainly underscores that risk, positioned as it is so near to Germany.

"It is important, Marie, for me to know your honest feelings. We have both spoken of engagement in the past but have postponed a decision for several reasons. Now, this new assignment seems to be an important signal for both of us to start to think of our future in more realistic and serious terms. Regardless of what we might decide, however, one reality exists that cannot be easily dismissed. I still have at least a twelve-month commitment of duty to the army before I can honorably resign my commission."

"Robert, to be very honest with you, I have become convinced that I don't have the makings of an officer's wife. I am afraid that I would not be able to control my fears if you were in a dangerous situation, and I worry that my behavior would reflect badly on you."

"I would never be concerned with your behavior, Marie, but I would worry about the concerns you might have about my work. Next year I will have much more freedom to address those concerns. For now, the only thing that we can do is try to devise a plan that will both serve the army's needs and alleviate your worries."

"Robert, I don't want to dictate what is best for you, but I know that our relationship cannot exist on fear and anxiety. For now, it is simply enough to know that you are aware of my concerns and are willing to consider a change when you are free to do so. I hope next year we can agree on something that can still provide you excitement and satisfaction while making our lives together far less stressful. For these next months, I am more than content to wait here in Paris, so you should simply consider what the best place is for you during that time."

"If it weren't for your concerns, if left solely up to me, I believe I would be of the most use with General Foch in Nancy."

"Well, if that is what you believe, that is what would be best. I never want to feel that you have compromised on account of me."

Having reached an accord—or at least a stay for the coming months—Robert seemed to visibly relax and for the remainder of the cab ride home was content to enjoy the sights of his beloved Paris. As they passed over the Seine, the sun glinting off its waters seemed to imply a bright future here, surrounded by so much beauty and opportunity.

———

After seeing Marie off for her evening engagement, Robert paused to pick up the evening edition of *Le Figaro* to catch up on the sordid details of the Caillaux affair. Stopping by the concierge's rooms, he obtained his back mail and retired to his rooms to attend to his affairs that he had been forced to neglect while in England.

As he sorted through the mail, his eye caught a thin letter with German postage and Sarah's unmistakable handwriting. They had seldom communicated in such a direct manner and, fearing some unfortunate news, he hastily opened the letter.

It read:

> Dear Robert,
>
> I hope that this not only finds you well but also in Paris for the fourth and fifth of July. I know that we had hoped to meet in September, when I will be in Switzerland, but unusual circumstances have come up that require my presence in Paris for these coming dates.
>
> Robert, I do so hope that you will be able to meet me sometime during that visit. Perhaps it is the lovely weather we are having here in Berlin, but I have been thinking of you more than ever. For no apparent reason, I will think of your eyes, or naked shoulders, or your smell in the morning, or even that infuriating smile of

derision that you get before you diplomatically dismiss one of my ideas as hopelessly unrealistic.

Of course, I have darker thoughts about the many obstacles that stand in the way of my being with you. I often think of that other woman who no doubt is the perfect mate for you. It requires a great deal to control such thoughts or else I might go madder than I already am.

Now too often my work seems far less important as my mind drifts off to thoughts of you.

I pray that you still share a small fraction of the love I have for you and that you will be able to meet me in Paris when I am there.

If you wish to be discreet, we can arrange to meet at the home of Lydia and Karl, whom you know well. I will leave Lydia more specifics if you contact her. If, for some horrible reason, you cannot or do not wish to meet with me, I would hope that you could leave a message with Lydia.

Until then, with all my thoughts and love,

Sarah

33

LESSONS

The brief time that Thomas had spent guiding Marie's study of the peculiar idiosyncrasies of logic had been pleasant and productive. He had attempted to structure her studies as he would with any of his other students, by assigning reading material and written assignments relating to the material that would then be reviewed together. This was a style that had shaped much of his own education and which he now used for a great deal of his teaching, since it allowed the teacher to tailor the content and pace of the studies to meet the needs and abilities of the student.

In these first meetings, Thomas had been surprised by Marie's enthusiasm and apparent aptitude for a subject that many of his other students found difficult or tiresome. What he now was coming to understand with Marie was that one could never take anything for granted. How far she had come since those days when Robert first introduced her to him; she had been little more than a schoolgirl embarking on her first great adventure in the larger world. During that time he had been captivated by her skills as a pianist and later intrigued by her curiosity and intelligence, traits that only served to add to her natural beauty.

He had subsequently had the great pleasure of watching her mature over the ensuing years as her relationship with Robert had become more serious. He was gratified to see her expand her knowledge in combination with her musical training and to note how these studies helped to enrich her understanding and mastery of her music. This intellectual growth, when accompanied by her physical maturation, made it all too apparent that she was now past her adolescence and maturing into a remarkable woman.

When he was in Paris, Thomas would stay at the home of his grandmother, as in his student days. She and several members of the staff had already left for the summer so that there was much available space to tutor Marie. Now, as the afternoon of their present session lengthened, he could sense the natural mental fatigue that comes from the intensive thought required to master a difficult subject. They had been wrestling with logic applications for more than two hours, broken up by a small break for tea. Marie, however, had insisted that they continue until she felt that she had gotten the full measure of the material that she had been studying.

Finally, Thomas suggested, "I think that you have done more than enough for the day. You seem to have a good mastery of what we have discussed, so I think that this is a convenient time to stop. I have a few notes along with some readings and exercises that you can work on until our next session."

After sorting out a stack of papers and handing them to Marie, he said, "Now I propose that such a good effort should not go without reward. The cook is still in this afternoon and will prepare a delightful tea, if that is agreeable to you."

"That would be lovely, Thomas, but I am in a more

celebratory mood. How would it be if we went to some quiet café to conduct our postmortem of the session today?"

"That sounds even better," he agreed. "There are several in the area that will more than meet our need. We can decide where to stop as the mood hits us. Let me tell the cook not to worry about us, and then we can be off."

The warm afternoon sun and open air was a pleasant change from the previous hours cloistered inside, intensely considering the implications of various aspects of the day's lesson. As they walked, the exercise and the changing panorama that greeted them with each new block seemed to help them relax. At last, they settled upon a small bistro that Thomas spoke highly of from past experience and from his friendship with the owner.

Upon entering, they were greeted warmly and were given a quiet table looking out on the street.

As they waited for an aperitif, they saw a newsboy on the street with the latest edition of the evening paper, hawking the ongoing saga of the trial of Henriette Caillaux.

"Tell me, Thomas, what do you think now of all this business with Madame Caillaux?" Marie asked.

"I cannot get over how much it is sensationalized here in Paris. The news of the affair in Strasbourg was much more restrained. It seems to me there is much about this whole spectacle that is very unsettling."

"Why is that?"

"It is not the trial as much as the reaction to it by various groups that I don't like. It is as if the trial of this woman is no more than a means to increase the differences that exist among us. In the past, I had not been aware that there was so much bitterness held by people who oppose what this woman and especially her husband seem to represent. When I first moved to Strasbourg, one of the things that I found most disturbing in an otherwise lovely city with a wonderful university was the ethnic hostility. There were many times when the native Alsatian population bordered on open rebellion to the German ruling authorities. Recently, there has been an improvement brought about by the government's becoming more open to dialogue with the native Alsatian population. When forced to deal with one another as individuals, the people have often found many areas of common ground. As proof of this, I have developed a warm friendship with two young Lutheran ministers, and in our discussions, we have found that we have far more in common in our beliefs than the centuries of suspicion and conflict would lead us to believe.

"I used to look forward to coming back to Paris to escape from the mood of antagonism that hung over Strasbourg. Now, with this trial, I see much of the same anger and hostility here, and it has become every bit as bad as in Strasbourg.

"It really appears, for many, that Madame Caillaux's crime is less important than the past acts of her husband. Whatever her fate, it will be of little consequence to many if her husband's power and influence remains intact. How does someone come to believe the worst about someone or a group of people if they have little or no firsthand experience with them? This is an insidious poison that has affected humankind for too long. Have we not learned from all our miserable past the lesson of love and peace that Christ was sent to teach us?"

"You are a priest, Thomas, and you know the history of warring and conquest described in the Old Testament. It seems we humans have made little progress in controlling our worst instincts, despite Christ's message."

"Marie, you are really like a refreshing tonic. Your perspectives are those of an older and wiser woman. It may well be naive on my part to expect us to behave any differently than so many before us. We can only hope and pray that we live in a time when the voices of the peacemakers will be louder than those who sow division."

"That's what I like about you, Thomas. No matter how dark things may seem, you never give up hope. That, for me, is like a tonic as well. If I didn't know better, I would think that you are sympathetic to the murderer's cause."

"I am not and cannot be sympathetic to her ultimate actions, but still her crimes were not motivated from some preordained evil but from her feelings for her husband and from the humiliation that came with the public exposure of their affair. Murder and adultery cannot be condoned, but in such circumstances it is easier for me to turn a more sympathetic and forgiving eye on the perpetrator."

"That is a very unusual and ambivalent perspective for a priest," added Marie. "Many, if not most, of your brethren would have nothing but contempt for the woman's actions and her immorality. For them, there would be no basis for equivocation."

"I don't know for sure what has influenced my thinking on this affair. Perhaps it has been my friendship with the Lutherans, who take a more liberal view of such matters and constantly remind me of Christ's friendships with less-than-model citizens such as Mary Magdalene. For some reason, I cannot help but feel sympathy for Madame Caillaux. If love motivated her hateful actions, perhaps God will weigh them on a different scale than those with baser motives."

"You are always a surprise to me, Thomas. I can take nothing for granted with you, even a blanket condemnation for murder."

"There are many times when there can be no compromise in such matters. That is the tone of the Old Testament. With the coming of Christ, we receive a new message from God, speaking of tolerance, humility, love for one another, and forgiveness. In its time, it was a revolutionary message shaking the foundations of Roman power, and it is no less revolutionary today."

"So what would you do with this woman if you had the power?" asked Marie.

"She should submit to the state's authority and be judged according to the law. That is a matter between her and the republic. My hope for her would be that she recognizes the heinous nature of her actions and makes a sincere attempt at atonement and forgiveness. If she does that, I pray that God will view her more favorably than many fellow sinners."

"Thomas, I apologize if what I might say embarrasses you, but I feel I have to say it. You are like no one I have ever met. It is not that you don't see the world with all its sins and imperfections but that you see it and still hope for the best. When I am with you, your beliefs give me hope for the future."

"Marie, you should be careful in placing too much trust in any one person, regardless of his beliefs or effect on you. If you only knew of my many inadequacies and doubts, I am afraid they would be far from inspirational. I am honored that I can help you, but you are truly fortunate to have many others who care for you, such as Robert, who is far more capable than me."

"Believe me, Thomas, I know how truly fortunate I am, but Robert is not the same as you. I know that he cares for me, but it is very difficult for him to share his feelings. Often it is hard for him to sense my concerns, which you seem to understand almost intuitively. Don't mistake this for criticism, which it is not meant to be, because he has so many wonderful traits. It's just that at times he seems so reserved that it makes it difficult to feel close to him. In the time that I have come to know him, I believe I understand him better, but still, many times it is difficult to know what he is thinking, since he is so guarded about what he says."

"I have been around him for what seems like my whole life, so it is almost intuitive for me to know what he might be thinking or feeling," added Thomas. "I can see for most people how difficult it might be to feel some genuine connection to him, as he is instinctively a private person. Knowing him as I do, however, I know that he has a passionate side to him for the things that he likes and respects that is quite real and genuine. It is just that he keeps those feelings well hidden."

"That is where the two of you are so different, Thomas. You are far more outgoing, able to speak easily about your thoughts and feelings. That makes you seem warmer and more easily approachable than Robert and most every other person that I know. It is probably foolish to value certain aspects of a person's personality more than others, but I am more at ease with people who can honestly express their feelings. When I am with you, Thomas, I am seldom in doubt about how you feel about any given matter, and that makes it easier to feel close to you."

"This conversation has veered far from your mastery of logic, I am afraid," Thomas said, as if embarrassed to continue. "Let's think more of what you have accomplished in the last day's lessons and what we need to do in the next weeks, rather than trying to analyze our perceptions of each other. As you may have already discovered, we can be easily mislead if we veer from the strict practices of logical analysis that you are trying to master."

"That sounds more like your cousin Robert speaking than the Thomas I know," Marie replied with a note of disappointment in her voice. "Is there no concession with the d'Avillard men for uncertainty and emotion?"

"If it makes you feel any better, Marie, I will concede that an occasional lapse from logic to emotion has a place in providing for a more enjoyable life. For the moment, however, the only concession beyond that I am willing to make is to suspend all rational judgments so as to better enjoy the good fortune of being with you at this wonderful café."

"If that is a concession, Thomas, it is a minor one, but one, for the moment, I will certainly accept."

34

BALKAN MADNESS

On the morning of June 29, all the world learned the news that Archduke Franz Ferdinand, heir to the Austrian throne, had been approached by a young radical while visiting the Bosnian capital, Sarajevo, and had been mortally shot at close range. In Paris, details of the assassination were marginalized to a small front-page notice, hidden by the ongoing news of the Caillaux trial. Elsewhere in Europe, where news from the Balkans for the last several years had tabulated ongoing wars and murders, the assassination of such a prominent person was treated almost as routine.

In Berlin, however, given their proximity to many of the prime players, the news was greeted with more caution. Many details were not yet known, and the reporting, aside from a brief description of the known facts, left much unsaid. Despite this, for Sarah and her colleagues, what little was known was both perplexing and worrying.

Sarah had never been to the Balkans and had, at best, a poor understanding of the geography and most certainly the people who inhabited this complex and turbulent region. Until recently, much of the region had been under the control of the Ottoman Empire and only with its evident decline had the ferment of multiple nationalities and religious beliefs been allowed to be manifest in various short-lived wars that had served to realign the political geography of the region. Despite these changes, the industrial revolution that had transformed much of Europe was virtually absent there, and so there was virtually no workers movement that otherwise would have drawn Sarah's interest to the region.

She also had little knowledge of the assassinated archduke, aside from some recollection that he was perceived in some quarters as a rather aloof and somewhat quarrelsome heir to the crown of Germany's most prominent ally. She had been on an outing to the Wannsee when she first heard the news and now was returning to the office as quickly as the transportation to the area would allow.

Upon arriving, she found the bureau abuzz with activity, something that was distinctly unusual for this time of day. In the editor's office, she found Stein surrounded by a stack of papers, overseeing the coming and going of many junior associates.

"Stein, I suppose you have seen the news out of Sarajevo?" she asked jokingly.

"And what might that be? That some dimwitted Austrian prince happened to pick one of the most sensitive days for Serbian nationalists to make a state visit. Such an idiotic gesture on the hated anniversary of the Serbian defeat by the Turks at Kosovo—did he not understand how many Serbs hate Austrian dominance in this area as much as under Turkey before?"

"So you think that the Serbs are behind this, rather than the Bosnians?" asked Sarah.

"I once knew two brothers from Belgrade, and from that acquaintance I came to learn many things about Serbians and the Balkans or at least the Serbian view of the Balkans. In listening to these brothers, it became apparent to me that the whole Balkan Peninsula was a giant dysfunctional region, racked by constant and bitter blood feuds between the various ethnic factions, all magnified by differences in religion. The Serbs, who are Orthodox, hated the Croats, who were Catholic, and hated even more the Bosnians who were Muslim. As much as they disliked these groups, they hated the Austrians even more, as unnatural interlopers who seized Bosnia during the weakness of their Russian protectors in the aftermath of their disastrous war with Japan. From all of this, I concluded that the vast majority of the residents must be mad and that any rational person or nation should go to any length to avoid becoming entangled in their affairs. I also concluded that assassination was as natural to them as breathing."

"So what do you expect will come from all of this?" Sarah asked.

"In this region, violence begets violence. No doubt the Austrians will find some pretense to blame this on Serbia, although on the surface it appears that the perpetrator was Bosnian. Someone I spoke to who is well connected in the Foreign Ministry suggested that there was already evidence linking certain elements of the Serbian army with the activities of the assassin, as well as other possible accomplices. This will no doubt lead to an escalating crisis between the two and the very real possibility of a war."

"This would not be unusual," Sarah added. "The Serbs have been at war with someone in the region for the last two years."

"We can only hope that the rest of Europe will have the

sense to remain disengaged, as they have for these other Balkan wars," replied Stein.

"What do you mean?" asked Sarah. For the first time, she caught a note of concern in Stein's voice.

"If Austria attacks Serbia, this might be different from any of the recent wars. Serbia does not have a likely ally in the immediate region to face the Austrians, certainly not Bulgaria or Romania. Austria also has a powerful alliance with Germany, which might have wider implications."

"Such as?"

"What worries me this time is Russia. When Austria annexed Bosnia, Russia, having been humiliated by the Japanese and with widespread domestic unrest, was in no position to oppose such an intrusion into the area. Besides, the Bosnians were predominately Muslim and of far less concern to the Russians than the Serbs, who are Slavic and Orthodox. What I fear most is that if war comes between Austria and Serbia over this killing, then the response of the Russians, who have long believed themselves the protector of the Orthodox people in the region, will have to be a serious concern."

"What, if anything, did the Russians do when Austria took control of Bosnia?"

"They made some threatening noises, but at that time they were in no position to do anything more than that. Humiliation by the Japanese and an ongoing domestic revolt saw to that. What resistance they may have offered was chased away when the kaiser came out in open support of the Austrian efforts."

"Ah, I remember now; they called him the Teutonic knight in shining armor."

"Exactly."

"So what keeps us from repeating this whole scenario this time?" asked Sarah.

"Potentially, nothing; that is what the worry is. If only Bismarck were still around I would not be concerned. He understood all too well the futility of dealing with large groups of barely rational individuals, like my two Serbian friends, and found no value in engaging in the region. He also understood, however, that there was potential for great calamity if others foolishly did so."

"Like the case of an Austrian invasion of Serbia?"

"Exactly; it has all the potential for the complications that Bismarck feared. The most crucial question of all in the coming weeks will not be the Austrian or even the Russian response to these events but the position of the kaiser and the German government. I have begun to work my sources to get some feel for what the German Foreign Ministry and army are doing in response to this news; specifically, what they are prepared to do in light of a Russian threat of reprisal against Austria for actions against Serbia. This interests me greatly, as, unfortunately, this kaiser is not Bismarck and may remember all too well how his protection of Austria's first intrusion in the region was so warmly received throughout the German-speaking world."

"If I have not said it before, I will say it now, Stein: you are the best."

"That is debatable, but the success I have had comes from my enjoyment of uncovering all the details of what plays out behind the closed doors of the powerful, especially here in Berlin. Fortunately, I have collected a few keys to help unlock those doors."

"So what have you found out so far?"

"At present, there is calm in all of those areas that would be most involved, should any overt support of Austria be imminent. It may be too early to judge from the look of things at present, but for now, there does not appear to be any evidence that anyone in the critical positions of power is treating this as anything more than yet another irrational event in an erratic and unreliable region."

"That is comforting to hear," Sarah replied. "I guess all that remains for us at the moment is to allow the events to unfold and trust that those in charge will have the sense of Bismarck and not get drawn deeper into the affair."

"That may be, but I would be dusting off contingency plans, in case our present group of leaders is far more foolish than the previous generation."

For the next several days the weather was unusually warm, and the days were ideal for escaping to the lakes and countryside that surrounded Berlin. Despite this, Sarah kept a close vigil on the affairs in the capital through her own contacts, as well as those that Stein and the others in the office had. She was pleased to hear from all of these sources that little increase in activity throughout the German government had been observed.

She and Stein had also cultivated several contacts in Vienna, and these were proving valuable as well in gauging the actions in that other critical capital. She was pleased to note the communiqués coming from Austria were rabidly sought by the home office in Paris as a valuable addition to their daily editions. This could only increase the reputation that the Berlin office was acquiring in Paris, especially if they could continue to provide new and valuable information about neighboring Austria. She recalled the many meetings that had been held in discussing ways in which the Berlin office could be more closely integrated with Paris, and now she was gratified to see the results of this planning come to fruition.

From their Austrian sources it was learned that indeed a great public outcry had arisen after the archduke's assassination, resulting in harsh language emanating from the Austrian Foreign Office, accusing Serbia of being behind this despicable action. These communiqués demanded not only an act of public apology but extensive compensation, and they threatened that a failure to satisfy Austrian demands would provoke more severe measures, including possible military reprisal. This aggressive tone was amplified by the media and apparently was being well received not only in Austria but in Hungary and the outer realms of the empire, including even Bosnia. Apparently, much diplomatic activity had been taking place at the same time with the Bulgarians and Romanians, in the hope of attracting them into a coalition to engage in a third Balkan war, if satisfactory retribution was not forthcoming from Belgrade.

Stein, who seemed to have meaningful contacts throughout Europe, including the faraway and often opaque Russian Empire, had uncovered no significant basis for alarm from the information that he had been able to gather so far. To date, in Germany and elsewhere, little official comment had been made of the matter, except to condemn the assassination and to send official condolences to Emperor Franz Joseph.

"I am, by nature, a pessimist in matters such as these, expecting the worst of humankind, but at present, I am pleasantly surprised by the restraint shown by both the Russians and our own government," Stein commented one morning, nearly a week after the assassination. "If we are lucky, this will continue and, just possibly, Austria will gain a satisfactory resolution to this by diplomatic maneuvering."

"I am told," Sarah added, "that there is a strong belief by many in the Foreign Office and even by the kaiser, that though the Russians are sensitive to their position with respect to their fellow Slavs in Serbia, should Austria threaten attack, they are in little better position to lend support to Serbia than they were for Bosnia."

"All of this might seem so to the logical German mind, but logic has always been in short supply in the Balkans," replied Stein. "What I fear most is that Russia will abandon such logic and feel compelled to be the defender of the world's Slavs. Their government is not well entrenched in power, and there was a great deal of resentment in many quarters that the czar had stood by idly while Austria seized control over Bosnia. We must hope that their influence will once again be ignored, because if not, it could be a disaster."

"Well, it's too nice a day for me to dwell on such a disastrous scenario, especially when the facts to date, even after nearly a week, do not support such actions by the Russians or any other major governments. Still, it might not be imprudent to pay a visit to Bertha Suttner this afternoon to hear her thoughts on the matter and to enjoy a pleasant afternoon tea."

"Rank has privilege, no doubt. While the rest of us toil in this office, trying to ignore the rare sun of summer, you will be content to converse in far more appealing surroundings."

"It will not be all pleasantries, as you think. Baroness Suttner has lived in the Crimea and has a far better understanding of what their thinking might be to another Austrian threat in an area they have always believed crucial to their interests."

"Well, please think of me and the rest of us toiling away on your behalf while you take your tea."

"I most certainly will, Stein. You may be assured of it."

35

SUMMER'S EVE

In Paris, the murder of the heir to the throne of the Austrian Empire had commanded the attention of those figures throughout the government charged with the security of the republic far more than the popular press or the public. The public interest, what little there was of it, soon died down in the absence of events that might threaten the tranquility of a glorious early summer. Not only the weather but the economy and the overall mood of the country seemed to be at levels that few could remember. In such an environment, it was natural that a murder in a distant corner of Europe, an area known for its instability and violence, would be ignored or downplayed, so to better turn to the pleasures of the season and the spicy tales coming from the trial of Madame Caillaux.

Within the government and military, the first concerns that the assassination elicited through various government and military agencies were lessened by ensuing events. Reassured by their sources, many of the most responsible members of the ruling ministers made plans for their August summer vacations, while at the same time President Poincaré left the city with an entourage to meet with the czar in Russia for a conference of allies.

This pervasive optimism in Paris was clearly evident to Sarah, especially in contrast to Berlin, where in recent days her struggles with the somber and at times irascible population of the German capital had been more intense than usual. Just before Sarah was to leave on her previously scheduled visit to Paris, Stein had sent a shiver of worry throughout the bureau when he discovered a special meeting called by the kaiser to host a special delegation of the most senior Austrian diplomats and military officials in Berlin. As Stein so quickly noted, such a gathering could have but one purpose and that was to discuss Germany's relationship with Austria, should the latter declare war on Serbia. The tension only seemed to ebb after the Austrian departure from the city was quickly followed by the most senior members of the German government and general staff of the army leaving the city to attend to their summer holidays. Furthermore, in Paris Prime Minister Poincaré also departed to visit the czar at virtually the same time.

Reassured that General Moltke would not have left Berlin so quickly if pressing military matters were looming, Sarah's relief was only exceeded by joy as she planned for her anticipated departure for Paris. Upon her arrival, the moment she stepped from the train in Paris, Sarah was aware of a vitality and élan that was seldom evident in more stolid and somber Berlin. She had sensed this difference in the past, but now it seemed more apparent than she could ever remember. On her ride home, she thought that the neighborhood near her parents' home had seldom seemed more affluent and fashionable. Arriving home, her mother appeared genuinely happy to see her, and Sarah sensed an unusual sense of empathy from her mother, who took pains to praise her carefully cultivated style and beauty.

On his appearance from work, it was apparent that her father had not been spared from the ravages of time and the pressures of his business life. His hair seemed to become grayer with each visit Sarah made to Paris, and he seemed less animated and more constrained. Yet he too had been pleased, as usual, to see Sarah. Always interested in her work and relationships, he listened intently as she related her activities in Berlin and the nature of her visit to Paris to help facilitate closer integration of the two bureaus. He had kept many of her recent dispatches from Berlin dealing with the Austrian crisis, as well as other articles, and had proudly posted them in a scrapbook of increasing girth.

By the end of the night, they had had a more pleasant reunion than Sarah could ever remember. Naturally, the conversation touched on issues of her social life, which she was able to skirt with a bright optimism concerning her prospects with a young man that she knew both would be interested in. She was able to end any further speculation by suggesting it was far too early to say any more about him, and so satisfied, they all seemed quite content to draw whatever conclusions that they might hope for.

At last, Sarah, pleading the need to get some sleep in preparation for a busy day, excused herself and retired at an hour somewhat earlier than she was used to. Not only would her next day be full with meetings at the paper, but she had promised to stop to visit Lydia that evening, and if all went well, she hoped desperately to meet the mysterious young man she had mentioned to her parents. With such dreams in mind, she found it difficult to go to sleep.

———————

That following evening, Sarah's dreams began to materialize when Lydia Rothstein-Gold answered a knock at her door and greeted a young man whose presence would normally be unusual for her normal circumstances.

"Good evening, Robert. It is good to see you again. I see since the last time we met, you have had a change in your status. Congratulations on your promotion, Major," Lydia noted as she greeted Robert warmly.

"Thank you very much, Lydia. It is perceptive of you to note such a minor change, but it is appreciated nevertheless."

Robert was happy to see Lydia's warm, reassuring face, as it helped assuage the anxiety and guilt he had been dealing with ever since he had received Sarah's letter announcing her visit to Paris upon his return from England. In the ensuing days, he could hardly remember a time when Marie had been so warm and spontaneous in the entire time of their relationship. He had tried to match her mood but felt instinctively that the strain of his concealed relationship with Sarah could not help but be appreciated in his manner. He had considered rebuffing Sarah's request for their meeting, out of respect for Marie, but the mere thought of the affront this would be to Sarah made such an option impossible. So it was that he had notified Lydia of his intent to make his rendezvous with Sarah, and here he was, fully accepting whatever consequences might follow.

"I might hope that you are here to visit me, but I am wise enough to suspect otherwise," Lydia continued. "No doubt it is Sarah that you have come to see, but she is not here yet. You may relax, however, as she has let me know some complications have come up, and she will be a little late. Can I offer you something to drink while you wait?"

"Thank you, but I'm fine right now."

Robert actually welcomed the wait, as it seemed most of his day had been spent rushing from one project to another in order to extricate himself from his office in time to meet Sarah. To his great relief, he had been able to finish just in time to make a hurried trip across town to arrive at the home of Lydia and Karl, only to find that Sarah herself was late.

Alerted by a note that a uniformed messenger had delivered yesterday announcing Robert's intention of making the rendezvous and to urge patience should he be late, Lydia had already made extensive plans for his arrival.

"I saw Sarah earlier for a brief lunch," Lydia continued. "If it is of any consolation for her being late, I know that she was so excited to hear of your message that afterward she could talk of little else. I was given explicit instructions about what I was to say and do, as if she was planning a top-secret operation."

"It sounds as if she has been around the German authorities too much," replied Robert. "If it is permitted in her instructions, might I ask where Karl is?"

"Karl has so many irons in the fire that I'm surprised that he was able to get home earlier for lunch. He and his old friends from Alsace have been involved in this taxi company, which seems to take more time than any of his other activities. It is his night to spell the evening dispatcher while he gets some supper, as the usual backup is off, having fallen and broken his arm. I don't know whether he or Sarah will get back here first. If I didn't know him better I would think he might be out with some young thing, but having been married as long as we have, we know what each other is thinking without even having to ask."

"How long have you been married, might I ask?"

"Going on twenty-five years now."

"You must be a perfect match."

"It might seem that way, but it is never as easy as appearances might indicate. We were fortunate to have the same values, which helps when reality comes after the first blush of love fades. Now that both of us have aged, our beliefs and shared experiences provide far more to our marriage than the passion that we knew when we were young."

"Did you feel drawn to Karl when you first met?"

"It seems like there was always an attraction that I had for him, but the real love came with a feeling of ease in being around him and comfort in trusting his ideas as much as my own. Even with all of that, being married for as long as we have been takes continued work and compromise."

"It sounds that you might think that a successful marriage for two people of very different backgrounds might be very difficult."

Lydia looked with increased intensity at Robert and then replied, "It may be that two people from different cultures might have a more difficult time in being accepted, but ultimately I believe happiness has far less to do with their families and social circles than it does in their feelings for and compatibility with each other. Love is a mysterious and powerful force, perhaps more powerful than most anything that shapes our lives. When it is real and genuine, it should not be compromised by the expectations of others or of polite society. If your question pertains to Sarah, I know only this. I have never seen her more excited than I have when she is thinking of you. I can only hope that you share her feelings, and if that is the case you should not let anything or anyone keep you from each other."

Before Robert could say anything further, their conversation was interrupted by the appearance of Karl.

Just as Robert rose to greet Karl, both were surprised to see Sarah enter hurriedly behind him. Upon seeing Robert, she seemed to hesitate for a moment when her eyes met his. Then, casting aside the bags that she was carrying, she rushed to pull him to her and embraced him passionately. Then, unexpectedly, she began to sob, at first softly and then more loudly, drawing Robert ever closer as she seemed to lose all control of her emotions.

36

SANCTUARY

For Robert, seeing Sarah break down like this was perplexing and a cause for concern. He had never seen her this way.

Slowly, Sarah's sobbing abated, and she was able to talk, at first hesitantly and then more evenly. "I had hoped and dreamed that it would not be this way," she began.

"Now, child, settle down and compose yourself," Lydia quickly advised. "Nothing can be as bad as you make out when you are here with all of us."

"I had hoped to get home early to dress, but now all he can see is this."

"Sarah, I am thrilled to see you, no matter how you may look," Robert said.

"Robert, it does matter. I had bought a new outfit from one of Berlin's best stores so that I might surprise you. Instead, just as I was hoping to leave the office, news came from Berlin that shook all of us and required that we spend the rest of the afternoon and early evening dealing with it."

"What is past is past," Robert said, trying desperately to

comfort her. "What is more important than any new dress is that you are now here. Besides, when did you become so concerned with your fashion?"

Sarah smiled and seemed to relax, loosening her hold on Robert and standing back to straighten her hair and appearance. "If you must know, Robert, it was when I began to think of you more than I did of my work or the rest of my life."

"Well, the two of you are here now, so I would think that the best thing is that you make the best of your time together without two old people like me and Karl getting in your way."

"You could never be in my way, Lydia! You and Karl should know that."

"Perhaps, my dearest, but we are old enough and wise enough to know that we are in the way tonight."

"Sarah, everything is going to be all right. Whatever it is that has so upset you is gone for the moment," continued Robert. "Take all the time you need to prepare yourself. I will stay here with Karl and Lydia, who will be good company. You ought to know me well enough by now to know that it is you that I came to see, not some idea of what you should be."

Sarah's look showed Robert how much she appreciated his words. "I apologize to all of you for showing my disappointment as I did. All of you have enough to worry about without having to concern yourselves with my outbursts."

"Sarah, you may not be able to imagine this, but I was once young like you, and I can still remember very well how I felt back then when it came to this man," Lydia said, nodding to Karl. "I have prepared your old room for you to use and change in, if you feel it necessary. You know where the bath is from there. I even fixed you and Robert a bit of a meal when I heard that you would be late. It is nothing as fancy as you might be used to, but a good beef stew, an honest baguette, along with a nice bottle of Medoc are nothing to sneeze at. Madame Perrault at your favorite patisserie also contributed one of your favorite tarts to the cause when she heard that you would be visiting tonight. You might have other more elaborate plans, but sometimes simply being alone is more fulfilling than even the finest that Paris can offer."

"I don't know what I would do without you, Lydia. Keep Robert busy, and I promise I will be back as quickly as I can."

With that, she gathered up the bags that she had brought with her and left, transformed from the distressed state she had been in only moments earlier.

Soon, Lydia returned to join a conversation between Karl and Robert that was being dominated by Karl's description of the demands that his taxi venture were placing on his time, especially now that it was becoming more successful. Robert felt at ease with the pair, and it appeared that they were comfortable with him as well. He could see why Lydia had become such a confidant of Sarah's, with her wisdom and reassuring manner.

Sarah returned much earlier than any of them had anticipated, looking radiant in the dress she had bought for the evening.

"I don't know what you are thinking, Robert, but I would say that her worries about her appearance seem ridiculous," said Karl appreciatively.

"I never thought it was a real concern in the first place," added Robert.

"Karl, it is time that we leave these two alone to do what young people in their circumstances do," Lydia insisted as she tugged at her husband's sleeve, leading him from the room.

At last Sarah and Robert were alone for the first time in months. They could restrain themselves no longer and embraced passionately as soon as Lydia and Karl had left the room.

At last, Sarah pulled away and straightened her dress.

Robert, looking perplexed, asked, "Is anything wrong?"

"Certainly nothing that you can fix, my darling. If we didn't stop, we might never have time to eat, and I am starved."

"I hope that I mean more to you than your next meal," Robert said plaintively.

"Don't be ridiculous. I just need a bit of sustenance to see me through the night."

"Where do you want to go for dinner?" he asked.

"Robert, was it true what you said to Lydia in your message yesterday about seeing me?"

"Of course it was."

"Then that is all I need to make me happy. After that, I could not improve on one of my favorite dishes: Lydia's beef stew."

"Since when do you like beef stew? I have never seen you order it."

"My preferences are influenced by circumstances."

"What about your dress?"

"What about it? Do you like it?" she asked playfully.

"Of course I like it, but it seems to be wasted here. I would like all of Paris to see you in it."

"The only one in Paris that I care to see me wear it is here with me now."

Grabbing his hand, she led him to the door leading to the other part of the house, where they soon found themselves in the dining area, which Lydia had carefully prepared in a manner as romantic as many a fine salon. Soon, they had opened a bottle of Medoc and set about enjoying their meal, which was often interrupted by their need to touch each other or to kiss in increasingly long, deep embraces.

Robert tried to broach the subject of the matter that had set Sarah into such an unusually distraught mood, but he was gently rebuffed.

"I am sure that you will find out about this very soon, but I don't want to discuss it now. I want nothing more than to concentrate all the present on you, and I cannot do that if I dwell on other matters. I have spent too much of my life doing that already. My time with you is too valuable to have it stolen by things that I can't control."

As their hunger eased, it was rapidly replaced by their rising passion. It soon became difficult to think or talk of anything. Following a passionate kiss, Sarah arose from her chair and, taking Robert's hand, drew him up to her. Pressed against each other, all their senses merged into an ecstasy of arousal. Slowly, they separated, pausing to catch their breath. Then Sarah once again took his hand and led him quietly down a back hallway to the room that Lydia had carefully arranged for her.

There, in the faint light of a small lamp, Robert could see Sarah outlined in a soft golden aura, and he gasped as he saw her drop the straps of her lovely dress and reveal her bodice engorged with her remarkable breasts. From that moment on, he was possessed by a singular thought of possessing and loving the sensual apparition that miraculously became tangible in his arms. There, for the next hour, all concerns faded away, replaced by a present so intense that the lovers, as if in a spell, could think of nothing else but each other.

Then, no longer able to sustain the physical demands of their lovemaking, they lapsed into a blissful state of contentment. In this state, suspended between fatigue and arousal, the realities of their worlds slowly crept back into their consciousness. At first they both resisted the intrusion, but at last Sarah could not hold back.

"Robert, you will soon find out the news that so disturbed me. This afternoon we received an urgent message from Stein, who effectively runs the Berlin bureau and whom I trust fully. He stated that conditions in the Balkans had deteriorated rapidly and dangerously. The Austrians had suddenly made a series of demands to Serbia that were so extreme as to virtually ensure war."

"That is not unexpected, given Serbian complicity in the assassination of the archduke."

"That may well be, but Stein has learned that the Serbians have turned to the Russians for support and that there are strong indications that the Russians are planning to aid their fellow Slavs in the event that Austria goes to war with them."

"If that is the case, the obvious question is, what will the Germans do?"

"Stein believes, and I agree, that the Austrians would not have sent such an ultimatum without an understanding of German support."

"What plans did you make in response to the news?" asked Robert.

"It was surprising how different the news was received by those present. Monsieur Jaurès believed that this was yet another manifestation of the regional instability of the Balkans and that the major powers of Europe could likely avoid such a cataclysm using good judgment and diplomacy."

"And what do you think?" asked Robert.

"I have come to trust Stein's instincts, and he feels, from what he is hearing from sources inside the government, that this has the potential to be very dangerous. If the Russians mobilize their army in response to Austrian measures, then the Germans will have to follow, and if that happens, then all will likely be lost. The concerns here were such, however, that everyone agreed that it was essential that all necessary actions should be initiated as soon as possible to put in place effective antiwar measures."

"So what does that mean?"

"That means that instead of staying here in Paris for the next several days, I will be leaving late tomorrow morning for Berlin."

"Why must you go? Can't you depend on your German contacts and associates?"

"Will you be staying here, Robert? If that were the case, then I might have to make a hard decision, but both of us know what will happen to you in the next few days. What reason is there for me to stay here if you are gone? You of all people should understand how important it is for a leader to be present during such critical times. I have dedicated too much time and effort to help prevent just such a war as this, and I could not live with myself if I stayed away at this crucial moment."

"I know how you feel about this matter, Sarah, but for once you should consider the risk to you, rather than some great cause."

"Robert, if I had not taken risks for my beliefs, you and I might have been together here in Paris for a number of years. If I could value my beliefs so dearly then, how can I turn my back on them now?"

"Would it change your thinking any if I told you how much I would worry about you and how much I want you to stay here in Paris? I cannot stand to think of you being harmed for any cause, even one you feel passionately about."

"Robert, to hear you say that is more wonderful than you can imagine. You don't know how many times I have worried that I might lose you. If this were only normal times, I would not think of doing anything but stay here and wait for you. Yet, if I ran from my commitments now, could I still be the person that you say you love? I know in my heart that if our relationship is to survive all the challenges that will come from it, then neither of us can be anything but true to our ideals."

"This is all madness, Sarah, but I should have known that it would be this way; it seems there is always this force that pushes us apart."

"I don't ever intend to let whatever that force is to keep us apart forever, Robert! You will always be with me, wherever we may be, but I must go to Germany now, just as you will no doubt be called away from Paris. When we finish with whatever we have to do, then seeing you again will be all the sweeter."

"I was only being selfish to expect you to do anything less, Sarah. I love you and will be thinking of you every day."

Then, overcome with emotion, they fell into each other's arms, spending what little time was left to them pressed close together until the early gray light of morning announced the intrusion of a painful reality into their blissful solitude and yet another unwanted separation.

37

AUX ARMES

Sarah was right. Robert arrived at his office at an unusually early hour after quietly stealing out a side door as the day was breaking, in order to avoid any awkward meeting with Lydia. Within the hour, Foch's adjuvant Colonel Devereux entered his office.

"Major, I'm glad that you are here early this morning, as we will have a full day of it. As you may have heard, the Austrians have delivered an ultimatum to the Serbs that may well be rejected. The Serbs have now turned to the Russians, who apparently have given them assurances that they will support them in any way possible, should they be attacked by Austria."

"I have heard similar information as well, Colonel, and that is why I came in so early this morning."

"You amaze me sometimes, Major, with what you know."

"Colonel, all I can say is that I have unusual contacts."

"I have been told that by General Foch. Major, it is essential that we be on a special two-thirty train to Verdun this afternoon. I know this doesn't give you much time to get your things together, but time may be something that we don't have much of if Russia plans to go to war with Austria."

"Do you know any further details of the Austrian ultimatum?" asked Robert.

"I do not, but I suspect that the Austrians have carefully calculated it to expire at a time that will give them the most military advantage. That would suggest a period short enough to prevent any full advantage from Russian mobilization and intervention."

"No doubt we will know more by the time we arrive at the train this afternoon. I'll see you then at Gare de l'Est. We will be on train number 227 and further instructions will be coming in a memo from the staff later this morning."

———

So began a day that Robert would later recall as one of the most hectic that he had ever experienced. He quickly set about finishing the final details for the plans he had been working on but not before asking his orderly to notify Thomas and Marie of his impending departure. What a life of duplicity he was now living! Fresh out of the arms of his lover, he now reverted almost instinctively to the obligations and expectations of convention.

Finishing his work, he barely had time to rush to the train station to see Sarah off. The need to see her one last time was so powerful as to make Robert suspend the remaining demands for his time that morning, just to get one last glimpse of her before they would part on their separate uncertain paths.

As he pushed his way through the crowds onto the quay where the train to Berlin stood ready to depart, he at last saw her standing aside from the crowd, staring intently at those passing by. As she recognized Robert, she broke out in a smile and rushed to greet him, embracing him with the passion of the previous night.

"I am so thankful to see you," she mumbled.

"I could not miss your leaving, though the army has done everything that it can to prevent me from being here."

"I knew that they would have to react to the Austrian news. What is going to happen to you?"

"I am supposed to leave for Verdun this afternoon, which barely leaves me enough time to see you off and then rush home to finishing packing for the train."

"My God, Robert, how can it be this way? After a night like last night, and now we are madly rushing off to God knows what."

"I hope that all of this blows over soon, Sarah, but even if I can't be with you in Berlin, you should know that I will be thinking about you and praying that you will be safe."

"You will be with me too, Robert. I can face any challenge now, just thinking of the day that I can hold you in my arms again."

As the last call for boarding was announced, they embraced one last desperate time, and then, within moments, she was gone.

———

As Robert sped home by taxi, he began to tabulate the essentials that he would need to assemble for his afternoon departure. Shortly after his arrival, in the midst of his hurried packing, he was interrupted by Marie's arrival. Already worn down by the day's hectic pace, Robert was surprised by how muted his reaction was at Marie's sudden appearance.

It was clear that she had not had the time to prepare herself in her usual manner, as her hair was slightly askew, and her dress was more casual than she would normally wear on the occasion of his leaving for an assignment.

"Thomas sent me word that you are being suddenly called up to Verdun this afternoon and that your leave for next month has been canceled," she said in a rushed manner that belied her anxiety. "I suppose it is something serious for you to be called away so suddenly."

"I really don't know much more than that it has something to do with the increasing tension in the Balkans between Serbia and Austria."

"Can't people just let the Austrians give the Serbs the lesson that they deserve? They seem to me a bloodthirsty lot and certainly not worth concerning us in France with their affairs."

"If it was only as simple as that, it would be much better for us and most other people in Europe. The trouble is that the Russians seem compelled to side with Serbia. If war breaks out between the Serbs and Austrians, and if the Russians actually mobilize in response to Austrian actions, then there is serious risk that the Germans will follow."

"Let them all destroy themselves, then. They deserve it for being such fools to kill themselves over this no-account country and region."

"You and much of France may feel that way, but unfortunately, we have a treaty with Russia that binds us to come to their aid if they are attacked, as foolish as that may be."

"Then we should revoke it!" Marie exclaimed.

"Poincaré has just returned from Russia. No doubt they talked at length about this alliance and the need to protect each other from the Germans, should war break out. I am afraid as much as this appears to be folly, those in power here in France may feel compelled to honor this commitment, thinking it to be not only in the interest of Russia but also of France."

"That cannot be," complained Marie. "How is it in our interests to go to war over Serbia?"

"Serbia is just the flash point," continued Robert. "If Russia declares war on Austria, then a chain of events may well follow, drawing all of Europe, including us in France, into war."

"The Russians might be able to succeed without us," she suggested hopefully.

"It is possible but not probable. They showed themselves as poorly led and organized just a decade ago, when the Japanese humiliated them. The Germans are infinitely stronger than the Japanese, and if left to oppose the Russians alone, the outcome would likely be swift and decisive. I am afraid that if war comes, our leaders know that we will be next, and the decision has already been made that it would be better to face the Germans this time with allies than alone, as we did in 1870."

As the implications of what Robert was saying slowly began to sink in, a look of defeat crept across Marie's face. "It seems that we as individuals are left with little more than to accept our fate, whatever it might be."

"We may not be able to control what the future might bring in these next days, Marie, but we never have to simply accept it passively. If war does come, I know you can handle hard challenges, but if Paris is ever threatened, I want you to promise me that you will go with your parents somewhere much safer, such as Lyon or Provence."

"Robert, don't say such frightening things."

"It may be frightening to hear but it is important to consider all possibilities, as distasteful as they might be. When I am away, it would give me great comfort to know that you were out of danger."

Fortunately for Robert, Thomas arrived at that moment.

"Thomas, I am so glad to see you!" cried Marie. "I had hoped to be composed in seeing Robert off, but the reality of his leaving makes it hard for me to deal with alone."

"I did not mean to frighten you, Marie. I was simply trying to be sure that you would be taken care of in the worst of circumstances. I am glad that Thomas is here in Paris because I know that I can trust him to look out for you."

"I suppose this affair in Serbia is the cause for all this concern?" Thomas asked.

"I'll try to explain while we go to the station. Help me with my bags, Thomas, and Marie, please ask the concierge to get us a cab."

As they traveled to the Gare de l'Est, Robert outlined what he knew of the present situation to Thomas. He chose his words carefully so as not to further worry Marie.

Thomas quickly grasped the implications of Robert's forced departure and the concern his leaving would now have on Marie.

As Robert stood among the crowd, ready to board his train, Thomas tried to appear as optimistic and resolute as he could be.

"Well, my cousin, I hate to see you leave without a more formal send-off, but this will have to do. I wish that I could assure you that things will work out as they should, but at this point, neither of us has much control over that. Whatever may come, however, I am confident that you will be able to handle it. In the meantime, I want you to know that I will try to look after Marie."

"That is a great relief, Thomas. I know if you are here, she will be with someone whose judgment I trust better than my own."

"Good luck, Robert, and God be with you," Thomas said. He shook hands with his cousin and then discreetly drew aside to let him talk to Marie.

As she drew near to him, Robert's feelings for Marie in seeing the sadness and worry in her face overwhelmed his fatigue and guilt. Her natural beauty and vulnerability perhaps had never been more apparent. He took her slowly in his arms, hoping to provide some comfort in any way possible.

"Robert, I don't know what to say. This is so sudden and frightening."

"Things will work out, Marie, but you must not dwell on the negative possibilities. I know that you are strong, and you must be even more so now. Thomas will be here as well, and no one could be as good a companion in difficult times."

"I know that, Robert, now more than ever."

Sensing that he must board the train, she drew him to her one last time and gave him a passionate kiss.

"Robert, I love you and will be thinking of you always in the coming days."

Looking into her eyes, Robert once again succumbed to Marie's immediate presence. Bending over as he boarded the train, he drew her near to him and whispered into her ear, "I love you too, Marie."

Afterward, as the train gathered speed, Robert reflected on his acts and words, unable to escape from his duplicity and failure to act in a manner that he felt these two women deserved. Now, as he faced yet other serious responsibilities in the coming days, he worried whether such ambivalence might compromise his ability to act effectively in the face of even graver challenges.

It was not the mind-set he hoped to be in, should war break out. As the train made its way through the outer quarters of Paris, Robert closed his eyes, but his sleep was fitful, as images of the two women continued to come back to him. Finally, his fatigue overcame his obsession with the futility of his attempts to reconcile his divided loyalties, and he eventually lapsed into a deeper and blessedly dreamless sleep. He was given this fortunate reprieve for more than an hour before he was awakened with some difficulty by a young lieutenant.

"I'm sorry to disturb you, Major, but I have further orders for you. Upon reaching Verdun, you and other members of the Twentieth Corps are to transfer to a train that will take you to Nancy. Further details are included in these instructions." With that, he saluted smartly, leaving the papers with Robert, and moved swiftly to finish his duties.

The station at Verdun was filled with trains and disembarking military personnel when Robert arrived. He soon found the train to Nancy and within the hour was on the last leg of his day's journey. In Nancy, he joined a crowd of disembarking soldiers whose ranks had swollen beyond the station into the neighboring surroundings. He had passed through Nancy in the past on several occasions but had seldom seen more than a company of soldiers at any time. This evening he saw few civilian travelers in the station. Even the stately Stanislaus Square in the heart of the city and near the hotel where he had been directed seemed to have been converted to a military base, so many were the number of soldiers present on its streets.

Arriving at the Hotel de Lorraine he scarcely had time to wash and unpack his light travel bag before he left for a scheduled staff meeting with General Foch, which fortunately included a meal, as by this late hour his fatigue had been replaced by hunger.

Surrounding Robert were men that, for the most part, he had just recently come to know during the weeks of transition to his new post. He was the youngest of the group, which included officers who had spent the majority, if not all, of their careers in the metropolitan or home forces. As far as he knew, he was the only one with any real experience in the colonies and one of the few with combat exposure, even though it was primarily against the disgruntled natives of Madagascar. To a man, however, they were some of the leading acolytes of the War College and fervent believers in the supremacy of offensive tactics so dear to General Foch.

All the men had the haggard look that came from a day, already too long, of attending to countless tasks that the crisis demanded. The group had hardly settled before General Foch arrived, looking unruffled in a freshly pressed uniform and a presence seemingly vitalized by the challenges of the moment.

"Gentlemen, I am pleased to see that all of you were able to get here on such short notice. I have just spent the brunt of the afternoon with General Castlenau at Second Army headquarters, and it seems quite possible that your presence here may be badly needed. As you have no doubt deduced, the urgent change in your status has been dictated by the Austrian-Serb crisis. We at headquarters were briefed within the last two hours on the most recent intelligence regarding the positions of the various parties to this dispute, and all that can be said with certainty is that at present the situation seems fluid and uncertain.

"What is currently the prime concern for us is not the Austrian complaint with Serbia, which seems to have a valid basis, but the Russian position to the threat of an Austrian attack on Serbia. Political instability seems to provoke military adventurism in some quarters, and this seems true with both Austria and certainly Russia. There are many there who believe that Russia must respond to an Austrian attack on Serbia, a fellow Slav Orthodox state. Failing to do so would virtually cede control of the region to Austria and underscore the czar's weakness. It is not completely clear at this time but those who advocate Russian resistance to Austria seem to have the upper hand at this time.

"If this opinion persists and Russia declares war on Austria, I need not remind you that that will provoke Germany to enter the picture and thereby drag us to brink of war. This scenario is far from inevitable, but its consequences for us, allied as we are through our pact with Russia, are unmistakable. It is not my province or anyone's in the army to dictate our preferences in this matter. It is our responsibility, however, to prepare fully for the consequences. Much of my discussions today have dealt with the role that we in the Twentieth Corps will play, should war be declared with Germany.

"Therefore, a brief review of an anticipated timetable is in order. If confrontation with Germany seems imminent, it will necessitate general mobilization, which for all practical purposes will be a de facto state of war. We have received near hourly intelligence reports of the buildup of German troops along our eastern frontier. This very afternoon, apparently to avoid an accidental confrontation with these German forces, we received an order from Premier Viviani to withdraw all French troops ten kilometers from the border. I have been informed that this corps in particular will be closely monitored to ensure our compliance with this directive.

"Should general mobilization be ordered, we can anticipate the arrival of a full contingent of troops by day seven. Until that time, with the troop strength available to us we will establish defensive positions as close to the frontier as orders allow. Upon coming to full strength, we will be capable of initiating Plan 17 for the engagement and conquest of Germany. I cannot disclose at this time our full responsibility, but suffice it to say that the Twentieth Corps has been given a preeminent position in the initial attack on German lines. For now, it is imperative that we have twice-daily cavalry patrols over our sector to obtain information on German activity on their frontier. It goes without saying, given the order to avoid troop deployment in the area, that such reconnaissance will be done discreetly in small groups, so as to avoid any provocation with German troops. Our troop strength will be deployed as far forward as possible in positions chosen to optimize our defensive capabilities.

"Robert, in conjunction with the intelligence being gathered, it is important that you and your engineering corps do what is necessary to provide the necessary infrastructure to defend this sector. Also, you will need to collaborate with the intelligence bureau to gather and process information on German troop strength and deployment as quickly after its arrival as possible."

"I have a great deal of information on the topography of our French sector and the existing rail and fortifications present," Robert said. "We already have good topographic information of the Vosges and the plain before Strasbourg from the days when they were part of France. At present, there are few better natural fortifications than the ring of hills we are already deployed upon around Nancy. Unless the movement of the German forces dictates otherwise, I would advise that we remain in this location until the time is chosen for an offensive. We are getting remarkable information from aerial photography that will allow the intelligence bureau and Colonel LaCrosse an even better idea of the region in order to plan an offensive. Given the terrain surrounding the Vosges Mountains, however, these options may be limited."

"Major d'Avillard is correct to suggest that the aerial photos are proving quite important," replied LaCrosse. "At present, German troop strength has increased in the area, but it is by no means at a dangerous level. There appear to be two armies arrayed in front of us. The Seventh Army is to the south, deployed in front of Strasbourg, and the Sixth further to the north, deployed to the south of Metz. Few, if any, of these troops are Prussian, with the Sixth Army being exclusively Bavarian and the Seventh primarily composed of Bavarians and Western Germans."

"Well, Colonel LaCrosse, that is a fitting note of optimism to wrap up the day's activities," said Foch. "Let's break up for now and try to get some rest, as tomorrow will likely be as hectic as today. We will meet at seven in the morning for breakfast in the salon."

With that, the group quickly finished their meals and moved off for a welcome night's rest.

38

CONTINGENCIES

In light of Marie's evident distress in the aftermath of Robert's departure, Thomas had avoided mentioning a letter that had come that very day from the Bishop of Strasbourg. He had written to alert Thomas of the deterioration in the relations between the German and French populace of Strasbourg, sensing that the old tribal passions, which recently had seemed to have abated, were now returning with even greater intensity as the Balkan crisis worsened. In closing his letter, the bishop had suggested that if the circumstances allowed, he hoped that Thomas could return to Strasbourg at the earliest possible moment.

The bishop was a kindly man with a keen awareness for the feelings of his large flock of followers in the region. Thomas and the bishop had developed a close relationship, in part based on the bishop's appreciation for Thomas's skills in communication and mediation with the students and others in his circle of influence.

Thomas knew that the bishop's words were true, as he had never known him to embellish or overreact. He also realized that much of the student populace he knew so well might be readily influenced by the passionate rhetoric of the crisis. He felt instinctively that he could help in calming the mood of many of the groups that he had come to know, and therefore realized how important the bishop's request might be.

Under normal circumstances, he would drop everything and return to Strasbourg as quickly as possible, but now he found it impossible to leave until he could be more certain of Marie's safety. If matters really deteriorated, as the bishop seemed to fear, Thomas could not leave in good conscience without being assured that Marie and her mother were on the train out of Paris back to Lyon.

He had hoped to better understand the immediate risks ahead by talking with Hervé DeLarmé, one of the few people he knew in France who might be able to help him in deciding the timing of his return to Strasbourg.

Unfortunately, his meeting with Hervé had left as many questions unresolved as answered.

Hervé had been deeply embroiled in the crisis ever since word came of the Austrian ultimatum to Serbia. He had grown tired of the confines of the Foreign Office and welcomed the opportunity to meet with Thomas as a diversion from the tensions and uncertain possibilities encountered there. Consequently, he had been a willing source of information during their lunch; it was just that whatever was known at the Foreign Office was subject to nearly hourly revisions, thereby making any understanding of the immediate consequences increasingly an exercise in speculation.

The now-familiar ground of entangling alliances was revisited, with little need to expound on the obvious. The potential vulnerability and lethality of those alliances had now become all too apparent in ceding the initiative of the present diplomatic process to the whims of the two least responsible members of their coalitions. As much as one could now shudder at the prospect of czarist Russia and the decrepit Austrian Empire determining the fate of Europe, it was ever apparent that this was the present reality, unless some inspired last-minute answer would come forth to extricate everyone from overt conflict.

What Thomas took from the meeting was more of Hervé's subjective perspective on the course of events and the news of the emergence of the British proposing a last-minute solution that held promise for changing the very dynamic of the crisis.

In the last few days, Hervé had sensed a fatalism that he had never seen among many of the senior diplomats with whom he had served. The sense that events were getting out of control was a powerful one that seemed to have transformed many key diplomatic personnel. Only yesterday, with word from Lord Gray in London proposing an emergency conference with the three members of the entente as well as Germany, there had been reason for optimism. This was reinforced by Germany's prompt acceptance to the proposal. Now, Hervé hoped that matters could be restored to a more rational footing.

Afterward, in light of the information he had received from Hervé, Thomas resolved on a plan of action. He planned to inform the bishop that he would return to Strasbourg as soon as he could attend to personal obligations. The most pressing obligation was Marie, whom he was to meet later this afternoon for a scheduled lesson. Thomas planned to discuss the bishop's request with Marie, knowing that he could not leave until he was certain that Marie both understood the risks of the present the situation and had a plan in place to deal with the worst possible outcomes.

———————

From the first moments of their meeting, Thomas's lack of enthusiasm for Marie's lesson was evident to her.

"Thomas, you seem to have much more on your mind today than this lesson. If you have more important matters to deal with, then I am happy to reschedule our meeting for another time."

"I'm sorry, Marie. You'll have to excuse me for my lack of attention. Unfortunately, I do have a lot on my mind, much of which concerns you."

"In what way?" she asked

"Recently, I received a request from the bishop to return to Strasbourg as soon as possible. Since then, I have been doing a great deal of thinking about his request and especially as it relates to you. I am concerned that this present crisis in the Balkans has the potential to turn quickly into something far more serious. The bishop is more worried than I have ever known him to be, and having spoken with Hervé DeLarmé yesterday, he was unable to totally ease my concerns."

"What are you talking about, Thomas?"

"Marie, Europe could be on the threshold of a major catastrophe, and if the worst should happen, there will be much suffering and danger. It is painful to think that here we are, trying to go over lessons that are based on reason, believing it to be an important part of civilized activity. I have spent much of my life believing that reason, empowered by the Holy Spirit, would nourish our lives. Now, there are dark forces at work that threaten that ideal. If my worst fears are correct, then I have been naive and, worst of all, may have left you less prepared to deal with the ultimate consequences. Instead of arguing points of logic, I should have provided more pragmatic advice in dealing with matters that are so terrible that we instinctively avoid talking about them. How could I ever leave for Strasbourg without being assured that you and your mother will be safe?"

"Thomas, you are acting just like Robert. Have neither of you any respect for my own intelligence or abilities?"

"That is a ridiculous question, Marie. It has nothing to do with you as much as it does our concern that you be safe."

"Then I would ask you not to mistake my fear and hatred of war as a lack of capacity to deal with such a disaster."

"Marie, I am not sure that you—or any of us, for that matter—know what may come from such a catastrophe. Believe me that my concern is not a lack of belief in you as much as it is a worry for your safety and the safety of us all."

"Thomas, none of us can know how we will react to great danger, and I would be dishonest if I said that I did. I am not some helpless person, however, incapable of dealing with serious matters. What is it that so worries you?"

"I have promised Robert to look out for you in his absence, and that is what I have been doing in trying to think through the many probabilities that might be ahead of us in the next few weeks."

"What worries you most, Thomas? Your promise to Robert or to me?"

"My promise is only an affirmation of how both Robert and I feel toward you. Without Robert here, I must act for both of us."

"Then you don't trust me to look after myself?"

"Of course I trust you, Marie, but if matters deteriorate, I fear that you and your mother might be in danger. I could not

411

stand that thought without knowing that I had done everything that I could do to prevent that."

"Thomas, you are suffering from the ignorance of manhood. Women have had to survive without their men throughout history, and my mother and I are as capable as any others who have lived through difficult times in the past."

"No doubt that is true, Marie, but this may be different."

"What is it that you would have us do, Thomas?"

"I want you to promise me that at the first inkling that Paris might be in jeopardy that you and your mother will pack your belongings and leave for Lyon or wherever it seems safest. You cannot wait too long to leave, Marie, because when it becomes apparent that the danger is real, then all of Paris will try to flee, and you will be caught up in the flood."

"Neither I nor my mother are interested in being at the mercy of the Germans, heaven forbid. I can assure you, Thomas, that we will be very prudent and will move, if that is best."

"Will you give me your word on that?"

"Thomas, you can be assured of it. Now clear your mind of these worries. Both of us have too many real concerns to deal with to worry about the silly notion that I am not capable of acting in my best interests."

"Thank you for reassuring me about what might seem obvious, Marie."

"If you are reassured, then our discussion has been very worthwhile, Thomas. I know how important your work must be in Strasbourg if the bishop is asking you to return so quickly, and I would not want to feel responsible for any delays here in Paris. Still, I am thankful for your concern for me and my mother. You don't know how much it means to me."

Somewhat perplexed by the formality of Marie's reply,

Thomas answered defensively, "Marie, you never need to thank me for my concern. It seems it is a natural part of me now."

"Oh, Thomas, how strange it is that such fearful times can expose our feelings." Overcome by his honesty, Marie drew Thomas close to her in a passionate hug.

They both looked at each other for a long moment, unable to speak or move. Then Thomas, as if straining to pull himself from a path that he feared to follow, spoke first.

"I was wrong to think that you were vulnerable and unable to care for yourself, Marie. In reality, I think what upsets me most is the idea of leaving you alone."

"That is absurd, Thomas. You know that you have an important obligation in Strasbourg, and it is something that we both must accept. I just pray for a time that we will again be able to do what we want, rather than what we must."

"That is called paradise, Marie. Until then, we must bear this purgatory as best we can."

"Then that is how it must be, Thomas. I don't know about you, but I think that this has been our best lesson to date, even if we veered from the all-too-ordered path of logic."

"You may very well be right, as usual, Marie. There is far more richness to life when not bound too tightly to the constraints of logic. Now, we both have to attend to important matters, so we can discuss this more tomorrow."

Afterward, as much as each looked forward to the prospect of their meeting the following day, neither could escape from the memory of that afternoon.

39

NEW REALITIES

In the brief time that she had been away in Paris, Sarah returned to find both Germany and especially Berlin dramatically changed. This was first evident at the border, where the usual routine was now replaced by a much more thorough interrogation of any non-German travelers crossing the border. The young border guard at first was concerned with Sarah but then seemed reassured by her excellent command of German and her listed address in Berlin. Nevertheless, he made it a point to carefully go over the new regulations that had been issued in her absence, requiring that all foreign nationals register their presence each night, either at the hotel or guesthouse where they might be staying or at the nearest police station. He emphasized that failure to do so would be considered a serious offense and might make that individual subject to deportation or, even worse, incarceration.

The stations in the larger cities seemed to be changed as well, with a very visible presence of military personnel in and around them. This presence seemed to increase the further east that

Sarah traveled into Germany, until she was surprised to see in Berlin that major sections around the station at the Potsdammer Platz were now occupied exclusively by military transports, with soldiers far outnumbering the civilian population.

On arriving in Berlin, she stopped briefly at her apartment to refresh and leave her bags and then decided to stop at the local police station at, fittingly enough, Gendarmerie Platz to register, as she had been instructed at the border.

Here, she was directed to an office that appeared to be set up to handle the registration of foreign nationals and where she was soon met by a more senior official than she had encountered at the border crossing.

This officer was brusque and reserved in his manner. His questions came mainly from a list that had been universally distributed throughout the country. He changed his manner briefly when finding that Sarah was primarily employed as a manager of the bureau of a French newspaper. With little other indication of concern, he finished his inquiries and repeated to her the instructions that she had received earlier—to make a daily report of her whereabouts while in the country. With that, she was released, whereupon she set out for the office, hoping to find Stein in order to get an update on the present situation.

Upon arriving, she found not only the evening crowd but many, if not all, of the workers and reporters who normally would have left the office by this time. Stein, she was told, was out getting a bite to eat and checking on some of his sources, but he should return in short order, as a meeting was scheduled for nine o'clock. In the recent days, he had even taken to sleeping on a cot in one of the back rooms, essentially setting up residence in the office to better oversee the flow of news that was coming into the city from various sources.

Sarah did not have long to wait. She had hardly settled in,

sorting over her messages that had accumulated in her absence, when Stein returned, accompanied by two of his younger protégées. He was at first so interested in his conversation with the pair that he failed to see Sarah seated at her desk near the front of the bureau. Finally recognizing her presence, he quickly finished his conversation and turned toward Sarah's office.

"Sarah, I expected to see you in spite of this mess, but now that you are here, I almost wish that you would get back on the train for France as soon as you can arrange to do so."

"That is some welcome, Stein. You don't know how good that makes me feel."

"Seriously, when I telegrammed you in Paris, I was worried about the course that events had taken, but this is progressing much faster than I—and, more important, most of the members of the government here—have anticipated."

"I came back, Stein, because if things were as serious as you led me to believe, then there would be much that would need to be done here by the antiwar coalition and many others."

"You are brave, if nothing else, to hope that you and your friends can alter the course of this, but I certainly wish you luck. It now seems, as each hour goes by, that there is more and more evidence to suggest that this may be spinning out of control."

"Tell me what you know so far and what you think is going to happen. I hate to admit it, but there is no one I trust more than you to make sense out of all that information you have gathered."

"The truth is, Sarah, that I have had an uneasy feeling about this from the very beginning, when I heard that the Austrians were provoking another Balkan crisis. Now, it seems this whole affair rests on an inane decision by the kaiser to give the Austrians a guarantee of German support for whatever action they might take in the Balkans, without some oversight or final approval. In effect, control of the crisis has been ceded to an Austrian government and military that has a far different perspective from so many here in Germany. There is no doubt that most officials felt they had gotten some sense of a more reasoned and measured plan after the Austrian visit earlier this month. If you remember, most of the top military men and government ministers left Berlin after that visit and did not return until they received word of the Austrian ultimatum to Serbia.

"Suddenly, whatever had been discussed took on far more serious implications, and from what I have learned, it is only now that many of the major players involved, especially the kaiser, are beginning to understand the true implications for calamity that the Austrian actions have produced. Only in the last two days have Moltke and Falkenstyne returned from holiday, but even before their arrival, there was a tidal wave of activity throughout army headquarters and a wide-scale alert throughout the country. Now, not only the army and the government but the entire city and no doubt all the country have become aware of the danger brought on by our Austrian allies. People in East Prussia are being told of a possible invasion by the Russians, and already many of those in a position to do so have fled to the safety of Berlin. It seems strange that only a few days ago there was so much indifference to the Austrians' handling of their Balkan interests and now, almost overnight, people can think of nothing else."

"Russia has only threatened to come to the aid of Serbia, but it is by no means certain that she will," Sarah said.

"Many in the government felt strongly that Russia would not or could not effectively support Serbia and risk war with Austria and possibly with Germany. Based on recent intelligence coming out of Saint Petersburg, that may have been a major underestimation of the Russian willingness to accept the consequences of war with the Central Powers, rather than stand idly by and watch them take control of a region they view vital to their interests.

"With the Austrian ultimatum to Serbia, the information that the government has been getting from their sources in Russia suggests that if Austria declares war on Serbia, Russia will come to the aid of their fellow Slavs. This threat is what has put everyone here on alert and has even transformed the thinking of some who might not have supported the militarists in the past. The fear of a Russian invasion, with all the real and imagined possibilities that a horde of Cossacks and Mongols might perpetrate on the Prussian homeland, can overcome much resistance.

"One has only to look at the media to appreciate the extent of change in the public mood. Now, with a militant Russia casting its shadow over this whole process, papers with moderate or even leftist leanings are sounding the alarm, calling for the defense of the fatherland in an hour of threat. Even many of the workers have gotten swept up in the hysteria. When confronted by the threat of a Russian steamroller overrunning their towns and countryside, war is seen in a different light, with theoretical concerns being swept aside by a need to defend the homeland.

"We have tried to report the facts as they have occurred and have tried to lessen the public hysteria by downplaying the inevitability of a war with the Russians. I am by no means sure, however, that we have had much effect. In talking with many of the leaders of the workers in various plants throughout the city, there seems to be a growing perception of the inevitability of conflict with the Russians and their foreign allies. More important, the members of the Social Democrats in the parliament are coming under increased pressure to approve all measures of support, should war become imminent."

"Is there any evidence of resistance to this disaster, or are people simply resigned to letting the Austrians and Russians determine the fate of the entire continent?" asked Sarah.

"I have just gotten word from my sources in the Wilhelmstrasse that the government has received an urgent request from Lord Grey of Britain for a meeting of the major powers to discuss a means of settling this crisis. This has been well received in the Foreign Office, and I am told that a positive reply was forwarded to the British ambassador within the hour. Among some of the people with whom I just spoke, there seemed to be some optimism that this proposal could be very helpful in defusing this situation."

"That is a relief to hear. At least this shows the German government's willingness to make an attempt to avoid a war. With British involvement, France will no doubt be supportive as well."

"I hope that is the case, but too much still depends on what the Austrians choose to do and how the Russians react."

"Thanks for your insight, Stein. If I'm not needed here for now, I really must get in contact with Frau von Suttner as soon as possible."

"Good luck," replied Stein. "Even if you are not able to talk with Bertha Suttner tonight, try to get some sleep, as you will need to be rested for tomorrow."

The next day Sarah was pleased to see that the cloudy, threatening weather from the day before had been replaced after a hard rain during the night by a cool and sunny morning. She hoped that this would be an omen for the day. She had arranged to meet with Frau von Suttner early this morning and knew how important the plans that they might formulate would be. Her trip to the Suttners' subsequently proved pleasant and was uncomplicated by further discouraging news in the morning papers.

On first greeting Sarah, Bertha Suttner showed her concern for Sarah's presence in Berlin, just as Stein had done the previous night.

"Sarah, although I am glad to see you, I am worried about your being here in Berlin during such times."

"It is because of such times that I am here. The people that I trust most to help defuse this crisis are here in Berlin. I knew that if we are to be successful in avoiding a terrible tragedy, I could not be anywhere else."

"I admire your courage, Sarah. You give us older people the energy to act on our convictions rather than simply accepting what is forced upon us."

"No, it is you who inspire us with all your accomplishments, fighting these insane wars. Your success in the past is what gives me hope that we can stop this disaster before it becomes an awful reality."

"I certainly hope that will be the case," added Frau von Suttner. "I am cautiously optimistic this morning from the news I have heard from my friends in the government."

"Which is?" asked Sarah.

"It seems that the kaiser, of all people, is now having serious reservations about the risks of blindly supporting Austria in a Balkan adventure, if it would risk a wide-scale war with Russia and France. Even worse would be the addition of Britain to such an alliance. He seems to realize that all of his posturing may now be called into account, and he seems suddenly willing to find some means of escaping from the consequences of his threats, now that a day of reckoning may be at hand.

"Still, there are many here who either would welcome a coming war or see it as a necessity if the coalition that makes up the Entente makes a confrontation inevitable. The most militant of these have been pressing for action, which no doubt has fed this huge military buildup here in the last few days. Still, I am told that there are many in the diplomatic corps who are strongly hoping for a negotiated settlement, and it is to this group that the kaiser is now turning. You may be aware that an overture has come from the British for an emergency four-power conference to discuss the situation as soon as possible."

"I had heard of this as well last night, but I assumed that the Austrians would have to be included," Sarah replied.

"Apparently, the British assumed that the Germans were either behind the Austrian ultimatum, or they could force the Austrians to comply with an agreement for the region since, as of now, the Austrians have not been asked to the conference."

"Little good that meeting might do if Vienna decides to take matters into their own hands," added Sarah pointedly.

"If our government can be persuaded to withdraw their support for such an action until this conference can be convened, that may go a long way in preventing the Austrians from doing anything rash. That is reason enough to organize and act as soon as possible. Since yesterday I have contacted the leadership council and all other significant parties that have been involved in our activities in the past. We have agreed to meet here at nine o'clock tomorrow morning to assess what actions have already been planned and what further needs to be done. In the meantime we would welcome any proposals from you and your colleagues in France to assist in our efforts."

"Before I left Paris, we had a lengthy discussion on this

matter, and I know that my colleagues there are willing to support us here in any way that might be asked of them. When we know more fully what you are planning to do, I will communicate that to them."

The two women worked hard through the morning, drawing up a list of essential activities for the following day. Later, with the purpose of her visit accomplished, Sarah excused herself without staying for the usual social visit that the two women commonly had over tea. Both knew all too well that unless matters could be changed, there would be little time in the future for such social niceties. Following final adieus, they separated, each resolved to focus her time so as to do as much as possible before their critical reunion the following day.

40

CONFESSION

In the span of several days, Marie's life as she had known it had been turned upside down. She had been warned, even as a young girl, that unexpected hardships and disappointments were an all-too-common feature of life, but surrounded by loving parents and the safety of an upper-class upbringing, she was spared from any significant travails throughout her years in Lyon. On coming to Paris to study, she had accepted the notion that she would be challenged by the competition inherent in her musical studies and by life in the most cosmopolitan of cities. Still, she had succeeded, even in this most demanding environment, with only minor setbacks. Her many natural gifts had contributed to her success, but perhaps more than any other attribute was an inner discipline and drive that helped Marie focus her talents to better overcome what difficulties she might encounter in reaching the goals that she had set for herself.

Now, as the specter of war suddenly disrupted the beauty of a remarkable summer season, it seemed to Marie that, for the first time, her life was being threatened by forces that were beyond her control. It had been a great shock when she was confronted by Robert's sudden reassignment, worsened by her fear of the uncertain risks she knew accompanied his departure. Now, as she had so many times in Robert's absence, Marie turned to Thomas for comfort.

In this moment of great uncertainty, Marie now realized even more how important Thomas was to her. Perhaps she had understood this all along but had tried to suppress the inconvenient realization that it was Thomas, far more than his cousin, who gave more meaning and fulfillment to her life. Yet the same forces that had led Marie to understand her feelings for Thomas were now compelling Thomas to return to his duties in Strasbourg.

Since Marie had last spoken with Thomas, she had spent an entire day and much of the night trying to deal with her feelings for him and Robert. To come to any resolution and to control the conflicting emotions that now dominated her thoughts was a task as difficult as any Marie had ever encountered. The tide of events that had unmasked her emotions had created so much uncertainty as to make it impossible to act decisively. She intuitively realized, however, that her only viable option at this time was to act with restraint and discretion. Such outward behavior no doubt would earn praise from both Robert and Thomas. Yet it was not praise Marie wanted but a means to mask her emotions until she had a better understanding of what she must do. She finally resolved to do as the cousins and accept whatever duties were necessary and proper for the moment. She would bravely see Thomas off, just as she had Robert, hoping and praying that afterward she would gain the time and wisdom to do what was right.

———

The following day, as Thomas attended to the final details of his packing, he was relieved to hear Marie's voice as she made an appearance far earlier than he had expected. While he finished, Marie unpacked a lunch she had brought for the two of them to share.

As they settled around the table, Thomas seemed unusually reserved, and though pleasant and polite, it was clear that he was preoccupied with other thoughts.

"Thomas, I know you have a lot to think about right now, but is there anything that I can do to help ease your mind?"

"I wish you could, Marie, but what worries me is beyond our control. I have an uneasy feeling about what I will encounter in Strasbourg when I go back. We have been blessed in our lives and spared much unhappiness until now. For most of history, that is a blessed exception. Humankind has a long history of self-inflicted misery, and I can't shake the dread that such times may be near."

"In all the time I have known you, Thomas, I have never seen you so pessimistic."

"I'm sorry to upset you, Marie. What good is it to worry about something over which we have no control?"

"It is only natural to feel this way, Thomas, no matter how much you try to dismiss it. To me, it only makes you seem more vulnerable and human. If it will make you feel any better, I want to reassure you that I am determined to do whatever is necessary in the coming days not to let you down. You and Robert may have mistaken my being upset as a sign of insecurity and weakness. My reaction is more out of anger at the failings and stupidity of those responsible for this condition than any dread for what I personally will have to face."

"You have reason to be upset, Marie, but you can't let your anger control you. We both need to focus on what we can do to make positive contributions in the days to come. I promise to work on my pessimism if it will help to decrease your anger."

"You have my word on it, Thomas. I could never willingly do anything to disappoint you, as your opinion means so much to me, and I hope that I will always be able to turn to you for support."

"As long as I have control of my wits, you can rest assured that will be the case, Marie. Now, perhaps we should get on our way, as the train will not wait for one reluctant passenger, even if he is a priest."

After finishing their lunch, Thomas gathered his bags while Marie tidied up. They then left for the station. No sooner had they progressed but a few blocks than they were greeted by the cries of the newsboys at the corner kiosk, announcing the verdict that Madame Caillaux had been exonerated by the jury on the grounds of temporary insanity.

"At last this trial is over!" Marie exclaimed. "Now we will be forced to endure the comments of those for her and against her."

"It is sad," added Thomas.

"That she was acquitted?"

"No, what I meant was how sad all this must be for the people directly involved. The murdered man's family will be embittered by this decision. Yet it was the very severity of his attack against Monsieur Caillaux, exposing his private life, that so poisoned the atmosphere and led to his murder. Can't we learn to treat one another with more civility? Now we have one wife widowed and another scandalized and forced to carry the memory of her sins for the rest of her days."

"Thomas, your empathy for the suffering of others, like this woman, whom you have never even met, is an inspiration to me. You like to think of yourself as some great logician like Aquinas, and I don't doubt for a minute that you have his gift of intelligence. I think of you, however, more like Peter Abelard, a man of great intelligence enriched by his passion. You must forgive me if what I say is a sin, but I cannot help myself. As much as I care for Robert, I have never met anyone like you, Thomas. It may be wrong, but I must tell you how I feel. Thomas, I love you more than anyone could ever imagine. Your warmth and love always give me courage and hope. Since the time that we first met, you have been willing to support me in anything that I have done. I cannot forget that ever. You must know, Thomas, that I will be here for you always."

"Marie, Marie, you must not say such things."

"I must if they are the truth. Do you love me, or am I just deluding myself to think you have feelings for me?"

"Marie, I don't know what to say. You thrill me and frighten me at the same time. Of course I love you, more than you could ever know, but I have taken a vow. What would become of us or you and Robert if I even think of breaking it?"

"Thomas, all I need to hear you say is that you love me. I am not an expert in religious matters like you, but I suspect God has a special understanding for people like us. I understand that you must act in accordance with whatever you understand to be his wishes. Someday, I hope that what God wants will be what I want. In the meantime, I will do my best to act so that you will be proud of me."

She then drew Thomas toward her, and for the first time in

his life, Thomas received a kiss of such passion that it would change his life forever.

The intensity of the moment was cut short by the arrival of the cab at the station. What time was left to them was limited as both rushed to the queue where Thomas's train waited for departure to Strasbourg. After one last embrace, Thomas quickly gathered up his things just in time to board the train as it began to set in motion.

Marie turned to watch, catching a glimpse of Thomas as he waved from a window seat, and then he was gone as the train passed from sight. She stood there on the platform alone for several minutes until gradually her sadness began to turn to resolve. As she made her way home, the cries of the newsboys had changed. They cried out the news that Austria and Serbia were now at war following the Austrians launching a series of artillery attacks along the Serbian frontier.

In the span of several hours, the curtain had been rung down on the farce that had dominated Parisian society for the last months. Now the first notes of the prelude were being sounded for a drama that had the promise of being for more tragic than the fate of Madame Caillaux.

41

DESPERATE TIMES

The first salvo fired by the Austrians against the Serbs rang out like a fire alarm throughout the capitals of Europe. In some, those responsible for the fate of their nations had long anticipated such a moment, and some even welcomed its coming. Others heard in these first shots the somber warning of a coming storm that threatened to overturn a protracted period of peace and prosperity virtually unknown in the long history of the continent and its people. Among the major powers, only in Britain was the news greeted with ambivalence and disgust that affairs could have reached such a perilous condition. As others braced themselves for the eventuality of war, British diplomats and statesmen sought any means possible to postpone any further outbreak of violence, in the fading hope that the looming outbreak of a continental war could be avoided.

In Berlin—except for the kaiser, who, at the last moment, had seemed to vacillate in his support for a conflict that he and his military had long planned—there could be little doubt where the military and the vast majority of the government stood. If Russia mobilized against Austria, it would be grounds for full mobilization of the German army, an act that would lead to war with the Russians if they refused to withdraw their threat against Austria. If mobilization should be ordered, it would also include the movement of troops to the western frontier in order to anticipate any possible French action in defense of her Russian ally. At this supreme moment of crisis, Germany, which had the most power and influence to affect the course of the crisis, had virtually ceded control of future events to the Russian government, to whom the kaiser was making last-minute appeals for restraint through the czar.

To Sarah, the entire mood of Berlin seemed to change almost hourly, based on the facts or the rumors of the moment. With the news of the Austrian attack on Serbia, she, like almost the entire populace of the city, realized how quickly the gravity of the crisis had changed. Upon hearing the news, she had spent most of her time in the bureau, where she was able to gain more information through Stein and his contacts, as well as through other news bureaus with which they were in contact. From the accumulated facts and rumors, there could be little doubt of the danger that lay ahead, increasing the tension in the office at times to almost unbearable levels.

The mental state of the citizenry, whose status she could assess in her travels through the city, was suffering as well. Many seemed withdrawn, scarcely smiling or offering any sense of emotion as they went about their daily activities. Others, however, had become progressively outspoken in their support of the cause of the fatherland and its right to defend itself against those who were gathering to suppress Germany's inevitable ascent. Often wearing patriotic insignias, such people readily lent their support to the increasingly militant rhetoric from some of the press and offices of the government. The effect of all this was to transform the city into a state of mass hysteria, populated by people of widely divergent emotions. Some people feared for the future; others welcomed the potential for a great battle that would leave Germany free, after an inevitable victory, to assume her rightful place of prominence on the continent.

Sarah was relieved when the time came to leave for her planned meeting with Frau von Suttner and the committee assembled to deal with the crisis. She welcomed the chance to do something that might help delay a terrible day of reckoning and to escape from the confines of the office that, during the last days, had taken on a depressing air with each bit of bad news.

Sarah arrived at the Suttners' early, only to find a large number of people already present. Many she knew from past years of organizing and demonstrating for peace. Many of the pacifists who were long associated with Bertha von Suttner's circle were present, along with some members of various worker-affiliated organizations, including the usual contingent from the dominant Social Democratic Party, the majority party in the Reichstag during the last year. Many more senior members of the Social Democrats were no longer present, although Herr Scheidermann, who Sarah knew from past meetings, was still the head of their contingent. There were other younger members present, however, with whom she had not worked in the past.

There was already a spirited conversation being carried on by those present, giving an intensity to the gathering that Sarah had seldom seen in the past. At the last minute, before the meeting was to begin, Sarah saw Rosa Luxembourg slip into the room and move quietly to a seat next to her, acknowledging Sarah's presence with only the slightest nod and smile.

With Baroness von Suttner's arrival, the meeting was called to order. Little time was lost in introductions before turning their attention to the present situation in the Balkans. As Frau von Suttner polled those present for any new information, she was interrupted by an inpatient Rosa Luxembourg.

"Baroness von Suttner, it seems clear that we are facing a situation that is graver than any in our recent past. The rapidity with which it has accelerated has given it a momentum that may complicate the tactics we have previously used."

"What are you suggesting, Fraulein Luxembourg?" the baroness asked.

"I am simply saying that all of our past tactics may be too feeble at this time to help stop a war that now seems imminent. We are in a time of the utmost danger, and consequently, with whatever little time might remain to us, we must adopt the most dramatic and radical measures to oppose those who would lead us to a war that few can doubt will be catastrophic for all of Europe."

"What do you propose, Rosa?" asked Sarah.

"It is not enough to simply demonstrate for peace as we have done in the past. Such efforts, while no doubt heartfelt, don't have the means to disrupt the war-making capability of the state. I fear they would be little more than the annoying bite of a fly to their collective bull neck. No, what is needed is the imminent threat of something far more disruptive to the nation's ability to prosecute war. What is needed is a general strike to show opposition to an imperialist war that would be a hideous crime committed against the workers of the world."

"Such a strike will not be easy to organize in the time that might be required. Furthermore, it will no doubt be viewed as treason by many, especially without some international coordination with the workers of the other countries involved," suggested Sarah.

"No doubt what you say is true, but time leaves us little alternative at this point," replied Rosa.

"Fraulein Morozovski is right about the political consequences," replied Scheidermann. "If war is declared, what right would the workers of Germany have to strike if our brethren in France and Russia failed to do so as well? We would be risking the fatherland's ability to defend itself from a Russian invasion and would be held responsible if those efforts were compromised."

"Herr Scheidermann, you and the members of your party are the largest elected group in the Reichstag. You will have to decide if you are representing the rights of the workers or the rights of the aristocracy, who will gain the spoils of an imperialist war from the slaughter of those workers. For socialists who have chosen to work within the framework of governments founded on the spoils of imperialism and capitalism, there has long been a danger to be tainted by their associations. One day you will have to decide if you are going to act as a defender of the workers or a defender of the status of the government of which you have knowingly become a part. For you and every one of your colleagues, Herr Scheidermann, that time is rapidly nearing, if not now."

Young Fritz Ebert, the nephew of the head of the Socialist Party, spoke up. "It is not so simple for my uncle or any of us representing our constituents in the government, fraulein. Not everyone—and especially not all the workers—believes that our interests lie in standing idly by while our country is invaded by the Russians. More and more of my constituents now believe that even if a war might be as harmful as you suggest that it is still not right that we abet the enemy by actions that would weaken the nation in a time of enormous threat."

"From what you are saying, Herr Ebert, I can assume that

you will approve any war funding, should the government bring that to the Reichstag, as it is required to do by the present constitution," Rosa challenged.

"I am not in a position to say what my uncle and the party will decide until the full circumstances that might accompany such a request are known."

"Then may I ask what you and your colleagues are prepared to do to support a general strike against war with Russia and her allies?" Rosa asked in an increasingly aggressive tone.

"I can answer that," replied Scheidermann. "We have had discussions even this very morning about such an eventuality. It was agreed by our policy committee that we would support the planning of such an event but cannot endorse it fully without knowing full details of the actions to be taken and, more important, details on the status of the crisis at the time. It was felt that to strike, when the country has already committed to war, would serve only to further endanger the lives of our own workers."

"May I speak as one such colleague from a potential enemy camp?" Sarah interjected.

"Please do," the baroness directed.

"It seems to me that we no longer have the time to debate all the potential ramifications of our actions. I agree with Rosa Luxembourg that these times demand the most drastic actions. I have conferred with my colleagues in Paris as recently as last night. I must confess that they were later than most of us in recognizing this threat. Even now, many believe that the last-minute attempt by the British will succeed diplomatically. Those same people recognize, however, that we cannot place our hopes exclusively on this outcome but must be aggressive in our planning. For that reason, even as we speak, plans are being made for a series of strikes culminating in a general strike in three days. I would suggest therefore that those of you who are in a position to organize German opposition should commit yourselves to that date. It may be our last chance to stop this tragedy by demonstrating the extent of opposition to war by men and women of two of the most critical nations potentially at the heart of this conflict."

"I endorse your suggestion, Sarah, and will work vigorously to that end, but I will need all the help I can get from some of those in this room to help mobilize the workers," replied Frau von Suttner.

"It is not my place to usurp this meeting, but at the end of our proceedings I would ask those willing to organize a general strike to meet with me to plan its implementation," Rosa interjected. "For those with little interest, there would be no further need to take any more of your time."

In a short time, the formalities of the morning meeting came to an end, and then Sarah joined Rosa and several veterans of past demonstrations throughout Germany, spending the better part of the afternoon setting the groundwork for a wide-scale strike that would be coordinated with the effort in France. Some members of the SPD remained for the discussions, but the little support they provided was to acknowledge an empathy with the effort if certain political contingencies could be met. During the planning, Sarah gained a new appreciation for Rosa Luxembourg and her unwavering commitment to oppose a coming war by whatever means remained. Almost subconsciously, she began to lend support to nearly all of Rosa Luxembourg's proposals for the days ahead.

As the meeting broke up, Rosa motioned Sarah aside. "I appreciate all of your support today. Without it, we would not have gotten as far as we did. We could make an excellent team."

"This strike is the only course left to us at present. I am proud to support you on this."

"You know how dangerous this will be if we fail," Rosa added.

"If I had been worried about that, I would not have come back to Berlin."

"It seems that I am always apologizing to you, Sarah. I have always thought that incremental socialists would make undependable allies in a time of crisis. I underestimated your courage. For those without your courage and commitment, their cowardice will be manifest in political expediency. Look at the SPD. There is little doubt in my mind that if this crisis worsens, they will throw in their lot with the kaiser's henchmen in the name of preserving the great German Reich, even though in so doing the workers will be damned.

"I have known the vast majority of these so-called socialists for too long now. Their first priority is to be socialists so that they can access political power. If that takes compromise with others whose aims are far different from that of their supposed constituency, they will cleverly manipulate the facts to make it look like their treachery is for the good of the workers. In truth, their greatest concern is mainly for themselves.

I must be honest with you, Sarah. If we fail and war does come in the end, it will do more for the workers than all the years of incremental gains that have been obtained so far. I believe a war will be so destructive for the workings of capitalism as to virtually ensure its overthrow by the proletarian. Unfortunately, this revolution will be realized only after the blood of countless innocent men has been shed, and that is why I am so ambivalent about its coming.

"If the war comes, you must believe me when I tell you, Sarah, that the ruling class will come after me, and if you are here in Germany, they will come after you. If so, you will need very dependable friends. Here is a list of names. Commit it to your memory and then destroy it. If they come for you, you cannot rely on those you know now. They will be arrested or closely followed themselves. If you cannot escape Germany by your own means you may turn to these people with no fear that they will betray you."

"I am touched and deeply thankful for your help," Sarah said, taking the list.

"It is what any good comrade would do. Now let's think no more of this. We have too much to do before we meet again tomorrow evening."

"Until then, Rosa, be safe."

"Until then, Sarah."

On her way back into the city on the tram from Frau von Suttner's, Sarah decided to stop by the police station to perform her required daily registration before proceeding to the office.

Upon her arrival, she was quickly directed to the same office of her previous visit, where the same young officious lieutenant was on duty. Upon taking her name, he checked a list of registered foreigners and then excused himself, leaving Sarah alone in the room. He soon returned with a sealed envelope with her name formally inscribed on the outside. As he handed it to her, he said, "This letter will inform you of the serious manner in which the government views your presence here in Berlin. I would urge you to take the contents quite seriously."

With that, he gave Sarah a curt bow and in so doing indicated that their conversation was finished from his official standpoint. He then turned and departed, leaving her alone to review the contents of the letter. She quickly opened it and slowly and deliberately, with all the training that her legal background had given her, studied its contents. The letter itself was quite brief and appeared to have been composed for the many people that the Interior Ministry felt represented a possible security threat in times of a national crisis. It simply stated that based on her known associates and past activities, should any formal state of war be declared against Germany, her presence would be viewed harshly. She was being notified that in that case, she would be considered a potentially dangerous alien and that she should expect to be detained in a manner that would ensure that she could not provide support to Germany's enemies.

What the threat could mean, Sarah could only speculate, but whatever it might be, it would no doubt be unpleasant. At that moment, she thought of Rosa's warning from earlier in the day, and rather than being surprised or even frightened by the threatening tone of the letter, she took it as a warning that she needed to take preventive action immediately.

Returning to her apartment, she quickly gathered her most essential belongings and packed them in a small traveling bag so that she would be prepared to leave, should it be necessary at a moment's notice. She then proceeded toward the train station to inquire about procuring a train ticket for France.

Having been out of the office for most of the day, she was unaware of the developments that seemed to be escalating the crisis with each passing hour. In the course of the early afternoon, word came that Russia had ordered limited troop mobilization along its Austrian border. Such an action did not convey the same commitment of full mobilization but clearly signaled Russian intentions to take an active role in the Balkan conflict. This action dispelled forever the notion that considerations of internal insurrection and military weakness would force them to the sidelines in a war between Austria and Serbia.

The Russian response was more than the German general staff could bear. Fearing the consequences of any further delay on their war preparedness, War Secretary Erich von Falkenhayn had become increasingly strident in his demands for an immediate order for mobilization of the German army. Falkenhayn was well aware of the logistics involved in full mobilization and the time it would take to bring the army up to full strength. Knowing what effect such an action would have on what remained for any hope of a peaceful resolution of the crisis, the kaiser vacillated. Finally, he agreed to a *Kriegesgefahr*, or a state of war readiness that allowed for many of the most critical first steps leading to full mobilization to be initiated.

The actions implied by this proclamation would soon become evident to Sarah. At the Potsdammer Platz station, she was informed of the new imperial directive and was told that as a consequence no nonmilitary transportation would be available for at least the next twenty-four hours unless she could produce a document from the transport ministry attesting to the critical nature of her travel. Sarah now began to more fully realize how far this crisis had progressed. Shaken by this news and the implied threat from the Interior Ministry, she was at first unable to organize her thoughts. Then, drawing on her inner resolve, she refocused and slowly tried to think of the means by which she might extricate herself from Berlin.

After a short time, she decided to return to the offices of the paper, where Stein greeted her with a look of relief and then, almost like a doting parent, scolded her for not keeping anyone in the office up-to-date on her whereabouts.

"Stein, I am always moved by your concern for my safety,

but I have been involved with so many important matters that it was simply not possible to get word back to you."

She then related to him the contents of the letter from the Interior Department and her failed attempt to obtain passage to Paris, which caused an even deeper look of worry to come over Stein's brow.

"Stein, you have enough to worry about besides my safety in Berlin. I have been thinking of some alternative options to get me to the west, should the trains not be running tomorrow. I have contacted an old friend in the taxi business to see if he can come up with a way, aside from the train, to get back to France."

"Whatever, Sarah, I hope it works, but you can't have enough people working on ideas that might be useful if things get really bad here."

"Stein, if things get really bad here, I don't want you or the staff to become too involved in trying to protect me. It might result in serious consequences for you as well, and that would be something that I could not tolerate. I can tell you I have some contacts who can help me in the manner that you are suggesting. For your own safety, I cannot tell you anymore, except that I am very confident that these people can be quite helpful if they are needed. That is all that you need to know at present. Now let's forget that we ever had this conversation and concentrate on getting this paper out for our readers."

42

AT THE PRECIPICE

In Paris, following the onset of hostilities between Austria and Serbia, a profound change had come over the population. For decades the country had been split by bitter struggles between the classes, struggles that had, at times, pitted aristocrat against bourgeois and more recently, the bourgeois middle class against the working classes. At their extremes came the bloodshed of the great revolution and the violent days of the Commune. Crisis had weakened many of the institutions of the country, such as the profound loss of prestige and credibility by the army in the aftermath of the Dreyfus affair. Many had feared, including those now most responsible for national security, that these bitter divisions would so weaken the nation's ability to defend itself that France might easily fall, should war come again with a unified and vigorous Germany.

The Austrian invasion of Serbia made it apparent that France could also be drawn into the conflagration. This realization seemed suddenly to bring a new awareness throughout France and all of its many divisions of a higher duty to defend their homeland, should it be threatened by an old and hated enemy. Even those elements that had been opposed to military conflict in the past now seemed to instinctively feel an obligation to do what was necessary to protect France in the face of such a threat.

Of this latter group were many of the elements of the workers movement that had long resisted the threat of a European war. Their leaders were among the most able of the socialist movement in Europe. Jean Jaurès was the philosophic as well as personal inspiration for a number of the most ardent members of that movement, and as the crisis advanced, many turned to his leadership, which had guided them so well in the past. For some reason, perhaps due to his success in past crises, he had seemed somewhat less concerned by events than many of his younger colleagues, believing that the continent's leaders would ultimately be motivated by self-preservation to draw back from the abyss of war.

When news reached Paris that Russia had declared a state of general mobilization against Austria, many sensed that any news to follow would be dire. The wait was short-lived when word came of Germany's demand for Russia to cease such actions within twelve hours or suffer significant consequences. Few could doubt that at the very least this would be full German mobilization, which would necessitate a response from the French government.

That government, unfortunately, like many before it, was populated by many ministers who were ill equipped for the crisis at hand. Premier René Viviani, though not in Jean Jaurès's immediate circle, was a lifelong socialist with a commitment to workers' rights and virtually no experience in foreign affairs. He brought a socialist antipathy to the prospect of war that made him, along with many of his inexperienced ministers, tentative in both thoughts and actions in the face of an increasingly hostile Germany. As the crisis accelerated, the premier and many of his cabinet became ever more agitated, making their judgment more erratic at a time when experience and sangfroid were essential.

During this time, however, General Joffre the army chief of staff, was well aware of the military implications of the chain of events in the east, measuring each new announcement against the timetable necessary for full mobilization. Once a critical point of German readiness was reached, any delay in implementing this process might place his army at a significant disadvantage against a German enemy. He remembered all too well the disaster at Sudan that virtually assured the French defeat in the Prussian War. In the face of Viviani's uncertainty and the cabinet's vacillation, he made certain to keep close contact with them through Messimy, providing critical information on German troop movement into the regions along their frontier with France. He also began agitating for full French mobilization as this German buildup became more evident.

Now, as the crisis escalated, Joffre, aided by the redoubtable President Raymond Poincaré, began to lobby more forcefully to begin the first critical steps necessary for full mobilization. Reluctantly, Viviani finally agreed in part to Joffre's demands, committing France to a course somewhat similar to Germany's, thereby providing more instability to a rapidly deteriorating situation. Once initiated, mobilization, even on a more limited scale, had a momentum of its own, sensitizing those in power to any future activity of a potential enemy.

In Paris as well as the other great capitals of Europe, the populace was now well aware of these developments through well-founded rumors and a press that was kept busy in publishing new facts in frequent special editions. The effect was to increase tension to extreme levels in the city and throughout all the country. All of this was easily appreciated at the offices of *l'Humanité*, where the entire staff struggled to keep up on and report the details of the rapidly changing events. Aside from trying to provide timely coverage of the facts of the crisis as they became known, Jaurès and the editorial board urged calm and restraint to counter the ever-larger number of voices arguing for war.

Sarah later would learn what would follow from close friends present at the office that afternoon. Jean Jaurès had been absent from the paper for most of the day, conferring with a circle of influential antiwar activists on plans to help diffuse the tension in France and to coordinate these actions with others throughout Europe. Late in the afternoon he returned to the office, where he appeared clearly exhausted by his effort. Despite the worsening news of the afternoon, however, he apparently still remained optimistic, believing that a British initiative, if supported by the force of people such as Viviani, might still lead to a peaceful solution.

Following a staff meeting that lasted for more than an hour, the editorial board, along with Jean Jaurès and other associates, set out for a favorite café to try to restore their energies with an evening meal. Afterward, most of the group returned to the office to attend to the ever-pressing needs necessitated by the crisis. Several members stayed, however, to languish over a brandy while continuing to discuss potential actions for the following day. Jean Jaurès remained and sat prominently in an accustomed seat at the front of the café, well outlined in the evening sunlight.

The tensions of the day, coupled with the appearance of this champion of peace so readily apparent to any casual passerby, proved too much for a radical young nationalist who spied Jaurès in passing. How is it that fate often uses the insignificant and mad to facilitate its grand design? At that moment, as the summer sunlight faded, all the young man's radical ideas fused in hatred. He fired five shots through the window of the café, mortally wounding Jean Jaurès and the cause to which he had dedicated his life.

———

That same day in Berlin, Sarah, unable to sleep well, had arrived at the bureau at an early hour. She hoped to gain some news of the course of events that might have transpired during the night, as well as to get an early start on trying to obtain some means of getting out of Germany, especially if rail transportation continued to be disrupted. Above all, she hoped for some lull in the frantic pace of events that had drawn the continent to the brink of war so suddenly and with such little warning.

She was out of the office when word came to the Berlin bureau of Jean Jaurès's tragic assassination. She returned shortly afterward, where she found Stein and everyone there visibly shaken.

"Where have you been, Sarah?"

"I have been at the police station, trying to convince that officious young policeman that despite my desire to be out of Berlin, the present circumstances, with virtually all the transportation in the city shut down, prevents me from leaving for Paris."

"What did he say?"

"He said it was beyond his control to make concessions for transportation difficulties, implying that if I was found in

Germany, should war be declared with France, then I would suffer the consequences."

"Sarah, you must leave by whatever means you can as soon as possible. We have just received terrible news, and it is no longer safe for you here," Stein added almost inaudibly.

"What is it? You and everyone here look terrible."

"We have just received word that Monsieur Jaurès was assassinated earlier this evening in Paris."

Stein saw a look of emotion come across Sarah's face that he had rarely seen. She usually accepted bad news with a trained, calm, almost mechanical demeanor. Now, he saw her grimace as if she had been shot herself.

"I was afraid this would happen one day. He was too large and eloquent a figure to simply ignore. He would never have been quiet in his opposition to a war that he considered senseless, unless, of course, some monster did the unthinkable and silenced him."

"You have done all you can here, Sarah. You must get back to Paris as soon as possible. You will be needed there much more than here now."

"I know that now very well, my dear Stein. It seems that anyone able to transport me to France at this time, however, cannot guarantee my passage any farther east than Franconia in the next twenty-four hours. Who knows what will become of the world in that time? Stein, if events force me to do so, I will go underground. I can tell you today that I have been preparing for that contingency. You may not hear from me in the morning or in the near future. If you do not, you will no doubt be hearing from the German authorities, and because of that, I cannot tell you any more. Until you hear from me in Paris, pay close attention to any communication from our Polish correspondent Miriam Cohen."

"I understand," Stein replied with a sly smile, recognizing Miriam Cohen as the pen name of a fictional Warsaw correspondent, who on occasion would release particularly sensitive information in the hopes of avoiding incriminating anyone in the Berlin office.

"Now, Stein, with Monsieur Jaurès murdered, if I am gone, you will be in charge of this bureau and all it represents. When I get back to Berlin, I expect to see you here and the paper having distinguished itself in my absence."

"You can depend on that, Sarah."

"I know I can. Now if you don't mind, I'm very tired and need to get home and get some rest. I'll see you around, Stein."

"I'll see you, Sarah, and if by chance it is not in the morning, it will be in the future in better times."

"Well, until then," she said and gave him a passionate hug and kiss, which served to hide the tears that had welled up in her eyes.

"Until then, Sarah," Stein answered, taking care to hide his own tears.

43

UNDERGROUND

At dawn the following morning, Sarah rose early, making sure the bag she had so carefully packed the night before was in order, if needed, and departed for the nearby district of Prinzlauer Berg. The news of the previous evening made her realize how imperative it was to find a safe harbor as soon as possible.

She drew upon the information Rosa Luxembourg had given to her, realizing that it offered the best option for her present circumstances. It was a testament to how desperate her situation had become that Sarah would turn to unknown friends of her most radical acquaintance. It was Rosa's notoriety, however, that made such friends essential, and so if she were to escape from the clutches of the German Interior Ministry, then, Sarah realized, at this time Rosa's clique offered her the best chance of success.

Traveling slowly so as not to arouse suspicion Sarah arrived at a small but well-kept residence in the Prinzlauer Berg district near the old Jewish cemetery, along a quiet street abutting a small park. There, she was told she would find a woman named

Marta. Sarah was sufficiently concerned with her situation by that time and took great caution in surveying the premises around the home. Fortunately, the hour was still early, so by sticking to the shadows she felt confident that she had concealed her features.

At the address she had been given, her knock was answered by a young woman looking no more than twenty years old. When Sarah asked for Marta, she was promptly ushered into a parlor by the young woman, who seemed to study her for some time before asking her name and the reason for her visit. When she heard that Sarah had been sent by Rosa Luxembourg, she left the room and soon returned, accompanied by a rather small elderly woman, who gave the impression of a rather typical German grandmother.

So it was that Sarah first came to meet Marta Frisch. Marta promptly dismissed the younger woman and directed Sarah to another smaller room, where the two could speak more intimately. Their first meeting was fairly brief, during which time Marta asked the same questions as the younger woman but in greater depth. Satisfied by Sarah's response, she seemed to soften her demeanor and to warm to her new guest.

After a little more time, Marta excused herself, stating the need to attend to pressing commitments that had come up only this day. She urged Sarah to get her affairs in order and to return that evening, prepared to stay as long as was necessary until the situation was better clarified. She also cautioned that Sarah should make herself as inconspicuous as possible by limiting any luggage and traveling during the peak of rush hour.

By that evening, the crisis seemed to have increased throughout the day, only making Sarah's dilemma more pressing. Realizing the gravity of her situation, she avoided the office to minimize the risk to her old associates and checked in with the local police station, as required by recent law. The officer with whom she dealt seemed almost bored with the procedure, which seemed to help lessen her concern.

That evening Sarah set out, casting one last glimpse at her apartment, not knowing when she might return, if ever. Her anxieties for the journey were fortunately not realized, and she arrived at Marta's without incident. She was greeted on this occasion without any of the suspicion of her first visit. Marta was able to meet with her for only a short time, but it was evident that she was happy to see that Sarah had arrived without complications.

After a brief discussion, Sarah was turned over to Marta's young assistant from the morning, Ruth, who showed her to her bedroom and gave her a brief tour of the facilities, including a library that already included some of the day's journals. Later that evening, Sarah shared a small but satisfactory supper with Ruth and then, exhausted by the events of the day, retired early and slept surprisingly well in the comfort of her new surroundings.

The following morning, Sarah was greeted in the dining room by Marta, who was already up and, from her appearance, already fully engaged in her morning activities.

"I am pleased to see you so early this morning, Sarah, if I might call you by your first name. I hope you slept well."

"Good morning, Frau Frisch. I certainly did. No doubt it was due to the relief of being here."

"Please call me Marta, if you would. From all that I have heard about you from Rosa, I already feel as if I have known you for some time. Could I offer you some coffee and breakfast?"

"That would be wonderful."

"Ruth, please bring us some coffee and breakfast while I get to know our guest better."

SOME DAMN FOOL THING

The young woman parted through a swinging door, while Marta led Sarah to a window overlooking a courtyard in the back of the quarters.

"This all must be very difficult for you, Sarah, but I can assure you that your coming here was very prudent. As you may know, Russia has mobilized its army, and it seems that Germany will do the same before the day is over. I am afraid we will be at war with the Russians soon thereafter. As you may have found by now, it will be virtually impossible for anyone not in the army to move any distance outside of the city."

"That difficulty is what ultimately led me to your home, Marta. I must confess that it is a bit unsettling to be dependent on strangers, as I have always prided myself on my self-reliance. All of this has happened so quickly, however, that all of my best plans have been dashed."

"I can see how this would worry you, as I have always looked out for myself as well, especially after my husband died four years ago. Let me tell you a little about myself, and maybe that will help set your mind at ease."

"That isn't necessary, Marta. When Rosa gave me your name it was apparent that you were someone she trusted."

"I can assure you that the trust is mutual and has been well earned on many occasions. I first met Rosa when she was a young protégée of my husband, Harold Frisch."

"I know that name from reputation. Although I never had the pleasure of making his acquaintance, I heard Monsieur Jean Jaurès speak well of him on several occasions in the past."

"Ah, the great Jean Jaurès, may God rest his noble soul. I remember dining with him and my husband on an occasion when he was in Berlin. He was a great man and one who will be greatly missed."

"He was one of the finest men I have ever known," added Sarah.

"Well, Harold came to know both Jean Jaurès and your friend Rosa through his long career as an advocate for the working men with whom he had been associated from his earliest days. I understand, Sarah, that you are a lawyer. He was also an attorney but having come from one of the working-class areas of the city, after he obtained his training he felt an obligation to use his knowledge to help those friends and early acquaintances he had known growing up.

"His life was spent protecting the rights of the workers against the designs of the wealthy and powerful by whatever means he could devise. I am proud to say he was quite effective at what he did, which ultimately brought him much respect and authority in the workers movement. This very room in which we are sitting was the site of many a gathering of such men and even women such as Rosa, where many a fine meal was shared along with the fellowship that came from their shared interests.

"Such a situation proved highly advantageous to me as well, as it forced me to become a gracious hostess to these many dedicated people and their close families and friends. Through the years, this led me to develop close friendships with many of them. Indeed, in times of stress I became as involved with the struggles of the wives and families as much as Harold was with their husbands."

In listening to Marta, Sarah began to see in her a German incarnation of her own dear governess and confidant Lydia Rothstein Gold. How strange that in this faraway city of Spartan customs and Lutheran values another woman, endowed with great common sense and a feminine sensitivity to the needs of those close to her, could exert an influence similar to that of

SOME DAMN FOOL THING

Lydia. It was easy to see how Marta could come to be trusted by someone as worldly and skeptical as Rosa Luxembourg.

As they chatted over their breakfast, their relationship and respect for each other seemed to grow by the minute.

At last Marta interrupted herself, saying, "How thoughtless of me to keep going on about myself. I hope that your accommodations are satisfactory."

"They are far more than I need or could have asked for. I hope that you will allow me to reimburse you for all your costs."

"Sarah, you have paid your share with all of your selfless work in the past on behalf of all of our comrades. You can repay me by not losing sight of our mutual goals, despite what we might face in the days to come."

"That is an obligation that I can gladly fulfill."

"Then it is settled. I would suggest you remain here and avoid showing yourself outside at a time when you might be observed by inquiring eyes. My friends and I will begin to work on a plan to get you home whenever it is possible. In the meantime, take the time to freshen up and make yourself at home here. Ruth can help you with any of your needs or questions. We will have our lunch around noon. You must excuse me for now, but I will see you then."

"I cannot thank you enough, Marta, for your kindness."

"You're more than welcome, Sarah. I will see you at lunch."

―――――――

For the rest of the morning, Sarah explored the common areas of the house, noting the arrangement of rooms and the decor. Marta had used restraint in decorating her home, yet her good taste was evident, even though tempered by practicality and economy. Sarah soon settled in the library with its large collection of books and journals and a seating arrangement that could lend itself to a moderate-sized gathering. She was pleased to see that the morning's copy of the *Daily Worker* was already there.

This paper, which had long served as the organ for the Social Democrats, outlined clearly the anticipated timeline of the ultimatum to the Russian government on its front page, along with many comments attributed to the kaiser and Chancellor Bethmann-Hollweg. In its editorial commentary, Sarah was surprised and disappointed to note a position increasingly sympathetic to the notion of Germany's being forced to act in response to the threat of a militant Russian-Serbian coalition, backed by the tacit encouragement of their French allies. It seemed that the specter of a Slavic invasion of Prussia and the territories of Austria Hungary was far more threatening to the editor than the threat that war among these various nations represented to the interests and very lives of the workers they had long represented.

At lunch, little further information had come regarding the ultimatum to Russia, but all realized that if the Russians failed to acquiesce to the German demands by that evening, the kaiser would declare full German mobilization, with all the implications. Sarah knew that given the thoroughness of German military planning, the army would be moved into key positions not only along the eastern frontier but also along the western frontier in direct opposition to France. Such actions would almost certainly bring full French mobilization as well, if they had not already, which would result in a situation where a declaration of war would be almost impossible to avoid.

As the day progressed and as bits and pieces of information

filtered in from various friends of Marta and the day's journals, the tension increased by the hour. By evening, it was almost certain that all the major armies on the continent would be mobilized within the next days, placing all the inhabitants of their nations at great risk of a tragic conflagration. At present, only Britain seemed uncommitted, and it was with Britain that those who prayed for peace held out hope for some relief.

The gravity of the situation seemed even more significant in Berlin. With full mobilization, Germany risked being surrounded by an armed and hostile France and Russia. Such a threat, long dreaded since the formation of the Franco-Russian alliance, would compel the German army to rush troops to both its eastern and western frontiers as the first step in a war plan long in the making. Before the day was over, those fears came closer to reality, as, failing to receive concessions from the Russian government, the kaiser authorized full mobilization of the German military forces.

Shortly, the inevitable aftermath of these actions followed with a formal declaration of war between Germany and Russia. All knew that a war declaration against France would soon follow. Sarah had witnessed this through the unusual prism of her residence in hiding, surrounded by Marta and kindred spirits who viewed each development with revulsion and trepidation. She would remember in great detail the afternoon when, gathered in Marta's library, they had heard the announcement of the German declaration of war against France.

On hearing the news, Sarah lowered her head but tried not to show the bitter disappointment she now felt.

Marta, sensing the vulnerability of her new friend, took her hand reassuringly. "Don't worry, Sarah. This will not change our plans for you but will make it more important than ever that we act with prudence and caution. This may complicate our actions in the next few days, but it will not deter us in the end."

Sarah could only shake her head in silent acknowledgment, as her emotions at that moment had muted her ability to voice her outrage.

44

A CONTINENT ENSNARED

Now the great trap that had been years in the making had been sprung. The leaders of France and Russia, followed by Britain, frightened by the specter of a rising and unified Germany, had pledged to link their collective fates to oppose German aggression. For the past decade, peace had been threatened by episodes of German aggression with each, increasing the collective dread of all involved. Calamity had been avoided by concerted diplomatic efforts, enhanced by a rising tide of economic prosperity across the continent.

All these efforts had been put at risk with the first shots fired by Austria against Serbia. The pleasant days of the early summer that seemed to reflect an emerging optimism about the continent and its future were suddenly threatened by a storm of frantic activity by a disparate collection of states in which irrationality, fed by nationalism and many of humankind's darkest fears, would threaten to usurp that future.

On August 1, failing to receive a guarantee from Russia to cease hostile actions against Austria, the kaiser's government announced full general mobilization of its forces on both its eastern and western frontiers. The following day, with the announcement of full German mobilization, a state of war was declared between Russia and the two central powers, Germany and Austria. What remained was a frantic attempt at this last hour somehow to keep France and Britain outside the conflict. By this time, however, the fear and distrust were too great.

It was France's turn next. German mobilization of their western frontier was too much for even Viviani to ignore. Full mobilization was ordered, and in response Germany quickly declared war on France, thereby sealing the fate of neutral Belgium, whose lands were essential to Germany's long-planned westward offensive.

As news of the war declarations spread throughout the various capitals of Europe, it was greeted by many with enthusiasm and public delirium. Crowds wildly applauded the parading troops, showering them with flowers on the way to their appointed rendezvous with their new enemies. Young men felt the momentum of the moment was too much to resist and quickly formed into long queues in hastily formed enlistment centers.

Yet there was by no means universal acclaim for this sudden and dramatic continental conflict. Throughout the soon-to-be-embattled nations, those who had actively opposed such a war and those who simply feared it were somber, reflective, and saddened.

Lord Grey, the British foreign secretary, nearly exhausted by his efforts to turn the continent away from war and filled with despair by the futility of his actions, observed the gas lamps below his Whitehall office and noted plaintively, "The lamps are going out all over Europe. We shall not see them lit again in our lifetime."

Compelled by a plan years in the making, German troops soon violated Belgium neutrality, and, in so doing, the trap was fully closed. Such a violation, which threatened their control of the Channel and the North Sea, compelled Great Britain to declare war against the German Empire and its allies.

In total, from the first shots fired by the Austrians against Serbia to the striking of the clock at midnight on August 4, when Britain declared itself at war with Germany, only a week had passed—a week that had seen frantic action by those responsible for the fate of their countries. In the end, their collective failure to resist the inexorable pull toward war threatened the progress that a century of liberalism had given the continent's citizens. At this hour, none of Europe's citizens could know how great that threat would be.

The trap had been sprung, and now the consequences would follow for Sarah, Robert, Thomas, Marie, and all the citizens of Europe, great and small. What few could know with certainty but none doubted, in this first week of August, was that they would be great. Time would prove just how great and how grave.